D0052141

HARLEQUIN Romance

LINDA GOODNIGHT

Married Under the Mistletoe

The Brides of Bella Lucia

$4.25 U.S./$4.99 CAN.

HARLEQUIN® *Romance*.

**From the Heart.
For the Heart.**

ISBN-13:978-0-373-03920-3
ISBN-10: 0-373-03920-4

AVAILABLE THIS MONTH:

#3919 HER CHRISTMAS WEDDING WISH
Western Weddings
Judy Christenberry

#3920 MARRIED UNDER THE MISTLETOE
The Brides of Bella Lucia
Linda Goodnight

#3921 SNOWBOUND REUNION
Barbara McMahon

#3922 PROJECT: PARENTHOOD
Trish Wylie

THE BRIDES OF BELLA LUCIA

A family torn apart by secrets,
reunited by marriage

When William Valentine returned from the war, as
a testament to his love for his beautiful Italian wife,
Lucia, he opened the first Bella Lucia restaurant in
London, England. The future looked bright, and
William had, he thought, the perfect family.

Now William is nearly ninety, and not long for this
world, but he has three top London restaurants with
prime spots throughout Knightsbridge and the West
End. He has two sons, John and Robert, and grown-
up grandchildren on both sides of the Atlantic who are
poised to take this small gastronomic success story into
the twenty-first century.

But when William dies, and the family fights to control
the destiny of the Bella Lucia business, they discover a
multitude of long-buried secrets, scandals, the threat
of financial ruin and ultimately two great loves they
hadn't even dreamed of: the love of a lifelong partner,
and the love of a family reunited.

This month, curl up and fall in love
with gorgeous Daniel Valentine in…
Married Under the Mistletoe **by Linda Goodnight**

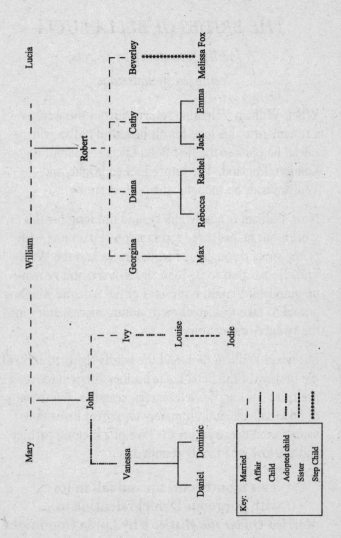

LINDA GOODNIGHT

Married Under the Mistletoe

The Brides of Bella Lucia

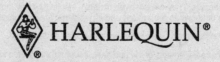

HARLEQUIN®

TORONTO • NEW YORK • LONDON
AMSTERDAM • PARIS • SYDNEY • HAMBURG
STOCKHOLM • ATHENS • TOKYO • MILAN • MADRID
PRAGUE • WARSAW • BUDAPEST • AUCKLAND

ISBN-13: 978-0-373-03920-3
ISBN-10:   0-373-03920-4

MARRIED UNDER THE MISTLETOE

First North American Publication 2006.

Copyright © 2006 Harlequin Books S.A.

Special thanks and acknowledgment are given to Linda Goodnight for her contribution to *The Brides of Bella Lucia* series.

THE BRIDES OF BELLA LUCIA

A family torn apart by secrets, reunited by marriage

First there was double the excitement as we met twins Rebecca and Rachel Valentine

Having the Frenchman's Baby—Rebecca Winters
Coming Home to the Cowboy—
Patricia Thayer (Silhouette Romance®)

Then we joined Emma Valentine as she got a royal welcome in September

The Rebel Prince—Raye Morgan

There was a trip to the Outback to meet Louise Valentine's long-lost sister, Jodie

Wanted: Outback Wife—Ally Blake

Now, on these cold November nights, catch up with newcomer Daniel Valentine

Married Under the Mistletoe—Linda Goodnight

Snuggle up with sexy Jack Valentine over Christmas

Crazy About the Boss—Teresa Southwick

In the New Year join Melissa as she heads off to a desert kingdom

The Nanny and the Sheikh—Barbara McMahon

And don't miss the thrilling end to the Valentine saga in February

The Valentine Bride—Liz Fielding

To the children of Gorlovka Hope Orphanage
in Ukraine, who may never read the book
but who will benefit from its proceeds.
My prayers are with you.

CHAPTER ONE

IN HIS wildest fantasies, if he were given to such things, Daniel Stephens had never expected to be here, doing this.

He shifted the heavy canvas duffel bag from his shoulder to the pavement in front of the beautiful, light-washed building, slicked back a damp clutch of hair and gazed up at the Knightsbridge Bella Lucia Restaurant.

London pulsed around him, the genteel hum of the élite, the roar of buses, the swirling, thick moisture of a damp October night, all both familiar and foreign after so many years away.

This was his birth family's restaurant. One of three, if he understood correctly. Fabulously successful. Exclusive. Expensive.

His nostrils flared. Outward façades never impressed him much. To his way of thinking most were lies, like his own childhood, covering a multitude of sins. But he had to admit, the Valentine family had style.

A chic woman stepped out of a taxicab beside him, tucked her designer bag beneath her arm, and sailed past without a glance to enter the glass double-doors of the restaurant. Soft jazz wafted out briefly, then was sucked back inside as the doors vacuumed shut.

Daniel had blood here. Blood that hadn't claimed him or his twin until now when it no longer hurt so much to have no father, no extended family, no one to care. Now his father wanted him. Or so he said. People like John Valentine generally hid ulterior motives. If Daniel waited around awhile, he'd find out what his father was really after.

The notion of claiming John Valentine as father still rankled as much as Mrs Valentine's demand for a DNA test to prove it. He'd refused her request during his brief visit a week and a half ago and, furious, had returned to the familiar call of Africa. But his twin brother Dominic had obliged, proving once and for all that the father who had abandoned them before birth was a rich and respected man.

Now that his troublesome temper had cooled and he'd thought the matter over, Daniel was back. Not that he wanted anything from the family he didn't know or trust. Not at all. But he did want something he couldn't get in Africa. Money. Lots and lots of money.

But first, he needed a place to live. His father—and he used the word loosely—had all but insisted he stay here in the flat above the Knightsbridge restaurant.

Light rain patted against his cheeks. His lips twitched an ironic smile. Water. The most precious commodity on earth. One so abundant here in his native country and so desperately scarce in his adopted one. He'd spent his entire career trying to rectify that problem, but project funds always ran short at the worst possible times. Now he was determined to use his skills and contacts in the UK to change all that. Life's inequities had always bothered him.

He lifted the heavy duffel bag back onto his shoulder. Might as well go up. Introduce himself to the American restaurant manager who had somehow been persuaded to share her lodging with him. He still wondered how John had worked that one out, but the old man had assured him that the woman was not only in agreement but was delighted with the arrangement. After all, the flat was large and roomy and there was some sort of problem in the restaurant that might make a woman alone uneasy. He hadn't added, though Daniel was no fool, that the flat also belonged to the Valentine family and that Miss Stephanie Ellison had no real choice in the matter.

If not for his determination to sink every shilling he had into the new business and ultimately into the Ethiopian water project, he might have felt badly about intruding upon the restaurant manager. He might have. But he didn't.

Obsessing. Stephanie Ellison was obsessing. And she had to get a handle on it fast. She glanced at the stylish pewter clock above the sofa. Five minutes.

"Oh, Lord."

The pressure against her temples intensified.

She paced from one side of her flat to the other, stopping to straighten every piece of framed art, two fresh flower arrangements and a pewter bowl of vanilla potpourri. All useless, obsessive gestures.

The living room, like every other room in the luxury Knightsbridge flat, was immaculate. And why not? She had cleaned, re-cleaned, and triple-cleaned today. Even the cans in the kitchen cupboards were organized into groups according to the alphabet.

And yet the throb in her temple grew louder and her gut knotted as if something was out of order.

Something *was* out of order. Seriously out of order.

"But I can do this." She paced across the white-tiled floor and down the hall to her bedroom to assess her appearance—again. "Oh, why did John put me in this situation?"

Especially now, with the problems in the restaurant. Until the missing money was recovered, Stephanie needed to concentrate her attention there. After all, as manager she was ultimately responsible. But thanks to her employer, she had to deal with an even more dreaded scenario. An unwanted *male* flatmate.

A shudder rippled through her.

John Valentine had no way of knowing that thrusting his son upon her as a temporary roommate had the power to push her over the edge. John, like everyone else, knew nothing of the hidden shame that caused her to keep people at arm's length.

Oh, she was friendly enough. She'd learned from a master to put on a smile, keep her mouth shut, and play the game so that the world at large believed the masquerade instead of the truth.

That was why she'd never taken on a roommate. Brief visits by girlfriends such as Rebecca Valentine, yes. But a roommate? Never. Having someone invade her space for a few days was bad enough. A roommate was sheer terror.

Anyone who got too close might discover the truth. And she couldn't even face that herself.

Since hiring her a year ago as manager of the exclusive Knightsbridge restaurant, the Valentine family had given her carte blanche in remodeling and running the Bella Lucia. They'd even indulged her penchant for contemporary art décor. Her boss seldom interfered. Which was exactly why she hadn't been able to say no when he'd asked her to house the son who'd spent years doing charity work in Africa.

She chewed on that, allowing a seed of hope that Daniel Stephens was as noble as his work implied. From her boss's enthusiastic description, Daniel was one minor step below sainthood.

She laughed, though the sound was as humorless as the hammering in her head.

"A saint. Sure, he is. Like all men."

One other thing worried her. Actually, a lot of other things worried her. But in her flummoxed state, she'd failed to ask how long Daniel would be staying. With all her heart, she hoped not long. There was too much at stake to have him here indefinitely.

She swiveled around backwards, twisting her head to look at the slim, smooth line of her pale green dress. Everything was covered. Nothing showed. But she'd have to be extra careful with a flatmate lurking about. She hated that. Hated worrying that someone would discover the secret she kept hidden away beneath designer labels.

Someone tapped softly at the door.

Stephanie jumped, then gritted her teeth in frustration. She would not, could not, let anxiety take over. The willowy redhead staring back from the mirrored tub enclosure looked in complete control, unruffled, and well groomed. Good. As long as the outside appeared in control, let the inside rage.

She smoothed newly manicured hands down the soft, flowing skirt, realigned the toiletries on the counter for the third time, and went to greet her boss's son.

One look at the big, dark, wild-looking man filling up her foyer and Stephanie's heart slammed against her ribcage. The throbbing in her head intensified. Fight or flight kicked into high gear. Escape lay past him and down the elevator to the restaurant below. She had little choice but to stand and fight.

There had to be a mistake. This could not be Daniel. Mr Valentine had called him a boy, and, even though she had fully expected a grown man, she hadn't expected this… this…barbarian!

"My boy," John had said with an indulgent chuckle. "He's a tad rough around the edges. Too much time abroad living without the amenities of the civilized world."

A *tad* rough around the edges? A *tad*? That understatement was a record even for the British.

This was no boy. This was a motorcycle gang in battered jeans, bomber jacket and rough-out boots. A pirate with piercing blue eyes, stubble darkening his jaw and unruly black hair in need of a cut. She had expected him at the worst to resemble his twin brother, Dominic, who worked for her as a part-time accountant. But this man was nothing like harmless, middle-aged Dominic. There wasn't a bald spot or an ounce of fat anywhere on this guy. And he was anything but harmless.

Surely there was a mistake.

Another equally disturbing concern struck. If this was

Daniel, and she prayed he wasn't, could John have sent him to spy on her, suspicious that *she* was responsible for the money missing from the restaurant accounts?

Fighting panic and forcing a bland expression she didn't feel, Stephanie took a small step back. The stranger was too close, too threatening.

"Are you Daniel?"

One corner of his mouth quirked. "And if I say no?"

If he said no? What kind of introduction was that?

She blinked several times, then drew upon a glib tongue and a sharp mind to gloss over her real feelings. "Then I'll assume you're the plumber, at which rate you're five days late and fired."

He laughed, a quick flash of white teeth in a sun-burnished face. *Oh, my.*

"To save myself that indignity, I'll confess. I'm Daniel Stephens, your new flatmate."

She'd always enjoyed the British male voice with its soft burr in the back of the throat. But this man's voice was half purr, half gravel and all male, a sound that shimmied down her spine to the toes of her new heels.

Heaven help her. What had she agreed to? This could never work. Not even if she wanted it to. And she most decidedly did not. He was too rugged to be handsome and too blatantly male not to be noticed. And Stephanie did not notice men. Not anymore.

She couldn't meet his gaze but she couldn't take her eyes off him either.

Her silence must have gone on a bit too long because he said, "May I come in?"

Stephanie opened the door wider, determined to remain

as composed as possible under the circumstance. "Of course. Please."

She couldn't let him know how much his size and strength and sheer manliness unnerved her. She could handle him. Hadn't she determined long ago that no man would ever get close enough to hurt her again? Hadn't she rid herself of that fear by moving far, far away from Colorado?

"I'm afraid you caught me by surprise." A lie, of course. "The flat is…"

He poked his rather unkempt, and altogether too attractive head inside and finished her sentence. "Fine."

Her flat, like her person, was always ultra-clean and tidy. Outward appearances were everything. And having things out of place distressed her.

Stephanie turned and led the way to the living room. Her stomach jittered and her heart raced, but she was good at the pretense game.

Trouble was, it had been a while since she'd had to pretend quite this much. Or for quite this long. There was that troubling question again. How long would he be here?

Daniel's bulk filled up the large living room as if it were elevator-small. He glanced around with an unconcerned expression. The luxury of a flat that most could only dream of was apparently lost on him.

"Where should I stash my bedroll?" He swung the bag from his wide shoulder as if it contained nothing but packing peanuts. "Any place will do. A room, the floor, the couch. Makes no difference to me."

Well, it certainly made a difference to Stephanie.

"I've put you in the back guest room." She forced a smile. "I assure you, it's more comfortable than the floor."

And as far away from her room as possible.

She led the way down the short hall toward the back of the flat, pointing out the other rooms along the way.

"This is the kitchen here. You're welcome to make use of it anytime." She felt like a Realtor.

"I wouldn't think you'd need much of a kitchen with the restaurant below."

"A person tires quickly of too much rich food."

"I can't imagine."

She paused to look at him. Bad decision. "Are you making fun of me?"

"Am I?" Blue eyes glittered back at her, insolent eyes that challenged. Stephanie glanced away.

Perhaps her statement had been rude. The man *had* spent a lot of years in places where food such as that served in the Bella Lucia was unheard of.

He was the boss's son. She didn't want to get off on the wrong foot with him. "I apologize. I'm really not a snob. But you'll have to understand, I'm accustomed to living on my own." She pushed the door open to the last bedroom. "You have your own bathroom through here."

"Nice," he said, though his tone indicated indifference as he gazed from the sage and toast décor to the queen-sized bed and then to the pristine bathroom beyond. He tossed the duffel bag into a corner next to a white occasional table. "I can see you aren't nearly as happy to have me here as John thought you'd be."

Stephanie wasn't certain what to say to that. She loved her job and couldn't chance upsetting her generous employer.

"I'm sure we'll get on fine." She hovered in the

doorway, eager to have him settled, but equally eager to make her escape.

"I don't think you're sure of that at all."

He moved across the room in her direction. Stephanie resisted the urge to shrink back into the hallway.

"I don't know what you mean."

"Sure you do."

Before she knew what he was about, he touched her forearm. The gesture was harmless, meaning only to convey reassurance. It had just the opposite effect.

Try as she might to stand her ground, Stephanie flinched and pulled away, desperate to rub away the feel of his calloused fingers against her flesh.

Hand in mid-air, Daniel studied her, clearly bewildered by her overreaction.

"I meant no harm, Stephanie. You're quite safe with me here."

Right. As safe as a rabbit in a fox's den.

Forcing a false little laugh, she tried to make light of her jitters. "I'm sure all serial murderers say the same thing."

"Cereal murderers?" He dropped his hand and slouched against the door facing, too close for comfort. "Can't imagine harming an innocent box of cornflakes."

So, he had a sense of humor. She backed one step out into the hallway. "My oatmeal will be relieved to hear that."

"Ah, now, porridge. There's nothing innocent about horse feed cooked to the gooey consistency of wallpaper paste. I might be tempted to do in a few boxes of those, after all."

This time Stephanie laughed. For a barbarian, he displayed a pleasant sense of the ridiculous.

"There's tea in the kitchen if you'd like a cup." She started back down the hall.

"Sounds great. If you're having one too."

She hesitated in the living-room entry, not wanting to appear rude, but certainly not wanting to become friends. Her idea of a male friend was one that lived somewhere else. Preferably Mars.

The gravelly purr moved up behind her, too close again. "We might as well get acquainted, Stephanie. We're going to be living together."

She wasn't overly fond of that term, but it wouldn't do to offend the son of her employer. From the rumors astir in the restaurant, she knew Daniel and Dominic were John's only sons, the result of a fling he'd had as a young man. Though he'd only recently discovered their existence, Mr Valentine was trying hard to make up for lost time.

"All right, then. I have a few minutes." She really should go, get away from him while she could still carry on a lucid conversation. Trouble was he'd be here when she came back.

In the kitchen, she poured tea into two china cups and set them on the small breakfast bar.

Daniel, instead of taking a seat, made himself at home by rummaging about for milk and sugar. In the narrow kitchen, they bumped once. Stephanie shifted away, rounding the bar to sit opposite him. If Daniel noticed her avoidance, he didn't react.

Instead, he slouched into the straight-backed white chair and splashed a generous amount of milk into the cup. Stephanie had never embraced the English penchant for milk in her tea. She did, however, favor sugar. In abundance.

"Tsk. Tsk. Three sugars?" Daniel murmured when she'd doused her cup. "Bad girl."

An unwanted female reaction skittered through her. The words were innocent enough, but his sexy tone gave them new meaning. Either that or she was losing touch with reality.

She inclined her head. "Now you know."

A black eyebrow kicked upward. "Sweet tooth?"

"A decidedly evil one. Grabs me in the middle of the night sometimes." Why was she telling him this?

"You don't look the part." His laser-blue gaze drifted over her slim body, hesitating a millisecond too long.

"I jog. I also have enormous self-control." Like now, when I really want you out of my flat, but I can't say so.

"Don't tell me you never sneak down to the restaurant for cheesecake and chocolate sauce?"

She smiled in spite of herself. "How did you guess?"

Small crinkles appeared around his eyes. The African sun had been kind to him. "Because that's what I'd do if I lived over a restaurant."

"Which you now do." Unfortunately.

"But you hold the keys to the Bella Lucia."

She stirred the spoon round and round in her cup. "There is that."

"Think I can persuade you to make your midnight runs with me in tow?"

Perhaps not, big boy.

Without comment, she lifted her cup and sipped.

Daniel did likewise, eyelids dropping in a soft sigh of appreciation. Stephanie had a hard time not staring. Though she was loath to admit it, Daniel Stephens was a stunningly attractive man.

"Can't get tea like this where I've been," he said, clattering the cup onto the saucer.

"Tell me about Africa." As she'd done countless times, Stephanie slipped into hostess mode, tucking away real feelings to skim the surface of civilized conversation. "Your father's very proud of what you've done there."

His face, so full of pleasure moments before, closed up tight. "My father doesn't know a thing about my work."

And from the stormy look of him, Stephanie figured John might never know. Her boss might want to mend fences with his sons, but this one had some hostility that might not be so easily overcome.

Daniel's anger reminded her of the kids she sometimes worked with in special art classes. There, where she volunteered her time teaching troubled children to paint, she had learned to listen as well as to share simple techniques of line and color.

In the same quiet voice she used to encourage those kids, she said, "Would you tell me about it?"

Forearms on the table edge, he linked his fingers and leaned forward. Too close again. The man had an unpleasant habit of invading her space. Stephanie tilted back a few inches.

"The work is rewarding and equally frustrating," he said.

So he'd chosen to sidestep the issue of his father and move on to the safer ground of Africa. She didn't know why she'd felt compelled to dig into his personal life in the first place. The less she knew about him, the better.

"Is that why you quit?"

"I didn't quit. I'll never quit," he said vehemently. "But

I've finally realized that I can make more of a difference here than I can there."

She frowned, not following. "How?"

"To build sustainable, safe water systems takes money and expertise. I'm a civil engineer. I've spent my whole life dealing with the problem. I have the expertise. What I lack is that vulgar little commodity called money."

"So you're back in England to raise money, then."

"In a manner of speaking. I'm starting my own business, contracting water projects throughout England. The demand is high, especially in the area of flood control. A man who has the right skills and contacts can make a fortune."

Maybe he *was* as giving as John had indicated. "And you're planning to use that money to fund projects in Africa?"

"It's the best way I can think of." He shoved a hand over dark, unruly hair. "That's why I'm grateful to you for sharing this flat, and that's also why I agreed to the arrangement in the first place. I dislike accepting favors, particularly from my father, but the less spent on living expenses, the more I can spare for Ethiopia."

Despite her determination not to get too close, Stephanie's opinion of Daniel rose several notches. He had a caring heart, at least where the needy in Africa were concerned. This knowledge gave her hope that he would not be difficult to room with. If her luck held out, he would keep his distance until the business was started and he could afford his own place to live.

And this brought her to the question that had burned on her mind since that first telephone call from Mr Valentine. Just exactly how long would all that take? How long would she have this disturbing, intriguing, terrifying man living in her flat?

Because, for her own protection and peace of mind, the sooner he was gone, the better.

CHAPTER TWO

SURREPTITIOUSLY, Daniel watched the stunning red-haired woman from behind his teacup. The moment she'd opened the door he'd lost his breath, knocked out by the sheer beauty of her long legs, slim, shapely body, and the long, wavy just-got-out-of-bed hairstyle. Though her dress was mid-calf and modest, his first, very wayward thoughts had been of sex, a natural male reaction that he'd reined in right away. Mostly. He'd once had a penchant for redheads and, if his body's reaction was an accurate indicator, he still did. But he was here on business. And business it would remain.

A few minutes in her company, however, had told him what the old man hadn't. That she wasn't all that thrilled to have him here. But he was here and planned to stick around. And it didn't hurt at all that his flatmate was gorgeous and smelled incredible as well. He could look, but that was the end of it.

Long ago, he'd come to grips with his own shortcomings where women were concerned. He liked them, enjoyed their company, but he'd never been able to fall in love. After too many years, he'd finally faced reality.

Thanks to his mother, he lacked the capacity to love anybody.

"I need to get back down to the restaurant." Stephanie's teacup rattled against the saucer as she set it in place. "There's more tea if you want it."

"Thanks, but no. No time like the present to get started on the telephone contacts."

She reached for his cup and he handed it over.

"You should consider getting a mobile phone."

"Hmm. Possibly later." Right now he was conserving funds.

"I have a computer if you need one." She motioned toward the hall. "Sometimes I work on orders and supplies at night."

"I'll probably take you up on that." He pushed up from the chair and came around the bar to stand beside her at the sink. "Let me help with this."

Wariness flickered across her pretty face. "I have it."

"Okay." He backed off, wondering if his size intimidated her. She wouldn't be the first, though she reached his shoulders. He propped his backside against the blue granite counter several feet away from her. The tension eased.

With a grace that had him watching her hands, she washed the cups, dried them and placed them, handles aligned to the right, inside the cupboard. The orderliness of her flat was almost amusing. His idea of domestic order was keeping the mosquito net untangled around his face at night.

She tidied up, putting everything away until the kitchen looked as if no one lived there. In fact, the entire flat had that look. As if it were a photograph, a perfect, sophisticated, contemporary ad of an apartment. Not a lived-in place.

Folding a snowy tea-towel into a precise rectangle, she hung it neatly over a holder, straightening the edges while she spoke. "Is there anything else I can show you before I go? Anything you need?"

"I'm not a guest, Stephanie. No need for you to fret over me. I can find my way around." Hadn't he fended for himself as long as he could remember?

"Right. Of course." Her hands fidgeted with the edge of the towel. "I'd better go, then. The evening crowd begins soon."

"I may go out this afternoon myself. Do you have an extra key to the flat?"

She clasped the butterfly hands in front of her. "I'm sorry. I never thought of having another key made."

"Give me yours and I'll go to the locksmith."

"I'll get it." She looked none too excited about the prospect of sharing her key with him, but she disappeared down the hall and was back in moments, key extended. "This also fits the doors leading out onto the balcony. In case you didn't notice, there are two entrances to the flat. A staircase up the outside as well as the elevator in back of the restaurant."

"Good to know. Thanks." He pocketed the key, keeping watch on her fidgety movements. She'd relaxed somewhat since his arrival, but Daniel had the strongest feeling her tension was more than the normal discomfort of acquiring an unfamiliar flatmate. Though good breeding or schooling gave her the right words to say, her real feelings lay hidden behind the serenely composed expression. And yet, her hands gave her away.

With an inner shrug, he dismissed the idea. Stephanie's

problems were her own. He wasn't interested in getting past the pretty face and tantalizingly long legs. His business here was exactly that—business.

"You're welcome to come down to the restaurant later and get acquainted if you'd like," she said, heading for the door. "Some of your family may come round. They often do."

The comment brought him up short. He still had trouble thinking of the Valentines as family.

"Is Dominic working today?" He'd had little time with his twin since returning to England. Discovering that Dominic had become a part-time employee of the restaurant below added to the appeal of living here. They'd been apart a very long time.

Stephanie glanced at her watch. "He should be in his office about now. I'm sure he'd enjoy a visit."

And so would Daniel, though he was every bit as eager to begin setting up appointments. The list of contacts in his bag was impressive. With it, his business should be up and running in no time.

His flatmate was halfway out the door when she stopped and turned. "Oh, one more thing, Daniel."

"Yes?"

Cool aqua eyes assessed him. "If you don't mind my asking, how long are you planning to be here?"

"Why, Stephanie—" he playfully placed a hand over his heart "—I'm crushed. Already trying to get rid of me?"

"No, no, of course not. I didn't mean that at all. I was just thinking…"

He knew exactly what she was thinking, but he couldn't accommodate her. "New businesses take a while to get off the ground. A year. Perhaps longer." He watched her, hoping to gauge her true reaction, but she gave nothing away. "That won't be a problem, will it?"

"That will be…fine," she said.

Daniel didn't believe a word of it.

Several hours later, Daniel exited the tube in high spirits, returning to Knightsbridge after a successful afternoon. He'd found a locksmith to cut a new flat key and afterwards had spent an hour chatting up a former university mate about business prospects. All in all, a good beginning.

Above ground, the rain had begun in earnest. Though he'd failed to bring an umbrella, the smell of rain in the air and the feel of it on his skin were a pleasure after years in the African sun. He resisted the childish urge to lift his face and catch the drops on his tongue.

At the back door of the Bella Lucia, he shook himself off to spare the floors a puddle. A kitten, no bigger than his hand, meowed up at him in protest.

"Sorry there, little one." He scooped the ball of fluff into one hand and slid her inside his jacket while he looked about for a dry place. She snuggled close, a warm, damp ball against his shirt, and turned her motor on. Daniel spotted an overhang and withdrew the kitten from his jacket. She meowed again.

"Hungry?" he asked, crouching down to set her beneath the overhang. Her yellow eyes blinked at him. With a final stroke of the small head, he decided to steal a bite for her later, and then went inside the Bella Lucia to find his brother.

To the right of the wide entry were the lift and a door marked "Storage." On his left were the offices. Taking a guess, he tapped at the first one and went inside. Dominic sat at a desk, intently staring at a computer screen.

Daniel stood for a moment, observing his brother at work. Fraternal twins, they had once shared similarities, but now, beyond the blue eyes and tall stature, they bore little resemblance. Domestication and long hours in a high-pressure accounting firm had taken a toll on Dominic's once powerful physique.

"Careful there, brother. You'll be getting eye strain from all that hard work."

The balding head lifted with a smile and a brotherly jab. "No chance of that happening to you, now, is there, mate?"

"Not if I can avoid it," he joked in return. Hard work was all he'd ever known, as Dominic well knew.

A bit wearily, Dominic removed a pair of reading glasses and rubbed at his eyes. "Are you settled in, then? Finding the flat upstairs to your liking?"

Daniel flopped into a chair. "You know I don't care about the flat. Why didn't you warn me about my flatmate?"

"Warn you?" Humor glinted on Dominic's tired face. "About what?"

"That she was young and beautiful. And not nearly as willing to have me move in as John let on."

A slow smile crept up Dominic's cheeks. "You always were a sucker for redheads."

"Getting this business off the ground is my first priority. The flat is just a step in that direction."

"Then why is Stephanie a problem? Did she try to toss you out?"

"No, nothing like that." Quite the opposite, actually. "She was polite, accommodating." She'd put on the pretense of welcome, but her fidgety movements told a different story.

"Then what's the problem?"

He wasn't sure how to answer that one. "I make her nervous."

Dominic guffawed. "Look in the mirror. You make everyone nervous."

Daniel shoved a hand through his unruly hair. He never could figure out why his appearance concerned people. Just because he didn't care about the usual conventions of dress or style, people sometimes shied away. Or maybe it was the darkness. Dark skin, dark hair. Bad attitude.

But this wasn't the feeling he had with Stephanie. "I think the problem is deeper than the way I look."

"Shave. Get a haircut. See if that helps."

He'd skip that advice. Unlike his conservative, by-the-book twin, Daniel had never been a suit-and-tie kind of a man. Perhaps that was why he meshed with Africa so well. That, and the fact that Africa needed and appreciated him.

"Is there a boyfriend lurking around to punch my face for moving in with her?"

"I thought you weren't interested."

"I'm not dead either."

Dominic chuckled. "Good. You were starting to worry me."

"I gave up on love, not on life."

Dominic knew better than anyone about Daniel's empty heart.

"Sometimes they're one and the same."

The profound statement stirred the old restless longing,

the feeling that, no matter how much good he did, life was passing by without him.

"Are you going to annoy me about my nonexistent love-life or tell me about Stephanie Ellison?"

"Well, let's see." Dominic gnawed at the earpiece of his glasses, pretending to think. "She doesn't allow staff to smoke anywhere near the restaurant. Says it projects a bad image to the customers."

"That's not exactly the kind of information I meant."

"None of us know much about her before she came here. She's a mystery really."

A mystery. Hmm. Better steer clear of that. He had enough puzzles to solve with the new business. "What kind of manager is she? Demanding? Difficult to work for?"

Though Dominic had only been in this job just over a week, he was good at gathering information, a knack that also made him a good accountant. Most of the time he knew more about a company than the owner.

"Stephanie's a bit of a workaholic, a real control freak about tidiness," Dominic said, "but she treats employees well. She gives every appearance of being an excellent manager."

Daniel heard the subtle hesitation. "What do you mean by 'gives every appearance'?"

"Nothing really. She's doing a fine job." Dominic glanced away, fidgeted with his glasses. He was holding back.

"I know you, Dominic. What are you not saying?"

"I don't want to spread unsubstantiated rumors."

"I'm your brother. I've just moved in with the woman. If she's trouble, you have to tell me."

"All right, then, between you and me." He sighed and rolled a squeaky chair back from the desk. "You've heard about the money missing from the restaurant accounts?"

Daniel nodded, frowning. John had mentioned the problem. "You think Stephanie's involved?"

"No. I don't. Someone kind enough to take sick waiting staff to her flat, give them an aspirin and take over their shift while they rest isn't a likely thief. Plus, she's meticulous to the point of obsession about every detail of running this place. I can't see her dipping into the till."

"Yet, someone is responsible."

"Right. And she's the newcomer, the outsider."

"Not the only one," Daniel pointed out.

Dominic blinked, clearly shocked at the suggestion. "You think I—"

Daniel laughed. "Not in a million years." His straight-down-the-line brother was so honest, he'd often confessed to childhood mischief before being confronted. "Have you talked to John about it?"

"Actually, the first clue came from him. He asked me to balance the dates when the money disappeared with all the other transactions filtering in and out of the three restaurants. There were some interesting inconsistencies, but nothing definite yet."

"So what's your decision? Is our pretty manager guilty?"

"I'm still watching, but, like I said, I don't want to think Stephanie is involved. She isn't the type."

Daniel didn't think so either, though he barely knew the woman. He'd much rather believe her anxiety around him was personal than an embezzler's guilty conscience.

The idea gave him pause and, before he could stop the words, he asked, "What about her personal life? Does she see anyone?"

Dominic tossed his glasses onto the desk and tilted back, his gaze assessing. Daniel shifted in his chair. Okay, he'd admit it. He wanted to know about his flatmate as a woman, not as a restaurant manager.

"She goes out now and then, though the gossip mill says she never dates seriously."

"Why? Too busy with work?"

"That's my guess. But Rachel thinks she's had her heart broken."

"Rachel?" Daniel frowned. "Employee or relative?" He was having trouble keeping track.

"A cousin. Our uncle Robert's daughter. Her sister, Rebecca, is a close friend of Stephanie's. I think she may know more about your lovely manager than anyone."

"She's not *my* anything," Daniel groused. "I was just asking." And he didn't know why, so he decided to let the subject of his flatmate drop. "So, tell me about you, Dominic. How's the job? The family?"

Dominic's gaze flicked to the computer screen. He picked up a pen and twirled it in his fingers.

"Alice is pregnant again."

Daniel tried not to let the surprise show. Dominic looked stressed enough without being reminded that his other kids were nearly grown. "How many does this make? Four? Five?"

Daniel spent so little time in England that he couldn't keep up. Never fond of his brother's wife, he hadn't tried too hard. Alice's well-to-do family had vigorously protested when she had married a nobody like Dominic, and since then she had maintained an air of superiority that rankled Daniel.

"This makes four." Dominic ran a hand over his face, and Daniel noticed again how much his brother had aged. "Alice is thrilled. She thinks another baby will keep us young. And a new addition also gives her a reason to shop."

As if she needed one. Daniel remembered his sister-in-law's propensity for spending. Luckily, his brother had done so well that his family could afford the best of everything. They lived in a fashionable area of London. His children attended private school, and both Dominic and Alice drove a Mercedes. Holidays in Rome or Madrid or anywhere they fancied were the norm. Daniel was glad for his brother's success.

Dominic had only taken the extra position here at the restaurant as a way to get acquainted with the family he'd never known, and now to help ferret out the thief in the ranks. He certainly didn't need the money.

"What about you? How do you feel about a new baby?"

Dominic drew in a deep breath and let it slowly out. "Stunned. I never expected to be a father again at forty."

"Forty's not too old."

"Easy for you to say," Dominic said with a rueful grin. "You aren't losing your hair."

Daniel returned the grin. "Is Alice all right, then? The pregnancy going well?"

"Sure. Everything's fine. Great. You'll have to come to the house for dinner one night and see for yourself." He gave a self-conscious laugh. "Get that haircut first, though."

In other words, Alice would have a fit if her uncivilized brother-in-law embarrassed her in front of her friends.

"How about one night next week?" Dominic went on. "I'll invite John as well."

"I don't think so."

"Come on, Daniel. Don't be a hard case. We wanted a father all our lives and now we have one. He wants to get to know us."

Tension coiled in Daniel's gut. John Valentine was not his favorite subject. "He has a daughter—he adopted Louise; he wanted her. Why would he want to know us?"

"Because we're blood. You and I have a right to be in this family."

"Not according to Ivy." John's wife had thrown a fit to discover her husband had two sons with a former lover. "And maybe she has a point. Being adopted is better than being illegitimate." The word left a nasty taste in his mouth.

"Louise doesn't think so. She's very upset. She's even started one of those birth-parent searches. Has John worried sick. He says she's not herself at all."

"Do you blame her? This must be a terrible shock to her." It had been to him. And he blamed the parents, not the children. Though he'd only briefly met Louise, she seemed nice enough, a quiet, accommodating woman dedicated to her family. She didn't deserve to be blindsided by two long-lost brothers and the revelation that she had been adopted by John and Ivy Valentine.

"Maybe." Dominic lifted a doubting brow. "Maybe not."

"Meaning?"

"John phoned earlier, fretting over her as usual. Which is very bad for his heart, by the way, and she well knows that. Says Louise is planning to leave for Meridia tomorrow for some nonsense. A make-over, I think he called it, for Emma."

Daniel searched his memory banks but came up empty, sighing in resignation. "Am I supposed to know Emma?"

"Cousin. Yet another of Uncle Robert's numerous offspring. Emma's the chef. Quite a renowned one, I hear. She was commissioned for a king's coronation. That's why she's in Meridia though who knows why Louise thinks she needs a make-over."

"Ah." Not that Daniel comprehended any of this. After living a lifetime with a handful of family to his name, he was now swimming in relatives he didn't know. From Dominic, he knew that their father John and his half-brother Robert were at odds. He also knew that the recent death of their grandfather William had increased the rivalry and battle for control of the restaurants. Beyond that, Daniel was lost. Even if he cared, which he hadn't yet decided if he did or not, sorting out all the Valentines would require time and exposure. "So how does this relate to our sister?"

"Our father thinks Louise is going off the deep end and needs him more than ever." His nostrils flared. "I think she's an attention seeker, drumming up sympathy to keep a wedge between John and his blood children."

"You and me."

"Right. She's on the defensive, trying to hold John's allegiance. After growing up in the wealth and society that actually belonged to us, she's unwilling to share. I, for one, think it's time you and I reaped the benefits she's had all her life."

The answer bothered Daniel. Though he didn't necessarily feel the same, he could understand his brother's emotional need to embrace their birth family. But he and Alice were well set. They didn't need the Valentine "benefits", either social or financial.

Settling back against the plush office chair, he studied his twin. They had always been different, but in the years since they'd spent any real time together the differences had increased tenfold.

Daniel wasn't sure he liked the changes.

CHAPTER THREE

FEET propped on a chair, Daniel slouched in broody silence on the too-small red sofa. His belly growled, but the half-eaten fish and chips on the table had long ago grown cold and greasy. Papers, phone numbers, business cards and other evidence of a budding business venture lay strewn around him in the darkness. He should be satisfied. But he wasn't.

Except for a few, brief conversations Stephanie Ellison had avoided being alone with him since his arrival. She was friendly enough when he went into the restaurant. She even smiled indulgently at his feeble jokes and brought him a drink. But long after the restaurant closed, she remained downstairs.

And he wanted to know why. This was her flat. She should be comfortable here even with him present. Worst of all, he didn't enjoy feeling like an interloper. He'd had enough of that when he was a kid and Mum brought friends to their hotel.

So tonight he'd waited up for little Miss Manager.

When her key turned in the lock and she walked in, Daniel was ready for her.

Light flooded the room.

"Are you avoiding me?"

Stephanie looked up, manicured fingers on the light switch, clearly startled to find him still awake, sitting in the midnight darkness. "I beg your pardon?"

"You heard me."

She didn't answer. Instead, she took one glance at the flat and started her incessant tidying up.

"Leave it," he growled, annoyed that once again she was trying to sidestep him.

She kept working. "My goodness, you're in a mood tonight. What's wrong?"

"You." Actually, she wasn't the only problem, but the one he wanted fixed first. The others could wait.

Her fidgety hands stilled on the fish and chips wrapper. "And just what have I done that's so terrible?"

"You skip out of here at pre-dawn, seldom come up to your own flat throughout the day, and then sneak in long after I've gone to bed."

"Managing a restaurant requires long hours." She tossed his forgotten dinner into the bin and then turned on him, green eyes flashing. "And I do not sneak."

"Have you always worked eighteen-hour days? Or only since taking me on as a flatmate?"

She gathered the papers from the floor and made a perfect stack on the table. "Why are you asking me this?"

"Just answer the question. Are you avoiding me?"

"Of course not. How ridiculous."

"Good. Then stop clearing up my mess and come sit down."

"I've worked all day and I'm very tired."

"You *are* avoiding me. All I'm asking is a few minutes

of your time. We are flatmates, after all. We live together, but one of us is not living here." Daniel didn't care that he sounded like a nagging wife. He wanted to know what her problem was.

She rolled her eyes. "Okay. Fine. I'll sit."

And she did. Like a gorgeous red-plumed bird, she perched on the edge of a chair opposite him ready to fly away at any moment. Her hands twisted restlessly in her lap. He had the strongest urge to reach over and take hold of them.

"I haven't ax-murdered you in your sleep, have I?"

Her lips twitched. "Evidently not."

At last. He was getting somewhere, though why he cared, he couldn't say.

"So stop being so jumpy." It irritated him.

"I am not—" But she didn't bother to finish the denial. "What do you want to talk about? Is there a problem with the flat? A problem with the new business?"

"Do you ever relax? Maybe read a book or watch the telly?"

"When I have time."

Which he doubted was ever.

He pushed. "How much of London have you seen since you've been here?"

"Not nearly as much as I'd like, but I love it. The museums, the history."

"We're steps away from some of the finest museums in the world. Which ones have you seen?"

"The Royal College of Art," she shot back.

No surprise there. He knew from looking at the walls in the flat and in the restaurant that she fancied modern art, the kind he couldn't begin to understand. There wasn't a realistic picture anywhere in the place.

"Where else?"

She shrugged and went silent.

"That's it? You've not done the palace or the Victoria and Albert Museum?" They were right around the corner.

"Not yet. But I will."

"What about Hyde Park?"

"I jog there."

"A picnic is better. What say we have one?"

Her hands stopped fidgeting. "A picnic?"

Was that longing he heard?

"Yep. Tomorrow afternoon. Hyde Park."

She shook her head; waves of red swung around her shoulders. "I'm too busy."

"So am I." Suddenly, he wanted a picnic more than anything. "But real life happens in between the busyness, Stephanie."

Her gaze slid up to his, slid away, then came back again. She wanted to. He was certain of it.

He gave her a half smile. It probably looked sinister but he hoped for charm. "Avoiding me again?"

"No!"

He lifted a doubting brow.

She sighed. "All right, then, a picnic. Tomorrow after the noon rush."

Triumph, way out of proportion to the event, expanded in Daniel's chest. At last. He was getting somewhere with the cool and aloof one. Though why it mattered, he had no idea.

* * *

"You're going on a picnic?" Chef Karl, slim and neat in his burgundy chef's coat, froze with one hand on the parmesan and the other on a giant pan of fresh veal.

"Yes, Karl, a picnic," Stephanie said coolly, though her nerves twitched like a cat's tail. "Not bungee jumping from the London Bridge."

"But—" his wide brow, reddened by heat and concentration, puckered "—you never take time off."

"She is today." Daniel, purring like an oversized pussycat and resembling a pillaging pirate, burst through the metal swinging doors that led into the kitchen from the back of the restaurant.

Stephanie's twitchy nerves went haywire. She had to grab on to the stainless-steel counter to, literally, get a grip.

My goodness, that man takes up a lot of space.

Karl, who hadn't a subtle bone in his body, looked from Stephanie to Daniel. "Oh. I see."

Exactly what he saw, Stephanie didn't know and didn't want to know. The staff had no right to poke into her personal life, although she now realized she and Daniel would become this afternoon's gossip.

Great. She was already struggling with last night's decision. What had she been thinking to agree to such a silly thing? Such a dangerous thing? But the truth was she wanted to go on a picnic. With her new roommate. And she did not want to obsess over the reasons.

When she'd come in last night to find Daniel sitting in the dark surrounded by his usual mess, she'd been tempted to run back down the stairs. He was right. She *had* been avoiding the flat, partly because of him. Partly because she dreaded the nightmares that had begun with his arrival.

She was exhausted both physically and mentally. When he'd goaded her, she'd been too tired to think. And now, here she was, both dreading and longing for a picnic with a pirate.

"Don't worry about it, Karl." She patted the chef's arm. "I'll prepare the lunch myself. This is a restaurant, you know. We're bound to have something picnic-worthy around here. You go ahead with preparations for this evening."

"Anything I can do to help?" Daniel asked, eyes dancing with a devilish gleam that said he didn't give a rip about becoming the latest fodder for gossip.

"You could let me off the hook." But she hoped he wouldn't.

The gleam grew brighter. "Not a chance. Be ready in ten minutes. We're walking."

Then he shouldered his way out of the kitchen, slowing long enough to hold the door for one of the hostesses.

"Bossy man," Stephanie muttered half to herself.

"The macho ones always are," the blonde hostess said. "But they are *so* worth it."

Stifling a groan, Stephanie settled on simple picnic fare, which she packed into a bread basket before going out to check the restaurant one more time.

Only a few stray shoppers sipped lattes or fragrant teas at this hour of the day. The dining room was quiet except for the efficient staff preparing for later when things really got hopping. Everything was well-organized. Stephanie's sense of order was intact—except for the little matter of an afternoon with a most disorderly man.

She passed by the bar, scanning the stock, the glasses, the bartenders. A lone customer sat at the bar sipping one of their special hand-mixed drinks. As was her habit, she stopped to offer a smile and a welcome.

From the corner of her eye she spotted Daniel's dark head. He poked around behind the bar and came out with a bottle of wine. He held it up, arching an eyebrow at her.

She pointed a finger in chastisement, but he only laughed and tapped a wide-strapped watch. "Two minutes. Back door."

As soon as he was out of hearing distance, Sophie, one of the bartenders, leaned toward her. "You and Delicious Dan seem to be hitting it off nicely."

Stephanie frosted her with a look. Grinning, Sophie slunk away to polish glasses.

Two minutes later, basket clenched in chilled fingers, Stephanie joined Daniel in the hallway. Her pulse, already racing, kicked up more when John Valentine walked in the door.

Her boss's portly face lit up. "Daniel. Stephanie. What a delight!"

Beside her, Daniel stiffened. "John."

They exchanged greetings, but Stephanie could feel the tension emanating from Daniel and the disappointment from her boss.

"So," John said, somewhat too jauntily. "Are the two of you off somewhere, then?"

"Hyde Park and the Serpentine. Stephanie hasn't been." Daniel's response was almost a challenge, as if he expected argument.

Guilt suffused Stephanie. She shouldn't be running off to play with the boss's son. "I hope you don't mind, Mr Valentine."

"Mind? Why should I? You hardly ever take an afternoon."

Since his mild heart attack a few weeks back, Stephanie thought John looked tired. With all that was going on, she wondered how his health was holding up. Missing money was bad enough, but the family problems continued to mount. John's wife was still angry about the arrival of the twins, though John longed to get to know them. Then there was his daughter, Louise. She'd had a whirlwind trip to Meridia and then, instead of working through her problems with John, had already jetted off again. This time to Australia to meet a woman who could be her biological sister. And none of that included the lifelong bitterness between him and his brother, Robert. How much more could the poor man handle?

"Are you sure, Mr Valentine?" she asked. "I can stay here if you prefer." In fact, considering the way Daniel got under her skin, working would probably be wiser.

"I'm available if any problems arise in the dining room. Go on. Have a lovely time. I'm going to pop in and say hello to Dominic. He thinks he may have some news for me."

With a fatherly pat to Daniel's shoulder, he left them. Daniel stared at the closing door, expression wary and brooding.

"Are you all right?" Stephanie asked.

His jaw flexed. "Why wouldn't I be?"

Then he took the basket from Stephanie's hands, pushed the back door open, and led her out into the overcast day.

The walk to the park was much more pleasant than Stephanie had anticipated. After the encounter in the hallway, she'd expected dark silence. Instead Daniel provided a wickedly humorous and totally cynical commentary on élite London that had her laughing when they entered the beautiful park.

The laughter of children sailing toy boats along the Serpentine Lake wafted up to them from a hundred yards away. A cool breeze, in line with the glorious autumn day, played tag with the curls around Stephanie's face. Daniel's hair, too, rugged and unruly, was tossed by the wind. His was the kind of hair a woman wanted to touch, to smooth back from his high, intelligent brow, to run her fingers through.

The thoughts bothered her and she forced her attention to the wonders of the historic park, breathing in the scent of green grass and fall flowers. "This is a gorgeous park."

"You can thank Henry VIII. He acquired it from the monks."

"Acquired?"

The corners of his eyes crinkled. "In much the way he *acquired* everything."

"Ah, bad Henry."

"Not all bad. We're here, aren't we?"

Well, there was that.

They passed kite flyers, strolling mothers, moon-eyed lovers, and other picnickers before finding a clear shady area to spread their blanket.

Daniel did the honors, flapped the red and white cloth into the breeze and then collapsed on it as it settled to the grass.

"Here you go, m'lady," he teased. And with one jean-jacketed arm, he exaggerated a flourish. "The finest seat in all of London."

Legs carefully folded beneath her, Stephanie sat on the edge of the blanket as far from her companion as was polite. He puzzled her, did Daniel Stephens, vacillating from broody and cautious to light-hearted in a matter of minutes.

Stretched out upon his elbow like some big cat basking in the sun, he seemed happier in the outdoors, as though the inside of buildings couldn't quite contain all there was of him. His mouth fascinating in motion, Daniel chatted tour-guide style about Rotten Row, famous duels, kings and queens, regaling her with stories of the famous old park while she emptied the contents of her picnic basket.

"I suppose we could have got food here," he said motioning to the eating places sprinkled about.

"I wouldn't have come for that. Only a picnic."

"Woman, you crush my fragile ego. I thought you came for my charming company."

She snorted. To her delight, he fell back, clutching his chest. "And now you laugh at my broken heart."

Relaxed and enjoying herself more than she'd thought possible in the company of a barbarian, she thrust a sandwich toward him. "Here. Try this. Karl's tarragon chicken salad is guaranteed to cure broken hearts as well as crushed egos."

"Yes, the way to a man's heart and all that." He unwrapped the sandwich and took a man-sized bite. "Mmm. Not sheep's blood or lizard's eyes, but it will do."

"You haven't actually eaten that sort of thing?"

He arched a wicked brow. "When in Rome, do as the Romans. When in Africa…"

She lifted a bunch of fat grapes. "Suddenly, these don't look too tasty."

"Very similar to lizard's eyes. Right down to the squish."

She made a stop-sign with her palm. "Hush."

Unrepentant but thankfully silent, he reached for the grapes. With an air of mischief he studied one closely, then met Stephanie's gaze before popping it into his mouth.

Refusing to watch, Stephanie said, "If we have time later, I'd like to walk awhile."

"We'll make the time." He tossed a grape into her lap. "A long walk after a picnic is good for the soul."

She could certainly use that.

"I wouldn't know. I've never been on one." She tossed the grape back to him. It thudded against his chest.

"You've never been on a walk?" Head back, Daniel threw a grape high into the air and caught it in his mouth.

Stephanie tried to look away and failed. "No, silly. A picnic."

Another grape had winged upward. Daniel let it plop onto the blanket uncaught.

"Never? No childhood jaunts to the country? No egg sandwiches in the garden?"

"No. My family was far too stuffy for that. Little girls sat at the dinner table, learned to play hostess, and never, ever got dirty."

"Unbelievable."

"Yes." And I don't want to talk about it. Some things didn't merit conversation at a girl's first picnic. "You, on the other hand, look perfectly comfortable sprawled beneath a spreading chestnut tree with a sandwich and a bunch of grapes."

"Far more my style than your fancy London flat."

"Is that why you're so messy?"

He tapped her shoe. "I'm not messy. You're far too tidy."

"That's been said about me before. I'm just a perfectionist."

"What makes you so obsessive about it?"

She wasn't going down that road either.

"There's nothing wrong with order," she replied, more defensively than she'd intended.

"Never said there was." He levered up to rummage in the basket, coming out with the wine and two glasses swiped from the restaurant. Following another foray into the basket, he extracted a corkscrew. With little effort on his part, the cork slid out with a pop.

Daniel widened his eyes at her. Stephanie giggled. She didn't know why, but a popping cork always made her laugh.

He poured, handed her a glass and waited while she sipped.

"You have good taste in wine," she said, savoring the rich flavor on her tongue.

"I have good *luck* in wine. Don't know a thing about the stuff."

"Really? I thought a son of John Valentine—"

"I wasn't always John's son. Remember? My mum was a club singer. Not the worst, but not the best either. Our upbringing wasn't quite on par with the Valentines." He made the admission easily, but some of his conversational ease had seeped away.

"Did you grow up here in London?"

"All around England. Wherever Mum could get a gig."

"That must have been an interesting life."

"Not really. Hotel staff make good nannies for a day or two but they don't substitute well for parents." Bitterness laced his words, telling Stephanie she'd touched a nerve. His meaning was clear. Two boys left alone to fend for themselves in strange hotels could not be the best situation.

"I'm sorry you were unhappy." And she was. Very sorry.

He shifted his attention from her to a red-dragon kite floating overhead. "Being alone all the time is scary to a little kid. And confusing."

Stephanie's heart squeezed. It couldn't have been easy for him to tell her such a thing, but the peek into his unhappy childhood made him seem less intimidating, more approachable. And she liked him for it.

"What about when you were older?"

"Then we were terrors." The mischief was back. "Pounding on guests' doors at two o'clock in the morning. Dumping ice over the balconies onto unsuspecting passers-by. We got our mum kicked out of more than one fine establishment."

Stephanie chuckled. "I can see you doing that. You bad boy."

He toasted her with his glass and knocked it back in one drink. "All Dom's idea, I assure you."

"It was not." She couldn't imagine easygoing Dominic coming up with any mischief on his own. If ever there was a by-the-book, rule-following man, it was Dominic Stephens.

"You're right. I was the rabble rouser." He sighed, a happy sound, and flopped onto his back. "Poor Dom."

She smiled down at him, trying to imagine him as a child. He was so completely man. But he'd been a little boy once, and he'd been wounded in the process.

Something in that knowledge caused her to relax. She had nothing to fear from Daniel. He knew about heartbreak too.

Daniel reached up and wrapped his fingers around a lock of her hair. He tugged, pulling her down toward the blanket. Slowly, she gave in to the gentle pressure and reclined on the soft flannel, the wineglass discarded in the grass.

He didn't touch her, for which she was grateful. She wasn't ready for that yet.

The thought caught her by surprise. *Yet?* She would never be ready for that. Daniel might have an alluring charisma about him, but so had Brett. Worse yet, so had Randolph.

She shivered and pulled her sweater closer.

Though Daniel didn't move or speak, she felt him there, warm and appealing. After a few seconds, she gave in to the quiet and closed her eyes, relaxed by the wine.

The breeze whispered against her face. In the distance a victory shout went up as one boater bested another. In her imagination, she could hear the clip-clop of royal carriages and envision the elegantly clad ladies from times gone by.

Something tickled her nose. She wiggled it. The tickle came again. She pushed at it and received a purring chuckle for her efforts.

Lazily, slowly, she opened her eyes to see Daniel hovering above her, a blade of grass between thumb and forefinger. Before she could stop the instinctive reaction, she cringed.

He pulled back. "Hey. I didn't mean to startle you."

Her heart hammered crazily. "I must have dozed."

He continued to hover, muscled forearms holding him above her. His eyes darkened in concern. "You're shaking."

She managed a false laugh. "It's nothing. A sudden wake-up."

Daniel brushed a hair from the corner of her lips. He let his fingers linger on her cheek, his gaze searching.

Stephanie froze, breath lodged in her throat. She didn't want him to remove his hand, though common sense said to do so. She lay there, examining the emotions as the therapists had taught her, until she knew—*she knew*—she wasn't afraid of Daniel. At least, not for the usual reasons. If she had fear, it was of herself, because she couldn't start a relationship with this man. She couldn't go there again and face the inevitable rejection. Years of counseling had brought her this far, but she'd long ago decided being alone was easier than risking heartache.

And Daniel could easily be a danger to her fragile heart.

"Let's walk," she said, her voice a breathy murmur.

Though obviously full of curiosity, Daniel helped her to her feet without comment. Shakily, she gathered the remains of their picnic, looking around for a garbage can. She'd hardly touched her chicken salad. No wonder the wine had rushed to her head.

They fell in step, strolling toward the long bridge spanning the lake. Daniel didn't try to take her hand and she was grateful. She knew he wanted to, but he must have known she would pull away.

In silence now, they walked over the bridge, pausing at the top to lean on the rails and look down. On the shore two lovers lay stretched upon the grass. The young man kissed his girlfriend with such tenderness that Stephanie's chest ached. She glanced away. But the view of a young family, doting over an infant in a stroller, was no better.

Today seemed to be the day to stir her latent domestic urges. Perhaps it was the amazing and romantic news that Emma, one of the Valentines and head chef at the Chelsea restaurant, had married a king. Or worse, maybe Daniel was to blame.

She slid a glance in his direction. The brooding Daniel had returned, staring in dark silence at the kissing lovers.

Being with him turned her thoughts in strange directions, down roads she'd closed long ago.

Unintentionally, she sighed. Daniel's dark head slowly swiveled in her direction. She kept her focus trained on the happy little family below.

Once, a long time ago, she'd believed she could break free from the past and embrace the future with a loving husband. She'd even dreamed of having a child to cherish. But Randolph had made sure that could never happen. That no man would ever want her.

Yes. Long ago, she'd come to grips with her inevitable destiny. So why did the thought depress her so much today?

CHAPTER FOUR

IN THE days to follow, Daniel had a hard time getting that picnic out of his mind. Correction. He had a hard time concentrating on business instead of his copper-haired flatmate. He had discovered that he was not only attracted to Stephanie, he also liked her. She was witty, and when she let her guard down, she was warm. It was that guard that puzzled and challenged him, and he reckoned the challenge was the fascination. That was why he couldn't get her out of his mind.

He loved challenges. Why else would he try to single-handedly solve the water-shortage problems of African countries?

He watched her flit around the living area, doing her usual fussy tidying-up thing. The television blabbed in the background and lemon furniture polish fragranced the air.

Daniel was supposed to be working at the desk he'd set up in one end of the large reception room, but he watched her instead.

Tonight, she'd come up from the restaurant early, claiming the flat needed cleaning. Yeah, right. The only mess was his and he couldn't bring himself to feel bad over it.

She'd changed into casual trousers and top and pulled her hair into a loose, sexy knot on top of her head. Wispy tendrils played around her elegant cheekbones, tempting him.

He shifted restlessly and tossed down the pen. He'd been celibate too long.

Last night, he'd heard her in the throes of a nightmare. He'd wanted to go to her but had resisted. What help could he offer? That sort of involvement required emotion, and he didn't have that in him. Besides, he doubtless would not be welcome in Stephanie's bedroom, bad dream or not.

He pushed up from the desk and stretched to relieve the kink in his back. When he turned, Stephanie knelt on the floor, polishing an end table. She looked up, luscious mouth curved in a smile. Daniel experienced another of his wayward, unflatmate-like thoughts.

"You've been working hard," she said. "Any progress?"

"Actually, more than I expected. My father—" he could barely say the word with civility "—has offered his support."

"Daniel, that's awesome." Her eyes glowed with true pleasure. "He has contacts that can give your business a real boost."

Daniel didn't answer. How did he admit that he didn't trust the man who had given him life?

Stephanie stopped polishing to study him. "You don't exactly seem overjoyed."

"I don't understand why he wants to do this."

"Because you're his son."

"He doesn't even know me. He has no idea if I can do the work, or if I have the integrity to carry out these projects in an ethical manner."

"That's right." She aimed the cloth at him. "Yet, he's willing to introduce you to some influential people. He's willing to put his name and reputation on the line."

"Yeah." And Daniel didn't get it. What did the old man expect in return? What was his game? Nobody did something for nothing. "He's set up a lunch meeting with some important investors over at the other restaurant."

"Are you going?"

"I haven't decided." He didn't like favors. They obligated.

Folding the polishing cloth into her usual crisp rectangle, Stephanie stood and faced him. "You didn't ask my advice, but I'm giving it anyway. Go. From all I've observed in a year of working for the man, John's a good guy."

Yeah? Then where was he when I was a kid?

"I'll think about it." He turned his attention to the television, hoping for distraction. All this talk about his father annoyed him. "Let's watch a movie."

She put away the cleaning materials and surprised him by coming into the living room instead of scuttling off to hide in her bedroom. Perhaps he could thank the picnic for this new acceptance of him. Though she'd fallen into some kind of mood at one point, they'd had a great time.

He still couldn't imagine that a woman her age had never experienced a picnic. Must have come from a weird family. He pointed the remote and clicked. Who was he kidding? His hippie mother had been super-weird. They'd gone on lots of picnics, though hers had usually been Woodstock-style outings that had lasted days during which he and Dominic had wandered around on their own.

He flipped through the channels, stopping at a comedy program.

"How's this?"

"Anything's okay with me. A brainless way to relax."

"You actually do that on occasion?" he asked.

She made a face at him. The curled nose and squinted eyes looked cute. The long legs curled under her looked pretty interesting too. Who knew naked toes could stir a man's libido?

Better concentrate on the comedy instead. He did, but his attention kept straying back to his companion each time she laughed.

Eventually, the program finished and the barrage of advertisements began. When he was about to give up and go back to his desk, a news brief flashed across the screen. A beautiful little girl, no more than six, smiled from a photo while the reporter intoned a gruesome story of neglect and abuse and violent death.

Stephanie slapped both hands against her ears and squeezed her eyes closed. Daniel was tempted to do likewise.

"Horrid, isn't it?" he asked, stomach roiling.

"Dreadful." She pushed off the couch and turned away from the television, her complexion gone pale, tears glistening in her eyes. "That poor little angel."

He knew she had a heart for troubled kids and sometimes taught an art class for some kind of scheme. Naturally, she'd be disturbed. Who wouldn't be?

"Yeah." He scrubbed a hand over his face, repulsed at the inhumanity of some people. If a hard-heart like him was troubled, tender-hearted Stephanie would make herself sick if she dwelled on the story.

He switched the telly off. The room went dark except for the dim hall light. Quiet, broken only by the traffic on the road below, enveloped them.

"Would you like some tea?" he asked, feeling the inexplicable need to comfort her.

She shook her head. "I need to run downstairs."

Her comment felt odd somehow. He squinted at her, tall and slim and composed, and wondered if he'd missed something. "At this hour?"

"One of the dishwashers was acting up earlier, had a small leak. I want to check it."

Daniel frowned at her. Why hadn't she mentioned this earlier?

"I could have a look. I'm handy with water pipes and such."

"No need. Really. I'll handle it."

In other words, she didn't want his company, a truth that caused an unwanted curl of disappointment.

"All right, then. Ring me if there's a problem."

Without answering, she headed out the door.

Daniel jumped into the shower for a quick scrub and had just stepped out when the telephone rang. He grabbed for the receiver.

Stephanie's breathy voice said, "Daniel, come quick. I need you badly."

He didn't hold back the chuckle. "Well, that's more like it."

"I'm serious. Please, if you think you can help, come down here."

A surge of renewed energy zipped through him. "The dishwasher?"

"Leaking everywhere. I'm slopping up water now."

"Will you feed me cheesecake afterwards?" referring to the time he'd asked her to take him down for a midnight snack and she'd frozen him with silence.

"What?"

"Never mind. Be right down."

Stephanie squeezed out yet another mop full of water and watched in dismay as more seeped from beneath the industrial-sized dishwasher. She'd called the plumber again about this a week ago and still he had yet to show up. Ordinarily, she'd have followed up and called someone else, but she'd had too many other problems on her mind. One, the money missing from the accounts.

Two, Daniel Stephens. Since the moment he'd arrived, the man had occupied her thoughts in the most uncomfortable way. Then he'd taken her on that picnic and she'd realized why. She liked him. His passion for Africa stirred her. His relentless pursuit of an incredibly lofty goal stirred her. Looking at him stirred her.

A voice that also stirred her broke through the sound of sloshing water. "Ahoy, mate. Permission to come aboard."

Stephanie looked up. All she could think was, *Ohmygosh. Ohmygosh.*

She'd known he was coming. She'd been expecting him. But she hadn't been expecting this.

Barefoot and shirtless, Daniel waded toward her in a pair of low-slung jeans, a tool belt slung even lower on his trim hips.

Close your mouth, Stephanie. Mop, don't stare.

But she stared anyway.

Daniel Stephens, dark as sin, chest and shoulder muscles rippling, black hair still wet and carelessly slicked back from a pirate's forehead, was almost enough to make her forget the reasons why she could not be interested in him. Almost.

Slim hips rolling, he sloshed through the quarter inch of water to the dishwasher. Dark hairs sprinkled his bare toes.

The sight made her shiver. When had she ever paid any attention to a man's toes?

"You forgot your shirt," she blurted, repeating the slogan seen everywhere in American restaurants. "No shirt, no shoes, no service."

He grinned at her, unrepentant. "You said you needed me. *Badly.* How could I not respond immediately to that kind of plea from a beautiful woman?"

He thought she was beautiful? The idea stunned her. Beautiful? Something inside her shriveled. How little he knew about the real her.

He, on the other hand, was hot. And he knew it.

"Are you going to fix that thing or annoy me?"

One corner of his mouth twitched. "Both, I imagine."

He hunkered down in front of the washer, tool belt dragging the waist of his jeans lower. Stephanie tried not to look.

"Do you think it's bad?"

"Probably have to shut down the restaurant for a week."

Stephanie dropped the mop. It clattered to the floor. "You've got to be kidding!"

He twisted around on those sexy bare toes and said, "I am. It's probably a leaky hose."

"Can you fix it?"

He smirked. "Of course."

"Then I really am going to fire that plumber."

"Go ahead and sack the useless lout. Tell him you have an engineer around to do your midnight bidding."

Now, *that* was an intriguing thought.

She retrieved the mop. "Which is more expensive? A plumber or an engineer?"

White teeth flashed. "Depends on what you use for payment."

Time to shut up, Stephanie, before you get in too deep. Do not respond to that tempting innuendo.

Metal scraped against tile as he easily manhandled the large machine, walking it away from the cabinet to look inside and behind. Stephanie went back to swabbing the decks. Watching Daniel, all muscled and half naked, was too dangerous. Thinking about that cryptic payment remark was even more so.

"Could you lend a hand over here?" he asked.

Oh, dear.

The floor, dangerously slick but no longer at flood stage, proved to be an adventure. But she slip-slid her way across to where Daniel bent over, peering into the back of the machine.

"What can I do?"

"See this space?"

Seeing required Stephanie to move so close to Daniel that his warm, soap-scented and very nude skin brushed against her. Thankful for long sleeves, she swallowed hard and tried to focus on the space in question.

"Down there where that black thing is?" she asked.

"Your hands are small enough, I think, to loosen that screw. Do you see it?"

"I think so." She leaned farther into the machine, almost lying across the top. Daniel's warm purr directed her, too close to her ear, but necessary to get the job done.

"That's it. Good girl."

His praise pleased her, silly as that seemed.

He pressed in closer, trying to reach the now-unfastened hose. His breath puffed deliciously against the side of her neck. Stephanie shivered and gave up trying to ignore the sensation.

Their fingers touched, deep inside the machine. Both of them stilled.

Her pulse escalating to staccato, Stephanie's blood hummed. As if someone else controlled her actions, she turned her head and came face-to-face with searing blue eyes that surely saw to her deepest secrets.

She needed to move, to get out of this situation and put space between them. But she was trapped between the machine, the hose, and Daniel's inviting, compelling body.

"I think I have it," she said, uselessly. Foolishly.

Daniel's nostrils flared. "Yes. You certainly do."

His lips spoke so close to hers that she almost felt kissed.

Daniel held her gaze for another long, pulsing moment in which Stephanie began to yearn for the touch of his lips against hers. How would they feel?

All right, she told herself. That's enough. Stop right now before you venture too close to the fire and get burned.

With the inner strength that had kept her going when

life had been unspeakable, she withdrew her hand and stepped away.

As though the air between them hadn't throbbed like jungle drums, Daniel didn't bother to look up. He finished repairing the hose while Stephanie completed the mopping-up and tried to analyze the situation. Daniel was interested in her. Big deal. In her business, she got hit on all the time.

But it wasn't Daniel's interest that bothered her so much. It was her own. Something in Daniel drew her, called to her like a Siren's song. One moment he was cynical and tough. The next he was giving and gentle. There was a strength in him, too, that said he could—and would—move a mountain if one was in his way. He was different from anyone she'd ever met.

Metal squealed against tile again as Daniel shoved the washer back into place.

"All done." He gathered tools, dropping them into the proper slots in his belt. "You'll need to order in a new hose right away, but that should hold for now."

"Thank you. I really appreciate this."

He came toward her, all cat-like muscle and unquestion-able male. "How much?"

"What do you mean, how much?" She took a step back.

He took one forward. "Remember your promise?"

Mind racing, she held the mop out like a skinny shield. What had she promised?

He stopped. "Cheesecake?"

"That's it? Cheesecake?"

"Why, Stephanie, whatever were you thinking?"

She laughed and playfully shoved the mop at him. He ducked, one hand out to ward off the pretend blow.

And then the slick floor took control. Daniel's bare feet slipped. Tools rattled and swayed, throwing him more off balance. He reeled backwards, caught the counter with one hand but not before his head slammed against the jutting corner.

Stephanie dropped the mop and rushed to his side. "Daniel. Oh, my goodness! Are you hurt?"

He righted himself, rubbing at the back of his head. He felt ridiculous. One minute, he was about to kiss a beautiful woman. The next he was thrashing around like a landed salmon.

"Only my pride," he admitted.

But when he brought his hand forward from the aching lump on the back of his head, blood covered his fingers. "Uh-oh."

"Let me see." Stephanie tugged at his shoulders. "Bend down here, you big lug."

With a half-grin, half-grimace, he lowered his head. A minute ago she'd been backing away as if afraid he'd touch her. And now her hands were all over him in gentle concern. Puzzling, infuriating woman.

"A scratch, I think. It's nothing." But her cool fingers felt good against his skin.

"Let me decide that." All business, she guided him to a chair. "Sit. We keep a first-aid kit beside the stove."

"I'm all right. It's only throbbing a bit."

But he sat anyway while Stephanie got the kit and went to work cleaning up the wound.

As soon as her fingers touched his hair, he forgot all about the throbbing pain. When had a woman last touched him with such gentleness?

The throb in his head moved to his heart.

"How bad is it, Doc?" he managed, though her touch was causing more reaction inside his head than outside.

"Irreparable brain damage. I fear there's no hope."

He hid a smile. If this was what it took to get her to touch him and joke with him, he'd bash his head every day of the week.

"Can't you kiss it and make it all better?" A man could always hope.

Her fingers stilled, only a fractional second, but enough for Daniel to know the question got to her. Good. She was thinking about it, too. He'd thought of little else tonight. Well, other than cheesecake. He still had hope in that department.

"Kissing spreads germs," she said lightly. "Can't chance infection."

"I'm already hopelessly damaged. A few extra germs won't hurt." He twisted around. "What if I said please?"

Their eyes met and, for once, held. Yes, she was thinking about it every bit as much as he was. What he couldn't work out was why he didn't just go ahead and kiss her. He wasn't shy with women. He didn't feel shy with Stephanie. But she kept a barrier up at all times, a wall that held him back, that scared him a little, as if kissing her would open a Pandora's box he was unprepared to handle.

Stephanie broke the stand-off by bopping him playfully on the shoulder. "Behave yourself or I'll use this alcohol cleanser."

"Evil woman." But he leaned his head forward so she could examine the cut.

Her stomach brushed against his bare back as she gently

separated layers of hair to dab away blood. Her scent, as clean and elegant as the woman herself, wrapped around him. Her fingers, light, deft, flitted over his scalp with exquisite care, as if she feared hurting him.

Daniel closed his eyes, soaking in the sensation. His own mother had never touched him with such infinite tenderness, and the truth of it brought a lump to his throat. A yearning, far greater and more complicated than desire, expanded his ribcage with a hot ache.

He wanted her never to stop, and that worried him. He, who'd made a point never to need anyone ever again, needed something from Stephanie.

He slept in the same house with her, breathed in her perfume, wondered what she wore to bed. But while he knew her on the surface, he sensed a secret heartache hidden behind the serene face. He needed to know what had hurt her. And that worried him even more.

"This would be easier if you had less hair."

Instantly, Daniel roused out of the pleasant lethargy that enshrouded him.

"Are you saying I need a haircut?"

He hadn't expected her to be like his sister-in-law, so concerned about appearances. But then, of course she was. Didn't her magazine-perfect flat prove as much?

"Maybe a trim."

She was probably right. He rubbed at the whiskers around his mouth. Lately, they'd taken the shape of a Fu Manchu. "What about this?"

"Your stubble? I like it."

Once again, he twisted around, this time surprised and far too pleased. "You do?"

"Sit still." She pressed gauze against the back of his head and held tight. "Yes, I like it. Very much. It's…" Her voice trailed off as if she had already said too much.

"Sexy?"

"Roguish." She gave his shoulder a soft pat. "There. All done."

Daniel caught her wrist. "Roguish?" Slowly, he pulled her around the chair to stand in front of him.

"Daniel—" She lifted a finger in warning.

He was tempted to bite it. "I only want to say thank you."

"Workman's compensation," she teased. "You were wounded on the job."

She started to pull away but he held fast. Her playfulness became a flicker of worry. Puzzled, he released her. He didn't want her to be anxious. He wanted her to be… What *did* he want?

She didn't move, and he was even more puzzled.

He studied her, trying to gauge what was going on inside her head, wondering why she fascinated him so much.

He wanted to reach out and bring her closer, but, more than that, he wanted her to come to him. He wasn't even sure where this was going, but, for purely selfish reasons, he longed for her to make the first move.

Something was churning behind that pretty face and he was willing to wait her out.

In that split second when he thought she might relent and move closer, a commotion erupted outside the restaurant.

CHAPTER FIVE

STEPHANIE jerked as if she'd been shot.

"What on earth—?"

Daniel leaped to his feet, grabbed a pipe wrench from the counter, and stormed through the swinging doors toward the back of the restaurant.

"Be careful, Daniel." Seeing no other weapon, Stephanie yanked a copper pot from the overhead rack and followed closely behind, too jittery to remain in the kitchen without him. After all, the hour was late, they were alone, and someone *had* been stealing money from the restaurants.

"Stay back," Daniel cautioned, putting one hand behind him in the dark hall to stop her.

"No," she whispered fiercely, bumping up against those wide, strong fingers.

Her own hands trembled on the pot handle, though she wasn't certain if they trembled from fear of the noise or from the unsettling episode with Daniel. She couldn't stop thinking of the feel of his hair, the soapy scent of his skin, or his bereft expression when she'd started to pull away.

Yes, something in him called to her, a loneliness she understood and wanted to erase.

"Stay behind me, then," he murmured. And the command made her feel protected in a way she'd seldom experienced. No one ever protected her except herself. And many times she'd done a sorry job of it.

At the back exit, they paused to listen. The racket had subsided. Slowly, Daniel eased the door open. In one swift motion he flipped on the light and leaped outside, wrench at the ready.

Then he laughed.

"Daniel?" Stephanie lowered the pot.

"Come out here."

She did. Two garbage cans lay on their sides, spilling trash on the concrete. A tiny kitten tore at a discarded meat wrapper.

Stephanie gazed at the pot in her hand and the wrench in Daniel's. "Look at us. Aren't we brave?"

"Positively formidable."

"Two giants bearing weapons against this terrifying intruder."

They both looked at the little kitten and burst into laughter.

In the crisp autumn darkness, with a soft breeze carrying scents of exhaust and the promise of winter hovering above, Stephanie and Daniel stood in the alleyway and laughed like lunatics left too long beneath the moon.

The kitten took note of their presence and, with a plaintive cry that resembled recognition, abandoned the trash heap to weave zigzags through Daniel's legs.

"Daniel," Stephanie said, pretending scandal. "Have you been feeding this cat?"

"Apparently not enough." And they laughed some more,

letting the tensions and questions brewing between them be washed away in the ridiculous.

"Come on," she said when she could once more breathe. "Let's feed your protégé."

"What about me? I'm still craving that payment you offered. Engineers don't work for free, you know."

Stephanie figured the moon had stolen her sanity. "Cheesecake?"

"Unless you have something else in mind." He grinned wickedly. "Terms are negotiable."

Her stomach fluttered. She really should send him upstairs for a shirt, but, at this point, what did it matter?

They scavenged the kitchen, found some smoked salmon for the kitten and two large pieces of cheesecake and a jar of chocolate sauce for themselves.

Rather than turn on the lights of the dining room and alarm security patrol, Stephanie lit a candle. Encased in a ruby globe, the candle glowed red and fragrant on the small table next to the kitchen door.

"Good cheesecake." Daniel laid down his fork. "But I need more chocolate."

She handed him the jar. "Karl is an excellent chef, especially with the desserts. They tell me your cousin Emma is every bit as good. Too bad Bella Lucia has lost her."

"She's the one that married the king, right?"

"Yes. In Meridia. Wherever that is."

Daniel poured the sauce on his plate, watching the chocolate drip with a mesmerized expression. "If I were the King of Meridia, there's no way my new wife would be commuting to a job in England. She'd definitely stay at home."

"Hey, don't hog all that." She playfully grabbed the jar

from him. "So you're going to make someone a very bossy husband?"

"I'll never know the answer to that." He caught a final drip of gooey sauce on his finger and licked it. "Daniel's rule number two. Never waste good chocolate."

She added another dollop to her plate. "What's rule number one?" she asked, expecting him to elaborate on his marriage comment.

"Empty your boots before putting them on." When she laughed, he said, "I learned that one the hard way. Scorpions." He gave a fake shiver.

"Africa must be an astounding place."

"You'd love it, Stephanie. The different countries, all the colors and sounds and smells. And the people I met. Amazing. Especially in the small villages. They may only have a small bowl of food for the entire family, but they'll insist on sharing with a stranger."

Everything about him changed when he spoke of Africa. The cynicism slipped away. His face lit up with an energy that came from loving what he did.

"How did you end up working so far from home?"

"Adventure. A chance to get away from a troubled upbringing." He hitched a bare shoulder, an action that flexed the muscles of his chest. "All the usual reasons of reckless youth."

"Interesting that your twin didn't join you."

"Dom and I have always been different." He licked the back of his fork and then studied it. "He's even more different these days, though. More intense, stressed."

She could hear the concern in his voice and admired him for that. Never having had a sibling, she couldn't imagine the bond twins might have. "I assumed that was his personality, him being an accountant and all."

"Didn't used to be. Oh, he's always been a stickler, always following the rules."

"Unlike you?" Stephanie teased.

"Exactly. That's why he's a great accountant and I'm not." Daniel's mischievous eyes twinkled. "But in the past, he was looser, more relaxed, a real joker at times." He shook his head and made another stab at his cheesecake. "He has a lot on his mind, I guess. A baby on the way, teenagers."

"That's trouble enough right there. But the restaurant has also added to his workload. That could be part of the problem. John has him auditing all the accounts in search of the money that's gone missing." She leaned her elbows on the table and admitted, "Did you know I thought you were a spy?"

His fork clattered to the table. He touched his chest, an eyebrow arched in question. "A spy? Like 007?"

Stephanie laughed. "Not quite, but I wondered if John thought I had something to do with the missing money."

"You do have access."

His words stunned her. Did he think she was responsible? "I don't need money, Daniel. And I love my job. I would never do anything to jeopardize these restaurants."

He held up a hand to stop her defense. "I know that now, Stephanie. I didn't when I first came here."

"So you *were* a spy? John set this little arrangement up as a means to keep an eye on me?" The notion mortified her.

"Not even close. In fact, it's a silly idea. John and I aren't on what you would call intimate terms."

"Am I a suspect?" Her stomach hurt just thinking such a thing.

"The subject came up, but Dominic doesn't believe you're involved, and he says John feels the same."

Some of her tension ebbed away in the gentle reassurance. She respected her boss. To think he might suspect her hurt. But she appreciated Daniel's honesty in telling her. "You had me scared for a minute. I thought the Valentine clan had turned on me."

"I don't consider myself a Valentine, Stephanie. John hasn't discussed any of this with me at all. I'm not part of the inner circle."

She could see that bothered him. "You really should try to get to know them. Especially your father and your sister."

A shadow, caused by more than the candle, fell across his handsome face.

"Adopted sister," he said firmly.

"And pretty upset to learn that, from what I hear. She's always been the darling in that family, Daniel. The sweet, good child doted on by all. To suddenly discover she's adopted must have totally rattled her foundation, her sense of self."

"I can relate to that," Daniel said. "But I can't understand why John and Ivy kept the adoption secret in the first place. Now they have to deal with the unpleasant consequences."

Glad to leave the unsettling subject of the missing funds, she said, "You mean the trip to Australia to find her biological sister?"

He nodded. "That's great from my viewpoint, but John's ranting that he doesn't want her poking into the past. Thinks she should be content with the life he gave her. Rather selfish of him, don't you think?"

Stephanie shook her head. "I think he's afraid she'll get hurt. That these biological relatives won't be what she expects or that they'll somehow take advantage of her."

His mouth curled cynically. "He's more likely worried about how this will affect him and his business. He doesn't need Louise creating more difficulties for him."

"So bitter, Daniel. John's made mistakes. Who hasn't? But he cares for Louise. You and Dominic, too, if you'll give him a chance."

Daniel twirled circles in the chocolate sauce on his plate. "Why bother? He seems to make a habit of hurting his children. Louise had a right to know she was adopted, just as Dominic and I had a right to know who our father was."

"Agreed. But that's the past. There is nothing you can do about it now." She was a fine one to be talking. "But you *can* affect the future."

"My future is set." But his tone was defensive, uncertain.

"Is it? Don't you want family, Daniel? Don't you need people around you? People who care for you and will be there for you when life sends a crushing blow?"

He grew quiet, thoughtful, and she knew, for all his arguments to the contrary, Daniel needed to connect with his family. Like her, he was held back by the fear of getting hurt. Strange how knowing that made her feel closer to him.

Who was she kidding? She felt closer to Daniel than she'd felt to anyone in a long time. They were kindred spirits, both having childhood hurts that still hampered them as adults. A bond like that was a powerful thing.

"Change of subject, okay?" he said gently, tapping her

fingernail with one tine of his fork. "My strange life doesn't concern you."

Oh, but it did. More and more every day.

The dark restaurant, the ruby candle glow, created an ambience of intimacy and, inevitably, personal conversation began to flow, moving away from the hazard of discussing his estranged family. He told her more about his gypsy lifestyle growing up. Stephanie sensed the hurt and loneliness interspersed with the funny stories.

In turn, she told him bits and pieces of her life in Colorado, her work in Aspen before coming here. But some things didn't warrant discussion, even with Daniel.

Long after the cheesecake was gone and the saucers pushed aside, they talked on. Stephanie knew the hour must be terribly late, but she didn't want to move, didn't want to leave this cocoon that had spun around them in the darkened restaurant.

Daniel leaned corded forearms on the table, his folded hands inches from hers.

"Tell me about the art classes."

"They're great. The kids—" She shrugged. "I like to think I'm helping, but I don't know." Some of them had been through far more than she had. "I want so badly to make a difference. Sometimes I dream about them, about their situations, about the things that have happened to them."

"You're doing a good thing, Stephanie. A good thing." He touched the back of her hand. "How did you get involved in that to begin with?"

"I've always had a heart for people who were down and out. I guess it stems from—"

She'd gone too far this time, letting the intimate setting and fatigue affect her usual reserve.

"Stems from what?"

Playing the pretense game didn't work too well with a bright man like Daniel. And in truth, she wanted to tell him. She was just too afraid, so she took the easiest way out.

"There was a child once, a little girl. A victim of abuse." The inner trembling started up, but Stephanie didn't let the nerves stop her. She could tell Daniel this much. And maybe by doing so, some of the lingering shadows would be driven back. "I should have told someone. But I didn't."

His voice deepened, incredibly gentle. "Why not?"

She lifted a shoulder. "She was afraid telling would make the problem worse. I didn't know what to do." And she still didn't.

Sometimes that was the worst shame. Knowing she might have stopped it, but she'd been too young to understand that.

As if he read her thoughts, Daniel asked softly, "How old were you?"

"Nine." She shook her head, recognizing the denial in his eyes. "But I should have told someone."

"You were a child. You can't feel responsible."

"I know. But it bothers me." Ate at her, if she told the truth. Had turned her into a woman who couldn't let anyone close enough to see the real person inside. "Children are powerless, Daniel."

He reached out, covered her hand with his. She soaked in the comfort of his spontaneous gesture.

"You were a child, too, sweetheart, as powerless as that little girl."

"I know. That's why I want to make a difference now. To help these kids, to show them a better way, a way out. I can't change the past, but I can help now."

The warmth of his skin against hers, his quiet understanding seeped into her battered heart like fresh rain into the cracked, parched earth. And like that dry ground, Stephanie felt renewed, refreshed, almost whole again.

For a split second, a blink in time, Stephanie considered telling him the rest, but as courage formed the words Daniel spoke again. "Life's injustices drive me crazy."

"Me, too. Obviously."

"Why is it, do you suppose, that some people have everything going for them and others have nothing?"

With relief, Stephanie recognized that she'd raised no suspicions. Daniel saw the conversation on the surface, as two adults discussing a troubled world.

"You're doing all you can to make a difference, Daniel, just like I am. In fact, more than I am. You've spent your whole life trying to help. That has to mean something."

"But the need is so vast, sometimes I feel like I'm trying to empty the ocean with a spoon."

Tenderness gripped her. "You have such a good heart."

"Stephanie, my love, let me tell you a fact about your flatmate. He doesn't have a heart." He said the words lightly, easily as though teasing, but she knew he was serious. "I'm a civil engineer. Developing water projects is what I do."

Stephanie didn't accept his reasoning. Pure self-interest would have lined his pockets long ago.

"What about feeding that kitten? Or coming down here in the middle of the night to fix my dishwasher? Is that for selfish reasons, too?"

"No. That's cheesecake."

The silly answer made them both chuckle.

"You ate that entire jar of chocolate," she said, smoothly, glad to move away from topics that could only lead to trouble.

Daniel took the empty container and scraped the inside with a spoon. "Wasn't I worth it?"

"Absolutely." She stole the jar from him and ran her finger around the edge.

Daniel grabbed her finger and licked it. The energy from the touch of his tongue against her skin raced through her body faster than a breath. For a guy without a heart, he had a habit of doing strange things to hers.

She pulled her hand into her lap, but the feel of that warm, moist tongue wouldn't go away.

"Don't try to steal my chocolate, buster."

Was her voice really that breathless?

"All's fair in love and chocolate."

"Now there's a subject we haven't discussed." She blamed the dark, intimate atmosphere for her bravado. But why not talk about love? They'd discussed everything else.

"Love?" Daniel shook his head. His hair, now dry and in need of a comb, flopped forward. "I'd rather have chocolate, thank you."

Her heart began to beat a little faster. "Haven't you ever been in love?"

"Thought I was once, but it didn't work out. Since then. Well, a man realizes his shortcomings. What about you? Any boyfriends wanting to bounce my head against the concrete?"

His airy tone gave her the courage to answer honestly. "I suppose I've realized my shortcomings as well."

"I beg to differ. No shortcomings from my perspective."

Though his observation did wonders for her self-esteem, it showed once again how little he knew of the real Stephanie.

"I was in love once, but…" Her voice trailed off. Why had she admitted that?

"And he hurt you."

The sentence was a statement, not a question, and Stephanie accepted that he understood what she'd left unsaid.

"Yes. In the worst possible way." Brett had rejected the real Stephanie, unable to see beyond the scars.

Compassion flared in Daniel's flame-blue eyes. She thought he might touch her. And she realized just how much she yearned for that. He, like no one else, found a way past her guard and into her heart.

"What did he do? Cheat on you?"

"No. Not that." Stephanie wished she hadn't brought up the subject, but didn't know how to stop now without drawing suspicion. They were tiptoeing far too near her secret shame.

Daniel's fingers flexed against the tabletop, his expression fierce and dangerous. "Don't tell me he hit you."

Stephanie tried not to react too strongly. She should have known he'd follow that line of thought. He was too smart not to make the leap of logic from cheating to abuse. She had to end it now.

"Let's don't go there, okay? This is not something I like to talk about."

He studied her in the dim candlelight for several heartbeats while her pulse thumped in warning. Finally, his rich voice quiet, he said, "All right. I'll let it go for now. But a woman like you shouldn't give up on love just because some fool didn't have sense enough to recognize a treasure."

"I thought you didn't believe in love."

"For myself, Stephanie. Only for myself."

Was he warning her off? Telling her not to feel anything for him? Not to fall for the gentle and kind man beneath the pirate's tough exterior?

If he was, she had a very bad feeling that his warning came too late.

From somewhere on the dark streets of London a clock chimed the hour. "Oh, for goodness' sake, Daniel. It's two o'clock."

She hopped up and began clearing away their dishes.

Daniel followed her into the kitchen where he stretched like a waking lion. "Doesn't feel a moment after one to me."

"We'll both be terrors tomorrow on so little sleep." She dumped the dishes in the sink and turned toward him. "Let's go. These will wait."

Daniel pretended shock and disbelief. "You're leaving the dishes undone?"

Stephanie raised a defiant chin. "Yes, I am."

"Will wonders never cease?" he said mildly. A smile quivered at the corners of his mouth.

As they left the kitchen, heading to the elevator, Daniel reached out, palm upward in invitation.

The night had been revealing and wonderful. And she'd begun to feel things she didn't want to feel again. Things that could get her hurt. Only she worried that this time, with this man, the hurt would be too much to bear.

She slipped her hand into his, accepting the fact that, regardless of what the future held, Daniel Stephens might be worth the risk.

CHAPTER SIX

"SCISSORS. Scissors. My kingdom for a scissors."

Daniel rummaged through the kitchen drawers, came up empty and decided to breach the inner sanctum of Stephanie's bathroom. Surely the woman owned a pair of scissors.

Without a second thought, he charged into her bedroom and came to a sudden halt. Though he had passed by and glimpsed the sleek blue and gray interior, he'd never come inside this room. The essence of Stephanie filled the space.

The bed was fluffy, white, and feminine. A dressing table against a wide window that looked out over the city contained the usual pots and jars that he couldn't comprehend. The curtains were open; light flooded the room.

He drew in a lungful of Stephanie-scented air. That gentle, expensive scent had driven him quite mad last night in the restaurant. He could stand here all day breathing it in.

Above a white painted chest of drawers, a single painting compelled him to a closer look. In startling contrast with the elegant, oriental-influenced artwork in the rest of the flat, slashing colors tore at the canvas in a violent assault. Perfectly centered within the storm of blues and violet was a shattered heart. On each broken piece was a tiny tormented face, dripping blood and tears.

Puzzled over why Stephanie would choose such a disturbing print for her bedroom, he squinted at the name scrawled in one corner.

His mouth fell open in surprise. "S. Ellison."

He'd known she painted, but this turbulent look inside the artist was startling to say the least. As if beneath the aloof exterior lay an unreachable depth of emotion screaming to be released.

Intuitively, he knew she would not be pleased by his observation. Backing away, he went into the bathroom, once more to be assaulted by her scent. Perfume. Shampoo. Soap.

"Scissors, Daniel. Scissors." Annoyed, maybe even unnerved that Stephanie occupied so much of his thinking, he found the scissors and got out of her private space. The hall bathroom was safer.

"Where to start..." he murmured, peering intently into the mirror. He lifted one long section of hair and snipped. Not so good. But it was too late to turn back now.

A few chops and curses later, he heard the front door open and close.

"Daniel."

He poked his head around the doorway. "In the hall bathroom."

Stephanie's heels tapped against the tile.

"I just wanted to tell you—" She paused in the open doorway. "Oh, dear."

Their eyes met in the mirror. "That bad, is it?"

Her mouth twitched. He gave her his fiercest glare,

which only made things worse. The twitch became a full-blown smile.

She took the scissors from his hand, an action that ensured he looked every bit as bad as he feared.

"Come in the kitchen and sit down."

"Why?"

She laughed. The woman actually had the audacity to laugh. "I'm going to save you."

"Can you?" he asked hopefully, feeling like an utter idiot, but relieved to know she could, and would, help out.

"I think so." She pulled a chair out. "Sit."

"Didn't we do this last night?" He squinted one eye up at her while she wrapped a towel around his neck and secured it.

"You seem to be having problems lately with your head."

"Tell me about it." She had no idea just how bad the problems *inside* his head were becoming. He looked doubtfully at the towel. "Does this have to be pink?"

"I will never tell a soul that the great Daniel Stephens, conqueror of Africa, marauding kittens and leaky dishwashers, wore a pink towel." She slid a comb through his hair, taking extra care over the cut from last night. "May I ask what brought this on?"

Hadn't she said he needed a trim? Not that he'd ever cared about appearances, but some people did. "Need to spruce up for that lunch meeting with my father."

She dipped around him, pleased. "You've decided to go?"

Thanks to her influence, but he didn't mention that. "Good business sense, don't you think? Those men own companies that could easily fund a water system for an entire village."

"Good sense, indeed." She combed his hair toward his face. It fell over his eyes. "How much of this do you want off?"

"My fate is in your hands."

She giggled. "Oh, Daniel. Pink towel and all, you do live dangerously."

Curiously happy, Daniel settled back into the chair and closed his eyes. Having Stephanie's hands on him, however he could get them there, was worth the humiliation of a botched haircut.

He let that thought linger for a while, studied on it. She was good for him as well as good to him. Being with her settled some of the restlessness. Maybe even some of the anger.

Last night had been a turning point of sorts when she'd let him come close, and he'd exulted in the knowledge that she'd trusted him, at least a little.

Though she'd stopped short of telling him all he wanted to know about her former lover, Daniel wasn't obtuse. The man had hurt her badly, maybe even physically abused her, though he hoped he'd misinterpreted that part. The idea of a man hitting her sickened him, but it explained why she'd been jumpy and wary in the beginning. Trust wouldn't come easy after that.

Stupid as it was, he'd been glad for that leaky dishwasher. Was even tempted to tear up some of the other pipes so he could fix them for her and watch her face light up with gratitude and admiration. Sharing secrets and cheesecake with Stephanie was worth the lump on his head.

"You have wonderful hair." Her voice had grown quiet.

He tried to think of a witty comeback but failed. How could he when her slim, sweet-scented body kept inadvertently bumping his as she moved around the chair, snipping and combing?

He'd had plenty of haircuts in his life, but none like this. None with a woman who interested him so much, whose touch warmed a cold place inside him. He tried to shake off the feeling. He didn't do emotional commitments and, from what Stephanie had told him last night, he sensed her reluctance in that area as well.

He couldn't understand why the idea of commitment even occurred to him. He enjoyed women. Always had. So what was the big deal with this particular one?

A lock of hair tumbled down, tickling. Stephanie brushed it away, then unfastened the towel and whipped it off.

He opened his eyes.

The tingling in his scalp moved lower.

She was bent at the waist sweeping a mountain of black hair into a dustpan. He silently cursed the calf-length dresses she always wore.

"There you go. All presentable..." Her voice trailed off. Must be the dopey expression on his face. She slowly put the dustpan aside.

At the moment, Daniel didn't care if he had hair or not. He did care that Stephanie was standing in front of him looking incredibly kissable.

He wrapped his fingers around her wrist. The bone felt fragile, delicate within his work-strengthened grip.

"We started something last night that we never finished," he said. "I'm a man who leaves nothing undone."

"Daniel," she warned without much conviction.

Stormy green eyes held his and he saw a yearning there as strong as the one in his own heart. He waited until she made the decision to come to him and then guided her onto his lap.

He wanted this moment to last. Wanted to watch her face and eyes. Wanted to see the desire flame up in her. He'd seen the painting. He knew she was a woman who hid deep passion behind this perfect, cool demeanor.

She touched his cheek. Fingers of silk stroked from cheekbone to the corner of his mouth and rested there. And then she smiled. Tremulous. Uncertain.

Uncertainty?

An ache of exquisite tenderness squeezed the breath from him. No, it couldn't be tenderness. He didn't *do* tenderness. Must be desire.

And to prove as much, he kissed her.

She was more than he bargained for.

Her mouth was far sweeter, far hotter, and far more willing than he'd imagined. She kissed him back with so much passion, his head reeled. His pulse thundered like rampaging elephants, and a swirl of some frightfully unfamiliar emotion pushed inside his chest. *Sweet, sweet, sweet* was all he could think.

And then as quickly as the kiss had begun, it ended. Stephanie yanked back from him, her mouth rosy and moist and horrified. Her eyes, wide and stormy as the Indian Ocean, darted frantically around the kitchen as if she had no idea where she was. She was shaking, though he didn't think from passion.

She leaped from his lap and rushed out of the room. Her bedroom door clicked shut with a little too much force.

He blinked at the empty kitchen. "What was that all about?"

With a vengeance, he kicked aside the chair and followed.

"Stephanie." He rattled the doorknob. Locked. "Let me in."

"Give me a minute." Her voice was shaky, strangled.

Oh, boy.

"Look. I'm sorry." Only that he'd upset her, not that they'd finally kissed. He shoved a hand over the top of his head, startled to have considerably less hair. "Will you tell me why you're upset?"

"I'm not upset."

An obvious lie. He blew out a breath.

"If you're worried about what people will think if we get, um, involved. I mean, because we're sharing a flat…"

"I'm not worried."

He gripped the back of his now hairless neck. "Okay, then. Good. I'm not, either."

When she didn't answer, he pecked at the door. "Steph. Listen. Remember what you told me last night, about the idiot that broke your heart?"

"Yes." Was that a smile in her voice? Maybe he was getting somewhere.

"No need to worry. The last thing I would ever want is to get involved. Emotionally, I mean. We both know up front that we aren't interested in that sort of thing. So we're safe. Right?"

With an abruptness that had him backing up to the far wall, the door opened and Stephanie came breezing out, every hair in place, lipstick refreshed, and no hint that anything had occurred. A warm, impassioned woman had gone into that room. The elegantly untouchable restaurant manager came out.

"Everything's fine, Daniel. Sorry for the overreaction to a little meaningless kiss." Tiptoeing, she kissed him on the cheek and then tip-tapped down the hall. "Gotta run."

A little meaningless kiss? Meaningless?

Daniel blinked at the slender backside disappearing around the corner.

He had never been so confused in his entire life.

Stephanie still shook as she entered the empty elevator. She hoped she looked more composed than she was feeling at the moment. Daniel had rocked her world. Completely. One kiss and she was lost for ever. Dear heaven above. She'd wanted the kiss to go on for ever, to always have Daniel's strong arms hold her as if he could shield her from the whole world. She'd felt so secure, so protected.

"I'm falling in love with him." Her throat tightened around the muttered words.

She'd suspected as much last night when they'd teased and talked in the restaurant. When the real man behind the pirate's face had revealed his true colors. Oh, she'd suspected her feelings for a while, but today had clinched it.

That was why she'd been so anxious not to let him ever touch her, kiss her. Deep down she'd known he had the ability to break down all her barriers and make her vulnerable again. Vulnerable, the one thing on earth she could never afford to be.

Daniel didn't want any part of love. Had even told her as much. She should be glad of that, considering her past. He probably wanted an affair. She didn't. Not that she didn't want him. But an affair meant revelation, and she couldn't allow him to discover the real Stephanie and be repulsed, as Brett had been. Besides, in the light of her deepening emotions, an affair that led to nowhere would never be enough.

What was she going to do now? He was her roommate, for crying out loud. She would see him every day without fail and fall more and more in love with him.

With a groan, she banged her head against the elevator doors. As if awaiting that cue, the lift stopped and rattled open. No one was in the hallway, thank goodness.

More out of habit than need, she straightened the neckline of her dress and started toward her office.

Her heels tapping along the tile corridor, her mind raced with indecision. What should she do? Tell Daniel the truth and risk rejection? Lie and say she wasn't interested so would he please not kiss her anymore? Admit her feelings? Find another flat?

One by one she examined each idea and tossed it aside. There was no answer to her dilemma.

For years, she'd kept an arm's length from every man. Now, in the space of a short few weeks, Daniel had crowded past her guard and seeped into her heart. She couldn't escape that fact any more than she could escape him. She wanted to be with him. She wanted to be kissed and held and loved again.

Okay. There was her answer. Not a perfect solution, but one she could live with. She could enjoy his company, accept his kisses, but make her intentions clear—she would never agree to an affair. That was the only way she could keep her sanity and also keep her secret. When he tired of her and moved on, she would survive. She always had.

As she passed the accounting office raised voices caught her attention. She slowed to a stop, listening, relieved to focus on something besides her tumultuous emotional state.

"Don't worry about it," Dominic was saying, his tone strained. "I can take care of the problem by Friday."

A voice she didn't recognize muttered something in reply. She couldn't make out the words, but the tone was tense. Curiosity lifted the hairs on the back of her neck.

What was going on in there?

She moved closer but noise from the kitchen blotted out the conversation. She caught bits and pieces, a word here and there, and, after a few minutes of unsuccessful eavesdropping, began to feel silly. If she wanted to know what was going on, she could ask, not stand in the hall lurking like a criminal. Ever since John had questioned her about a vendor transaction she'd made from her flat, she'd been suspicious of everyone and everything. Add Daniel's confirmation that her name had come up as one having access and she was jumping at shadows.

She went into her office and waited until she heard the door of the accounting office open. Then she stepped back into the hallway.

Dominic stood in the entry of his office watching the pair depart. He ran a finger beneath his shirt collar and took a deep breath.

"Dominic."

He whirled around, noticing her for the first time. "Stephanie, hullo. You startled me."

"I thought I heard angry voices. Who were those men?"

His eyes, so like Daniel's and yet so different, shifted toward the back door. "Those men? Mr Sandusky and Mr Richardson?"

He seemed reluctant to tell her more, but she remained silent, waiting. Finally, Dominic gave a short laugh and rubbed a hand over his head. Daniel had that same habit, but the effect was quite different on a balding pate. "That wasn't arguing. That was debate over a very important topic. My brother."

Now she was taken by surprise. "Daniel?" What did he have to do with this?

"Sandusky and Richardson are investors. I'm trying to convince them that Dan's water ventures could eventually be nice moneymakers for their group."

And here she'd been thinking bad thoughts. "What a wonderful thing to do, Dominic. Daniel will be touched."

A modest blush stained his cheeks. "He's my twin. I want the best for him. And if sweetening up some business investors will help, I'll do it."

"You really should tell him. He has videos, photos, statistics, all kinds of information that could seal the deal."

"No. No. Not yet." He stood up straighter, fidgeted with his tie. "I'd rather wait until they've committed. I don't want Daniel disappointed if they don't come on board."

"Oh, I see." And she did. She also felt terrible for the ugly doubts that had popped into her head. "Well, let me know if I can be of any help. Daniel will be thrilled by this."

Then she went inside her office and shut the door.

Poor, sweet Dominic.

All day she'd been worrying about the tampered

accounts and trying to pinpoint suspects. In hopes of affirming her own innocence, she'd begun to wonder about Dominic.

The problem had begun shortly after Dominic came to work for the restaurants. But that was all the so-called evidence she had. Well, except for the two times she'd walked into his office unannounced and seen him scramble to log off the computer.

She chided her runaway imagination. The guy was probably looking at sexy pictures and was embarrassed at being caught. She had no business thinking the worst of Daniel's brother.

Thank goodness, she hadn't said anything. An unfounded accusation could alienate both John and Daniel. Worse yet, it could hurt them. And the last thing she ever wanted to do was hurt her boss or the man she was falling in love with.

But someone was responsible. If she wasn't guilty, and Dominic wasn't guilty, it could very well be, as John feared, someone else in the family. But who?

CHAPTER SEVEN

LIFE was starting to go his way.

Daniel softly punched a fist into his palm, excited about the new agreement with AquaSphere Associates. Even the cloudy day couldn't dampen his enthusiasm.

He stopped in the restaurant's back doorway to scratch the kitten under the chin.

Stephanie had been right. Meeting with his father's business contacts had resulted in the first of what should be many more contracts for his fledgling company.

For all his reluctance to attend the lunch meeting, Daniel had to admit his father seemed genuinely committed to helping him. The issue still made him uneasy. A lifetime of neglect couldn't be made up in weeks, and money wouldn't fix the hurt of having no boyhood father. He wasn't sure what to feel for John. One thing for certain, trust had to be earned. And the jury was still out on that one.

The kitten arched her back and rubbed against his calf as he walked away, leaving stray hairs on his dark trousers. It had been a long time since he'd dressed in a suit and tie. He didn't much care for the discomfort, but the new haircut seemed to demand more conservative attire.

His thoughts drifted pleasantly from the meeting to the afternoon Stephanie had trimmed his hair. He ran a hand over his head, grinning at the memory. Not surprisingly, she'd done a good job of taming his unruly locks, at least to some degree. A perfectionist like her wouldn't have offered if she wasn't sure of the outcome.

It was the minutes after the haircut that stayed with him, though. That first kiss was imprinted on his mind as permanently as a tattoo. At the time, he'd thought it was the only kiss he'd ever get, but she'd surprised him the next day by kissing him. Not on the cheek as she'd done before, but on the lips, proving that she'd forgiven whatever wrong he'd done.

He didn't know why that pleased him so much, all things considered.

Now that she didn't jump every time he came near, Stephanie was great company. She was intellectually stimulating, witty, and generous to a fault. He knew she befriended her staff almost to excess, loaning money, listening to sob stories, filling in when someone needed time off. But she was also generous to him in ways that boggled his already confused thought processes. Without his knowledge, she'd spent hours developing a PowerPoint presentation from his slides. The exceptional work had most certainly made the difference in today's meeting.

If that wasn't enough to get any man thinking about her, she was also the most coolly gorgeous thing he'd ever seen. He could deal with that. But living under the same roof with a woman who stopped at kisses was driving him quite mad. And she would never agree to the only kind of relationship he could give, a physical one. He wished he had more to offer, but he didn't.

Ah, well, kisses were better than nothing.

Maybe he'd ask her to celebrate today's success with him. Perhaps take her to a football match, or they could head to the West End for dinner and a play. Stephanie would like that, he was sure, and he did own a decent suit now.

Happy and full of excess energy, he decided to take the stairway up to the flat. Pounding the steps two at a time, he reached the top without breaking a sweat.

Stereo music blasted through the glass balcony doors. Classic hard rock. Daniel laughed as he stepped inside the living room. The insistent, driving sound was so unlike the smooth jazz Stephanie preferred in the restaurant.

Only slightly winded, he drew in a deep breath. Stephanie's perfume swamped him.

Yes, it was a good day. A good, good day.

"Stephanie," he called, but wasn't surprised when she didn't answer. Superman couldn't hear over that music.

He followed the sound down the hall, thinking to knock on her bedroom door until she heard him.

When he saw that her door was already open, he slowed.

And then he froze.

Back to him, she stood at the closet, rifling through a rack of clothes encased in clear plastic cleaner bags. Her long wavy hair was piled on top of her head with the usual stray curls tumbling down. Tall, slim, and lithe, the beautiful redhead was nude.

But it wasn't the nakedness that had his heart slamming against his ribcage with the force of a freight train.

It was the scars.

From shoulder blades to mid-thigh, long, white scars marred the perfection of an otherwise beautiful body.

Daniel rocked back. What on earth—?

He stood in the dim hallway for several more stunned moments before realizing he had to get away. He couldn't let her catch him here, not like this, not when his face must register the storm raging inside.

Wheeling on the heels of his shiny new shoes, Daniel raced out of the flat and thundered down the stairs. Right now, he couldn't face anyone. He needed time alone to assess what he'd just witnessed.

The alleyway was thankfully empty except for rubbish bins, the kitten, and an illegally parked car. Weak in the knees and breathless, he leaned against the brick wall at the back of the restaurant and closed his eyes. The image of Stephanie's battered skin arose like a bad dream.

What had happened? Fire? A car crash?

He saw the scars again, the long, slashing stripes that lay like ritualistic lashes across her entire backside.

Ritualistic lashes.

As if he'd been slammed in the gut with a sledgehammer, all the air whooshed out of him.

Oh, my God.

A trembling started down his soul. He fought the tide of emotion, scared of what it meant. Pity. This must be pity. And rage. He had never been so angry. Not at his mother. Not at John. Not even at the inhuman conditions he had witnessed in the course of his work.

Some vile, evil maniac had intentionally beaten Stephanie until she was terribly, irreconcilably scarred. Not once, not even twice, but many times in a ritual of abuse.

Their conversation in the restaurant came back to him, sharp and in focus, making sense now. When she'd said her boyfriend had hurt her badly, he'd suspected violence, but this was unfathomable. Only a monster could have done this.

Why had she stayed with him? Why had she let this happen, not once but many times? Had she been controlled by him in some way? Threatened and afraid? Was this why she'd come to England? To escape a maniac?

His temples throbbed with a dozen questions he couldn't ask. Stephanie didn't want him to know. She'd be destroyed if she thought he had discovered her secret.

The scars explained so much. The reasons she had avoided physical contact with him, the fear in her eyes until he'd finally proven himself trustworthy. Even the elegant dresses that showed so little skin now made sense.

Stephanie's wariness wasn't from a cold heart. It was self-preservation.

He squeezed his eyes shut against the onslaught of emotion rising up inside him, swallowed the vile sickness in his throat. His poor, beautiful, broken Stephanie.

The devil who had committed this heinous crime deserved to die. And Daniel would have gladly done the deed without a blink of remorse.

Daniel walked the streets of Kensington for more than two hours before returning to the restaurant. Long shadows of evening fell across the alley. The kitten greeted him as usual. This time he picked her up and rubbed his face against her fur, soaking in the purring comfort before opening the back door.

His shirt was rumpled and untucked. His shoes were

now scuffed and dirty. He'd long since shoved the silk tie into a pocket and loosened the top shirt button.

The smells emanating from inside the Bella Lucia made his stomach growl. To a man who hadn't eaten since lunch, the scent of Italian food was pure heaven—ironic considering how sick he'd felt earlier.

The need to talk drove him to stop at Dominic's office, but his brother had already gone home to Alice and the kids. The knowledge that his twin had someone to go home to struck Daniel with a loneliness he seldom experienced. He'd never know that pleasure of family, never have someone to share his life and troubles.

The moment he walked into the dining room, he spotted Stephanie. His gut clenched.

Cool and smooth as the terracotta tile beneath her feet, Stephanie moved from table to table, dropping a warm greeting, a welcoming smile, a complimentary bottle of wine. The restaurant pulsed around her with the beat of unobtrusive jazz, trendy, chic, a respite from the busy streets outside.

No one would ever guess the pain and betrayal she'd lived through.

His admiration edged upward. She'd suffered far more than he ever had and yet she'd chosen not to wither, but to bloom.

Out of sight of customers, Daniel leaned in the doorway, watching her, the perfect manager, perfectly groomed, perfectly poised, perfect in every way except for the terrible sorrow she hid from the world.

Tenderness threatened to choke him.

Regardless of what had happened to her, Stephanie had

KIMANI
ROMANCE

An Important
Message from
the Publisher

Dear Reader,

If you'd enjoy reading contemporary
African-American love stories filled with
drama and passion, then let us send you
two free Kimani Romance™ novels. These
books will keep it real with true-to-life
African-American characters that turn up
the heat and sizzle with passion.

By the way, you'll also get two surprise gifts
with your two free books! Please enjoy the
free books and gifts with our compliments...

Linda Gill

Publisher, Kimani Press

Peel off Seal and
Place Inside...

FREE GIFT
PUBLISHERS
SEAL
THANK YOU

We'd like to send you two free books to introduce you to our brand-new line – Kimani Romance™! These novels feature strong, sexy women, and African-American heroes that are charming, loving and true. Our authors fill each page with exceptional dialogue, exciting plot twists, and enough sizzling romance to keep you riveted until the very end!

KIMANI ROMANCE ... LOVE'S ULTIMATE DESTINATION

Your two books have a combined cover price of $11.98 in the U.S. and $13.98 in Canada, but are yours **FREE!** We'll even send you two wonderful surprise gifts. You can't lose!

Two NEW Kimani Romance™ Novels
Two exciting surprise gifts

I have placed my Editor's "thank you" Free Gifts seal in the space provided at right. Please send me 2 FREE books, and my 2 FREE Mystery Gifts. I understand that I am under no obligation to purchase anything further, as explained on the back of this card.

PLACE FREE GIFTS SEAL HERE

168 XDL EF2L   **368 XDL EF2W**

FIRST NAME	LAST NAME

ADDRESS

APT.#	CITY

STATE/PROV.	ZIP/POSTAL CODE

Thank You!

(KR-TL-11/06)

BUSINESS REPLY MAIL

FIRST-CLASS MAIL   PERMIT NO. 717-003   BUFFALO, NY

POSTAGE WILL BE PAID BY ADDRESSEE

THE READER SERVICE
3010 WALDEN AVE
PO BOX 1867
BUFFALO NY 14240-9952

NO POSTAGE
NECESSARY
IF MAILED
IN THE
UNITED STATES

made a success of her life. She went right on caring about the people around her, nurturing those in need, giving, loving.

And unless he'd missed something, she had no one in her life to reciprocate. Who tended her when she was sick? Held her when she cried?

With a sigh, Daniel wondered if life would have been different if he'd ever learned to love someone other than himself. But no matter. He hadn't. His heart was as empty as the devil's soul, whether he liked it or not. He wasn't the kind of man Stephanie needed. He wasn't the kind of man any woman needed for more than a night or two, an admission that left him emptier than ever.

Stephanie disappeared into the cloakroom. Unfamiliar tenderness crowding his better judgment, Daniel pushed away from the wall and followed.

He eased up behind her and placed a kiss on the back of her neck.

"All work and no play—"

Stephanie spun around. Her skin tingled from the feath-erlike touch of Daniel's lips, from his warm breath on her skin. Since the first time they'd kissed and she'd realized she loved him, something had broken loose inside her. Though she would eventually pay with a broken heart, she hungered for the touch of another human being. But not just anyone. Daniel.

"I wondered where you were. How did things go today?"

"Great." He told her about the contract, but his mind seemed somewhere else. "I need someone to celebrate with me. How about you?"

A celebration with Daniel sounded lovely. "I'm working."

He took her hands and pulled her toward him. The

usual mischief danced in his eyes, but tonight she saw something else in those blue depths that she couldn't quite define.

"So," he said as he nuzzled her temple. "These excellent employees of yours can't finish the evening without you?"

Stephanie resisted the longing to lean closer and soak him up like the dry sponge of need she was. "Of course they can."

"Good." He stepped back, still holding her hands in his warm, calloused grip. "Grab your coat and let's go. I'll take you anywhere you choose. Say the word and I'll even put the cursed tie back on."

She laughed. "This is your celebration."

"Right. So indulge me. You choose."

He stroked a finger along her cheek, smiling at her in the strangest way. There it was again, that subtle difference, as though he really cared about what she wanted.

"You're in an unusual mood."

"Nothing unusual about taking my favorite lady out for a good time."

His favorite lady? Where had that come from?

He ushered her from the cloakroom, skirting around the diners to slip out the front door.

"I need to let Sheila know I'm leaving," Stephanie protested.

"Call her from the flat." Without warning, he backed her against the wall. On the streets, traffic pulsed and somewhere a car honked, but the air around the two of them grew silent. That gentle, questioning expression appeared on Daniel's face again. Then his lips covered hers with such exquisite tenderness Stephanie almost felt loved.

What in the world was going on with him tonight?

* * *

Whatever was going on didn't relent in the days to come.

On a blustery afternoon when November had shortened the days and the sky threatened a cold rain, Stephanie donned slacks and sweater for yet another outing with the indefatigable Daniel. The man had more energy than an electric company. He could spend the morning schmoozing clients, visiting job sites, and frequently working himself into a dirty, sweaty mess, then come breezing in to whisk her away from the restaurant for a few hours of adventure. Invariably, she protested out of duty to her job, but her protests grew weaker with every soft kiss and tender caress. She was helpless to turn down these special moments with the new, solicitous Daniel.

Coat and gloves in hand, she met him in the living room. All cleaned up in blue jeans and a turquoise sweater that turned his eyes to jewels, he helped her into her long leather coat. When he began to button it up with his large, competent fingers, a swell of pure pleasure filled Stephanie to the point of no return.

Head bent, a wayward lock of his dark hair fell forward. Stephanie pushed it away, then let her fingers drift down to the warm, whisker-rough curve of his cheek.

Lord, she loved this man.

"All done." But he didn't step back. Instead, he took her scarf, draped it around her neck and used the soft flannel to bring her face in line with his. The whisper of his breath, minty and fresh, kissed her lips. "Ready, then?"

"Ready." She was as breathless as if she'd run six flights of stairs.

Hand holding hers, he led the way to the elevator.

"Where are you kidnapping me to?" she asked when they were inside the lift.

He pressed the floor indicator and, with a wicked grin that set her heart thudding, said, "Secret."

He'd told her only that they wouldn't be back until late and she should dress casually. A twinge of guilt said she shouldn't be gone during the dinner rush, but John had told her more than once lately that she worked too much and should take more time off. She wondered if Daniel had anything to do with that.

"Let me check in with Sheila and make sure everything is running smoothly before we go."

Still grinning in that wicked, wicked manner, he backed her against the metal wall. "No."

She pushed at his chest. "I can't enjoy myself unless I'm sure everything is covered."

Sighing an overly dramatic martyr's sigh, Daniel slumped. "Woman, have you never in your life done anything irresponsible?"

On tiptoe, she kissed him. "Humor me. I might be worth it."

"Kiss me again and I'll believe you."

She obliged, and Daniel, the naughty man, deepened the kiss, holding it while the elevator pinged open and then closed again.

"Daniel!" Stephanie cried when he finally let her come up for air. Something had definitely come over him tonight.

"What?" His handsome face was a study in innocence.

She whacked him playfully on the arm. "Are we going to spend the entire evening in this elevator?"

He cocked his head as if giving the idea serious thought. "Can't beat the privacy. Let's do it."

Doing it would be wonderful, but Stephanie couldn't ever go there again. Not even with Daniel. She leaned around him and pushed the down button.

"Spoilsport." But he draped an arm around her waist and snuggled her close, nuzzling her neck in the seconds from her flat to the restaurant.

"You're making this very difficult."

"That's the plan."

When they finally exited the elevator, laughing like two sneaking teenagers, Stephanie felt lighter and happier than she had since the day she'd left Denver.

With Daniel's hand at her back in the most protective way, they went into the restaurant, spoke briefly to the competent Sheila, and then retraced their steps to the back door.

"We could use the front entrance, you know," Stephanie said.

"What about the motorcycle I have waiting?"

"You do not," she said, but, knowing Daniel as she did, he probably did.

His eyes gleamed with mischief. "Try me."

A thrill of excitement raced along Stephanie's spine. She couldn't think of anything more wonderful than riding behind Daniel, her arms around his waist as the cold wind whipped her hair and stung her cheeks.

He paused outside Dominic's office and reached inside his coat pocket to extract a small box. "Let me drop this off first. Dominic's eldest is having a birthday."

Before Stephanie could comment on his thoughtfulness, Daniel pushed the door open. Two men whirled around. Anger sizzled from them as palpable and menacing as a nest of vipers.

Stephanie's breath froze in her throat. The investors were back and none too happy. Dominic sat behind the desk perspiring profusely.

She didn't know what was going on, but something was badly wrong. The tension in the room was thick enough to choke an elephant.

Daniel's hands fisted at his side. He looked from his brother to the two men. "Is there a problem?"

His tone was tough and protective, leaving no doubt about whose side he was on.

A pair of the hardest, coldest eyes she'd ever seen glared back. "No problem at all." The reptilian glance shifted to Dominic. "Isn't that right, Dom?"

Dominic pushed up from the squeaky chair. Stephanie couldn't help noticing a tremble in his hands. "Everything is fine. Just a bit of unfinished business." He hustled around the desk to usher the two men to the door. "I'll call you tomorrow about that project. You have my word."

Daniel looked at Stephanie and murmured, "What's going on?"

She lifted her shoulders, afraid he wouldn't appreciate her thoughts.

The rumble of voices in the hall told her that Dominic's unfinished business was quite a serious topic.

When Dominic returned to the office visibly shaken, Daniel asked, "What was that all about? Who were those guys?"

"Old friends." His face was pale. "No one you know."

Now Stephanie knew he was lying. The ugly suspicion

rose again, this time with enough strength to give the doubts validity. Dominic wasn't soliciting investors for his brother's business. He was up to no good. He had to be. Otherwise, why behave so strangely and lie so blatantly?

This time, Stephanie had no choice. She had to inform John that something was not right with the accountant. Maybe he wasn't embezzling funds, but something was definitely amiss.

Stephanie glanced at Daniel, her heart sinking lower than the Alaskan sun. She was about to accuse his brother of a crime.

He was going to hate her for this.

CHAPTER EIGHT

"LIKE it?" Daniel shouted over one shoulder, his voice yanked away by the force of wind and speed.

Stephanie leaned forward, mouth all but touching Daniel's ear. "It's wonderful."

The motorcycle sped through the streets and alleys of London, dodging in and out of places they probably shouldn't have ridden. But Daniel, confident and competent, had no fear. With him in control Stephanie didn't either. Hands locked over the smooth, supple leather of his jacket, she reveled in the energy racing through her bloodstream. For the first time in a long time, she felt carefree and alive.

She could have ridden for ever and been happy, but Daniel slowed and pulled into a parking bay.

"We're going to be tourists tonight," he said, helping her off the bike.

"Like this?" She shook her hair out, knowing she looked wild and wind-kissed.

"You're beautiful." Daniel bent to kiss her nose. "But your nose is cold."

She tiptoed up and returned the kiss. "So is yours."

He growled deep in his throat and made a teasing grab

for her. With a squeal, she jumped back, stumbled and was quickly righted by his strong hands.

"Careful there. We have lots of walking to do."

Pulse tripping, more from Daniel's touch than the near fall, Stephanie slipped her hand into his. "Where are we headed?"

"There." He pointed upward at the huge, rotating London Eye. "And then other places."

Even this late in the fall, the area along the South Bank of the Thames was alive with visitors, the smells and sounds almost carnival-like. They bought tickets, joined the growing line, and boarded an enclosed glass pod of the giant observation wheel. Buildings and people grew tiny as the Eye slowly ascended.

"I feel like I'm inside a bubble," she said.

Daniel smiled his reply and moved them closer to the window. Other visitors sharing the pod oohed and ahhed, pointing out landmarks as the wheel continued its climb.

A little boy with a posh accent carried on a running commentary to his parents as various sites came into view. Daniel shrugged and stuffed his guidebook into a pocket.

"Nothing like a personal tour," he muttered against her temple.

For Stephanie, the landmarks weren't the important part of the ride. Being with Daniel was. Yet, the panorama was breathtaking.

Through a moisture-smeared veil, she glimpsed London spread in every direction around the mighty river. In the west, the sun was setting. Though the fog and haze obscured the sunset, rays of diffused light penetrated just enough to cast a glorious glow over the city.

The South Bank, a cultural Mecca for art, music and

theatre, was a place she'd been wanting to visit since coming to London, but had never had the time. She was glad. Seeing the area with Daniel made it even more special.

Positioned behind her, her favorite barbarian rested his chin atop her head and pulled her back against him. Through her coat she felt the press of his jacket zipper, the mold of his muscled chest and belly, and the strength of his arms lightly bracketing her waist, and marveled at how safe she felt. She, who never felt safe in a man's arms, wanted to stay here for ever, loving him always as she did this moment.

She closed her eyes, the panorama briefly forgotten, and focused on the essence of Daniel. He smelled of leather and fresh air and that manly scent that was uniquely his. Though a dozen or so other people occupied the pod, Stephanie felt as if they were the only two people around. Something magical had happened when he'd come into her life, as if the thick miasma of fear and distrust had blown away in the fresh breeze of a man without false motives.

She knew where she stood with him. He'd made no secret that they could never be more than they were now, a fact that both comforted and seared. Comforted because he would never see the scars and be repelled. Seared because she loved him and knew these moments with him could not last.

The quiet burr of his voice forced her eyes open.

"According to our worthy guide," he said wryly, "we can spy Buckingham Palace right over there." He dipped closer, his cheek to hers, and pointed in the general direction.

The touch of his skin against hers was electric. She

turned to face him, resisted the urge to kiss the corner of that sexy mouth. "I think we could see the entire city if the weather was clear."

"The view from right here is even lovelier." As if he wanted to memorize every feature, Daniel scanned her face.

"Why, Mr Stephens, are you trying to flatter me into another late-night trip for cheesecake and chocolate sauce?"

"Is it working?"

"Could be," she answered and was rewarded with a quick flash of white teeth against his dark skin.

And then the rest of the trip around the wheel was lost as they focused on each other instead of the London skyline. For Stephanie those moments staring into Daniel's handsome face defined the evening. Inside their own glass bubble, a real romance with the man she had fallen in love with actually seemed possible.

When the ride ended, they strolled the promenade along the waterfront, stopping to watch the cruise ships pass. Darkness had come and streetlamps illuminated the tree-lined path and reflected off the river's edge in a dance of shadows and light.

"It's a long walk around," Daniel said when she opted to walk to the Millennium Bridge.

"I don't mind." The longer they walked, the longer she would be with him, alone and having fun. And the longer she could pretend they had something special together.

"We can hire a cab back to the bike."

"Or walk." Like a happy child, she wrapped her arms around herself and spun around in a circle. "This is so awesome."

Daniel caught up to her, grabbed her hands and whirled

her again. "I thought you would fret over the restaurant all night."

"Shh. Don't tell a soul. I'm relieved to be away for a while." The Bella Lucia didn't worry her, but she couldn't get Dominic, and the coming conversation with John, off her mind. Daniel hadn't said a word more about the incident in the office, but he had to be concerned as well. Even if Dominic hadn't taken the money, something was not quite right with Daniel's twin.

She stopped spinning and the open lapels of her long coat swished against her boot tops. "What do you think is going on with Dominic?"

Daniel grew serious. "I think he may be in trouble, though he doesn't confide in me the way he once did."

"No guesses? No twin's intuition?"

He frowned, deep furrows in his sun-bronzed brow. "None."

She wanted to ask if he thought his brother would embezzle money, but feared Daniel would take offense. And the last thing she wanted tonight was to spoil the magical evening.

"It worries you. I shouldn't have brought it up." They started walking again. "Change of subject. Tell me about your work today. About the projects. What's happening?"

"One of the reasons for my good mood." He seemed relieved to sidestep the topic of his brother. "Today I hired two water technicians and another engineer to help carry the load on all the waste-water management projects I've taken on. Plus, I have a meeting set up next week with Lord Rathington."

She blinked up at him. "Should I be impressed?"

"Very." Daniel's proud smile pushed the Dominic dilemma to the back of her mind. "The man owns half of Britain, including WS Associates, the consulting firm that can make or break an upstart company like mine. And, rumor has it, he's made a few safaris to Africa."

"Ah."

"Exactly. He seldom meets personally with anyone, but he's agreed to see me."

Stephanie smiled. "You are the most amazing man to have achieved all this since coming to London."

He laughed. "You give me too much credit. I'm sure my father had something to do with it."

"Be that as it may, I think you're amazing, and I'm proud of you."

"Keep talking. You're good for my ego."

She was in the process of forming a snappy comeback when they rounded a curve in the river and a glorious display of lights blazed in the darkness.

"Is that St Paul's?" Stephanie stared in wonder at the elegant old cathedral.

"Glorious, isn't it?"

"I had no idea it was this impressive. I suppose it's closed at this time of night?" she asked, hoping.

"I'm afraid so. But there *is* something here in the neighborhood I want to show you."

Her disappointment at not seeing the interior of St Paul's turned to curiosity. There were so many landmarks in this section of London, she wondered what he could have in mind. Perhaps the Globe? Or the Tate Modern? He knew she loved contemporary art. He'd even teased her about it when she'd said she hated the masters but loved the abstract and avant-garde. Of course, she hadn't told him why she despised those classic paintings. Another secret better kept.

Instead of the Tate, however, he turned down a side street toward a closed and darkened business section.

"Where are we going?"

"You'll see," he said mysteriously, suppressed excitement in every word.

"Now I really am curious."

Boots echoing along the quiet street, Daniel stopped in front of a lovely older brick office building.

"Here we are. She has character, don't you think?"

"Yes. But exactly who is she?"

"*She* is the office space I leased today for Stephens International Water Design."

"Daniel! Oh, my goodness." She didn't know whether to laugh or cry. He looked so proud and so much like a small boy wanting approval.

She threw her arms around him in an enthusiastic embrace. "This is marvelous. A real office. Can we go in? Please."

Her reaction clearly thrilled him. He threw his head back and laughed. "Whatever the lady desires."

She desired, all right, something far more precious than a tour of an office building. But seeing Daniel happy was enough for now.

Inside the small but pleasant office space, Daniel stood with hands on hips waiting for her to comment.

"I can see a pair of plush chairs here along this wall, blue, I think," she said, moving around the room as decorating images flashed in her head. "And a nice wall grouping above them. Perhaps a black and white photo display of some of your projects. And the desk will go here. A very modern computer desk and—"

Daniel caught her in mid-sentence and spun her around. "You're a special woman, Stephanie."

Her heart caught in her throat. "Because I like to decorate?"

His chuckle raised warm goose bumps on her arms. "Because I needed you to approve."

Was that uncertainty? In a man as confident and strong as Daniel?

"This office is perfect. And what better place for a water-project engineer than along the shores of the Thames?"

"I knew you'd appreciate the symbolism."

Hand in hand, they took a brief tour of the office, then made their way back out on the street. All the way to the Millennium Bridge, Daniel talked nonstop about his plans and ideas for the fledgling business.

"You will succeed beyond your wildest dreams, Daniel," she said when he expressed a concern to the contrary. "I believe that with all my heart."

The long, water-washed pedestrian bridge stretched across the river and welcomed strolling couples. Stephanie and Daniel walked to the center and stopped to look down at the river below.

Lights from the shore gleamed on the water, and fog twisted and smeared the panorama into an impressionistic painting. Gentle music from a passing cruise ship wafted up to them. With a half-smile that made her pulse race, Daniel inclined his head.

"Dance?"

A few other strollers passed by, but Stephanie paid them no mind. She lifted the edge of her long coat and dipped a curtsey, then stepped into Daniel's beloved arms. For a few glorious minutes while the boat hovered nearby, they swayed and swirled on the pedestrian bridge. Resting her cheek in the crook of his neck, she reveled in the scent of his skin and delighted in the beat of his heart echoing hers.

Could he be feeling the same thing she was? This incredible surge of joy, this new willingness to be vulnerable to another person regardless of the past? Her heart swelled with the hope that both of them could lay aside their hurts and move forward together. She loved him. Dared she admit her feelings?

Everything he did tonight spoke of caring, but he claimed to have no love to give. With each passing moment in his company, Stephanie found that harder and harder to believe. If this continued, she would have to tell him.

But not tonight. She couldn't chance shattering the lovely fantasy of tonight. Here in Daniel's arms along the bank of the Thames, she could pretend that he loved her, too.

"Telephone call, Stephanie. The man says it's very important."

The evening rush was on and the restaurant was alive with trendy Londoners. Stephanie didn't mind. She was still walking on air from the incredible date with Daniel the evening before.

"Okay, thanks, Sheila."

She scribbled "zucchini" on a notepad beside the kitchen door, then caught herself and wrote "courgette" instead. The dish had come back to the kitchen uneaten on several plates. And whether she called the vegetable courgette or zucchini, less than marvelous food was not acceptable in her restaurant.

"He's calling long distance. From Colorado."

Her pen clattered to the tile.

"Colorado?" Was that squeaky sound coming from her? "Tell the waiting staff to downplay the courgette and recommend the potato-aubergine tart as an alternative. I'll be right back."

With a heavy dread, Stephanie went into her office, closing the door behind her. She took several long, steadying breaths, then punched the hold button.

"Stephanie Ellison speaking."

She braced herself for the horrid voice.

"Miss Ellison?" Relief shimmied through her. It wasn't him. "George Howard Whittier here. I hope I haven't caught you at a bad time."

Her stepfather's law partner. She glanced up at the clock, calculating the time in Colorado. Afternoon, if she figured correctly, though the sun had set in London. "Is something wrong?"

"I'm sorry to break the news so abruptly, but I've had difficulty tracking your whereabouts. I do hope you're not alone." Gentlemanly hesitation hummed across the ocean.

"What is it, Mr Whittier?"

"My dear, your father passed away two weeks ago."

Stephanie dropped the telephone and slithered to the floor.

Daniel tossed restlessly in his bed. He'd had a bad feeling all day, a kind of premonition that something was amiss.

In the sometimes dangerous situations he had been in while working abroad, he'd learned to trust his gut instincts. The simplest clue, such as a sudden hush of animal sounds in the darkness, often meant trouble ahead.

Tonight he felt that same hush brooding over the flat. Stephanie had come in an hour ago, claiming exhaustion, and had gone straight to bed. He knew the restaurant had been hopping tonight, but he was disappointed. He looked forward to the evenings when they had time to talk.

All day, she'd been on his mind. Her sweetness, her scent, the taste of her skin. When he'd shown her his future office space, she'd reacted just as he'd hoped, with the same excitement he'd experienced when he'd signed the lease.

He flopped over on the firm mattress and punched his pillow into a fluffier lump. If the noise wouldn't bother Stephanie he'd get up and work on the new monitoring design for flood control in North Yorkshire.

If she weren't so tired, he'd wake her and they'd sneak down to the kitchen for a midnight snack.

He slammed the pillow again. Might as well admit, Stephens, you're miffed. After last night when they'd had such a great time, he had expected a repeat performance or, at least, a recap. There had been that moment on the bridge when they'd danced and the world had seemed to fade away, leaving only the two of them. He relished the idea of being alone with her, frequently and for long periods.

He sat up, feet over the side of the bed, and shoved five fingers through the top of his hair. What was happening to him? His mind should be on work and water and fund-raising. Those things were his life. A woman was only a passing fancy, but Stephanie no longer fit his carefully structured view of women.

Frustrated, he flopped backwards on the bed and lay staring at the shadows dancing on the ceiling.

A sharp cry yanked him up again.

"Stephanie?" he called, knowing she couldn't hear from this far away. He got up and opened his bedroom door. A scream pierced the night. Whimpering sobs began. And then a terrible pleading.

"No. Please. No."

Hair rose on his arms.

He'd heard her nightmares when he'd first arrived and had done nothing. In time, the bad dreams had subsided. But now he couldn't stay away. Not after he'd seen the scars.

Heart thundering, he rushed into her bedroom.

"Stephanie. Love. Wake up."

Eyes accustomed to the darkness, he could see her, feel her thrashing in agony. Without a second thought, Daniel climbed onto the bed and pulled her into his arms.

"No. Please." She fought him like a wild thing, but his strength was far greater—just as someone else's had been. An awful sick lump formed in his throat.

"Stephanie. Love. It's Daniel. Wake up. You're safe. You're safe." He held fast, pressing her face into his naked shoulder until she went limp against him, and he knew she had awakened.

Her body trembled while Daniel crooned meaningless words of comfort against her hair. Even sweat-soaked, she smelled of exotic flowers.

When at last she quieted, he stroked the damp hair from her face and kissed her forehead. "Tell me."

She shook her head and shrank back as if only now aware that they were in a bed together. "A nightmare."

That was obvious. "About?" he urged as gently as he knew how.

Using the sheet for a tissue, she dabbed her damp eyes, then drew in a long, shuddering breath. "Something happened tonight. A phone call from my family's attorney."

Daniel waited, saying nothing, but trying to put the two events together.

"My father died two weeks ago." The words came out flat and wooden. "And I didn't even know."

For Daniel, missing his father's funeral wouldn't have mattered even a month ago, but now that family had intruded into his life he knew he would care if something happened to John. He didn't want to care and wasn't about to let John know as much, but he would. Stephanie hadn't been home for her own father's funeral. Understandable that news of his death would set off a bad dream.

"I'm sorry, love. Truly." He wanted to hold her, but she seemed not to want that, so he settled for touching the back of her cheek with his knuckles.

"I have to go to Colorado," she whispered, "and settle the estate."

"So soon?" Daniel flipped on the bedside lamp.

Stephanie's eyes were red and wild as she blinked against the sudden flood of light.

"Yes. Now. Tomorrow." Her hands began to pick and twist at the sheet in a way that Daniel recognized as deep anxiety.

"Is it that urgent?"

"I don't want to go back, but I have to."

A quiver of worry intruded. "Is he still there? Your ex?"

"Brett?" She looked bewildered. "No. No. Not any-more."

He felt a measure of relief. If the monster who'd abused her wasn't there, she'd be safe.

She shoved off the bed. Silk pajamas whispered against her skin. She paced to the window and back. The trembling started again and Daniel wasn't sure what she needed.

He offered all he could. "You've had terrible news. You're distraught. Come here. Let me hold you."

As if he were the lifeboat in a stormy ocean, she fell upon him, knocking him onto his back. He took her with him.

Her wild tangle of curls fell across his face. He pushed them aside, trying to read her expression, to understand what she was feeling.

"Come with me, Daniel," she murmured, the request urgent, almost frantic. "I can't do this alone."

"Love." Beyond that, he was at a loss. The old fear rose up. What was she asking?

"Please, Daniel. I need you beside me. I need your strength. I love you. You have to know that by now. And I need you with me. I can't get through this alone."

Daniel stiffened. She loved him?

Oh, no.

Stephanie's warm, slender body lay atop his and yet he had no sexual urgings, just the terrible need to run. He was a coward of the worst kind, but the word love scared him out of his mind.

"Stephanie, sweetheart. Listen to me." He rolled them to the side so they lay face-to-face. Her stormy sea eyes were wild and distraught. "You don't love me. You can't."

He wasn't lovable. And he had no love in him. Hadn't he told her as much?

"But I do," she whispered. "I didn't mean to. I didn't want to. But I love you."

Daniel released a groan of dismay. What had he done? Stephanie needed far more than he had to give. She deserved far more than a man with no heart, no soul.

He squeezed his eyes closed against the onslaught of despair. No matter what he did now, she would be hurt even more than she already was.

The best thing he could do for both of them was get away. He sat up, putting distance between them. If he touched her much longer, he'd do something stupid. She didn't deserve the kind of misery a life with him would bring. He was too empty. He had nothing to give her. Nothing.

"We agreed early on that neither of us wanted emotional commitment." He couldn't look at her. "You can't love me, Stephanie." His own mother hadn't. How could she? "I can't love you. I don't know how. I don't have it in me."

She touched his bare arm. "You're wrong. You have so much love, it scares you."

He shook his head. She didn't understand. He didn't expect her to.

"Don't you see, Daniel? A man who gives his entire life to improve life for others has plenty of love. You're afraid. That's all. So was I, but you're not like him."

She was afraid of loving, too, and now he'd ruined her for good. She would never chance letting another through her force field of protection.

"I'm sorry, Stephanie. Truly." She'd never know how sorry.

"Go with me, Daniel. No strings. I can't do this alone."

But she loved him and love always expected something in return.

"The meeting with Lord Rathington," he said feebly.

Drawing the sheet up like a coat of armor, she sat up straighter in the center of the bed. Her expression went cool, her body still as stone. "Of course. How thoughtless of me. You can't miss that."

He stood like the stunned fool he was, wishing he had something more to give her. Something that mattered. In the end, he said the only thing he could. "I'll move my things into the new office while you're gone."

Red-eyed and flushed, she nodded with the regal grace of a queen. "I think that's best."

She was right. It was for the best. He had nothing to offer her, and prolonging the relationship would serve no good purpose.

Then why did he have the strongest need to crawl back onto that bed and beg her forgiveness?

CHAPTER NINE

COLORADO was as beautiful as ever. But even the majesty of the snow-covered Rockies couldn't lift the dark mood hanging over Stephanie like a London fog as she maneuvered her rental car through the streets and inclines of downtown Denver.

As much as she dreaded the days ahead of settling the family estate, the heartache of that last fight with Daniel tormented her most.

Why had she said those foolish words? Why had she tossed her heart out on that bed for him to reject? What was it about her personality that navigated toward men destined to hurt her?

And yet, Daniel was nothing like Brett or Randolph. For all his denials and sharp cynicism, Daniel cared deeply about people. And after that wonderful, magical night along the Thames, she'd even believed he cared about her.

Over and over, for the entire international flight, she'd puzzled over Daniel's behavior and called herself ten kinds of fool. She'd walked right into that opportunity for Daniel to break her heart.

But Daniel had suffered hurt, too. Somehow, from his

mother's and father's mistakes, he'd come to think of himself as unlovable and unloving. He was wrong. But Stephanie was too tired and weak to fight anymore. She wasn't even sure she had the emotional strength to face the meeting with the Ellison family lawyer.

Her grip on the steering wheel tightened as the tall glass and steel building came in sight.

Might as well admit the truth. She was scared out of her mind.

She pulled the rental car into a parking garage filled with cold air and exhaust fumes, then rode the elevator up to the eighteenth floor to the law offices of Whittier, Ellison, and Carter. The suites, ultra-conservative, just like her stepfather, occupied one end of the floor.

An immaculately groomed brunette receptionist and a security guard manned the entrance. Randolph had always been paranoid about security. To Stephanie's way of thinking, his own conscience had known he deserved to be shot.

"Stephanie Ellison to see Mr Whittier," she told the receptionist.

The action was nothing new. Even as a child, she and her mother had been expected to check in at the desk and wait their turn as if they were nothing but business appointments instead of family. Randolph Ellison had never cut her a bit of slack. Not in any way. She wasn't expecting today to be any different.

"Miss Ellison?" The brunette assessed her with an open curiosity that would have displeased her now-dead employer. Underlings were to maintain professional decorum at all times. "Mr Whittier is expecting you. I'll buzz him and you can go right in."

"I know the way, thank you." Without waiting, Stephanie pushed through the heavy double doors and knocked at the inner office marked "George H. Whittier, Attorney at Law."

"Stephanie, my dear child, come in. Come in." Mr Whittier, tall and angular in his gray business suit, came around an enormous oak-and-glass desk to greet her. As bony as he was, she expected him to rattle.

He seated them both. "You look wonderful, positively luminous. London must agree with you."

"Thank you. I'm happy there." Or she had been until she had allowed Daniel to break her heart. She ran damp palms over her royal-blue designer suit, chosen specifically to provide the confidence needed to get through this meeting. "If you don't mind, Mr Whittier, could we get down to business? I'd like to get back to England as soon as possible."

The jovial expression turned somber. "You do realize that there is a great deal to be done before the estate can be settled. I'm afraid this may take some time."

She gripped the tiny designer purse in her lap. "How long?"

"Several weeks at least. Maybe longer with the holidays coming on. Business moves much slower at this time of year."

The holidays. She'd hardly given them a thought with all that was happening in London. But here in America, business came to a near standstill from late November through the New Year.

Her stomach began to churn. How could she face dealing with Randolph's estate for more than a day or two? The nightmares had come nonstop since she'd first gotten word of his death. It was as if he had the power to reach from the grave to torment her.

"I don't want any of it, Mr Whittier. Give everything to charity."

"That's not possible, my dear. Your father made certain you couldn't do that. You see, he was very concerned about your state of mind after you went away to college."

Concerned? Yeah, right. He was concerned that she'd tell someone the truth about the powerful, respected attorney turned local politician. But she never had. She'd been too ashamed then and she was too ashamed now.

Face carefully composed, she asked, "What do I have to do?"

"Randolph set the trust up very carefully. There are stipulations regarding distribution of certain properties."

A chill circled her heart like cold fingers. "He couldn't touch the trust my mother left me, could he?" Knowing Randolph as she did, he had tried.

"No, of course not. But the bulk of the estate is in a trust of Randolph's creation. You have control, of course, but some of the holdings come with stipulations." He picked up a sheaf of papers and cleared his throat. "Your father left a letter addressed to you."

Stephanie wanted to ask him to stop calling Randolph Ellison her father. But there was another carefully preserved lie that she wasn't ready to admit to the world.

She reached for the letter and was surprised when the attorney did not hand it over. "I'm sorry." She dropped her hand. "I thought you said it was addressed to me."

"It is. But your father instructed that I read it aloud in your presence." He shifted, clearly uncomfortable. "I know

the contents, Stephanie, and I want to apologize in advance.
I tried to convince Randolph not to include this, but he
insisted. Just as he insisted that it be read aloud."

One last opportunity to humiliate her, no doubt.

"You have to understand," Whittier went on. "After you
left, Randolph became quite bitter. I'm afraid he never got
over your abandoning him after your mother's death."

Stephanie held back an angry retort. She hadn't abandoned him. No longer afraid for her mother, she'd escaped
from hell. But knowing Randolph as she did, she wasn't
surprised that he had become the injured party, playing her
as the ungrateful, heartless daughter.

Her head began to pound, but she kept her expression
empty and her voice cool and calm. "Read the letter, please."

"Very well." Whittier gave her another long look before
bowing his head to the missive and beginning to read.

My dear Stephanie, he read.

Your best interest and that of your beloved mother
has always been the focus of all I do. You know this
is true. I never wanted anything but the best for you.

The old hypocrite. If he'd wanted her to react to that
outright lie, he would be disappointed. She sat still and
straight. Randolph, good lawyer that he had been, had
begun his attacks gently, saving the zinger for last. She had
to be ready for anything.

Your mother and I gave you the best life possible.
We raised you in the best society, with the finest ed-
ucation and all the material things money could buy.

Yet, you never appreciated any of it. You are an ungrateful, disobedient young woman who does not
deserve my generosity.

Thank you, Daddy Dearest. You always were so very,
very generous with money as long as the other price was paid.

The lawyer's gray gaze flickered up to hers, a warning
that the worst was yet to come. Stephanie braced herself.
The cold trembling started deep in her stomach.

The letter went on for several pages of hideous vitriol
until Stephanie wanted to bolt from the room and never
return. But, after all she had suffered at Randolph's hands,
she was not about to give him that satisfaction.

The trembling spread to her knees. Though her face
blazed with humiliation, she sat straight and stiff in the
armchair and waited until the diatribe ended.

Mr Whittier lay the paper aside and looked up. "Again,
my apologies, Stephanie, for the remainder of this
document. Would you like some refreshment, tea perhaps,
before we continue?"

"No, thank you. Just get it over with. After the last few
pages, I can handle anything."

She wasn't sure if that was exactly true, but she had no
choice. On the outside she remained poised. The inside
raged with anger and hurt and a sick dread.

After another moment of hesitation, Whittier pushed his
glasses on and finished.

Under the circumstances, I should turn you out in
the street penniless. But I am a generous man whose
charity extends beyond the grave. Considering that

your real father was nothing but trash who seduced
your mother and left me with his bad seed, I am not
surprised by your disgraceful behavior. I'm only
thankful that my blood does not flow in your veins.
Nevertheless, I tried to keep you from following your
mother's same wanton path. But just as I forgave her,
I am forgiving you.

Whittier glanced over his bifocals. "You can rest
assured, my dear, that this meeting is entirely confidential.
Nothing in this letter will ever leave this room."

The heat of embarrassment deepened. She swallowed
past the cotton in her throat. No one outside of her mother,
herself and Randolph had ever known the truth about her
parentage—until now. "Thank you."

The quiver in her voice angered her. She would not let
Randolph get to her, not now.

Whittier carefully folded the letter in thirds and replaced
it in the vellum envelope. "I need your signature to indicate
the letter was read to you. Then I must sign before a notary
as proof that I followed Randolph's instructions to the letter."

"He was always thorough." Hands trembling, she
dashed her signature across the indicated line. "Is this all?"

The sooner she had this settled, the sooner she could sell
that house of horrors and go home to England.

"The will itself is quite straightforward. We've only to
clear the house, decide on what you want done with other
properties, and wait for probate. All the properties, bank
accounts, and holdings are already in your name."

She stared at him, stunned. "You're kidding. After that
horrible letter, he left me everything? No strings attached?"

His expression was sympathetic. "He left you everything, but Randolph always attached strings."

Of course. The loud banging inside her head intensified. "And that would be…?"

"You are to personally clean out the family home, and neither it nor the acreage around it can ever be sold as long as you live. Randolph said you would understand his reasons."

Black spots danced in front of her eyes. The devil. Oh, yes, she understood why he had done this. He knew how much she hated that house. That she never wanted to cross that threshold again. So he connived to punish her one final, lifelong time.

Daniel slapped the lift button and waited impatiently for the door to ping open.

He didn't think his week could get any worse. After supervising a job site east of the city, he'd come back to find problems with another project. Then word came that his furniture couldn't be delivered for at least a week, and now this urgent call from his brother.

His black mood deepened. Annoyed with waiting, he abandoned the lift and pounded down the stairs.

Stephanie had been gone a few days and since she'd left, his mood had been black as midnight. Nothing was going right, and he was going crazy living in that flat. If he had to sleep on his bare office floor, he was moving out.

The flat screamed Stephanie's name, her scent, her belongings. Even her art and the fastidious organization of her kitchen cabinets reminded him of her.

He couldn't sleep either, something he'd always been

able to do, even under the most adverse environmental conditions. Then last night, he'd completely lost it. He'd suffered the stupid urge to crawl into Stephanie's empty bed. At the last minute, he'd camped on the floor of the living room, her pillow cradled in his arms for the entire sleepless night.

Yup. He was losing his mind.

And to top it all off, something serious was happening with his brother. In the urgent phone call just now, he'd heard fear and desperation. All Dominic would say was, "I'm in trouble, Dan. Get down here fast."

So here he was, out of breath, cranky, and worried as he entered the small accounting office.

Dominic sat at his desk, complexion gray as ashes. Their father, John, sat across from him. Daniel glanced from one to the other and back again. They were both as grim as a double murder.

He felt a protective need to stand between the two.

"What's going on?" he asked.

The question was meant for Dominic, but John replied.

"For the past few weeks money has slowly disappeared from the Bella Lucia accounts."

"Yeah?" He knew that. Stephanie worried about the issue all the time. He also suspected what was coming, and the idea that his own father would accuse Dominic of stealing got his hackles up.

"Stephanie came to me with her suspicions," John said quietly.

Daniel felt as if he'd been struck by lightning. "Stephanie?"

How could she do that? Why hadn't she at least warned him?

John waved off his protestation. "Don't blame her. She didn't want to say anything, but she had to. It took a bit of work, but we finally figured out how the money was being diverted."

John's sad gaze settled on Dominic. With a start, Daniel saw the physical similarities between his fraternal twin and their father. "Your idea was both simple and brilliantly clever. Set up false service accounts into which the money, in the guise of payments, was electronically diverted from a remote location, so that any of the other people with access could be blamed. Why, son? Why would you do this?"

Eyes downcast, Dominic rested his forehead on the heel of his hand, his voice desperate. "I only meant to borrow the money. I was going to put it back, I swear." He lifted his head and looked at Daniel. "You have to believe me, Dan. I was in a pinch for cash and borrowed heavily from some individual investors. After that, things got out of hand."

"Loan sharks," John said flatly. "They always find a way of making you pay and pay."

And suddenly Daniel recalled the two men he and Stephanie had encountered in Dominic's office.

"I didn't know they were shady. And even if I had, I was so desperate for the cash, I would have agreed to any amount of interest. The problem came when I couldn't repay them fast enough and they began pressuring me, threatening to hurt Alice and the children."

Daniel slid down into a chair. Hell. His brother was in deep trouble. If he hadn't been so focused on his new business and in pursuing Stephanie, maybe he would have noticed in time to help. "Why? You're well-heeled. Why would you be in a pinch?"

"You don't understand," Dominic said miserably. "When the economy began to flounder my company cut back. I was one of the higher salaries, so I was expendable. And with the new baby coming and Jeffrey entering university, Alice spent more and more. I couldn't bring myself to tell her that I'd been sacked. She's always expected the best. She wouldn't understand."

Yes, Dominic's wife was quite a spender and, though Daniel hated to think it, she was a self-centered social climber who might not stand by her man in a financial crisis. Not like Stephanie, who didn't care how much money Daniel invested or how much he gave away. She'd liked him—correction: loved him—for who he was.

A sharp pain stabbed through his heart, cutting off his air. He couldn't think about Stephanie. He was here to help his brother. With concerted effort, he focused in on the terse conversation between John and Dominic.

"So working here wasn't a means of getting acquainted with the family?"

"I'm sorry, John. It wasn't. This job was all I had."

John leaned forward in the chair, elbows on knees, fingers steepled out in front of him. Intense emotion, whether anger or disappointment Daniel couldn't say, radiated off him. "So you set up false service accounts and embezzled money from your own family?"

Daniel tried to read John's face. What was going on behind their father's tired eyes? What would he do with this information? Was he the kind of man who could send his own son to prison?

Daniel clenched his fists. Probably. But he'd have to do it over Daniel's dead body.

"I'll pay the money back. I swear." Dominic's voice was hoarse with desperation.

"This is a huge sum, Dominic. The restaurant is in serious jeopardy because of the losses. We have little choice. We must take action and we must do it now."

Daniel leaped from his chair, jaw tight, blood rushing to his head. "I'll repay the money myself, but I won't see my brother in prison."

He could cancel the furniture. As much as asking for favors would grind against him, he would even cancel the office lease and ask John for a small office space in one of the restaurants.

Energized by the hope that he could help, he spun toward Dominic. "I have a little savings put back and my company is under way. I can borrow against it."

"Absolutely not!" John's reaction thundered through the room. He rose and moved to stand next to Dominic, clasping a hand upon his son's shoulder. "I'm your father. Helping you is my place, not your brother's."

Dominic's mouth fell open. "Sir? Are you serious?"

Daniel had the same reaction, staring in speechless bewilderment. Was the man serious?

Jaw set in determination, John nodded. "When you were small lads, I wasn't there. And I regret every day and every year that I missed. I never had a chance to buy you a bicycle or your first car. I never bought your school uniforms or paid for your food or took you to a football match." His voice dropped as he studied Dominic's face. "Don't you understand, son? I need to be the one to see you through this difficulty. No matter how great the expense, I will find a way to cover the loss."

All the air went out of Daniel. Deep inside, in that place that had been frozen for so long, a layer of hurt and anger melted away. Was this what family was supposed to be? Was this what he'd shut out of his life for so long?

John had every right to be furious and to call the police. But instead, he behaved as if—as if—he cared. He behaved like a loving father.

Dominic, as stunned as Daniel, slowly rose from his desk chair. "Sir. I don't know what to say. I'm grateful beyond words."

Moisture glinted in John's eyes. "I don't want gratitude. I want my sons."

In that instance, Daniel watched a weight of worry lift from his brother as he experienced for the first time the healing power of a father's love.

His own chest expanded to the point of bursting. He, who hadn't cried since grammar school, blinked back tears.

Maybe family was a good thing after all.

Forty-five minutes later, still reeling from the scene in Dominic's office, Daniel finished packing his business materials in preparation for the move. He'd promised to have dinner with the family at John's house later tonight. The idea that he looked forward to an evening with his father no longer surprised him. Stephanie was right. John was a good man. Daniel felt privileged to have that good man's blood running through his veins.

Regret pulled at him. He'd realized something else, too.

He wasn't half the man his father was. Unlike John, he'd let someone down in her hour of need. When Stephanie had needed him most to help her through the loss of her only parent, he'd walked away.

"Nice guy, Stephens," he muttered.

Maybe he should call her, apologize. See if she was all right. Make sure her ex hadn't discovered her return to Colorado.

He gnawed on the idea, all the while jamming items in boxes. Somewhere in this mess of papers was a number she'd left in case the restaurant needed her. A tiny smile tugged the corner of his mouth. Stephanie would have a fit if she could see the mess he'd made of her flat.

The telephone jangled. He dropped a handful of files into a box before answering.

"Stephens International Water Design."

After a momentary pause such as is common to overseas transmission, a very feminine American voice spoke. "Oh, hello. Is that you, Daniel?"

"It is. Who's this?" He balanced the receiver between chin and shoulder and went on packing.

"Rebecca Valentine. Well, Rebecca Tucker now. Your first cousin, I believe?"

Rebecca. Another relative that he had never met. But Stephanie spoke fondly of his uncle Robert's oldest daughter, and they chatted regularly by telephone.

"Rebecca. Hello, then. How's married life?" Stephanie had talked with excitement about her friend's unexpected romance with a Wyoming rancher. He'd even seen some wedding photos.

A soft laugh danced over the long-distance wires. "Wonderful. There's nothing like love to slap you upside the head and make you look at life in a whole new way."

Talk of love made him uncomfortable, especially considering the crazy thoughts he was having lately.

"If you're calling for Stephanie, I'm afraid you've missed her. She's in Colorado."

This time the pause was pregnant. "You're kidding."

He wished. "She left a few days ago. Her father passed on, and she had to go back to settle the estate."

"Not alone. Promise me she didn't go alone."

The stab of guilt was all too real. "She did."

"Oh, but that's horrible, Daniel. Someone should be with her. She shouldn't have to face that house alone."

Cold fingers of dread crawled up his spine. "That house? What do you mean?"

"Something terrible happened to Stephanie in that house. I just know it. She never talked about it. You know how she is. Very private, almost secretive about her past. But she said enough for me to guess that her father may have abused her. She despised him and she despised that house."

"But I thought…" His stomach rolled in revulsion as the truth hit him. He'd blamed the ex-boyfriend when all along the scars, her fears, her nightmares, all stemmed from whatever had happened to her in the family home in Colorado. She was that little girl, the victim of abuse. "Oh, no."

She hadn't begged him to go with her out of grief for the loss of her father. She'd been afraid to face the past alone.

"I am a fool," he breathed. "I should have gone with her."

"Go now, Daniel." Rebecca's voice deepened with

emotion. "If you care about her, please go. She needs you. Go."

She needed him, in much the way Dominic had needed John. And, heaven help him, he needed her, too. His very bones cried out for her and he'd been too blindly wrapped in self-preservation and selfishness to realize the truth.

If he cared, Rebecca had said. Oh, he cared all right. He loved her. Daniel Stephens, man without a heart, loved the strongest, most amazing woman on earth.

He sank to his knees amidst the mess of papers on the living-room floor. As soon as he could breathe again, he was going to America.

CHAPTER TEN

SHE couldn't do it.

Stephanie lay on the bed in her room at the Adam's Mark Hotel. The room had grown too cool, but she hadn't the energy to get up and adjust the heat. Outside the window a soft snow fell, pure and white and silent.

Fully dressed in a turquoise and black ski sweater, black pants and boots, she had readied everything needed to make the trip out to the suburbs. The portfolio of legal papers. Telephone numbers to call. She'd even contacted the auction house to sell off Randolph's extensive art collection and her mother's collection of antiques. They were prepared to begin cataloging as soon she could let them into the house.

Until the house was cleared of all furnishings and personal belongings, she couldn't leave Colorado. But after a few days of watching the Weather Channel she still hadn't mustered the courage to drive out to Littleton.

Randolph's final, hideous attack on her emotions had taken a toll. Immersed in a depression unlike anything she'd ever experienced, she wondered if her mother's mental fragility was a part of her internal makeup, too.

She squeezed her eyes tightly shut, only to find her mother's haunted eyes and Randolph's mocking smile behind her eyelids.

"You killed my mother," she whispered. "I won't let you kill me, too."

With every bit of effort she had, Stephanie tried to rise from the bed.

Halfway up, she dropped back with a sigh. Maybe tomorrow would be better.

Turning on her side, she stared out the window at the drifting snowflakes.

When her room phone rang, she jumped. For a nanosecond, her foolish heart hoped the caller might be Daniel. But she knew better. Daniel was gone from the Bella Lucia flat by now, and that was for the best. He would have turned away from her eventually anyway. Better now than later.

More likely the call was her attorney, urging her to get on with it. She let it ring into silence.

Five minutes later, someone tapped at her door.

"Who is it?" She wasn't in the mood for housekeeping.

"Open the door and see for yourself."

Her heart slammed against her ribcage. Only one man possessed that purring burr in the back of his throat. "Daniel?"

Here? In Colorado?

What could he want? Had something happened in London?

Her stomach twisted into a knot. No matter what his reasons for coming, seeing him was going to hurt. And she just couldn't take any more of that today.

Trepidatiously, she opened the door.

At the sight of him, big and dark and all man, she felt her knees wobble and the ache of love she wanted to escape rose up like a tidal wave.

"Why are you here?" Darn her voice for quivering. She blocked his entrance. No way was he coming into this room.

Daniel had different ideas. Gently, he pushed inside and closed the door behind him. "I made a terrible mistake and I want you to forgive me."

Stephanie crossed her arms protectively and turned away, going to the window. She felt him, all six feet four and muscles, move pantherlike up behind her.

Eyes squeezed tight, she prayed he wouldn't touch her. She'd crumble like a dry cracker if he did.

He didn't. And she was both relieved and disappointed.

"Stephanie. I've come across the ocean to find you. Hear me out."

A snowflake the size of a silver dollar swirled like an autumn leaf in front of the window. She focused on it. Cold, fragile, dying.

"You were right all along. I do have the ability to love. You taught me that. Maybe I'm not all that lovable, but I believe you love me. I've just endured four plane changes and six thousand kilometers without sleep to tell you that—" he paused and the air pulsed between them "—I love you."

Not now. Please not now. She'd spent almost a week coming to grips with the fact that the breakup was inevitable and for the best.

Feeling colder than death, Stephanie rubbed her hands up and down the soft mohair sleeves. Her father's voice yelled inside her head. "Worthless. Bad seed. If he knew the real you, if he saw the scars, he wouldn't be here."

Better to leave the break in place and move on than to chance rejection again when he discovered her ugliness.

"No, Daniel. You were right. It's over between us."

"Don't do this, Stephanie." He sounded as ragged as she felt and so desperate, she hurt for him. "I beg you. I know I made a mistake. I know I hurt you. But please don't give up on something as good as what we have."

"You can't love me, Daniel. It won't ever work."

"Why?" he whispered and moved closer.

"Because you don't really know me. The real me. If you did, you'd run back to London."

He touched her shoulder, tugged gently at the loose, stretchy neck of her sweater.

Horror tore like a whip down her back. She dipped away, pushing at his hand. "Don't."

But Daniel proved relentless.

With a tenderness that melted her resistance, he pulled the neck of her sweater down just enough to reveal the crisscross of flayed, damaged shoulder.

Afraid of the revulsion she would see, Stephanie couldn't look at him. Blood rushed to her head, pounding, swishing, pressing until she thought she would faint. Shame filled her.

"Look at me," his beloved voice demanded. "I love you, Stephanie. I love you. All of you."

"I'm so ashamed," she whispered, her voice raw and thick with the need to cry.

When she didn't look up, Daniel forced her chin up with his opposite hand. She felt humiliated, shamed, and afraid; tears filled her eyes. She shook her head and tried to pull away.

"Don't hide from me, love. I know. I saw." Head bent so the dark, unruly locks of hair tickled the side of her neck, Daniel kissed her shoulder.

"And you can still say you love me?"

"I love you even more. Your strength. Your courage. A man who didn't appreciate you would be a fool. I've been a fool."

A dam burst inside her then. With a sob, she fell against him. His two powerful arms caught her up, kissing her face, her tears, her hair; murmuring all the words she'd longed to hear.

After the first fierce storm had passed, Stephanie pulled away. Drawing in a shuddering breath, she asked, "Do you want to know?"

Daniel took the question as a test. She had to know if he would balk now, when the worst was yet to come.

Determined not to blow this chance to prove his love, he kept his gaze steady and sure, his eyes not leaving hers as he led her to the bed.

He was scared out of his wits to know the horror she'd been through. But he loved her. And he wanted to be strong enough to carry her pain so she could let it go.

He lay down, then pulled her down beside him. She stretched out, full-length, staring up at the ceiling.

Daniel leaned up on an elbow to look down into her aqua eyes and told her about the day he'd come into the flat and seen the scars. Then, he said, "Tell me what happened."

She studied his face for the longest time. He could read all the fears, the worries, the doubts that telling the story held for her. But gradually the wall of wariness slipped away and was replaced by trust. She trusted him. At last. And in the power of that realization, his love grew tenfold.

"I loved my mother," she said simply. "She was kind and sweet, but emotionally fragile. I blame Randolph for that."

"Your father?"

She shook her head and red hair fanned out over the white pillow. "No. Thank goodness. He was my stepfather, though I didn't know until I was nine years old. That day I came home from school and heard them arguing. My father was browbeating Mother as he always did in his snide, cruel, controlling way. He called her a whore. I'll never forget how awful the word sounded, though I barely understood its meaning."

"What were they arguing about?"

"Me, it turns out. Mother thought he was too strict, too harsh. And he was. He would punish me for the least thing. A book left lying on the table. A spot of dirt on my dress." Her gaze glued to the ceiling as if she watched a movie overhead. "The night before he'd whipped me with his belt because I couldn't remember the title of a painting."

"All this time I thought your ex—" He slid down to lie beside her, hiding the horror he felt.

She shook her head. "No. Brett did hurt me, but not that way. He couldn't handle my past. And I was afraid you'd be the same."

"Oh, my sweet." With an arm around her back, he rolled her towards him. Tremors rippled through her, tearing at Daniel's self-control. "You've carried this burden alone for too long. The man must have been a maniac."

"Yes, he was. But only Mother and I knew. He was so

smooth, a politician, a social success. He took pride in parading his possessions, especially his collection of the great masters, before company. My job was to recite the names and artists in his vast repertoire. Heaven help me if I forgot one."

Daniel fought to stay silent though he wanted to rage at the evil man who'd hurt her so. Randolph Ellison had scarred more than her body. He'd scarred her soul.

"He'd always told me I was bad and worthless. That was why he punished me so much. I could never understand why he didn't love his own daughter. That day, he brought all my mother's sins out to throw them in her face. She'd had an affair, got pregnant with me, and Randolph used that indiscretion to control her—and me—for the rest of her life."

Now Daniel understood her obsessive tidiness. Keeping things in order gave her a sense of control. The more anxious she became, the more she needed the environment around her under control.

"How did he know you weren't his child?"

She gave a small, sad laugh that was no laugh at all. The warmth of her breath soughed against the skin on his neck.

"The great and mighty Randolph Ellison was sterile. An accident of some kind when he was a boy. He and Mother had never planned to have children."

"Surprise, surprise," he said softly.

"From what little she told me, he didn't seem angry at first. He'd told her they would pretend the child was his and no one would ever know. That was the way Randolph worked. His revenge knew no bounds, but he wanted to punish her slowly and completely. And that's what he did. Over the years, he picked away at her self-esteem, convincing her that she couldn't survive without him. He controlled her every movement, her social life, everything. She grew depressed and nervous, an emotional wreck until she had a breakdown. After that, I had to protect her, too. She was so fragile."

"Couldn't she have gone to your real father for help?"

She pressed one hand against his chest as if he was her lifeline. The urge to protect her hit him like a freight train.

"He was married, too."

"What a nightmare." He twined one of her curls around the end of his finger, calming the storm inside with the repetitive action. He'd be no good to Stephanie at all if he let go of the building rage.

"My finding out the truth infuriated Randolph. He didn't have to hold back his hatred anymore. That's when the real beatings began."

Daniel had seen the ritualistic scars. She didn't need to describe the torture for him to know what had happened.

"What about your mother?"

Stephanie swallowed hard. Her voice fell to a sad whisper. "She overdosed on antidepressants when I was seventeen. I still feel so guilty about that."

"You? Why? Your stepfather was the one who drove her to it."

"She was upset because of me. She'd tried to interfere during one of his…" Stephanie's voice trailed off. She stared out the window, unable to go on. Daniel wasn't sure he could bear to hear anymore.

"I understand, love. No need to elaborate." He stroked her hair over and over, offering the only comfort he could. "Why didn't you tell someone? Why didn't anyone stop him?"

"I tried to tell once. But Randolph was a very smart, very powerful man. He knew how to work the system to his benefit. No one believed the fabulous, charismatic attorney would ever do such a thing. I was branded a spoiled, lying child. And after he finished with me that time, I was afraid to ever tell again."

"So you kept the abuse inside all these years."

"Except for Brett. And that was a disaster. He was horrified, revolted by the scars and abuse. I felt ugly, untouchable." Her voice dropped. "Unlovable."

"He was an idiot. You are the most beautiful, incredibly lovable woman in the world."

She smiled, a tremulous, teary smile that broke his heart. And he felt such joy to know he could love someone this way.

"After Brett, I gave up on love for good."

"Not for good. I'm here now. And you will not give up on me. I won't allow it."

"What changed your mind?" she asked, stroking a hand over his bewhiskered face. He'd had the devil of a time getting here and no time to shave.

"You."

She raised an eyebrow.

"You haunted me. I couldn't sleep. And then something happened that woke me up to the power of loving someone." He told her about John's reaction to Dominic's embezzlement.

"So it *was* Dom. Oh, Daniel, I'm so sorry."

He was sorry ,too, but didn't want Stephanie to see how worried he was. "John seems set on seeing him through this."

"He will. Your father is both powerful and decent, a rare combination."

"Yes, I'm sorry for all the times I resisted getting to know him. My mum had poisoned our minds about him." But Stephanie already knew about his troubled relationship with his mother. No need to go through that again.

Tugging on a lock of her hair, he aligned her body with his. "Enough about them," he whispered against her soft, lush lips. "Let's talk about us."

"Is there an us?"

"Absolutely."

With a happy sigh of surrender, he lost himself in the pleasures of her sweet mouth. She responded so sweetly, so passionately that he was hard-pressed to break away.

"I have to ask you something."

"Mmm," she murmured dreamily, tracing his lower lip with one finger.

"You're distracting me, woman."

"My intention."

He grabbed her finger and kissed it, then held her hand prisoner against his chest. "Will you marry me? Will you put up with this moody Englishman who has nothing to offer except the promise that I'll spend the rest of my life giving you all that I am and all that I have?"

He loved the way her eyes, so sad moments before, sparkled now. He loved the way her face softened with happiness. He loved everything about his Stephanie.

"Well?" he persisted.

"When?"

"What do you mean, when?"

"When do you want to get married?"

"This afternoon."

She laughed. "This afternoon? Daniel! A girl has to plan."

He heaved a beleaguered sigh. "Okay. I'll give you a week."

"After the estate is settled. I don't want that or anything else to spoil our wedding day."

Yes, getting that painful experience behind her was necessary to her peace of mind as well as his.

"Deal. I'll help you get things settled. Meanwhile make your plans, because you are going to be my bride as soon as possible." He rolled to a sitting position and reached for the phone. "Let's call London. After the week he's had, I think my father could use a little good news, don't you?"

Smiling her answer, his beautiful bride-to-be sat up, too, wrapped her arms around his waist and gazed up at him with an expression that made him believe he could conquer the world.

Drawing her against his side where he always wanted her to be, he connected with the overseas operator and waited until he heard his father's voice.

"Hullo?" he said.

"Daniel? Son? Is that you?"

"Yes, Dad. It's me." And the joy that burst in his chest at finally saying that simple word erased the years he'd been a fatherless son.

CHAPTER ELEVEN

HE WAS whistling in the shower.

Stephanie pinched her arm to be sure she wasn't dreaming. Daniel, her love, her heart, had come all the way from England to propose. Imagine that! All the way across the Atlantic to tell her of his love.

Dressed in her usual long flannel pajamas, she stood at the hotel window, watching the snow dance around the streetlights and cast a white glow in the darkness. In a matter of a few hours, she'd gone from depressed to joyous, all because of Daniel. With him at her side, she could face anything, even the task of cataloging and dispensing the contents of her childhood prison.

A deep, rumbling baritone replaced the cheery whistle.

Stephanie smiled.

He had to be exhausted, suffering from jet lag, but he'd taken her to an elegant, wonderful tea at the gracious old Brown Hotel. Over tiny finger sandwiches and Earl Grey tea, he'd told her over and over again that he loved her. They'd talked and talked until their hearts were full and their jaws aching. The burden of her disturbing responsibilities had lifted just by sharing them with him.

Afterwards, they'd walked the snowy streets of Denver to the Molly Brown House and made the trek upstairs, amused at how such a tiny nineteenth century place could have once been considered the grand house of Colorado's wealthiest citizen.

Just then, Daniel came out of the bathroom, rubbing his face with a towel.

"How's this?" he asked, rubbing her cheek with his.

"Smooth." She sniffed. "You smell good, too."

He flipped the towel over one bare shoulder. "I suppose I should have done this before going to tea."

"We would have missed it if we'd waited any longer."

"The phone call to London took more time than I expected."

Stephanie smiled. "Good news takes time to share. Speaking of London, now that Louise is back, do you think she'll invite her new family to the Christmas party to meet the Valentines?"

"Can't say. I fear I don't know Louise that well. At least, not yet."

All either of them really knew about Louise was her reputation as the kind-hearted, conservative, good daughter of John and Ivy Valentine. She'd been traveling so much lately, having only returned to England the day before Daniel had left for America, that Daniel had had no time at all to become acquainted.

Whatever Daniel was about to say next was smothered by a huge yawn, and Stephanie laughed. "I think your body must be losing its battle with jet lag."

"Are you complaining about my body?" He flexed a muscled arm.

Playfully, she squeezed his biceps and gave an exaggerated shiver of admiration. "Your physique is magnificent, as you well know, Mr Conceit. But you *are* tired."

"Yes, I am. Exceedingly." Naked chest and all, he pulled her to him for a kiss. His skin was cool and damp and fragrant with soap. "My internal clock doesn't know where I am or what time it is."

He flopped onto the bed and tugged her down. "Come here."

Her pulse stuttered. She knew he expected to spend the night, and that was fine with her. Having him here was all she really wanted. But she hadn't spent the night in the same bed with a man in a very long time.

All her old fears and anxieties flooded in. What if he changed his mind? What if he only imagined he could handle the way her body looked?

As if he understood, Daniel clicked off the lamp, leaving only the dim lights from the streets. "Just lay beside me, love. Let me hold you."

The tension in her shoulders eased. Being held by Daniel was exactly what she wanted. And she knew he loved her. He wouldn't force anything she wasn't ready for.

Glad to be covered from neck to ankle, Stephanie slid beneath the sheet and nestled against Daniel's broad chest. It felt so good to be wrapped in his embrace, protected by his strength.

His calloused hand rubbed up and over her hair, her neck, her shoulder, then drifted down to massage her back. "Did I tell you lately that I am totally, madly in love with you?"

"Not in the last two minutes."

He shifted to his side and bracketed her face with his fingertips. "I love you. You can't imagine how good it feels to be able, finally, to say that. To feel that."

"I know."

"Are you worried about tomorrow?" he asked, eyes searching hers in the semi-darkness.

She swallowed a lump of tenderness. He was so wonderfully thoughtful.

"A little." A lot. Tomorrow she had to face the house. And she was scared. "But I don't want to talk about that. Not tonight."

Today had been too special to mar with tomorrow's worries.

"Enough talk then," he murmured, and his mouth found hers.

The kiss was sweet and hot and hungry. His intention was clear. He loved her; he wanted her.

And she wanted him. The rest should come naturally. For a normal person it would. But not for her.

"Daniel," she said, plucking nervously at the collar of her pajamas. "Please don't be angry, but I'd rather wait until our wedding night."

He looked pathetically disappointed. If she hadn't been so worried, she would have laughed.

"It's just—" She hesitated, afraid to say what was on her mind. Regardless of Daniel's claim to the contrary, Stephanie had a horrible fear that, somehow, the ugliness could still drive him away.

Daniel stopped her fidgeting hands with his.

"The scars?" he asked.

She nodded.

"I've seen them, remember? And you're still beautiful to me."

The awful truth rose in her throat like a sickness. She wanted to tell him. He deserved to know.

While she hesitated, he said, "My love, if you were scarred from head to toe, I would still love you. And because I love you so much, I'll try to be patient. I'll even take another room after tonight. Just remember, though, on our wedding night—" he tugged gently at her pajama top "—this will go. All of it will go. And I will see and love all of you. There will be no more secrets between us."

Long after Daniel's magnificent chest rose and fell in exhausted slumber, Stephanie lay staring at the ceiling.

He was so sweet, so understanding. And he'd asked so little of her. She only hoped that when the time came, she would have the courage to give him what he asked.

Daniel awakened disoriented. A sliver of glare had snaked between a pair of green drapes to laser him right in the eyes.

As he rolled over memory flooded in stronger than the glare. He was in America. With Stephanie.

Contentment expanded his chest. If he didn't have such a jet-lag hangover, he might shout with happiness.

Thrusting out one hand, he searched the sheets for his lady.

"Stephanie?" His voice was a morning frog.

No answer.

He pried open one eye, saw nothing, and opened the other.

"Stephanie?" He sat up, looking, listening.

With a frown, he shoved the covers away and padded through the room. "Where are you?"

The bathroom door stood open. No Stephanie, but a yellow note was stuck to the mirror. He yanked the paper down.

Just as he'd suspected. She'd gone to the property to begin sorting through her nightmare.

"Stubborn, independent female," he muttered, then stomped around the room, grabbing clothes and shoes in a fit of temper. "No business going out there alone."

In record time he dressed, found the address, and called a taxi. Stephanie shouldn't face that house alone.

The ride to the suburbs was beautiful and the snowy scenery cooled his hot temper. The snow had stopped and sun glistened off the fields of white. Kids had ventured out to roll huge balls into snowmen. City workers in oversized machinery pushed piles of the fluffy stuff to the sides of the road.

But while his eyes admired the Mile High city, his mind recalled last night.

He'd been disappointed. What man wouldn't be? The woman he loved had been in the bed beside him all night and he hadn't been able to do more than kiss and hold her. If his body hadn't been so tired, he'd have spent the night in a cold shower.

He hated what had happened to her. And he was going to prove his love by waiting until she was ready to trust him. The scars were horrid, not because of how they looked but because of how she'd come to have them. But they truly didn't matter to him.

The taxi slid to a halt outside a gated residence. "This is it."

Daniel paid the driver and got out. He stood at the opened gate, staring down a long, curving, snowy driveway toward a mansion set upon a knoll.

What a place!

An enormous house, built of some sort of golden-red wood, cedar perhaps, rose three stories high against a backdrop of the Rocky Mountains. The fresh snow decorated the roof and shrubbery, giving the place a fairy-tale appearance. Who would believe such a stunning home could hold such an ugly secret?

He spotted her then, standing beside her silver rental car. The driver's door was open as if she'd just stepped out. One hand shading her eyes, she stared up at the house.

Daniel broke into a trot and his boots crunched at the dry snow. Before he reached her, she whipped around.

Dressed in the long black leather coat, red hair spilling around her shoulders, cheeks kissed pink by the cold, she took his breath away.

"Daniel," she said simply.

"Why didn't you wake me?" he panted, out of air from the run and the unaccustomed altitude. "I didn't want you coming here alone."

She smiled. "This morning, for the first time, I finally believed that Randolph Ellison can no longer hurt me." A peace she'd never had before emanated from her. "You did that for me, Daniel. You made me strong enough to face anything." She reached out a hand gloved in black leather, and touched his cheek. "This house is my burden to bear, not yours."

He squelched another burst of temper. If she thought for one minute he would walk away and leave her to face this house alone, she was sadly mistaken. "Call me chauvinistic, but when you agreed to marry me, your problems became mine. I'm here. And I'm staying. Get used to it."

Her smile grew brighter than the glaring snow. She threw her arms around his neck. "You look positively fierce. And you've just reminded me of why I love you so much."

She kissed him, a full, smacking kiss that made him laugh.

"Come on, then. Let's get this job done."

She turned to face the house again and Daniel saw her hesitate as some of her bravado slipped away. She really was terrified of this building.

He took her gloved hand in his. "Together, my love."

With her cheeks a little rosier than usual, her eyes a little brighter, and her face set like stone, she led him up on the porch and inside the house.

The immaculate, enormous vaulted great room looked as if the owner were only away for the day. As neat and tidy as Stephanie's flat, the furniture was uncovered, the huge stone fireplace laid with logs, and the wood floors polished to a sheen. Even the potted plants lining the foyer looked green and healthy.

"Someone has been caring for the house?" he asked.

"I discontinued the service yesterday."

"So, what's the plan today?"

"Inventory. I brought a laptop." Her voice was quieter than usual. Her eyes moved from side to side as if watching, waiting for the bogeyman to appear.

Daniel ached for her, but he didn't comment. She had to confront this symbol of her past on her own terms before she could put it behind her for good.

As they moved through the rooms he noticed the magnificent collection of paintings and sculptures decorating the lavish interior. Unlike Stephanie's thoroughly modern works, these pieces were classics, several that he was surprised to see outside of museums. Stephanie saw them, too, and her hands twisted restlessly against the slick leather of her coat. This artwork, some pieces near priceless, had cost her far more than it would ever be worth.

When they passed in front of the massive stone fireplace, Stephanie took down a photograph of a beautiful red-haired woman.

"My mother," she said simply.

He stepped up close and looked over her shoulder.

"You look like her." Right down to the haunted eyes.

"A little maybe. Randolph said I resembled my worthless father."

"Randolph, as we well know, was an unmitigated fool." Anger hovered around the edge of his words. He wished Randolph Ellison were still alive because he personally wanted to make him pay for all the harm he'd done.

Picture held tightly against her chest, Stephanie continued to roam the house, saying little, doing nothing as far as inventory. Daniel held her hand and tagged along, letting her take the lead. This was her show. He wanted to do it her way. And he'd be here for whatever she needed.

Through two dining rooms, an enormous kitchen, a sun room, a hot-tub room complete with skylight, and a massive games room, Stephanie seemed to hold up well, though she was far quieter than usual. The old familiar way she had of distancing herself from other people returned, and it was as if she knew he was there, but he wasn't.

They started up the wide spiral staircase.

"Five bedrooms up here," she said woodenly. "All with private baths. Wasn't that wasteful in a family of three?"

They looked inside each one and Daniel noticed that each had its own balcony with exterior stairs leading down to a small garden. Beyond that, a wooded acreage led into the mountains.

"What about the third floor?" he asked.

She hesitated. A pinch of white appeared around her lips. "One dormer room. Mine."

"You were up there alone?"

"Yes. With no way down but these stairs that led right past the master bedroom. He made sure I couldn't run away."

Daniel bit back an angry curse. His poor, precious little rich girl. Alone in her ivory tower prison, except for the madman downstairs.

She hesitated another second longer, contemplating the dark landing above. Then she dropped his hand, put her mother's photo on the bottom step, and started up. She looked for all the world like a condemned queen on her way to execution.

A terrible foreboding started Daniel's blood racing. Suddenly, he didn't want her up there. He could inventory and empty this part of the house.

"Stephanie?" he said, just as she pushed open a cherry-wood door and stepped inside, out of his field of vision.

In the two strides he took to be inside the room, she had

started to come undone. She shook violently. Her chest rose and fell in agitation.

And then Daniel understood. This had been the room of her torture, of her beatings, and God only knew what else. He had to get her out of here.

He reached for her elbow. "Sweetheart—" he started.

She jerked away.

"Why?" she asked in a voice so anguished that Daniel's knees began to shake.

"Why did you hurt me? I was just a little girl."

As if in a daze, she moved forward, trembling, whimpering. When she reached the fairy-princess bed, she fell to her knees, arms thrust forward across the white bedspread in a posture of submission.

And then she raised her head and screamed.

"I hate you. I hate you! Do you hear me, you evil monster? I hate you! I'm glad you're dead. I'm glad you're dead. You had no right to hurt me."

Daniel slid to the floor beside her but she didn't seem to know he was there. His heart said to stop her, but his gut said she needed this. Throat aching, he bit down on his fist and kept quiet.

Stephanie shook so hard the bed quaked, but still she railed on against the criminal who'd made her childhood a living hell. Sweat broke out on her face. Her eyes streamed tears. Her voice grew raw and raspy, and yet she raged.

Her total brokenness terrified him. He'd never felt so helpless.

When at last the torrent ceased, Stephanie's exhausted body went limp. Daniel gathered her to him, heart shattered in a thousand pieces with the tender concern he felt for his woman.

"Shh," he crooned. "Shh. He can't hurt you ever again. Not ever."

"Daniel?" she said, still quivering.

"I'm here, love. Everything is okay, now."

"He's dead, isn't he? He's really dead?"

"Yes, love. Yes."

"I'm glad." She looked up at him, aqua eyes red-rimmed and teary. "Oh, Daniel, am I a bad person because I'm happy that someone is dead?"

The pressure inside Daniel's chest reached breaking point. "If you're bad," he ground out, "I'm worse. I wanted him to be alive so I could have the pleasure of killing him myself."

"Daniel," she whispered, her fingers touching his cheek. "You're crying."

Crying? Him? The tidal wave of emotions, love, anger, sorrow, overwhelmed him then. Now he knew he had a heart because it was broken. For her.

He crushed her to him, rocking her back and forth. He kissed her hair, her swollen eyes, her wet cheeks, and after a while he simply held her.

He wasn't sure how long they sat there on the floor, but eventually, Stephanie stopped trembling and sat back.

"Better?" he asked.

She nodded. "Much."

And then his brave, strong woman dried his tears and hers, and smiled. A wet, wobbly, sad effort, but still a smile.

"Let's go back to the hotel, Daniel. The nightmare is over. And I'm so very, very tired."

* * *

Three weeks and an enormous amount of work later, the last of the valuables from the mansion had been inventoried and readied for auction. Some days, after they'd done all they could with the property, Stephanie relaxed by shopping or jogging while Daniel spent hours by phone and computer doing business back in London.

The days passed, and as the remnants of her early life were catalogued and set aside Stephanie was amazed at how her inner spirit slowly healed. Confronting the memories locked in that house had freed her.

Even Thanksgiving, a holiday that normally held little meaning for her, had taken on a special significance. She'd told Daniel over a quiet dinner in the hotel, "I have you this year. For that, I will ever be thankful."

Now, as she sat on the hotel bed, up from a power nap, Stephanie sorted through the final pile of legal papers.

"I'm still not sure what to do with the house," she admitted, gnawing the end of a pencil. "I had originally planned to set it on fire and watch it burn."

Daniel, who sat at the small round hotel table perusing the newspaper, didn't seem the least troubled by that revelation.

The newspaper rustled as he lay it down. "A waste of perfectly good lumber."

"And some very costly furnishings." She pushed the papers aside and padded to the exterior vanity. "Ugh. Bed head."

"A charming sight, I assure you." Daniel grinned, causing her heart to flip-flop. "Let me."

He took the brush and gently began the job of untangling the mass of curls. "I have a thought about the house. Are you open to suggestions?"

"From you?" She gazed up at him in the mirror. His eyes were serious. "Of course."

"The estate has a legacy of hurt. Change that. Make it a place of helping."

And as suddenly as that, an idea popped into her head.

"Daniel, that's brilliant. I know exactly what I want to do." Excitement zipped through her blood stream. "I'll call my attorney and have him investigate our options."

"For what? Tell me."

"A safe house for abused women and children. A place for them to come without fear, to heal and get on their feet. There's enough money with the estate to keep it in perpetuity."

"What a terrific idea."

"I would never have thought of it without you." She whirled around and took the brush from his hands. On tiptoe, she kissed him. "I love you. You are so smart."

"Keep talking." He walked her backward toward the bed. "On second thought, don't talk. Kiss."

With a laugh of happiness, she did exactly that as Daniel tumbled them down.

After far too much kissing that left them both frustrated, Daniel groaned, "If you want to wait until our wedding night, we'd better get married today."

"Think you can wait until Monday?"

"This coming Monday?"

He looked so wonderfully hopeful that Stephanie laughed. "Yes. Most everything I have to do is taken care of now. My mind is clear of all those stressors. And I don't want to wait any longer to be your wife."

The corners of his eyes crinkled. "I hear Aspen is beautiful this time of year."

"Aspen?" A bubble of happiness rose in her chest. "I still have friends in Aspen." But Daniel knew that already, a reminder of how thoughtful and considerate her husband would be. "It's the perfect romantic spot for a wedding, however impromptu."

He pumped his eyebrows. "And a honeymoon?"

"Yes." She jumped up, pulled him up with her, and danced them around the hotel room. "A Christmas wedding in Aspen."

Unlike Denver, Aspen held good memories and a few friends she'd kept in touch with. A phone call or two to the Snowbound Lodge could set things in motion.

And if she had any worries about the wedding night, Stephanie was too happy at the moment to think about them now.

CHAPTER TWELVE

THE bride wore Christmas green.

Daniel's stomach dipped the moment Stephanie stepped out of the chapel's tiny dressing room to join him in the short walk down the aisle. She'd warned him that her dress was not traditional, claiming she looked terrible in white. Modest cut, chic and elegant, the long emerald velvet was the perfect complement to her flowing red hair. Her mother's diamond choker and matching earrings sparkled like Christmas lights against her peach skin.

He cleared his throat, found it uncommonly dry, but managed to say, "You are beyond gorgeous."

She smiled up at him, her aqua eyes gone as green as her dress. "Wanna marry me?"

Fighting the need to crush her to him and carry her off like some barbarian, he breathed, "Oh, yeah."

He was either going to marry her or kidnap her. One way or the other, she was going to be his today. He'd waited as long as he could stand it, a notion that still astounded him. He had never expected to marry, let alone love a woman the way he loved Stephanie.

"Then lead the way, handsome man. I wanna marry you, too."

He folded her hand, soft and smooth as the velvet fabric, over his elbow and led her toward the minister waiting at the front of the chapel. Behind the clergyman, floor-to-ceiling windows offered a spectacular view of the forest, and beyond that, the snow-covered Rockies. Stephanie had chosen this quaint little chapel, nestled in the trees near Aspen, for this view. But Daniel found the vision beside him far more breathtaking.

From somewhere came the sound of a harp playing "Ave Maria", so gentle and heavenly that he felt transported by the sheer beauty of the place, the melody, the moment. One glance at Stephanie's enraptured face told him she felt the same.

When they reached the minister, a graying, middle-aged man with smile lines, the music ceased and the ceremony began. The minister read from the Bible and spoke lovely words that roared in Daniel's head like the sound of the sea rushing in. He didn't care what was said as long as the end result was the same. But Stephanie deserved a special memory and he intended for her to have it.

The ceremony seemed to go on for ever and yet be over in a moment. During the exchange of rings, Daniel's hands trembled, not with anxiety or fear, but with an emotion so powerful he thought he might go to his knees. He, a man who had braved floods and droughts and so much more was reduced to tremors by the sound of Stephanie whispering her eternal promise of love.

At last, the moment came when she was his for evermore, and, with his heart near to bursting, Daniel kissed his bride. Not once, but over and over again until all of them, minister, witnesses, and the newlyweds, were laughing.

The harp music began again and to the accompaniment of "Ode to Joy", a fitting piece if ever he heard one, Daniel and his bride completed the formalities and prepared to leave.

"I have a surprise, Mrs Stephens." Daniel draped a long fur cape over her shoulders and opened the door.

A pair of large, hairy-footed golden horses waited docilely in front of a curved white sleigh.

Stephanie gasped and looked up, expression so full of love and excitement he knew he'd made the right choice. "Daniel, I love it. I love you."

She kissed him.

"Just the reaction I was hoping for."

A sleigh ride might be clichéd, but it was exactly the kind of romantic gesture he wanted to do for her. The sleigh was only the first of several surprises he had planned for this special night…and for his special bride.

Snow kissed their faces as the driver "tsked" the horses into motion. Snuggled beneath a heavy fur lap robe, Daniel held his lady-love close. All the while, his heart was singing.

Horse hoofs thudded softly against the packed snow; harness a-jingle, they journeyed out of the pines and into town.

"Aspen is a fairy tale at Christmas," Stephanie said as the sleigh glided down Main Street.

Every building in the quaint resort of the rich and famous was bathed in lights so that the town glowed with warmth and holiday cheer. Festive green and red decorated the storefronts, the streetlamps, the windows, the doors, and, as if the human effort weren't enough, nature supplied the constant cover of snow and the backdrop of majestic mountain peaks and stunning star-sprinkled sky.

Cheek against hers, he pointed upward. "Did you see that?"

"A shooting star," she said and he could feel her smile curve upward. "We have to make a wish."

But Daniel's wishes, even the ones he hadn't known he wanted, had all come true. A father. A family. And now a wife. He gazed down at her. Her eyes were squeezed tight in the pale moonlight. "What did you wish for?"

"You already know," she murmured, opening her eyes. "I wish for us to always be as happy and in love as we are tonight."

"Your wish is hereby granted." He sealed his promise with a kiss.

They rode along in silence for a while, snuggled close sharing warmth and smiles. The scent of wood smoke from nearby homes teased the air, and an occasional car motored past. Once, they heard snatches of Christmas carols coming from a brightly lit building—a country club party, he surmised.

The cold of Colorado made Daniel's skin tingle. He used the chill as an opportunity to hold his wife a little closer.

When at long last she shivered, he said, "You're getting chilled. Maybe we should go to the cabin now."

"This is so wonderful. I hate for the night to end."

"We'll ride as long as you choose, but remember, love…" he rubbed her nose with his "…the night has only just begun."

Stephanie's skin tingled, too, though not from cold. She loved the invigorating smell and feel of cold mountain air.

She tingled from the delicious suggestion in Daniel's voice, and the notion thrilled her. Even though the nagging worry about tonight didn't leave, with all her heart she wanted to be Daniel's wife in every way.

"I'm ready to go to the lodge when you are," she said and was rewarded with a heart-stopping kiss.

Daniel spoke to the sleigh driver and they began the trip away from the city proper.

When the sleigh turned north, Stephanie sat up to look around. "This isn't the way back to the lodge, is it?"

"We're not going to the lodge." Daniel's expression was smug and secretive.

"But our things are there."

"Not anymore."

A zing of excitement heated her blood. Daniel, her husband, her love, was making tonight a beautiful adventure.

The sleigh turned down a narrow, tree-lined lane and headed deeper into the woods. The horses slowed to a gentle stop in front of a small cabin, illuminated from without and within.

"Your honeymoon cottage, my love." Daniel hopped down and playfully bowed toward the small cabin nestled in the snow-laden pines.

"It's perfect."

And it was. From the wreath on the door to the romantic interior where a small fireplace already crackled.

Inside, Daniel slid the fur cape from her shoulders and dropped it onto a stuffed chair. "This is our little hideaway for the next week."

"How did you do this? Everything was booked when I called."

"That's because I called first."

"Sneaky." She trailed her fingers over a small wooden bar where a large basket of Christmas cookies, gingerbread men and foil-wrapped chocolates awaited them. "But very wonderful. I think I might fall madly in love with you if you keep this up."

"Admit the truth. You fell for me the minute I invaded your flat."

She smiled. "Maybe I did. But you also scared me to death. Such a barbarian, all dark and wild with those big muscles."

He stalked toward her. "Are you scared now?"

"Terrified." With a squeal, she danced away from his outstretched hands, laughing. Her heart raced a little faster.

She grabbed for the cookie basket. "Want a cookie?"

His grin was absolutely feral. "Nope. I want you."

He caught the sleeve of her dress and tugged. She catapulted into his arms, stomach fluttering with excitement.

"There's hot mulled cider," she teased, knowing that neither of them was at all interested in food. At least not right now.

His eyelids drooped to a sexy stare. "I'd rather have hot married you."

Stephanie felt the heat of a blush but loved knowing that her new husband wanted her so badly.

"So impatient," she said, a complete untruth. He'd been a paragon of patience since their engagement, giving her all the time and space she needed.

"Love the way you look in this dress." He ran a finger beneath the sweetheart neckline. She shivered with the thought that soon he would see her, touch her, everywhere. "I'd love it even more if you'd take it off."

Stephanie laughed, a husky sound that surprised even her. She tugged at his tie, enjoying the mating ritual.

"And you look so handsome and sophisticated in this suit."

"Handsome? Sophisticated?" He gave her a mock frown. "What about virile? Tough? Strong?"

She struck a pose, vamping for him, her voice intentionally seductive. "Manly, rugged, and, oh, so sexy."

"Want to find out how sexy I can be?"

"Maybe." She touched the diamond choker at her throat. "Would you help me with this?"

"We have to start somewhere," he murmured wryly. Then he unclasped the necklace, whisked it from her, and replaced it with his lips. His soft whiskers tickled deliciously. Stephanie let her head fall back. A low hum vibrated from her throat to his mouth.

"Are you trying to seduce me?" she asked when she could finally speak.

"How am I doing?" he murmured against the pulse dancing wildly beneath her collarbone.

Stephanie couldn't answer. She was too busy angling her neck this way and that to capture the luscious feel of his hot mouth and tongue on every inch of her skin.

"I have earrings too," she finally managed to say, though the words were breathy.

He chuckled. "Yum."

In turn, he removed each one and suckled her earlobes, nuzzled the sensitive skin beneath her ear, kissing her until they were both breathless.

"Anything else you want removed?" he whispered, his voice a throaty purr.

She loosened his tie and in a slow, sexy dance slid it from his neck. She trailed the narrow band of silk across his face. He caught the end with his teeth in a sensuous tug-of-war.

"Maybe I should slip into something more comfortable," she said.

Eyes widening, he dropped the tie like a hot potato.

"Meet you in the bedroom in five minutes?" he asked hopefully.

A tiny knot of anxiety formed in her stomach. Even though they'd been working toward this moment for weeks, some of her playful eagerness drained away. As much as she loved this man, she dreaded the moment he would see her.

"I'm a little nervous," she admitted. Actually she was a lot nervous, but telling Daniel the truth helped. He knew and he understood that her reasons were not about him, but about herself.

"Don't be, love. Don't be." He took the tie and looped it around her neck, using the strip of cloth to pull her close, swaying them from side to side. "I love you more than I can say. And want you just as much. Nothing is going to change that."

She hoped he was right.

"I want you, too. So, so much." Gathering her courage, she kissed his jaw. "Five minutes."

When she came out of the bathroom in a robe she'd bought especially for tonight, Daniel already waited in the bed, his broad chest nude and golden in the glow of the fireplace. The overhead lights were out and only a small lamp lit the room. She silently blessed his thoughtful concession to her modesty and fear.

"We can turn out all the lights if you'd rather," he said.

"What do you want?"

"Whatever you do."

Though she knew his preference, she loved him for giving her the choice. "Leave them on."

He reached for her, but she backed away, standing in the full light from the fire. If she was going to do this with lights on, she would do it all.

Gaze locked on Daniel's face, she untied the belt of her robe and let it drop. She had to watch his reaction.

"I haven't told you everything, Daniel."

"You don't have to."

"Okay, then. I'll show you. No secrets, remember?" She let the shoulders of the satin robe slither halfway down to her elbows.

Daniel levered up to watch, his pupils large and dark in the fire-glow, the sheet falling to his trim, rippled belly.

"More than my back is scarred," she whispered.

"Let me see." His voice was soft, compassionate, loving. She could do this. For him. For herself.

She let the robe slide ever so slowly past her arms, over her hips to puddle at her feet.

She stood, naked and vulnerable, heart pounding wildly as she watched his reaction. The revulsion she expected never came.

"You…are…so…beautiful," he ground out between jaws clenched with desire.

In that moment, Stephanie knew she had found the impossible. A man who looked past the horrible scars of her childhood to the woman inside.

All her doubts and fears fell away to join the robe at her feet when Daniel's nostrils flared and his eyes darkened in passion.

"Come here, woman," he growled.

Slowly, proudly, she moved toward him, reveling in the mounting passion she evoked in her new husband. Not pity. Not revulsion or sympathy or even anger. But love and passion.

"I love you," she said as he pulled her onto the bed with him.

His body trembled against hers, and she loved him even more.

And then with an exquisite tenderness that brought tears to her eyes, Daniel laid her back against the downy pillows and gently kissed every scar on her body until she no longer thought of anything except becoming one with her forever soulmate.

Daniel awoke to the warm, delightful smell of fresh coffee. For three glorious days now, his beautiful bride had managed to awaken before him and fill the cabin with delicious smells. Tomorrow he simply had to wake up first and make her breakfast in bed.

"Morning, my love." She swept into the bedroom, carrying two steaming cups. Her face scrubbed clean and pink, her hair tied back at the neck, she looked fresh as the mountain air.

He took the mug, sipped at the warm brew, and then said, "You're interfering with my plans."

She perched on the edge of the mattress. "How so?"

"I want to do the spoiling, but you don't give me a chance."

She pushed the hair back from his forehead with one cool, soft hand and kissed him. He loved it when she did that. "Daniel, you made our wedding day—" she paused to smile "—and night perfect. You've made every day since perfect. Fixing breakfast makes me feel like a real wife. I love it."

"Do you love me, too?" He could never get enough of hearing her say it.

"Oh, a little, I suppose." She grinned, and seeing her relaxed and carefree enough to tease filled him with enormous joy.

He was still on an emotional high from their wedding night. As hard as it must have been for her, Stephanie had undressed for him—had wanted to. And by that action, his beautiful, brave wife had given him the finest wedding gift of all—her trust. No one had ever sacrificed anything for him that he remembered. But she had.

After the initial shock of seeing what her stepfather had done to her body, he'd seen only the woman he loved more than life. With his heart bursting, he'd vowed at that moment that no one would ever hurt her again, beginning with him.

"What do you want to do today?" he asked, setting his cup on the bedside table. "The world is yours. I'll even get the universe if you want it."

"I'm sorry to bring this up, but—" she ran a fingertip around the rim of her cup "—we're going to have to think about going back to London soon."

"No-o-o." He flopped backwards on the bed in protest. But he knew she was right. They both had work to do that couldn't be done long distance, but being here with Stephanie was magical. He'd never been so fulfilled.

"Louise phoned earlier."

"My sister?"

She smiled, and Daniel lifted one shoulder in response. Referring to Louise as his sister was starting to feel okay.

"Things are chaotic. Your father and Robert are arguing constantly because Robert thinks Dominic belongs in jail. John won't hear of it, of course. Money is very, very tight and there is talk of closing one or more of the restaurants. She thought we should know."

The problem, thanks to his brother, was approaching crisis state.

"I talked to Dominic yesterday. He's worried, too. As he should be, but still…" He let the rest ride. Dominic was his twin. Regardless of the mistake he'd made, Daniel would stand by him just as John was doing. In the face of such desperate odds, Daniel was amazed at their father's steadfast loyalty.

"So what do you think we should do?"

He sighed. "Book our flights."

"Agreed." She rose from the bed and set her coffee cup beside his. "But first, I have a present for you."

He pumped his eyebrows. "You're coming back to bed?"

She laughed. "Maybe. But something important came by messenger a few minutes ago, and I can't wait to share the news with you." She left the room, only to return a moment later carrying a brown envelope.

"Remember all that fabulous art my stepfather collected?"

Yes, he remembered. And he also recalled the abuse she'd suffered when she hadn't been able to remember the titles and artists. He'd wanted to tear the paintings from the wall and rip them apart with his bare hands.

She handed him a legal-looking document. "That collection auctioned for an enormous sum of money."

"Good. Are you planning to add that to your Hope House?"

She shook her head. "This document creates a trust to help fund Daniel Stephens' water projects in Africa."

Incredulous, he stared from her to the document. "You're serious. That's really what this is."

"Yes. If I'd known a crisis would arise in the family, I would have saved some out for that. But I didn't. And this is already in motion. A trust of this kind can do an enormous amount of good."

"You put your inheritance into this? For me?"

"My wedding gift to you. I know how important those projects are to you. Now they're important to me." She climbed on the bed beside him, touched his cheek with her fingertips. "You changed my life, Daniel. You made me feel beautiful and desirable and worthy. You took away my shame. Nothing I give you will ever be enough."

Love, almost more than he could contain, exploded inside him. This woman, this incredible, generous, valiant woman had taken the ugliness of her childhood and created something beautiful. And in the process, she'd changed him, an empty, heartless shell of a man.

And as he contemplated the priceless gifts Stephanie had given him—her love, her fears, and now her inheritance—Daniel let go of the bitterness he'd carried so long.

CHAPTER THIRTEEN

"It's a Christmas party." Over the softly crooning music of "White Christmas," Daniel spoke close to Stephanie's ear. She was understandably nervous about tonight. "What bad thing could possibly happen?"

Daniel gazed around at the gathered assembly. Seated with them at the corner table were Daniel's cousins, Rebecca and Rachel, both pregnant and with their new husbands by their sides. Across the room, Rebecca's stepchildren played wide-eyed under the Christmas tree. A host of Valentines, of whom Daniel and his bride were both now a part, swarmed the gaily decorated interior of the Bella Lucia Mayfair. Beneath the outward gaiety, the strain was almost palpable.

"A Christmas party that is also an emergency family meeting. Things could get sticky before the evening is over."

She nodded toward Robert and his wife, ensconced at one end of the room, and then toward John, who'd taken a table at the other end. The two brothers, who'd never gotten along, were really at odds now.

"This is my first ever family Christmas," Daniel said. "I think I'll enjoy myself and forget the rest." He dropped a kiss on her hair, and filled his lungs with her fresh designer fragrance. He was only telling half the truth. He was worried, too. As hard as he'd tried to remain detached from his blood relatives, they had a way of sucking him in. And now they were in trouble.

Regardless of some happy news, including Daniel and Stephanie's elopement, bad news seemed to be the order of the day. Dominic's embezzlement had caused much greater damage than John had anticipated.

Without a huge infusion of money from Lord-knew-where, the Bella Lucia chain would be bankrupt. John was striving valiantly to protect Dominic and had drained his personal accounts in the effort. Robert was furious with them both and threatening everything from lawsuit to strangulation. All involved, including Stephanie, were concerned about their livelihoods. Daniel felt guilty to see his own dreams coming true when others were losing theirs.

"You two look cozy," Rebecca said, smiling toward Daniel and Stephanie. "How was the honeymoon?"

"Perfect," they answered in unison and then burst out laughing. No one would ever know how perfect. They'd skied, hiked, and gone sledding. They'd dined out and in. They'd strolled the woods and the streets of Aspen. But mostly they'd stayed in the secluded cabin and reveled in the joy of their love.

"Did I ever thank you for sending me to America?" Daniel asked.

Rebecca reached across the table to squeeze Stephanie's arm. "Seeing my friend happy is thanks enough."

"You look pretty happy yourself," Stephanie said, returning the squeeze.

"Delirious." Suddenly, Rebecca's eyes widened. "Daniel," she said in amazement, "is that your sister?"

They all looked in the direction of Rebecca's gaze. A tall blonde in a white angora crop top and red micro mini had entered the dining room. Mistletoe jewelry flashed from her belly button. At her side was a tall, tanned fellow who probably had every woman in the place staring at him.

Daniel choked on his drink. "That's not the Louise I remember."

Gone were the classic designer suits, subtle makeup and hairstyle. Miss Goody-Two-Shoes looked red-hot.

"We're not the only ones noticing her new look." Stephanie hitched her chin toward Max. Daniel's cousin, who helped Robert run the Bella Lucia Chelsea, glowered at the outrageously clad Louise and her escort.

"Don't mind Max," Rachel said. "The two of them have never gotten along."

"Hmm. I wonder." Rebecca's eyes sparkled beneath the white blinking Christmas lights. "Sometimes all that fighting is a mating dance."

Mitchell, Rebecca's husband, chuckled indulgently. "I'm afraid you'll have to overlook my wife. She sees romance everywhere these days."

Rebecca grinned up at him. "You complaining?"

He hooked an elbow around her neck and pulled, his besotted expression clear to all. "Nope."

"Romance or not, Louise is here for the same reason we are. Because this family has big problems." Rachel seemed set on fretting. And rightly so. She'd been a favorite of Grandfather William's and had invested her adult life in these restaurants. "I, for one, don't know what we're going to do."

"I've offered to take a cut in salary," Stephanie said. "Others have done the same."

"The business needs a lot more money than salary cuts can generate. Unless Uncle John and Dad come up with a plan soon, the entire chain will have to close. But the way those two quarrel, I can't see that happening."

"Surely, they can find an investor, Rachel. Doesn't anyone in this huge family have that kind of money?"

"There is one. But he won't help."

"Who's that?"

"Jack. Dad's other son, my other half brother, the estranged one. But he washed his hands of this place and all the Valentines a long time ago."

Odd. Daniel had never heard of this cousin. "Will he be here tonight?"

"Are you kidding?" Rachel shook her head. "Jack hasn't been to a family gathering in years. He hates this place. All the others may put aside their differences at Christmas, but not Jack. If this place sinks, he'd be the last person on earth to throw out a life-preserver."

Above the lilt of "Have Yourself a Merry Little Christmas" came the tinkle of metal against glass. Soon the room took up the chorus of tapping and conversation hushed.

John rose. His face was drawn and weary, his usual ruddy vigor gone, and Daniel thought with a start that his father looked old. He'd had a mild heart attack a few months back and now the strain of Dominic's misdeed was taking a heavy toll.

Still, he carried himself erect, and, with a determined set to his chin, he started across the room toward Robert.

"I would like to propose a toast," he said. The sound carried among the assembly now gone quiet except for the soft Christmas carols playing through the sound system. All eyes watched as John approached his brother's table.

Robert looked startled; an inward struggle played across his features. Finally, as if he had no choice, he rose, wineglass in hand. The rest of the crowd rose as well.

"Tonight," John said, his gaze intent on the other man's face, "is Christmas. All of us are here because we're family. If only for this one night, let's forget our problems, and celebrate all the good things that have happened to us this year." When Robert didn't protest, he went on, gathering momentum. "Here is a toast to all of us. Young and old. Old and new. We face some challenges, but the indomitable spirit of the Valentine family will prevail. Somehow, some way, we will prevail. May the coming year bring happiness, peace, and prosperity to us all."

"Hear, hear," someone in the crowd called. And a chorus of the toasts rose and fell. Glasses clinked.

Daniel used that diversion as an excuse to maneuver his bride beneath a sprig of mistletoe. "Merry Christmas, wife."

"Merry Christmas, husband," she said as his smiling lips melded with hers.

When the kiss ended and the clinks and good wishes faded away, the front door of the restaurant, closed to all but family, whooshed open. Cold December air flooded in.

The party, wineglasses held high, turned as one to see who the latecomers were.

A collective gasp emptied the room of oxygen.

For there in the doorway stood Madison Ford, Jack Valentine's assistant. And next to her, a cynical half-smile on his face, was none other than the prodigal son himself, Jack Valentine.

* * * * *

New York Times *bestselling author Linda Lael Miller is back with a new romance featuring the heartwarming McKettrick family from Silhouette Special Edition.*

SIERRA'S HOMECOMING
by Linda Lael Miller

On sale December 2006,
wherever books are sold.

Turn the page for a sneak preview!

Soft, smoky music poured into the room.

The next thing she knew, Sierra was in Travis's arms, close against that chest she'd admired earlier, and they were slow dancing.

Why didn't she pull away?

"Relax," he said. His breath was warm in her hair.

She giggled, more nervous than amused. What was the matter with her? She was attracted to Travis, had been from the first, and he was clearly attracted to her. They were both adults. Why not enjoy a little slow dancing in a ranch-house kitchen?

Because slow dancing led to other things. She took a step back and felt the counter flush against her lower back. Travis naturally came with her, since they were holding hands and he had one arm around her waist.

Simple physics.

Then he kissed her.

Physics again—this time, not so simple.

"Yikes," she said, when their mouths parted.

He grinned. "Nobody's ever said that after I kissed them."

She felt the heat and substance of his body pressed against hers. "It's going to happen, isn't it?" she heard herself whisper.

"Yep," Travis answered.

"But not tonight," Sierra said on a sigh.

"Probably not," Travis agreed.

"When, then?"

He chuckled, gave her a slow, nibbling kiss. "Tomorrow morning," he said. "After you drop Liam off at school."

"Isn't that…a little…soon?"

"Not soon enough," Travis answered, his voice husky. "Not nearly soon enough."

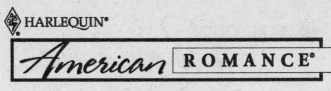

HARLEQUIN®

American **ROMANCE®**

IS PROUD TO PRESENT

COWBOY VET
by Pamela Britton

Jessie Monroe is the last person on earth
Rand Sheppard wants to rely on, but he needs
a veterinary technician—yesterday—and she's the
only one for hire. It turns out the woman who
destroyed his cousin's life isn't who Rand thought
she was. And now she's all he can think about!

"Pamela Britton writes the kind of
wonderfully romantic, sexy, witty romance
that readers dream of discovering
when they go into a bookstore."

—*New York Times* bestselling author
Jayne Ann Krentz

Cowboy Vet *is available from*
Harlequin American Romance in December 2006.

www.eHarlequin.com   HARPBDEC

Harlequin® Historical
Historical Romantic Adventure!

Loyalty...or love?

LORD GREVILLE'S CAPTIVE
Nicola Cornick

He had previously come to Grafton
Manor to be betrothed to the beautiful
Lady Anne—but that promise was broken
with the onset of the English Civil War.
Now Lord Greville has returned as an
enemy, besieging the manor and holding
its lady prisoner.

His devotion to his cause is swayed by
his desire for Anne—he will have the
lady, and her heart.

Yet Anne has a secret that must be kept
from him at all costs....

On sale December 2006.
Available wherever Harlequin books are sold.

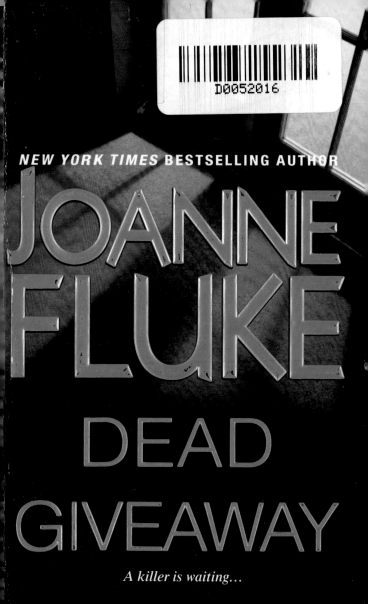

NEW YORK TIMES BESTSELLING AUTHOR

JOANNE FLUKE

DEAD GIVEAWAY

A killer is waiting…

KENSINGTON
U.S. $7.99
CAN $8.99

EAN

ISBN-13: 978-0-7582-8973-5
ISBN-10: 0-7582-8973-1

9 780758 289735

5 0 7 9 9

S

A Letter From Joanne Fluke

Years before Hannah Swensen unlocked the back door at The Cookie Jar, I went to visit a friend and her newborn daughter in Las Vegas. I flew out of Minneapolis in the middle of a snowstorm, happy to be escaping the cold Minnesota winter. When we landed in Vegas, I met my friend and switched to sandals for the drive to her place. As I stuffed my snow boots in my suitcase, I thought of how wonderful it was to breathe warm air that hadn't come out of a furnace vent!

We drove out of town and took the road to Mount Charleston. Soon there was snow on the ground and it got deeper and icier as we climbed higher. I thought I'd be relaxing by a pool in the warm sun, but it seemed that I was returning to cold weather much sooner than I'd expected!

We walked into their log cabin near the mountain top. Their access road wasn't plowed and residents had to park on the shoulder of the highway. It wasn't far and I marveled at the breathtaking scenery. How gorgeous! And how glad I was that I had my snow boots!

By the time we turned in for the night, I was imagining what might happen if someone lived in an exclusive, high-rise condo in this beautiful but terrifyingly isolated place. What if there was a blizzard? And what if a killer terrorized the residents who were stranded with no help from the outside world? This was the moment I knew I had to write *Dead Giveaway* and set it high on Mount Charleston. I hope you enjoy reading it. Even though I know it's fiction, I still can't re-read it without shivering!

Books by Joanne Fluke

Hannah Swensen Mysteries

CHOCOLATE CHIP COOKIE MURDER
STRAWBERRY SHORTCAKE MURDER
BLUEBERRY MUFFIN MURDER
LEMON MERINGUE PIE MURDER
FUDGE CUPCAKE MURDER
SUGAR COOKIE MURDER
PEACH COBBLER MURDER
CHERRY CHEESECAKE MURDER
KEY LIME PIE MURDER
CANDY CANE MURDER
CARROT CAKE MURDER
CREAM PUFF MURDER
PLUM PUDDING MURDER
APPLE TURNOVER MURDER
DEVIL'S FOOD CAKE MURDER
GINGERBREAD COOKIE MURDER
CINNAMON ROLL MURDER
RED VELVET CUPCAKE MURDER
BLACKBERRY PIE MURDER
JOANNE FLUKE'S LAKE EDEN COOKBOOK

Suspense Novels

VIDEO KILL
WINTER CHILL
DEAD GIVEAWAY

Published by Kensington Publishing Corporation

DEAD GIVEAWAY

JOANNE FLUKE

KENSINGTON BOOKS

http://www.kensingtonbooks.com

KENSINGTON BOOKS are published by

Kensington Publishing Corp.
119 West 40th Street
New York, NY 10018

All Kensington titles, imprints and distributed lines are available at special quantity discounts for bulk purchases for sales
promotion, premiums, fund-raising, educational or institu-
tional use. Special book excerpts or customized printings
can also be created to fit specific needs. For details, write
or phone the office of the Kensington Special Sales Manager: Kensington Publishing Corp., 119 West 40th Street,
New York, NY, 10018. Attn. Special Sales Department.
Phone: 1-800-221-2647.

Kensington and the K logo Reg. U.S. Pat. & TM Off.

ISBN-13: 978-0-7582-8973-5
ISBN-10: 0-7582-8973-1
First Kensington Mass Market Edition: May 2014

eISBN-13: 978-0-7582-8974-2
eISBN-10: 0-7582-8974-X
First Kensington Electronic Edition: May 2014

10 9 8 7 6 5 4 3 2 1

Printed in the United States of America

DEAD
GIVEAWAY

PROLOGUE

The meeting took place in a high-rise office building, twenty stories above the Vegas Strip. The five men wore fashionably cut business suits. There wasn't a bodyguard in sight, the strains of Italian aria did not fill the air, and no one's name was Guido.

The tanned blond man looked uncomfortable as he addressed the senior member of the group. "I'm sorry it has to be this way, but our only option is to take a hard line."

Reluctantly, the older man nodded, perspiring heavily. "I know, I know. She thinks she's in love and she won't listen to reason. She doesn't realize he's playing her for a fool."

"She's already talked too much." The short, thin man frowned. "We managed to take care of it this time, but we can't take another chance."

The older man peered into their faces for some sign of compassion, but no one would meet his eyes. "But she's my daughter! There's got to be some other way!"

The fourth member of the group, a heavyset man with a ruddy complexion, sighed deeply. "You know we're reasonable men. If there's another solution, we're willing to consider it."

"What if I personally guarantee her silence? Put a guard on her day and night?"

There was a silence for a long moment and then the heavyset man shook his head. "We know your intentions are good, but you can't control her forever. She'll manage to slip her guard sooner or later and then . . ."

The fifth member of the group, silent until this point, held up his hand. "I know that I speak for every man here when I say that we respect your feelings for your daughter." The heavyset man nodded along with the others. "And because of that respect which we all share, I have worked out a plan to keep her alive but eliminate the threat she poses."

They all leaned forward as he outlined the details. An expression of anguish came over the older man's face as he listened, but then he nodded reluctantly. It was better than nothing.

"It's settled then." The heavyset man sighed deeply. "So what about the boyfriend?"

The older man's expression hardened as he rose from the table. "Do what you think best. I have no interest in him."

Happy Smith wheeled another load of rubbish up to the industrial Dumpster. The wind whistled down the canyon and he shivered as he zipped up his jacket. The foreman would be plenty surprised when he came up the mountain tomorrow and found all the construction trash and debris hauled away.

A strange set of circumstances had prompted Happy to start work one day early. It had to do with the mission and their Sunday schedule. First they fed you the food, a nice chicken dinner with soup and mashed potatoes and little green peas. But then, after the apple pie that Miss Alden made in a big pan for the men she called her lambs, she herded them all into the chapel to say prayers all afternoon.

Happy had already resigned himself when he'd heard Miss Alden tell another man that he'd better hurry or he'd be late to work. And that had given him the idea. The slip from the foreman was in his pocket and he'd folded it over so the date didn't show. Miss Alden had been so excited about his job that she'd given him a nice yellow windbreaker and a pair of gloves from the charity box. And Sam, an old wino who'd been at the mission since they'd opened the doors, had loaned Happy his horseshoe ring for luck.

Happy turned around to stare at the building on Deer Creek Road. The foreman had told him it was almost finished, a high-rise with nine condos that took up a whole floor apiece. Even though he wasn't supposed to do any cleanup inside the building, Happy had been itching to see those million-dollar condos.

The parking garage was wide open, its iron security gates propped up by the entrance, waiting to be installed. Happy hurried in and climbed the stairs to the first floor. He knew he was snooping, but he wouldn't touch a thing. No one would ever know he'd been inside.

When Happy opened the door to the first-floor condo, he gasped out loud. It was carpeted with the thickest rug he'd ever seen, plenty soft enough to sleep on. And the rooms were so big they could hold every one of Miss Alden's lambs, without anyone ever bumping into anyone else.

There was a smile on Happy's face as he wandered through the rooms, trying to imagine being rich enough to live in such a place. The kitchen looked as if it belonged in a restaurant, with a walk-in freezer, a mammoth stove with four ovens, and enough shelves in the pantry to store food for a year.

After he had peeked into each of the rooms, Happy decided to head straight up to the penthouse. The foreman had told him they were putting a whole spa up there. Happy didn't see how they could build a pool without digging a hole in the ground, but the foreman had assured him that was exactly what they were doing.

It took time to climb up nine flights of stairs, and even though he stopped to rest at several landings, Happy was panting when he pushed open the door to the penthouse. The sight that awaited him made him gasp in awe. Metal girders curved around in a series of interlocking arches to make a domed ceiling. It wasn't finished yet, but several panes of glass were in place and Happy could see that there would be an unobstructed view in all directions. He stopped to look out at Mount Charleston and watched the pattern of the clouds just brushing its peak.

The view was so spectacular that, for a few moments, Happy lost himself in contemplation, forgetting the man-made marvels at his feet. Then he whistled in awe as he gazed down at the immense hole in the floor, lined with steel beams. He guessed they needed all that reinforcement because the pool was all the way up on top of the building. He'd watched some men put in a backyard pool once, but all they'd done was prepare the hole, install all the pipes, and drop in one of those premade shells.

There was the sound of a motor outside and Happy

looked out to see a brown van pull into the driveway. When the doors opened and two men got out, Happy ducked behind one of the girders. His heart was beating fast and he rubbed Sam's horseshoe ring for luck. If the foreman was down there, he'd be in big trouble.

The men walked around to the back of the van and Happy sighed, relieved that he'd never seen those two men before. They opened the back door and helped another man out. He was staggering a little and Happy could see that he'd had too much to drink. They must have gone to a party and now they were taking their friend for a little walk to sober him up before taking him home.

The men looked startled as Happy leaned out and shouted, but when he asked, they promised to give him a ride back to the mission. He should stay put and they'd come up to get him.

Happy was smiling as he walked back to explore the rest of the spa. If he'd watched just a moment longer, he would have seen that one of the men carried a gun. And that the third man was staggering because his hands were tied behind his back.

ONE

Lyle Marshall was smiling as he threaded his way past a group of high rollers at the craps table. He'd signed the papers this morning and now he was officially retired. Since he'd made a hell of a profit by selling his share of Paradise Development to his partner, Marc Davies, he could afford to plunk down a sizable bet, but Charlotte was waiting in the banquet room and he didn't want to be late to his own twenty-fifth wedding anniversary bash.

A short, stocky man in his early fifties, Lyle was dressed in a custom-made gray linen suit. Charlotte always went to the tailor with him, choosing the material and cut that looked best. She also picked out his shirts and ties, even the smoking jacket she insisted that he wear at home. Charlotte was a lady of impeccable taste.

A huge blond woman, slightly resembling Brunhilde in the one opera Charlotte had dragged him to, hit a jackpot on the nickel slots. Bells rang, lights flashed, and she let out a shriek that almost deafened everyone within earshot. Lyle grinned; definitely a soprano. Charlotte was the founder of the Friends of the Las Vegas Civic Light Opera Company and was always complaining about the lack of good strong sopranos.

Lyle sidestepped the gawking tourists and entered the restaurant. An almost palpable sense of relief came over him as the piped-in music muted the clatter of the slot machines outside. Vegas was hard on the ears. And on the savings account. If Charlotte ever guessed how much of their money had been converted into chips and scooped up by the croupier, she'd kill him.

They'd come here as newlyweds. Charlotte had wanted to stay near her parents in Arlington, Virginia, but he'd convinced her that a real estate agent could make it big in a town like Vegas. The casinos employed a lot of people and all of them needed housing. There was a huge turnover, too.

From day one Charlotte had complained about the glitz, the heat, and what she called the gambler mentality. It was true there wasn't much culture, and the young city had little historical heritage. All those things meant a lot to Charlotte, but she missed the change of seasons most of all. Smack in the middle of the desert, Vegas didn't really have much weather to speak of. The wind blew a little harder in the winter, and the nights got colder, but that was about it. Shifting sand, bright lights, dry heat, and the feeling of being caught in the middle of a never-ending party—that described Vegas.

Marc and Lyle had formed Paradise Development fifteen years ago and it had been a going concern from the very first day. Marc was a wizard at finding prime building sites at ridiculously low prices, and Lyle presold the houses he built. The only fly in the ointment had been Charlotte, but Marc had solved that one, too.

It had all started two years ago, when Marc picked up some great mountain property dirt cheap. One look at the land and Charlotte had fallen in love. There were trees that turned colors in the fall, snow in the winter, wildflowers in the spring, and real summer thunderstorms. They'd contracted with Paul Lindstrom, their architect of choice, to design the perfect apartment cluster, to feature an exclusive country club–type environment. Given the slope of their mountain site, Paul had designed a high-rise building, each unit consisting of an entire floor individually tailored to suit the occupant's needs. There were two common areas, the garage and the penthouse spa. The spa was complete with pool, Jacuzzi, sauna, tennis court, weight room, and jogging track. Totally enclosed by a climate-controlled glass dome, the spa afforded a spectacular view of the Mount Charleston area.

Charlotte and Lyle had moved in last year along with eight other couples who'd passed Charlotte's muster. Like one of those blue-blooded clubs back in Virginia, its members had to be perfect or they couldn't buy in. Charlotte loved the view from their eighth-floor condo, thirty-five minutes from Vegas on Deer Creek Road. "Mountain living at its finest" was the phrase she'd used two years in a row on their Christmas cards.

"Hi, Mr. Marshall." The hostess, a leggy blonde in a slit skirt that left very little to the imagination, greeted him with a perfect smile. "Everyone in your party is here except for Mr. Davies. He called and said he'll be delayed a few minutes."

Lyle grinned as he followed her to the plush private banquet room Johnny Day had reserved for the occasion.

Lyle had always liked Johnny. He seemed like a regular guy, and Lyle had recommended him for membership in their Deer Creek Development, even though there were rumors about his womanizing. An Italian lounge singer who'd had a couple of hit records, Johnny's passion was mechanical musical instruments, and he had a whole warehouse full of antique music boxes of all sizes, along with player pianos and giant orchestrions. The orchestrions were fascinating. Built in Europe before the turn of the century, the elaborately carved wooden cabinets contained string instruments, horns, woodwinds, and percussion. Johnny had explained that the orchestrions in his collection operated just like player pianos. The mechanical arms that drew the bows across the strings, the bellows that pumped air into the wind instruments, the levers that activated the drums and the cymbals were all cued by a roll of pre-punched music. Charlotte, though a loyal supporter of classical symphony, admitted that the sound the orchestrions produced was nothing short of incredible for its day.

It had been touch and go overcoming Charlotte's aversion to anyone in show business, but now Johnny owned the fourth-floor unit. Johnny's collection had done the trick. When Lyle had first introduced them, Johnny had presented Charlotte with a heart-shaped music box he claimed had belonged to Queen Victoria. It might even have been true.

Charlotte was sitting at the head of a table decorated with white satin wedding bells and roses, an empty chair next to her. Lyle stopped in the doorway and gaped at his wife of twenty-five years. The long brown hair, always worn high on her head in a French twist, was gone. Through the wonders of modern cosmetology, it had been lightened to a golden cap cut in a fluffy feathered style. Lyle blinked, and then he started to grin. Charlotte looked good. She was wearing a bright pink jersey dress with a short skirt and it clung to her in all the right places. Her figure had always been good, but she'd been going to exercise classes for the past six months and there was definitely something to be said for all the toning and tightening. Lyle felt as if he'd just been presented with a brand-new wife.

"Hello, darling! You're just in time." Charlotte had spotted him in the doorway and Lyle crossed the room to kiss her. Jayne Peters and Johnny Day were playing show tunes at the piano and Lyle noticed that Johnny was pale beneath his tan, a telltale sign to anyone who knew him well. Johnny had been gambling again and things hadn't gone well for him.

"Let's do our song, Jayne." Johnny switched on the microphone and they both started to croon.

Darling, when you're old and decrepit
And liver spots make you look like a leopard,
I'll stick with you through stormy or sunny
'Cause you're the one with all the money.

Charlotte giggled and pulled Lyle down into his chair. "That's awful! You must have written it, Jayne."

"Don't shoot. I confess." Jayne raised her hands in mock surrender. A petite woman in her late thirties with high cheekbones, her jet-black hair was pulled back into two long braids. She was wearing a white satin cowboy shirt embroidered with red roses, white jeans studded with rhinestones, and red high-heeled cowboy boots. Since Jayne wrote strictly country-western songs, her agent had insisted on the cowgirl image. Public admission that her family name was Petronovitch and her parents had emigrated from Russia could be disastrous.

"Good afternoon, Lyle." Jayne's husband and Paradise Development's architect, Paul Lindstrom stood up and extended his hand. A quiet man whom Jayne called her "textbook Norseman," Paul spoke slowly and precisely. As always, he was impeccably dressed in a snowy-white shirt and dress slacks. At slightly over six feet tall and in his early forties, Paul was slim and fashionable. The only discordant note was his unruly halo of sandy hair. It reminded Lyle of pictures of Einstein and gave Paul the look of a sleepy lion.

"Hi, Paul." Lyle reached out automatically to complete the handshake. Paul had never dropped his Norwegian habit of rising to shake hands whenever anyone entered the room. When Paul and Jayne had first moved into the ninth-floor unit on Deer Creek Road, Paul's polite ritual had driven Lyle crazy. There were handshakes in the sauna, on the tennis court, and in the hallways. It had taken Lyle quite a while to get used to Paul's curious habit, but all the women in the building, including Charlotte, found the ritual utterly charming.

"Look at the lovely flowers Darby brought us." Charlotte gestured toward the centerpiece, a massive bouquet of roses.

Lyle turned to smile at Darby Roberts. Clayton and Darby lived on the fifth floor and Paul had designed a large domed greenhouse garden for them.

"Your flowers?" Paul asked Darby.

Darby nodded. "The yellow ones in the middle are my own hybrid. I've been working on them for years, and Clayton registered them with the association last week. I named them Marshall Golds after you and Charlotte and that's my anniversary present to you. Smell 'em, Lyle."

Darby watched as Lyle bent over to inhale the fragrance. She was a small, dark-haired woman, so thin that her skin resembled white parchment stretched over a road map of blue veins. She looked so fragile that Lyle sometimes wondered if the mountain winds would pick her up and blow her away. In contrast, her husband, their resident lawyer, was as heavy as Darby was light. Clayton strived to look healthy, tan, and athletic and he gave his workouts the same priority as his appointments with clients. At eight every evening, Clayton arrived at the rooftop spa, spending five minutes in the tanning booth, followed by twenty-five minutes on the exercise bike. After that, came a fifteen-minute sauna and then thirty laps in the pool. Despite his efforts, Clayton still carried a hefty roll of flab around his waist, and Lyle knew why. Clayton indulged himself with three-martini lunches at Alfredo's, where the entree was always pasta.

"Here's the paperwork." Clayton pulled a legal document from his pocket and presented it to Charlotte. "I personally checked the registration form. Since it didn't cover several salient points, I constructed an addendum which gives you clear title and protection against unauthorized use."

"Thank you, Clayton." Lyle tried to match Clayton's serious expression. He didn't give a fig if anyone wanted to grow Marshall roses, but it was obviously important to Darby and Clayton.

"I've got a present for you, too." Johnny Day stood up and motioned to a waiter who was hovering in the background. Almost immediately, twelve silver ice buckets were wheeled out, each containing a bottle of Dom Pérignon.

"Oh, Johnny." Charlotte clapped her hands in delight. "My absolute favorite champagne!"

"Your absolute favorite caviar, too." Johnny nodded and the waiter produced a crystal bowl filled with the finest Beluga caviar. "This is just the appetizer. I'll let Marc tell you about the rest of the meal when he gets here."

Moira Jonas got to her feet. A large woman with more muscle than fat, her red hair was twisted up into a knot on the top of her head, making her appear even taller. Moira's physical appearance matched her imposing presence as Vegas's leading interior decorator.

"That's simply a stunning outfit, Moira. You look wonderful," Charlotte complimented her.

Lyle noted genuine envy in Charlotte's voice and couldn't imagine why. Moira was wearing one of the caftans that had become her trademark. This one was a vivid blue embroidered in bright red thread, and it was decorated with shiny gold beads interspersed with mirrored disks. Lyle thought she looked a little like the toy stuffed elephants found in a New Delhi bazaar.

"Aw, bullsh . . . I mean, horsefeathers! I know I look as big as a house." Moira caught herself just in time and her roommate, Grace DuPaz, did her best to suppress a smile. As the only daughter of a career army sergeant, Moira's choice of expletives had been pretty colorful when Grace had met her ten years before. Since then, Moira had made a considerable effort to clean up her language.

"Thanks anyway, Charlotte." Moira tried to accept the compliment gracefully. "Can we bring out our present now? Grace has sixteen dancers on hold out there."

"Sixteen dancers?" Lyle was clearly puzzled as Grace jumped up to join Moira. Thin and graceful, she was the exact opposite of Moira and wore her dark blond hair in a long ponytail. Grace had been the toast of Vegas, the featured dancer in all of the Castle's glitzy extravaganzas. She'd left the stage last year to become the head choreographer.

Charlotte had expressed her doubts when they'd wanted to buy into Deer Creek, as it was no secret that Moira and Grace were live-in lovers. Then, when Moira had offered to decorate all the units, Charlotte had quickly changed her mind. Since Moira and Grace never discussed their intimate relationship and Charlotte refrained from personal questions, the three women were now good friends.

"I wanted to stage it perfectly, even though Moira said it really didn't matter, that you'd appreciate it anyway. And then, at rehearsal today, I noticed these perfectly lovely costumes from last year's show just hanging right there on the rack. Naturally, once I explained the situation, all sixteen girls wanted to help, so I asked for volunteers and . . ."

"Gracie dear, you're babbling," Moira interrupted gently. "What she really means is that our present's too dang big for one person to carry."

Charlotte winced. "This doesn't have anything to do with your inheritance, does it, Grace?"

"Yes and no." Grace laughed. "It's not the moose head, if that's what you're thinking."

"Thank God!" Charlotte gasped. Grace's father had been a taxidermist and Paul had designed a special climate-controlled storage room for their unit. When Lyle had seen Grace's collection and wanted to buy a moose head for their den, Charlotte had objected strenuously. Moose were ugly in the first place and she certainly didn't want some horrid dead creature on her wall, staring at her with its glassy eyes.

"Okay, guys . . . hit it!"

At Moira's cue, Jayne began an African melody on the piano. Grace crossed the room to open the door and a crowd of dancers dressed in Zulu costumes and carrying spears came in, holding a tiger-skin rug, complete with head.

"Oh, Lord!" Charlotte began to laugh. "That animal has to be six feet long."

"It's actually a little over nine. I can take the head off if it really bothers you, but it adds such a nice touch of authenticity and it'll be on the floor, not the wall. Moira says it'll fit perfectly in front of your fireplace and I think it'll look very . . ." Grace stopped in midsentence as she felt Moira's hand on her arm. "Okay, Moira, I'll stop. But do you like it, Charlotte?"

Charlotte reached out to touch the fur. "It's beautiful and you can leave the head on. I can always put a sleep mask over its eyes."

"Since we're doing the presents . . ." Alan Lewis got to his feet. The owner of a chain of upscale building supply stores, Alan had provided Deer Creek materials at cost in return for his first-floor unit. An overweight man in his fifties with a cherubic face and a completely bald head, he placed his meerschaum pipe in an ashtray and cleared his throat. Alan's doctor had told him to quit smoking last year, and he'd tried everything: hypnosis, acupuncture, even aversion therapy in a famous clinic. Finally, the doctor had conceded that a pipe might be less harmful than chain-smoking unfiltered Camels, provided Alan didn't inhale, of course. Alan had left his doctor's office and ducked into the nearest pipe store. The salesman had been very helpful and Alan had emerged four thousand dollars poorer, with two hand-carved, antique meerschaums and a set of seven Dunhills, one for every day of the week, in a custom-fitted presentation case. His wife, Laureen, had picked out the tobacco, an aromatic blend that smelled a lot like cookies baking. Now Alan's doctor was happy and so was Laureen, and only Lyle knew that Alan still sneaked a Camel now and then.

"We wanted to give you something special." Alan beckoned to his wife. "Laureen? You do the honors, honey."

"I just want you all to know that this was Alan's idea." Laureen Lewis picked up a silver-wrapped box and carried it to Charlotte. An attractive blonde who was always watching her weight, she hosted a cooking show on the local Las Vegas television channel. Usually unflappable, Laureen's face was pink with embarrassment as Charlotte began to unwrap the package.

Charlotte lifted the lid and stared into the box with disbelief. "What is it?"

"It's a toilet seat." Alan grabbed it and lifted it out. "See? It's silver, that's in honor of your twenty-fifth anniversary, and it hooks on like this. The fixtures are genuine gold and that's mother-of-pearl inlay on the edges. I can install it in a jiffy if you tell me which bathroom you want it in."

Charlotte couldn't help it. She started to giggle. Leave it to Alan.

"I think it should go in the guest bathroom." Lyle took over when he saw that Charlotte was virtually speechless. "That way more people will get to admire it. Thanks, Alan. That was very . . . generous."

When Jack St. James stood up, Lyle gazed at him in shock. He was a short, muscular man in his early forties with light brown hair closely cropped in the military style. Today he was dressed for the occasion in a dark blue three-piece suit, quite a change from the chinos and NRA sweatshirt he usually wore. When Jack had applied for the job as live-in security officer, he'd told them that during his employment with a big security outfit, he'd designed the highly rated home security system that several of Charlotte's wealthy friends used. Jack was a lifelong member of the NRA, an organization that Charlotte abhorred, but his mention of a gold medal won in Olympic rifle competition had confirmed that Jack St. James was the man for the job. The tough little man inspired their confidence, important since their building was so isolated. In return for a small, one-bedroom apartment just off the garage and a reasonable salary, Jack had agreed to design a special security system for the entire building and to act as their in-house security chief.

"Twenty-five years and you're still together." Jack handed his gift to Charlotte. "I figure you and Lyle deserve medals for that."

Charlotte lifted the lid on the box and gasped, then held up Jack's gift for everyone to see. There were two silver medals inside, replicas of the ones from the Olympics. "Thank you, Jack. It says we won the silver in the marriage marathon. That's very clever! Wherever did you find them?"

"I didn't exactly find them. I just drew up the design and had a trophy place make them to order."

"It's your idea?" Alan Lewis put his pipe in the ashtray and got up for a closer look. "I bet you could market these. People are always looking for unusual gifts and these'd sell like hotcakes. It's a brilliant concept."

"And you could use silver for the twenty-fifth, gold for the fiftieth, and bronze for whatever the bronze anniversary is. What is it anyway? I've got a Hallmark date book at home and could look it up because they usually have a list of . . ." Grace realized that Moira was staring at her and she stopped. "All right, Moira. But I still think Jack is a genius."

As everyone began to tell him how clever he was, Jack sat there, obviously embarrassed, until Jayne took pity on him.

"Go fetch our gift, Paul. Jack's face is redder than a turkey waddle."

"A what?" Lyle turned to her in surprise. He hadn't been raised on a farm, but neither had Jayne. It must be a phrase from a song she'd written.

"A turkey waddle. You know, those gross little things that hang down on the . . . oh, never mind. Just get it, Paul."

"If you will all pardon me, please?" Paul got up and bowed. "This will take only a moment."

Everyone watched as Paul returned almost immediately with a large box. "Jayne has told me this is appropriate for your happy occasion. It is only a small token of our friendship and affection, but we hope it will meet your favor."

"Lord!" Lyle's eyes widened as Charlotte lifted a miniature house out of the box. "That looks just like 247 South Haven Street."

"It is!" Charlotte bent closer to read the house number on the tiny door. "Look, Lyle, a replica of our very first house. Is that why you were asking me all those questions, Jayne?"

Jayne nodded. "Paul got hold of the original blueprints and his model man built it."

Charlotte lifted the roof and peered at the tiny furnishings inside. "I still don't know how you did it, but it's simply perfect, all the way down to the awful living room rug."

"How'd you do it?" Moira leaned closer to look. "That pattern isn't even made anymore."

"Betty did the rug. That's her present."

"Our Betty?" Charlotte looked shocked by Jayne's emphatic nod.

"Dang-tootin'. I showed her what I needed and she hand-colored the pattern with felt-tip pens."

"That was so sweet." Charlotte sighed deeply. "I'll go up to thank her when we get home. Do you think she's getting any better?"

Moira shook her head. "That's impossible, Charlotte. I read a book on it. It says that some days are better than others, but it's an inevitable decline. Of course, Betty doesn't realize how confused she is and that helps, but Alzheimer's is a real b . . ."

"Bitch." Grace supplied the word before Moira had time to think of an acceptable substitute. With all these "shucks" and "dangs" and "horsefeathers" floating around, she sometimes felt like she was a character in a Jimmy Stewart movie. "Alzheimer's is a bitch of a disease."

Everyone was silent for a moment. Betty Matteo's lawyer had offered Marc the land on Deer Creek Road at a bargain price, provided it contained a unit for Betty and her full-time nurse.

Charlotte cleared her throat. "Well . . . Lyle and I thank you all for the wonderful presents. I think this is the nicest celebration we've ever had."

"It's not over yet." Hal Knight came as close as he ever had to smiling as he handed Charlotte a thin package. A handsome man who Charlotte thought resembled the young Henry Fonda in *The Grapes of Wrath*, Hal was saved from a too-pretty face by a hairline scar, two inches in length, running across his left cheekbone. Most people imagined that it was a dueling scar, but Hal freely admitted that it came from a fall off his tricycle at age three.

Hal lived and worked in the third-floor unit. He was the cartoonist who drew Skampy Skunk, Benny Bunny, and Chiquita Chicken, whose antics made the whole country laugh. Few people acknowledged the subtle sarcasm that ran through every strip.

They'd all grown to know Hal very well, and one night at the penthouse spa, after one too many glasses of wine, he had revealed the source of his bitterness. Because he was handsome and successful, beautiful women continually made overtures toward him. Flattered, Hal enjoyed their company, but that was as far as it went. He'd tried all the remedies. Therapy. Sex clinics. Potency drugs. Even a desperate attempt at a homosexual liaison. Nothing had worked. Apparently, Hal had informed them wryly, he was lucky. One therapist claimed that he was sublimating his libidinal urges in his work, and that if a certain particular part of his anatomy was functional, he might not be nearly so successful.

"This is sweet, Hal. Thank you." Charlotte reached up to kiss him on the cheek. "Look at this, everyone. It's Skampy Skunk and Chiquita Chicken congratulating us on our anniversary."

Hal nodded. "Better hang on to that, Charlotte. It'll be worth big bucks someday."

"It's worth big bucks now." Lyle took the drawing from Charlotte and studied it. "A signed Hal Knight has to be worth at least a grand."

Hal almost smiled again. "More like five grand, Lyle, and just wait till I croak. Look what happened to the sketches Picasso drew on restaurant tablecloths. I'm probably a better investment than IBM."

"Sorry I'm late." Marc Davies burst into the room,

shook hands with Paul, who had automatically risen to his feet, and took his place at the table. "Some idiot backed into my car at the baseball game and dented my bumper."

"My goodness! I didn't know they played baseball in February!" Charlotte looked confused so Marc hurried to explain.

"It was college baseball. They start early so they can finish before the end of the school year, and I went out to watch the new pitcher at UNLV. He's got one heck of a changeup and his slider's pretty decent, too. Those are pitches, Charlotte."

"Is he better than you were?" Lyle couldn't resist teasing his former partner.

"Of course not." Marc grinned. "I was the hottest thing the pros ever latched on to. Ask anyone who was around back then. This kid I saw today has got possibilities, though. All he needs is a little seasoning."

Charlotte frowned slightly. "I didn't know you played professional baseball, Marc. You never mentioned it."

"That's because I wasn't there long enough to brag. One season and I was retired. It's a long story, Charlotte."

"It sounds fascinating." Charlotte reached over to fill his glass with champagne. "Tell us about it, Marc."

Marc raised an eyebrow. "You're really that interested?"

"Of course we are!" Charlotte smiled at him. She wasn't, but she knew that a good hostess always listened to her guests.

"All right. Just let me wet my whistle first. I've got some catching up to do."

Lyle studied his former partner as he drank. At first glance, Marc looked the part of a builder, sporting jeans and a blue work shirt open at the collar. But Lyle knew that Marc ordered his jeans from a tailor in London, and that the shirt was actually cut from the finest silk with an elaborate blue-on-blue pocket monogram. Marc's loafers were handmade in Italy and his watch was a diamond-studded Rolex worth thousands of dollars.

Marc drained his champagne glass and set it down. His face was slightly flushed and Lyle was sure that he'd had a couple of beers at the game. He'd always been very closemouthed about his aborted baseball career before.

"On the night before the last game of the playoffs, I got a call from some guy who wouldn't identify himself. He said that if I came in to relieve, he'd give me a hundred big ones to throw the game."

"Do you mean a hundred thousand dollars?" Charlotte looked shocked as Marc nodded. "Whatever did you say?"

"I told him I wasn't interested, that there was no way I wanted to get involved in something like that."

"Well, I should hope not!" Charlotte pursed her lips together. "Did you report it to the authorities?"

Marc shook his head. "I figured it was a joke. We had some real bozos on the team and that was right up their alley. At the game the next day, I got called up to relieve in the sixth when the score was tied four-four. I got two strikes on my first man and then he caught a piece of my curveball and lined one straight at me. I had to dive to make the catch and I racked up my elbow so bad they had to take me out of the game."

Grace was sitting on the edge of her chair. "That's exciting! I just love baseball except that I'm always working when the games are on television and every time I try to tape one to watch later, Moira ends up telling me how it came out before . . . Okay, Moira. I'll be quiet. But did your team win, Marc?"

"Nope, we lost. And the next day I got an envelope in the mail with a hundred big ones inside."

"Good heavens!" Charlotte gasped. "They thought you got injured on purpose?"

"I guess so. I thought about turning it in, but the kind of guys who pay to fix a game don't like anyone to know about it, especially the police. And there was no way I could identify who'd sent it anyway. So I stuck it in a safe deposit box and went off to the hospital for elbow surgery."

"But the surgery didn't work," Lyle prompted. He'd heard this part of the story before.

Marc nodded. "That's right. After five different doctors had worked on me, they told me to forget about pitching again. And since my career in baseball was finished, I used the money to start my construction business."

"No one ever asked you to return it?" Charlotte's hands were trembling slightly as she refilled Marc's champagne glass.

"Of course not." Marc shrugged. "Everything turned out the way they wanted, even though my part in it was strictly unintentional. I've always regarded that cash as a kind of workman's compensation. And I've never told anybody about it before."

"Well, we certainly won't repeat it!" Alan nodded emphatically. "I don't blame you for keeping it, though. After all, how could you return it if you didn't know who'd sent it in the first place?"

"That's exactly the way I figured it. And that's enough about me. We've got just enough time for a few words from the happy couple before I present my gift." Marc drained his champagne glass again and motioned for the waiter to pour more. "You first, Lyle."

Lyle was solemn as he got to his feet. "Since Charlotte and I got married twenty-five years ago, I haven't regretted a single day."

"Isn't that sweet?" Grace started to applaud, but Charlotte reached out to grab her hands. She was well acquainted with her husband's sense of humor.

"And that single day was June fourth, nineteen eighty-nine."

"I knew it!" Charlotte was laughing as she got to her feet. "He doesn't mean it. At least, I don't think he does. And now, I have a surprise for all of you. My book is going to be published!"

"Your book?" Moira looked puzzled. "We didn't know you were writing a book, Charlotte."

Charlotte smiled modestly. "Well, some people might not call it a book, but I do. Remember the genealogy study I did last year?"

"Of course." Paul rose to his feet to shake Charlotte's hand. "I, for one, was very impressed. If I remember correctly, you traced your ancestors back to the fifteenth century."

Charlotte looked proud. "That's right, Paul. All the way back to Vicar William Henry Wingate's birth in fourteen thirty-one. But that's not the book they're going to publish."

"Tell us, Charlotte." Grace clapped her hands together, as excited as a child. "Who's your publisher? Is it a work of fiction, a murder mystery, or maybe a romance? You certainly could do one of those after being married for twenty-five years. No, I can't see you writing a romance. It's not cultivated enough. So I bet it's a family saga. I just love family sagas, I read one last week about some very valuable family jewels that were . . ."

Moira reached out to put her hand over Grace's

mouth. "Never mind, Gracie. Be quiet and let Charlotte tell us."

"Thank you, Moira. My book is going to be published by the Clark County Historical Society. And I'm not sure what category it is. Let's just call it a genealogical study of our land on Deer Creek Road, since I'm tracing the lineage of ownership."

"That sounds fascinating." Moira tried to look interested even though the very idea bored her silly. "How long have you been working on it?"

"I just started the research a few months ago and I've already discovered some things that are really quite shocking."

Laureen looked interested. "Like what? My mother traced the history of our family, but she quit when she came upon proof that my maternal great-uncle was a horse thief."

"Oh, it's much more shocking than that." Charlotte began to smile. "For example, I discovered that there was once a bordello right where our building stands."

Moira let out a whoop of laughter. "That's wonderful! Our own little red-light district. What else did you find?"

"I've barely scratched the surface, but I've been studying old assay records and I found several references to a silver mine that's reputed to be on our land. According to local legend, more than a dozen prospectors were murdered before they could stake a claim."

Alan began to grin. "Maybe Laureen and I should do a little exploring this summer. We'd own that mine if we found it, wouldn't we, Clayton?"

"Of course." Clayton nodded. "Our title includes all mineral rights."

Marc frowned. "Don't waste your time, Alan. The

odds of finding anything worth excavating are even longer than the odds at roulette. Right, Johnny?"

"Oh, I don't know about that." Johnny flashed his famous grin, the one that made middle-aged ladies ask for his autograph after every show. "I think the odds at roulette are pretty good."

Marc snorted. "Only if you own the house. Roulette's a sucker's game and you know it. How about the double zero?"

Jayne put her hand on Marc's arm. "Hush up, you two. What else did you find, Charlotte?"

"Well, there is one other thing." Charlotte lowered her voice. "Now, I'm not entirely sure about this, but one of my references alludes to some extremely unsavory individuals who may have held title previously."

Clayton, who was about to take a sip of champagne, set his glass down with a thump. "What on earth are you talking about, Charlotte? We went through a title search as part of our escrow and the title is clear."

"Oh, I'm sure it is, Clayton. What I'm interested in are the crimes that may have been committed while these individuals owned our land."

"What kind of crimes?" Hal leaned forward. "Come on, Charlotte. You can't leave us up in the air."

"I guess not." Charlotte's lips turned up in a mischievous smile. "All right, Hal. One more tidbit of information and that's it until I get the proper documentation. My reference alludes to several mysterious and unsolved murders."

"Holy . . . uh . . . cripes!"

Grace laughed out loud as Moira switched words in midsentence. "Go ahead and swear, Moira. What we just heard deserves more than a 'cripes.'"

"And I used to think genealogy was boring." Lyle put

his arm around his wife's shoulders. "How about a toast to Charlotte, the genealogical sleuth?"

As soon as the waiter had refilled their glasses, Marc stood up. "To Charlotte's book. Come on, everyone. Drink up. And then it's time for my present. I'm treating Lyle and Charlotte to the best dinner money can buy."

"Thank you, Marc. We love to dine out." Charlotte took a sip of her champagne. Then she noticed that everyone was leaning forward in anticipation. Marc must be taking them to a very exclusive restaurant. "Where are we going?"

"I made reservations at the fanciest restaurant I could find. And I arranged a special dinner, just for you two. How does *langoustes à la parisienne* sound? Followed by *canard à l'orange* and maybe a little strawberries Romanoff with crème Chantilly and candied violets?"

Charlotte sighed. "That sounds heavenly. But where are we going?"

"Well, that presented a little problem, but I found the perfect place. Come on. Let's go."

Lyle looked around at the half-empty bottles of champagne. He knew how much this had set Johnny back and it was too good to waste. "You mean we're leaving right now?"

"Right now." Marc drained his glass and stood up. "Come on, everybody. You all know the plans."

Charlotte and Lyle exchanged puzzled glances as they got up and followed Marc out the door. Johnny whisked them into a private elevator and seconds later they stepped out on the sidewalk in front of the casino.

"This way." Marc led them to a silver limousine idling at the curb. "Charlotte? Lyle? Climb in. I'm sending you to the Ritz for a romantic dinner."

"The Ritz?" Lyle frowned as the chauffeur held the door open for him. "Where's that, Marc?"

"In New Orleans."

"New Orleans? But . . . Marc!" Charlotte was so flabbergasted, she couldn't think of what to say.

Darby laughed. "Jayne and I packed your things, Charlotte. Your suitcases are in the trunk."

"That's right." Marc nodded. "You said you always wanted to go to Mardi Gras and this year you're going."

Charlotte looked confused. "But where will we stay? Lyle tried to get hotel reservations over three months ago and everything was booked solid."

"I've got a little more juice than Lyle." Johnny grinned at her. "I called in a marker from a friend of mine and you're all set up in the bridal suite at the Orleans Hotel. What's the matter, Charlotte? Don't you want to go?"

Charlotte began to laugh. "Of course I want to go! But . . ."

"No more buts.'" Marc reached out to give her a hug. Then he shook Lyle's hand. "Now climb in. The chauffeur has your tickets and you'd better hurry. Your plane leaves in an hour."

Lyle opened the French doors and stepped out onto the private balcony. There was another parade passing in the street below, headed by a group of jazz musicians in white suits, and Lyle groaned as he heard the familiar strains of "As The Saints Go Marching In." He'd always liked that song, but he was sure he'd heard it a hundred times since arriving in New Orleans. Mardi Gras was a perpetual party and Lyle was growing tired of celebrating. He felt like stretching out on the bed and going to sleep, but Charlotte was so eager to take part in the festivities that it wouldn't be fair to disappoint her on their last night.

He stepped back inside the suite, shutting the doors on the music, and glanced at his watch. Charlotte was still in the bathroom, putting the finishing touches on her makeup. If she didn't hurry, they'd be late for the costume party in the hotel banquet room. Lyle felt a little silly in black leotards, a black-and-white checkered tunic, and a hat with tassels and bells. But when he'd tried the harlequin outfit on this morning, Charlotte had convinced him that it was perfect for the occasion.

"Almost ready, honey?" Lyle sat down in the wing chair facing the fireplace and yawned. One more party and then he could go home and recover from this vacation.

The bathroom door opened and Charlotte stepped out. She was dressed in a powder-blue velvet dress decorated with lace and pearls. Tonight she had long, plump curls piled up on the top of her head. Since Charlotte's hair had been short when she'd gone in to put on her costume, she had to be wearing a wig. "Well? What do you think?" Charlotte raised a blue velvet mask to her eyes and twirled around. "Do I look the part?"

"You look gorgeous, honey." Lyle evaded the question. He wasn't sure who she was supposed to be, but guessed it was someone like Marie Antoinette.

"Let's go then." Charlotte headed for the door and Lyle stifled another yawn as he followed. Ten more hours until he could catch some sleep on the plane. He'd never guessed that a vacation could be so exhausting.

There were several people on the elevator, and Lyle nodded to another harlequin, two devils, and a woman in a dark red velvet dress that looked a lot like Charlotte's.

Charlotte frowned as she checked the other woman in the mirrored walls of the elevator and when her lips finally turned up in a smile, Lyle breathed a sigh of relief. Charlotte had decided that she looked better than the other woman.

The elevator descended slowly, and at every floor more people in costume got on. Lyle found himself holding his breath. The scent of mingled perfumes and colognes made him feel slightly dizzy.

As the elevator started down again, Lyle felt a hand in his pocket. About to yell that someone was stealing his wallet, he felt a burning pain just below his shoulder blades. He tried to turn to see what was jabbing him, but the elevator was so crowded he couldn't move. Then, as his vision began to cloud, he heard Charlotte gasp in pain, and then everything went pitch-black.

TWO

Ellen Wingate sighed as her clamoring first graders went through the lunch line. Macaroni and cheese with chocolate pudding for dessert. Chocolate always made Billy Zabinski hyper, which was fine if he could run off some of that energy during noon recess. But today the wind was gusting and it was below zero.

"Miss Wingate? Billy's playing around with my braids again!"

"Billy? I want you to sit here." Ellen caught Billy just as he was about to dunk Tina Halversen's long blond braids in his milk and moved him to another table.

"Are we gonna get out-thide today, Mith Wingate?" Tommy Barnes looked up from his plate and gave her a gap-toothed smile. Tommy was a dear child, freckle-faced with an unruly shock of bright red hair, and every time he lisped, he reminded Ellen of Ron Howard in *The Music Man.* Before she could answer, Billy Zabinski chimed in.

"Please, Miss Wingate? We've been real good all morning. Will you let us out?"

Ellen bit back her laughter. Billy made school sound like a prison and he did have a point. It was February in Minnesota, and for the second week running she'd had to amuse them after lunch. "I know you've been good, Billy, but it's much too cold. We'll have our recess in the classroom and I promise we'll do something extra special."

"We could play eraser tag," Colleen Murphy suggested.

"Perhaps." Ellen sighed. The last time they'd played eraser tag in the classroom, they'd tipped over a desk and Annie Benson had skinned her knee. It would be safer to read them a Dr. Seuss book, if Billy would shut up long enough to listen. "All right now, is everyone settled?"

Thirty-one heads nodded in unison and Ellen smiled. They were good kids, but a seven-hour school day was much too long without the regular breaks for recess. Actually, buttoning and snapping and zipping up thirty-one sets of winter clothes was a trial in itself. They waddled out onto the playground like little stuffed bundles for ten minutes, barely mobile until the bell rang and she had to go through the whole process again in reverse. The alternative was trying to have recess in the classroom without breaking either the furniture or their necks.

"Be good for Mrs. Heino now." Ellen turned to the lunchroom monitor, an elderly woman with a hearing problem. When Ellen first started at Garfield Elementary, she'd asked the principal whether Mrs. Heino's hearing loss had occurred before or after she'd taken the job as lunchroom monitor. But Mr. Eicht had no sense of humor, nor did the rest of his staff. Ellen wondered whether it had something to do with enduring the endless Minnesota winters year after year.

"Mrs. Heino?" Ellen raised her voice. "You can send Billy to get me in the lounge when everyone's through eating."

Mrs. Heino nodded and Ellen beat a hasty retreat. She had ten minutes, perhaps fifteen if Mary Christine Fanger dawdled over her food.

When the current year had opened, Ellen had been delighted to find that the first and the sixth grades had common lunch periods. That meant she'd see Rob Applegate in the teachers' lounge every day. Since he was the only male teacher, and single, and she was the only female teacher under forty, it seemed natural that eventually they'd get together.

Twenty-eight years old, Ellen hadn't been out on a date since her junior year in college, when her roommate's fiancé had buttonholed one of his friends to take her to their engagement party. Ellen's escort had danced with her dutifully, but the moment the party was over he'd dropped her off at her dorm and she'd never heard from him again. Men just didn't seem to be interested in tall, lanky women with glasses. Of course, she had plenty of men friends. She helped them write their term papers and study for their exams, but they'd never shown any signs of wanting a closer relationship.

Rob Applegate was different. A thirty-six-year-old bachelor who lived in an apartment over his mother's garage, he was as tall as she was, and almost as skinny. Alma Jacobson, who taught third grade and knew everything about everyone in Thief River Falls, said he didn't have a girlfriend, but that his mother was hoping he'd get married before she was too old to enjoy her grandchildren. And he seemed to like Ellen, always stopping by her room to ask how someone's younger brother or sister was doing.

One day over coffee in the teachers' lounge, Rob had mentioned that he didn't like to see women in slacks. Ellen had never worn them to school again. And when he'd said that his favorite color was aqua blue, she'd gone right out and bought an aqua-blue sweater even though she hated the color. She'd carried flowers to his mother when Mrs. Applegate had gone into the hospital for gallbladder surgery, the card signed by the whole staff so it wouldn't look obvious. And she'd roused herself out of bed to drive to the Lutheran Church every Sunday because his brother was the minister. She'd even volunteered to teach a Sunday school class, although the last thing she wanted was to face more children on the weekends. Not that any of it mattered, now.

On her long-anticipated date with Rob, they'd gone to see a movie at the only theater in Thief River Falls, a Saturday matinee. Ellen had thought it was rather good, a shoot-out between two rival gangs on the streets of New York, but Rob hadn't liked it at all. On the drive to a steak house out on the highway, he'd complained about its gratuitous violence, another example of the movie industry's lack of commitment to the younger generation.

Despite the fact that Rob drove slowly, obeying every traffic law and speed limit sign, they'd arrived at the restaurant early. The hostess had seated them in the bar and asked if they wanted a drink. Ellen said a glass of white wine would be nice, but Rob had ordered plain 7UP. Then he'd warned her that it wouldn't do for anyone in the community to see her drinking. She was a teacher, after all, and she should take her responsibility for molding young minds more seriously. She shouldn't get the idea that he disapproved, but he only drank at home, where no prying eyes could see him.

Though Ellen had kept her glass out of sight and there was no one else in the bar, Rob seemed to be terribly nervous. When the waitress had come to take them to their table, a lovely spot looking out over a snow-covered garden, Rob had insisted they move to a place in the center of the room. Windows could be drafty, he pointed out, and he didn't want to take any chances of catching a cold and having to miss work. Even though he always left detailed lesson plans, a substitute couldn't begin to teach his class as well as he could. They'd ordered a steak for her and chicken for him. Red meat was bad for the digestion and a man over thirty had to watch his cholesterol. No garlic bread either; he didn't believe in strong spices. Decaffeinated coffee, of course, since it was past six.

Ellen still wasn't willing to give up on the only bachelor she knew. As they ate, she attempted to make conversation. Had he seen the special on public television about ancient Rome? Rob didn't own a television set. He was firmly convinced that television had done more to corrupt the morals of the young than any other technological advance in their lifetime. Ellen scratched television off her list of possible topics and asked about his hobbies. There she struck pay dirt. It seemed Rob was an amateur photographer, specializing in local birds. Did she know that there were over seventeen varieties of finch in the three-mile area surrounding Thief River Falls? He'd recently acquired a very excellent telephoto lens, four hundred millimeters. And the first day he'd gone out with his motor-driven Nikon, he'd managed to capture the mating ritual of the North American crested grosbeak. He'd be delighted to show her his photographs after dinner.

Accepting, Ellen had spent the rest of the meal wondering whether being invited to a man's apartment to see his photos of North American crested grosbeaks was the same as being asked to view someone's etchings. She hadn't asked out loud. Rob had left a straight 15 percent tip and then they'd driven back to his apartment.

That was when the trouble had started. He'd asked her to duck down in the seat three blocks before they'd reached his mother's house. It didn't look good for a bachelor to bring a woman home at night; people might talk. Ellen had complied, what else could she do? He'd driven into the garage, shut the door behind them, and whispered for her to be quiet so his mother wouldn't find out she was there. And after they'd tiptoed up the stairs, he'd headed straight for the bottle of brandy hidden behind the sugar canister in his cupboard.

She'd seen his pictures, all of them, and learned much more than she'd ever wanted to know about birds. By then he'd finished the bottle of brandy. For a man who didn't drink in public, he certainly made up for it at home. The moment the bottle was empty, he'd grabbed her and kissed her. And then he'd passed out on the couch.

Furious, Ellen had grabbed her coat and walked the ten blocks to her own apartment, practically freezing in the skirt she'd worn to please him. Rob Applegate was a terrible stick-in-the-mud and a hypocrite to boot. He'd even had the nerve to come up to her after church the next morning to ask whether she'd had a good time.

As she headed down the hallway, Ellen caught sight of her reflection in the mirrored door of the multipurpose room. Wearing a new red pantsuit she'd ordered from the Penney's extra-tall catalog, she thought she looked much better than usual. Skirts always hung awkwardly on her boyish hips, and if she tucked her blouses in, only a padded brassiere gave her any bustline at all. This pantsuit's tunic masked her figure and her legs felt warm for the first time this winter.

Heading on down the corridor, Ellen frowned at the grimy handprints on the walls. They could do with a good scrubbing or even better, a bright, cheerful paint job. Everything outside was black-and-white, glaring white sheets of snow dotted with the bare black skeletons of trees. Children needed color in their lives and the school was decorated in dirty beige and anemic green. Red and blue stripes would be nice, or even a bright cheerful yellow. Billy Zabinski might be less of a problem if school offered a nice bright environment.

A bad draft whistled under the big glass doors that led to the playground, and Ellen shivered. The snow was blowing so hard she could barely see the pine trees at the far edge of the playground. If visibility grew severely limited, as predicted in the weather report, the buses might come early to take the children home. And if the wind kept on blowing through the night, they might just have a school closure in the morning. It would be nice to have a snow day, but in Minnesota the plows hit the roads the moment the snow started to fall and stayed out until it stopped. The whole system was very efficient. They'd had years to perfect it.

Ellen sighed. Three and a half hours to go. Tomorrow would be more of the same, and next week, and next month. This was her fourth year at Garfield Elementary and it already seemed like a lifetime.

Ellen loved the first two months of winter with its sparkling blanket of white snow. But when the mercury consistently dipped down below zero and every day tested her survival skills, she began to long for the spring that was still at least another four months away. By the end of January, she was sick to death of climbing into a parka and boots and heavy mittens just to empty the garbage, and of remembering to plug in the headbolt heater on her car every night so it would start in the morning.

Her first October in Minnesota, Ellen had taken the advice of her coworkers and gathered all the necessary survival gear. In addition to the ice scraper and snow brush she carried next to her on the passenger seat, there was a twenty-pound sack of kitty litter in her trunk to add ballast so she wouldn't get stuck in a snowdrift. There was also an empty three-pound coffee can containing a candle and a book of matches to provide life-sustaining heat and light in case her car broke down. And she'd put together a cache of candy bars and bottled water that lay frozen in a shopping bag in her trunk. An extra gallon of gasoline sloshed in its plastic container, along with a can of Instant Flat-Fix that probably wouldn't even work in subzero temperatures. Ready for the long Minnesota winter, she hated every moment of it.

Ellen stared out at the slide, a snow-covered hump that rose like a prehistoric beast out of a field of unbroken white, and wondered what would happen if she just pushed open the doors, ran across the playground, climbed into her car, and drove west to California or Nevada or Arizona, or anyplace warm and sunny and green.

"There you are!" Alma Jacobson ran down the hallway to intercept her, the sleeves on her gray sweater flapping. "Mr. Eicht's looking all over for you. You've got a long-distance call in the office and he said it was an emergency."

"Long distance?" Ellen frowned. "Did he say from where?"

"Las Vegas, Nevada. A Mr. Marc Davies. I'll take care of your class if they finish lunch before you're through."

"Thank you, Alma." Ellen realized that Alma was shifting from foot to foot, barely concealing her curiosity. "Marc Davies is my Uncle Lyle's partner."

"I hope there's nothing wrong." Alma looked genuinely concerned. "Take your time, Ellen. I'll herd them all into the multipurpose room and we'll sing "Froggie Went A'Courting." That should be good for at least ten minutes."

Ellen's heart was pounding as she hurried to the office. Why would Marc Davies call her? Uncle Lyle and Aunt Charlotte were her closest living relatives, but she hadn't seen them since her mother's funeral, ten years ago. Naturally, they exchanged Christmas cards and letters, but they'd never been close. She rounded the corner quickly and pushed open the office door. Mrs. Timmons, the school secretary, motioned her toward the principal's office. "Use Mr. Eicht's desk, Ellen. He said it's all right. Your call's on line two."

Ellen was surprised to find her hands were trembling as she picked up the receiver. They were trembling even more as she put it down, five minutes later. Mrs. Timmons took one look at her pale face when she emerged, and rushed her to a chair.

"Just sit right here, Ellen." Mrs. Timmons hurried off for a glass of water and watched anxiously as Ellen sipped. "Bad news, then?"

Ellen nodded. "I just found out that my aunt and uncle are dead."

An angular woman in her mid-fifties who was not given to any overt signs of affection, Mrs. Timmons patted Ellen's shoulder awkwardly. "Oh, dear! I'm so sorry, Ellen. Was it a car accident?"

"No." Ellen's voice was shaking slightly. "They went to Mardi Gras for their anniversary and they were attacked in a hotel elevator. The police think it was a mugging that got out of hand."

"I don't know what this world's coming to!" Mrs. Timmons sighed deeply. "It's gotten to the point where decent people can't even step out of their houses without taking their lives in their hands. Ellen, dear . . . you still look white as a sheet. Shall I call Mrs. Percy to come in and sub? I know she's home today."

Ellen was about to say that she could stick it out when she remembered that Mrs. Percy needed the work. A teacher's pension wasn't much to live on. "Good idea, Mrs. Timmons. Tell her my lesson plans are in the middle desk drawer, but she doesn't have to follow them if she'd rather do something else. Alma took my class down to the multipurpose room to sing."

"That's fine, dear. You just get your coat and run along. Alma can watch them until Mrs. Percy gets here."

In the teachers' lounge Ellen slipped into her coat, put her shoes into a carrying bag, and pulled on her moon boots for the walk to the parking lot. When she got to the car, she'd have to take off her moon boots, too bulky to drive in, and put her shoes back on.

The lounge was deserted. All the teachers were back in their classrooms and Ellen felt almost as if she were doing something illegal by leaving before the final bell had rung. She should be starting her reading class about now, printing new vocabulary words on the board for the Larks. Ellen had three reading groups, and despite their

euphemistic names, everyone in her class knew that the
Bluebirds were the fast group, the Robins were average,
and the Larks were slow. She was thinking about Billy
Zabinski as she let herself out the front door and walked
to her car. Mrs. Percy wouldn't have a speck of trouble
with him. She was his grandmother.

It was strange turning onto the highway at twelve-
thirty on a weekday. Ellen inched out carefully to pass
a Northern States Power truck and glanced in her
rearview mirror to make sure there was plenty of room
before she cut back into her own lane again. This would
be a very bad time to have an auto accident. She was still
a little dazed by the news.

Exactly seven minutes later, Ellen pulled into the car-
port at the Elmwood Apartments and got out to plug her
car into the socket on the post next to her parking place.
Without her electrical engine heater, the oil would
thicken and the water in her radiator would freeze in the
subzero temperature. The first time Ellen had used it,
she'd forgotten to pull the plug in the morning and
had trailed the extension cord down the highway, to
the amusement of everyone else on the road. By now the
whole process was part of her daily winter ritual, but she
still double-checked.

Ellen trudged up the stairs to her second-floor apartment and unlocked the door. Her familiar apartment
seemed suddenly strange to her, the wall hangings and
furniture and plants she'd chosen so carefully now
alien, as if she were viewing them through the eyes of a
stranger. There was a name for that phenomenon, the
opposite of déjà vu. She'd memorized it once for a psy-
chology class, but she couldn't remember it now.

In an effort to clear her head, Ellen walked down the
hallway to the guest room. She'd rented a two-bedroom

apartment so she'd have a place to work on her dolls, and the room was filled with her life-size creations. The hobby had taken hold when she was still in high school, something to keep her occupied while the prettier girls were going out on dates.

Her very first doll was propped up in a chair. She'd sewn nylon stockings together and stuffed them to make a doll big enough to wear one of her mother's old dresses. It wasn't a very professional job, but Ellen had kept it for sentimental reasons. Over the years, she'd made dolls out of any material she could find. One from an old patchwork quilt found in a thrift store reminded her of the illustration on the cover of her favorite children's book, L. Frank Baum's *Patchwork Girl of Oz*. Scattered all around her guest room were dolls made of velvet and silk and chintz. There was even one made of durable canvas that she'd propped up in the passenger seat as company on her long drive to Minnesota.

Ellen reached out to straighten a hat on her very best doll. Designed in a college art class at the University of Virginia, its molded plastic arms and legs could be locked into any position, much like department store mannequins. Its features were perfectly neutral, an inspiration prompted by studying her roommate's teddy bear. Teddy bears could look happy or sad, comical or serious, depending entirely on the viewer's perception.

She'd run out of flesh-tone dye one Saturday night, and rather than risk being late with her final project, Ellen had attempted to mix the dye herself from what was available on the workroom shelves. Mixing a flesh tone from basic colors was difficult, and she'd added a drop of this and a drop of that until she'd finally achieved a color that looked acceptable, despite the fact that it didn't exactly match the premixed color. She hadn't realized the result was anything out of the ordinary until she'd taken her project back to the dorm.

Her roommate, Ming Toi Lee, had gazed at it in awe. How had she ever achieved that lovely skin tone? She'd never seen a Chinese mannequin before and it was about time someone appealed to the Asian consumer. Jolette Washington, from the room next-door, had stuck her head in to see what all the fuss was about. Ellen had designed a black mannequin? How wonderful! Jolette's roommate, Toyo-San Kasawi, had turned to give Jolette a confused look. Ellen's mannequin was clearly Japanese.

Ellen's roommate had run out to get Mary Longbranch, a full-blooded Sioux, who'd sworn that it was American Indian. So they'd lugged it down to the lobby and invited in everyone they could think of to offer an opinion. Vietnamese, Russian, Hawaiian, African, plain old Caucasian, the list was endless. Everyone appropriated Ellen's doll for their own ethnic group.

Later that night, they'd discussed the possibilities. Everyone thought that Ellen should either sell her idea or go into business to manufacture it herself. Department stores everywhere would jump at the universal mannequin. Five years had passed, during which Ellen had been living as frugally as she could. She was still years short of enough capital to open a business, but that was her long-range goal.

The sense of unreality was still with her. Perhaps a drink would help. Ellen wandered into the kitchen and retrieved the half-full bottle of white wine she'd put in the refrigerator two weeks ago. Someone had told her that cheap wine didn't go bad as fast as the expensive kind, and less than five dollars for a bottle of Chablis was certainly cheap.

The wine tasted a little like vinegar, and Ellen poured it down the sink. Marc Davies had said the reading of the will would be held tomorrow. It wasn't critical that she be there in person even though the lawyer, Mr. Clayton Roberts, had said she was a beneficiary. Aunt Charlotte had always promised her the family china, which had belonged to her grandmother. The silverware, too, but how could she possibly afford to ship it out here? She really had no use for it, since she seldom entertained.

Ellen sighed as she peered at the field of blowing white snow outside her kitchenette window. Warm and sunny, Las Vegas offered palm trees and flowers and swimming pools. The prospect of flying out of this interminable winter was very enticing. It would be insane to even consider it, a total waste of money for a trip that wasn't the slightest bit necessary. Still, she had thirteen days' leave accumulated and this qualified as a family emergency. She had half a notion to take a week off work and go get her china in person.

"Well, Ellen. How does it feel to be a millionaire?"

"I'm not sure, Mr. Roberts . . . I mean, Clayton." Uncle Lyle's lawyer had told her to call him by his first name. "I think I'm still in shock."

"Understandable." Clayton took her by the arm and steered her out of his wood-paneled office. "What you need is a drink."

"But I hardly ever . . . all right." Ellen nodded quickly. She had been about to say that she wasn't in the habit of drinking in the middle of the workweek, but this wasn't exactly a normal week.

As Clayton pushed the elevator button, he turned to her. "I've got some work to finish here so Johnny Day's taking you to the Castle Casino for the show. Then we'll take you up the mountain to see your new home."

"Johnny Day?"

"That's right." Clayton's gold-rimmed aviator glasses slipped down slightly as he nodded. "He's your fourth-floor neighbor."

Ellen's knees were shaking slightly as she got into the elevator with Clayton. She glanced down at her sensible navy-blue dress with the white collar and cuffs and wished she was wearing something else. The other teachers would be green with envy when she told them she'd met the most famous singer in Vegas.

The elevator started to descend and Clayton turned to her. "Just relax and enjoy yourself, Ellen. Tomorrow we'll put our heads together and decide on the best way to move your things out here."

Ellen felt her head start to whirl. It was quite a shock to discover that she now owned a safe deposit box stuffed with Federal Treasury certificates plus her aunt and uncle's expensive condo on Mount Charleston, including what she'd expected to inherit, her aunt and uncle's silver and china.

"You're planning to move out here, aren't you, Ellen?"

"I'm not sure." Ellen's voice was tentative. "There aren't many jobs for teachers here, and I'm on a tenure track back in Minnesota."

"You don't have to teach, Ellen. Your certificates yield between seven and nine percent annually. If you continue to roll them over, you'll never have to worry about money again."

Ellen took a deep breath and tried to remember how much money she actually had. Any figure with more than four zeros seemed beyond comprehension.

"Mr. Roberts . . . I mean, Clayton . . . do you think I'd have enough money to open my own business?"

"I don't see why not. What did you have in mind?"

Ellen was almost breathless. "Mannequins. I'd like to manufacture them."

"Oh, yes. Charlotte had some pictures." Clayton frowned slightly. "You may have cash flow problems at first. It takes a large capital investment to open a manufacturing concern, and there's a sizable penalty if you cash in your certificates before the due date. My advice would be to secure another source of financial backing."

Ellen was about to ask him to be more specific when the elevator doors opened on a tall, dark-haired man pacing in the lobby. Ellen felt the color rush to her face as she recognized Johnny Day, even more handsome than on his record albums.

"You're right on time, Johnny." Clayton led Ellen over to be introduced. When Johnny reached for her hand and brought it up to his lips, Ellen thought she'd faint from sheer excitement. He was tall, well over six feet, and for the first time in her life, she felt delicate and feminine.

"I'm on in an hour, so we'd better hit the road." Johnny took her arm. "A bottle of bubbly's chilling at your table and I can join you for a glass if we hurry. Are you coming over, Clay?"

Clayton glanced at his watch. "I'll meet you there. Make sure Ellen has a good time. I'm trying to convince her to move out here and start her own mannequin business."

"So, Ellen . . . what do you think of Vegas?"

His speaking voice was exactly as she'd expected, deep and soft and incredibly sexy. Ellen tried to keep her mind on the conversation and ignore the way her legs were trembling as they moved toward the door. "I haven't really seen much of the city, except for the airport, of course." She was silent for a moment, trying to think of something intelligent to say. "The weather's wonderful, and everything's so nice and green. It's quite a change from the snowbanks of Minnesota."

"Hey, we've got snow on our mountain." Johnny flashed her a grin. "Just wait till you see the view from my bedroom window. It looks like one of those winter scenes they put on Christmas cards."

Ellen didn't dare meet his eyes. Was Johnny Day inviting her to his bedroom? Or was she jumping to a ridiculous conclusion? "It sounds beautiful. Is it very cold up there?"

Johnny nodded. "You bet! Forty degrees when I left his morning."

"That's even colder than Minnesota!" Ellen shivered slightly. "It was only twelve below when I got on the plane."

Johnny turned to her with a puzzled look and then he laughed. "No, Babe. It was forty *above* on the mountain. It never gets below zero here."

Ellen felt the color rush to her face and she was glad he was busy hailing the valet parker. Aunt Charlotte had written that the temperature was moderate. Johnny must think she was a real idiot.

Johnny handed over his ticket and smiled at her again. "So tell me about this mannequin business."

"There's not much to tell." Ellen stared up at him and wondered whether teeth that perfect could possibly be real. Her natural reticence evaporated as she began to describe her universal mannequin and her long-held dreams of marketing it to department stores.

"Sounds good to me," Johnny reflected when she had finished. "And Clay said you need a financial backer?"

Blushing, Ellen nodded. She knew she'd rattled on like an excited schoolgirl, but there was something about Johnny's intense brown eyes and friendly smile that invited her confidence.

"I could back you. I've got some loose cash to invest before Uncle Sam takes his cut. Think you'd be interested in having me for a partner?"

"I . . . uh . . . that sounds wonderful." Ellen felt her head start to whirl again. Compared to rural Minnesota, where it took people years to decide whether or not to repaint the barn, everything was happening much too fast.

"We could set up right here in Vegas and name it something catchy. Universal Mannequins is too much of a mouthful. How about Vegas Dolls?"

Ellen nodded. Vegas Dolls was a fine name for a business, especially if it summoned to mind the gorgeous showgirls who worked here.

"I'll look for a warehouse right away. Where do you want to work, in the warehouse or up on the mountain?"

Ellen took a deep breath. "Would there be room in the condo? I'm used to working at home."

"No problem, Babe. You've got the whole eighth floor and all you have to do is tell Paul Lindstrom how you want it remodeled. I've got some contacts so I'll set up the distribution network, but we'll have to move fast. The fifteenth's my deadline for reinvesting."

Ellen was too stunned to do more than nod. Without any effort on her part, her dream was turning into a reality.

"It's settled, then." Johnny leaned over to kiss her cheek. "You'll be too busy to go back and pack your things. Is there someone who could send them to you?"

"Alma Jacobson might. I gave her a key before I left. I'll call her tonight and ask."

They were walking out of the building now, and Ellen almost stumbled as she realized what she'd said. She'd just agreed to give up her teaching contract only months before she was eligible for tenure to move over two thousand miles across the country into a condo she'd never seen. And she was going into business with a man she'd met less than five minutes ago who also happened to be the singing idol she'd sighed over for the past ten years.

"Getting cold feet?" Johnny smiled down at her and Ellen shook her head.

"Not really. I only get cold feet in Minnesota. It's much warmer out here."

Johnny laughed and led her to his car, a white Ferrari convertible, so shiny that it looked brand-new. Ellen sighed in pure contentment as she slid into the bucket seat upholstered in immaculate, soft kid leather.

It was dusk and the huge neon signs blinked on and off as he drove down the strip. The people they passed looked slim in their summer clothes and Ellen felt almost weightless without her bulky parka and moon boots.

There was a smile on Ellen's face as Johnny turned into a circular driveway flanked by towering palm trees, and a huge casino with turrets and spires came into view. There were colored spotlights weaving their beams in patterns over the walls and the entrance was guarded by a moat and a drawbridge manned by footmen in gold livery. It was a scene straight out of a storybook: Miss Wingate in an expensive foreign car with her famous bachelor partner, pulling up in front of a castle. That would certainly make all thirty-one first graders at Garfield Elementary sit up and take notice!

THREE

February on Deer Creek Road
Fifty Minutes before 10:57 AM

Ellen frowned as she rummaged through her box of mannequin limbs. On days like this, when everything seemed to go wrong, she almost wished she'd never left Minnesota two years ago.

The morning had started off badly. Her thirty-cup pot was the old percolator type and only made good coffee if she filled it to capacity. It had been a parting gift from the Garfield Elementary faculty and Ellen was sure they'd chipped in their books of green stamps to get it. Perhaps they'd assumed opening a mannequin business meant she'd have plenty of employees. In any event, the coffee it made turned to tar before she could drink it all, and she'd finally geared up to go into town to buy a pot to use every day.

The saleslady had shown her the newest model, promising that all she had to do was put in the coffee and water, set the automatic timer, and she would have hot coffee. Ellen had set the timer for eight and gone to bed,

but when she'd come into the kitchen this morning
there was no coffee to greet her. Checking the instructions, she'd found that the digital timer had a red light
for PM and a green light for AM. Since the red light was
glowing, her coffee would brew automatically, but not
until eight in the evening.

Just as Ellen had switched the timer to manual, the
phone had rung. It was the Purple Giraffe in New York,
an exclusive chain of children's clothing stores, frantic
because their purchasing department had made an
error and they needed two dozen more mannequins by
the end of the week. Naturally, Ellen had promised to
deliver, and now she'd located twenty-four right arms but
no left arms to match. Since she molded the arms in
pairs and had never had an order for one-armed mannequins, they had to be somewhere.

Ellen stepped back to survey the boxes of limbs
stacked on her workroom shelves, all coded with numbers, the work of her business manager, Walker Browning. When he'd heard that Ellen was looking for a
business manager, Jack St. James had recommended his
black friend from Chicago for the job, and Ellen had
hired him sight unseen. Walker was extremely well
organized and he was also a whiz at finding new mar-
kets for Vegas Dolls. If Walker were here now, he'd go
straight to the proper box, but he was in Vegas picking
up supplies.

Deciding it would be a waste of time to look for the
arms herself, Ellen wandered back into her large sunny
kitchen. When she'd moved into the eighth-floor condo
two years ago, Ellen had mentioned that she didn't care
for the ultramodern black enameled cabinets that
showed every fingerprint and the gleaming white floors
that required constant cleaning. Moira Jonas, their

resident interior decorator, had offered her services and in less than a week, she'd faced the cabinets in oak and ordered an antique table and chairs to match. With lacy ferns hanging from wicker baskets, green and white gingham curtains, an array of copper pans and utensils mounted on the rack over the stove, and a braided rug on the new wooden floor, Ellen's kitchen had been transformed.

Then Moira had started on the rest of the condo, replacing Aunt Charlotte's stylish white leather furniture with comfortable overstuffed chairs and a couch and loveseat covered in patterned chintz. The black marble fireplace had been redone in aged brick. Matching chintz curtains now graced the floor-to-ceiling windows, and for her bedroom, Ellen had chosen a massive four-poster bed and a dresser set to match. An authentic nineteenth-century quilt in a Double Wedding Ring pattern covered the bed and Priscilla curtains hung at the windows. There was even a spool rocker in the corner to hold her patchwork doll, and a washstand complete with a blue bowl and pitcher.

The bathrooms had presented a problem. Moira had pointed out that in order to be authentic, they should look like privies, but had compromised with wood paneling and antique medicine cabinets. She'd found a claw-footed tub deep enough to accommodate Ellen's long legs and the shower was hidden behind wooden doors.

When it came to Ellen's workroom, Moira had consulted with Paul Lindstrom, the building architect. They'd knocked out the wall between Aunt Charlotte's sitting room and Uncle Lyle's office, converting it into a huge work space. Paul had installed rafters to give it the look of a farmhouse attic and the wooden floor was treated with several coats of polyurethane so it would be impervious to spilled dyes and chemicals. The high ceiling had been lowered in strategic spots to give the illusion of gables, and tall triangular windows gave Ellen the benefit of the spectacular view.

Ellen was just sitting down at her old-fashioned kitchen table when the phone rang again. It was Laureen Lewis from the first floor.

"Hi, Ellen. Do you have that recipe of your grandmother's handy? I tried it last night and had a terrible flop."

"What happened?" Ellen frowned. She knew she'd copied the recipe correctly.

"The caramels never set up. It turned out to be the most luscious chocolate frosting I've ever tasted, but that's not what I was after. It just doesn't work with a five-ounce can of Hershey's syrup."

"Hold on a sec." Ellen reached for the red loose-leaf cookbook on the shelf by the phone. Laureen was doing a chocolate program on her cooking show and had been very interested in Grandmother Wingate's recipes. Ellen flipped through the book until she came to the page with a smear of chocolate on the corner. She remembered making that smear as a child, helping Grandma Wingate make caramels for Christmas.

"Yes, it says five ounces. At least I think it's ounces. It actually looks more like a cent sign to me."

"That could be it!" Laureen sounded excited. "Does she have any other notations on the recipe?"

"Yes. At the top it says it's from Mrs. Friedrich, the Lutheran minister's mother. And Grandma wrote a note on the side. It says, 'Never serve to Bill Carr. False teeth.'"

"I love it." Laureen laughed. "Is there a date on the recipe?"

"No, but the one on the next page is for Mrs. Friedrich's

watermelon pickles and it's from the summer of forty-five."

"That's close enough. I'll call Hershey's in Pennsylvania and ask for an old price list. Thanks, Ellen. And I'll bring you some caramels this afternoon if they turn out right."

"That would be a real treat." Ellen's mouth was watering when she hung up the phone. She hadn't tasted Grandma Wingate's chocolate caramels in years and it was a sure bet she'd never make them. Grandma Wingate had been an excellent cook, and so had Ellen's mother, and both had looked cute in their ruffled aprons. Unfortunately, neither attribute had been passed on to Ellen. She'd learned to fry an egg and broil a piece of meat, but that was the extent of her talent in the kitchen. Everyone said that a man wanted a wife who was pretty and knew how to cook. She flunked on both scores. No wonder no one had ever wanted to marry her.

Forty-five Minutes before 10:57 AM

Laureen's stomach gave a protesting growl as she opened the refrigerator door. All this wonderful food inside and she couldn't eat any of it.

Harry Conners, her producer, had delivered an ultimatum when she'd shown up twenty pounds heavier after the Christmas holidays. If she didn't lose ten pounds by the end of next month, he'd have to replace her. Laureen had explained that there was no way to test a recipe unless she tasted it, but Harry wasn't one to listen to reason.

Naturally, Laureen had tried. She'd even gone on the newest fad diet, which promised miraculous results if she

ate only an unsalted rice wafer four times a day, washed
down by a vile-tasting concoction of food supplement
powder mixed with grapefruit juice. But three days after
she'd finished the recommended two-week stint, she'd
stepped on the scale and found she'd regained her lost
pounds and then some.

A package of thick-sliced bacon beckoned, and Laureen yearned for bacon and eggs for breakfast. She was
tired of being constantly hungry. Her stomach growled
at the most embarrassing times and all she could think
of was piles of creamy mashed potatoes awash with
savory brown gravy. Grace claimed that dieting was a
simple matter of balancing the calories consumed with
the amount the body burned up through exercise, but
of course that was easy for her to say. She was naturally
thin. And the daily exercises she'd recommended only
made Laureen hungrier.

As Laureen reached for the bacon, she had almost
managed to convince herself that her problem was
hereditary. One of Laureen's earliest memories involved
sitting on a bench in some kind of health club, waiting
for her mother to get out of a steam cabinet. She'd expected her mother to emerge thin and beautiful, but her
face had been as red as a lobster's and she'd been just as
plump as ever.

With a sigh of remorse, Laureen shoved the bacon in
the very back of the refrigerator. She'd have a small glass
of skim milk and a piece of diet toast with sugar-free
jam. And then she'd make her husband's breakfast, even
though he didn't deserve it.

Alan Lewis looked out his window and frowned despite the lovely scene, a glistening expanse of white snow

unbroken by human footprints. The pines in the grove loomed dark and tall, a frosting of snow on their branches and three bright blue mountain jays and a vivid red cardinal were pecking at the feeder Paul had designed. The whole picture was worthy of Currier and Ives, but Alan found it difficult to appreciate. Ever since Laureen had found out about Vanessa, his treatment had been colder than the icicles that hung from their balcony.

Alan flipped the lock on his office door and sat down at his father's desk. His office was his refuge, a replica of the one his father had maintained in the back room of his country hardware store. Moira Jonas had decorated the walls with antiques. There was an old red Flexible Flyer hung from the rafters over his head, along with assorted shovels and rakes and even a hand plow. Laureen thought the room looked cluttered, but Alan loved the sense of hands-on merchandising that was difficult to maintain in the modern world of computer-generated orders and automatic restocking. His father hadn't needed a computer to know what was on his shelves. Of course, his father hadn't owned fifty-three stores in six different states, either.

He pulled out the center drawer and felt in the back for the hidden compartment where a carton of unfiltered Camels was secreted away from Laureen's prying eyes. Opening a pack, he withdrew a cigarette, rolling it between his fingers almost reverently. As he touched the flame of his lighter to the tip of the cigarette, the intercom crackled into life.

"Alan? Do you want oat bran pancakes for breakfast? Or would you rather have egg substitutes and oat bran toast?"

Alan gave a guilty start and dropped the cigarette into

the ashtray. Laureen would confiscate his Camels if she knew they were here.

"Alan? Can you hear me?"

"I hear you, honey." Alan sighed deeply. The last thing he wanted was more oat bran. Ever since Laureen had read that it reduced serum cholesterol, she'd been sneaking it in everything she cooked. "I guess I'll have fake eggs and toast. But if you're working on something important, I can wait."

Laureen's voice was impatient. "Of course I'm working on something important. You know I'm doing the chocolate show next week."

"It's all right, honey. I'm not very hungry and I can always fix something later."

"Don't be ridiculous! I always cook for you when I'm home. Five minutes, and don't be late!"

The intercom crackled again and Alan was glad he couldn't see Laureen's expression. "Thanks, honey. I'll be there." Alan switched off the intercom and picked up his cigarette, coughing slightly as he inhaled. Laureen had been up late last night with the chocolate caramels, and her unaccustomed failure, coupled with the strain Vanessa had put on their marriage, had put her in a foul mood.

Alan leaned back and puffed on his forbidden Camel, wishing he could turn back the clock. Hal Knight had married two years ago and since then his wife, Vanessa, had gone after almost every man in the Deer Creek Condo complex. The moment Alan had recognized Vanessa's little game, he'd been very careful to give her a wide berth, even though she was younger than anyone in the building and probably lonely. He'd even begun to feel a little sorry for her, alone every day while Hal was off on his business trips.

Looking back on that day, a month earlier, Alan could

honestly say he hadn't suspected a thing. Vanessa had called to say her garbage disposal wasn't working right, so he'd grabbed his toolbox and headed right up to the third floor. When he found her waiting in a see-through pink negligee, Alan had thrown his previous caution to the winds. It had only happened a couple of times before Laureen had caught them, and Laureen wasn't the forgiving kind.

Almost time. Alan put out his cigarette and hurried to the attached bathroom to flush the evidence down the toilet. He brushed his teeth, used some mouthwash, and headed down the hallway to the kitchen to try to make peace with his wife.

Forty Minutes before 10:57 AM

Moira Jonas took a blue and gold caftan off the hanger and slipped it over her head, careful to avoid her reflection in the mirrored closet doors. Her newest outfit, decorated with ropes of shiny gold beads on a cobalt-blue background, had long sleeves and a high mandarin collar to hide the crepe that was beginning to show on her neck. She'd tried all the expensive creams and moisturizers, but nothing seemed to help, and Grace had noticed; she was sure of it. Of course Grace was much too kind to say anything critical, but she worked with gorgeous showgirls all day long and even though she insisted she loved Moira just the way she was, comparisons were inevitable.

Moira brushed her long red hair and pulled it up into a tight bun she'd been wearing lately. It hurt, but it smoothed out some of her wrinkles. Last night she'd casually broached the subject of a face-lift and Grace, ten years younger and blessed with skin as smooth and elastic as a baby's bottom, had been less than sympathetic. Didn't Moira realize that any surgery, no matter how minor, was dangerous? Subjecting yourself to elective cosmetic surgery just because you had a few character lines was totally insane.

As Moira walked through the bedroom, she stopped to study several swatches of material tacked to the wall. She'd vowed to decorate their unit by Christmas at the latest, but three rush jobs had come up and she'd put it off. What was the old adage about doctors' wives never getting the proper medical attention? Or dentists' wives having rotten teeth? Grace was probably sorry she'd fallen in love with an interior decorator since she was still living in a million-dollar condo with bare white walls.

"Damn . . . I mean, darn!" Moira ripped down the swatches and went to put on the coffee. Just as soon as she'd finished her breakfast, she'd make a final decision on the patterns and colors, drive into town to pick up materials, and start turning their condo into a showplace that would make Grace proud.

Thirty-five Minutes before 10:57 AM

Vanessa Knight sat on her pink satin bedspread and pouted. Today was her twenty-third birthday and her husband hadn't even bothered to say good morning. He was locked in his studio, working on that dumb comic strip of his, and he'd yelled at her when she'd knocked at the door. She wished she could drive into Vegas to have a birthday lunch with some of her friends, but Hal wouldn't let her go anywhere alone and he refused to take her along on his business trips since that silly incident with the bellhop. All the poor man had done was hold her arm a second too long when he'd helped her into the elevator, but Hal had been furious. He was insanely jealous when any man paid the slightest bit of attention to her.

She got off the bed with a flounce and the towel she was wearing slipped down to her waist. It was a pity there was no audience. Vanessa knew she had a dynamite body. When Hal had first seen her in the buff, he said that with her curly blond hair and vivid blue eyes, she looked exactly like a live version of Little Annie Fanny in the *Playboy* cartoon.

Vanessa walked over to the window and stared out at the snow-covered landscape. There was no one in sight except a curious squirrel, so she did a bump and grind just for the hell of it. Then she flipped off the towel and tossed it aside with a frown. This particular towel brought back memories, most of them unpleasant. It was royal blue with a pink satin border and it had cost Hal over a thousand dollars. Forty-nine dollars for the towel, twenty for the matching washcloth, and nine hundred and fifty-six dollars for Vanessa's public humiliation.

The saleslady at Heroldson's had been very impatient when Vanessa had been unable to make up her mind between royal blue and sunshine-yellow. She was an older, overweight woman with a blue rinse in her hair, the type who secretly envied Vanessa's beauty and made up for it by treating her with contempt. And when Vanessa had handed her the charge card to pay for the towel, the clerk had taken vicious delight in telling her that it was no longer valid for any purchase over fifty dollars.

Despite the long line, Vanessa had protested. That was ridiculous. She'd charged over fifty dollars just last week. She was Mrs. Hal Knight and her husband would be very angry when he heard about how Heroldson's had treated her.

The saleslady had smiled and said she didn't think Mr. Knight would be upset at all, since he'd called the store personally to place a limit on his account. Perhaps Mrs. Knight had been charging excessively?

Vanessa's face had turned red. She'd whipped out her MasterCard, but the saleslady had informed her that Heroldson's didn't accept any other credit cards. Vanessa would have to go up to the credit office on the fourth floor if she wanted to find out the details, but since the account was in Mr. Knight's name, he could monitor the charges in any manner he chose. And right now she was holding up the line. If she'd be so kind as to step aside?

Naturally, Vanessa had been furious. Her first instinct had been to drive right home to confront Hal. She'd been halfway across the parking lot when she'd remembered that a friend of hers worked in Heroldson's credit department. Turning around, she took the elevator up to the fourth floor.

Tricia had been only too happy to help. She'd told Vanessa that there were ways to get around the ceiling Hal had placed on his credit card. Since the limit applied to a single purchase, Vanessa could buy the towel on one charge slip and the washcloth on another. Tricia would write it up for her. And while she was at it, she'd be glad to help Vanessa find lots of other items under fifty dollars.

Naturally, they'd had a big fight when the charges had come in and now Vanessa was forced to ask Hal every time she needed anything, even a new toothbrush. She was right back where she'd been as a single girl—short of cash.

Vanessa knew everyone in the building suspected that she'd married Hal for his money, but she'd honestly loved him and thought that their marriage would work. Of course his money was the reason she was sticking it out, but it hadn't been the deciding factor.

When Vanessa was a child, her mother had told her that it was just as easy to fall in love with a rich man as a poor one. Money made everything easier. If her mother had married a rich man instead of the truck driver who'd deserted them before Vanessa was born, Vanessa could have grown up in a nice house with nice clothes and plenty of spending money. And she certainly wouldn't have been forced to drop out of school to take a job in a factory. She'd gotten out of the small Southern town eventually, but it had taken her three long years of punching a time clock and saving every penny to do it.

Things had started to look up the moment she'd rolled into Vegas. She'd bought herself some fake ID and landed a job as a change girl in a downtown casino, where she'd met the producer who had turned her into Vanessa Thomas, rising young starlet. Of course, it had been only one movie and she hadn't spoken any lines, but it had been a far cry from the plastic seat cover factory in Georgia.

And then she'd met Hal and fallen in love. He'd taken her out for dinner almost every night and sent her roses at least once a week. She hadn't guessed how wealthy he was, not then. Of course, she knew the places he took her were expensive, but lots of guys put fancy meals on their expense accounts.

Then, one night when her roommates weren't home, she'd invited Hal to her apartment for dinner. Afterward, she'd tried to seduce him and that was when she'd found out about his problem. Poor Hal had been so embarrassed that Vanessa's heart had gone out to him. She'd told him she loved him anyway, and Hal had said he was crazy about her, too. But there was no way he'd ever ask her to marry him. It wasn't fair to ask a healthy young woman to live without sex.

After Hal had left, Vanessa had settled down on the lumpy couch and done some hard thinking. She'd had a red-hot affair with the producer, but he'd treated her like an absolute nothing when they weren't under the covers. Hal was just the opposite. He said he couldn't make love to her, but he treated her just like a princess.

The next morning she'd told Hal she wanted to marry him anyway. The sex wasn't that important to her. She'd signed the papers he'd asked her to, and they'd gone off to a wedding chapel to make it legal. She hadn't found out Hal was rich until after it was all over.

Now, looking back on the whole thing, Vanessa knew she'd set herself up. She hadn't really believed that a good-looking, masculine man like Hal couldn't perform in bed. She'd simply thought that he just hadn't met the right woman yet. And she'd talked herself into believing that *she* was that woman.

Right after the wedding, she'd bought all kinds of books guaranteed to get results, and treated herself to lots of sexy negligees and kinky outfits. When the books and the clothes hadn't worked, she'd driven down to the strip and talked to a couple of hookers she knew. She'd tried every single thing anyone had suggested, but Hal had just gotten more anxious and uptight. So she'd moved into a separate bedroom and resigned herself to a celibate life. They would be loving roommates and that was fine with her.

In some ways, Vanessa was an old-fashioned girl. She'd taken her marriage vows seriously. She'd promised Hal she wouldn't sleep with anyone else, and she hadn't, not then. But Hal still got angry if he thought her dresses were too tight and someone whistled at her on the street. He stopped taking her to restaurants because he said the waiters leered at her. And he made her give up her acting classes because of a love scene, even though it was right there in the script.

Then he'd started to harass her about the other men in the building. Couldn't she see that Clayton was staring when she wore her pink bikini? She should wear a modest one-piece suit. And no more tennis in the mornings with Jayne and Paul. He was sure that Paul had gotten an eyeful when she'd bent over to lob the ball.

At first Vanessa had tried to please him. But one day last year, when he'd yelled at her about parading around in front of the man who came to repair the refrigerator, Vanessa had lost her temper. The refrigerator repairman was at least sixty years old and life was too short to put up with this kind of grief. She'd told Hal she wanted a divorce.

Hal had laughed and told her to talk to Clayton about that prenuptial agreement she'd signed. An honest lawyer, Clayton told her all the facts. She'd only get a small allowance if she divorced Hal, but she'd get half of everything Hal had if Hal was the one to divorce her.

Vanessa had set out to drive Hal straight to divorce court. First, she'd spent hours in town, shopping in all the expensive stores and picking out everything she'd ever wanted. But Hal had just cut off her credit. And he'd taken away the keys to her car so she was stuck up here on the mountain like some sort of prisoner.

When spending too much of Hal's money hadn't worked, she'd tried to play on his jealousy. Surely he'd divorce her if he knew she was sleeping with his friends.

Vanessa was a little ashamed of herself, but she'd set out to seduce them systematically, starting with Clayton. Ever since Darby had died of cancer, he'd been lonely and he'd jumped at the chance to take her to bed. Then there was Marc, who was always up for a pretty woman. And Johnny Day. But Hal hadn't reacted at all, even though she'd flaunted it.

Paul had been polite and friendly, but he hadn't seemed to understand what she wanted. Vanessa figured it was his Scandinavian background, so she'd finally given up and tried for Jack. He'd been impossible, too. One day, when she'd practically thrown herself at him, Jack had hugged her and told her that he was flattered. She was pretty and sexy and he didn't blame her for trying to drive Hal to divorce, but he wasn't about to play her game.

She'd picked Alan next, mostly because Hal liked Laureen. But sleeping with Alan hadn't worked, either. Hal had shouted at her and called her a tramp, but he hadn't filed any papers. There was only one man left, Walker Browning, but while Vanessa no longer had a Southern accent, she still had her Southern prejudices. There was no way she'd seduce a black man. At her wits' end, she'd figured that Moira was nice enough, and Hal might go crazy if she slept with a woman. So she'd spent the past two weeks cozying up to Moira, asking her advice on decorating and pretending to be very interested in learning about furniture arrangement and color schemes. Moira was flattered at all the attention, but Grace kept interrupting at just the wrong times.

Vanessa sighed as she tossed the towel into the hamper. Over a year old, its satin edges were already beginning to fray, just like her nerves. Something just had to happen to take Grace out of the picture for a couple of days so she'd have time to zero in for the kill.

Thirty Minutes before 10:57 AM

The phone on the fourth floor rang three times.

"Hello, this is Johnny. I can't answer the phone right now, but if you leave your name and number, I'll get back to you as soon as I can. Wait for the beep."

A woman's amplified voice filled the room. "Johnny? Are you there? This is Karleen and I'm sick of leaving messages on your damn machine! Are you avoiding me, or what?" There was the sound of a dial tone and a moment later, the machine clicked off. Less than two minutes later, the phone rang again. After the required three rings, Johnny Day's disembodied voice answered again.

This time the woman's tone was conciliatory. "Sorry, Johnny. I didn't mean to bitch, but I haven't heard from you in over a month and time's running out. I've got enough money, that's not it. But I need to know what you want me to do about our little problem. Please call me."

There was a dial tone and the machine clicked off. A moment later, it activated again and the tape began to rewind, making way for new incoming calls and erasing five weeks of messages that Johnny Day would never hear.

Twenty-five Minutes before 10:57 AM

Rachael stood in the exact center of Darby's sitting room, the best place in the fifth-floor condo to practice her Tai Chi. All the other rooms had the look of an exclu-

sive men's club with ceiling to floor bookcases, standing
floor lamps, and leather furniture. This sitting room had
been Darby's domain and she'd decorated it with pink
and white poof pillow couches and chairs, lightweight
and easy to shove back against the wall. When Rachael
had moved in, Clayton had offered Darby's sitting room
as hers to use as she wished. He seldom ventured inside
and Rachael presumed the room brought back painful
memories of his late wife's illness.

Dressed in one of her seven compulsory training uniforms, Rachael faced her reflection in the mirror over
the fireplace. Today's pajama-like outfit was green, a
color that would teach her serenity. She also had red
for courage, yellow for vitality, blue for patience, white
for purity, brown for modesty, and black for power and
determination. Rachael's dark curly hair was tucked up
in a green turban to match, and she looked a bit like an
oriental scrub nurse, except for her feet, which were
bare and getting colder by the minute. She'd turned
down the thermostat because her teacher claimed it was
healthier to practice forms in a cold room.

The expensive practice tape was playing something
that sounded like the soundtrack from *The Last Emperor.*
The music, guaranteed to focus concentration and clear
the mind of distracting influences, wasn't having its desired effect on Rachael this morning. All she could think
of was the Johnson case. She'd spent two arduous months
in preparation, but she knew Judge Ulrich would have to
be deaf, blind, and dumb to rule in favor of a slum land-
lord like her client.

Rachael exhaled and assumed the ready position.
She'd practiced four forms already and now she was
working on the fifth, something called *Stork Cools Its
Wings II.* As the music decreased in volume and her

teacher's voice announced the form, Rachael did her best to follow the complicated instructions. *The right foot steps to the side and takes the weight of the body, left toe touching for balance in front. Now the right elbow lifts to guard the throat while the left palm turns in to guard the hip, fingers pointing to the right.*

Rachael frowned and shifted from foot to foot. Did the left take the weight, or was it the right? Neither one seemed to work very well. This had all looked so easy when her teacher had demonstrated it in class last week. She was concentrating so hard on maintaining her balance that she didn't see Clayton as he came in.

"That's quite a sight, Rachael. You look like a drunken windmill."

Rachael turned to look at him, an action that turned out to be her undoing. Her feet got tangled and she would have fallen if Clayton hadn't wrapped his arms around her waist.

"Not fair, Clay," she protested. "I almost had it before you scared me."

"Sorry, Rachael." Clayton looked concerned. "I thought it was advisable to lend a hand before you fell flat on your face."

Rachael smiled up at him. After six months as his mistress, the sight of him still made her a little breathless, although Clayton wasn't really a handsome man. Of moderate height and weight, he had hazel eyes set just a little too close together and he tended to squint when he wasn't wearing his glasses. His light brown hair was streaked with silver at the temples and rather than lend him a distinguished air, it only served to emphasize the lines in his face. Clayton was far from the Adonis that Rachael had pictured in her dreams, but there was something about him, something she couldn't identify, that made her knees turn weak every time she thought of making love with him.

Rachael pressed her body back against his and wiggled a little, knowing precisely what effect it would have. "You shouldn't make fun of me, Clay. My teacher says that Tai Chi will help me get in touch with my body."

"I wasn't aware you had a problem in that area." Clayton's voice took on the slightly husky tone that Rachael had come to recognize. She loosened the belt on her uniform and guided his hand to her breast. When she'd first come to work in his law firm, he'd been all business. It had taken a full three months before he'd noticed that his new junior lawyer was also an attractive woman.

Clayton gulped as her fingers found the zipper of his pants. "Are you through with your karate for today?"

"It's Tai Chi, not karate, and I've done all I'm going to do for now. Just let me slip out of this and we can test what I learned about agility and balance."

Clayton's breath caught in his throat as Rachael shrugged out of her pajama-like outfit. Barely over five feet tall, her body was compact and utterly feminine. Her skin was darker than his even though she never used the tanning booth up at the spa, a phenomenon she'd attributed to her mixed-blood ancestry. Her father had been a mulatto laborer, and her mother an underaged daughter of a Spanish diplomat. Rachael had been given up for adoption the night of her birth, and the identity of Rachael's birth parents had been kept in strict confidence by the adoption agency. It was one of the reasons Rachael had decided to become a lawyer. Her first court appearance had been on her own behalf and the judge had granted her access to the adoption records.

"Come on, Rachael." Clayton reached out to grab her hands. "Let's go back to bed."

"What's wrong with right here? The rug's nice and soft."

"But, Rachael . . . I don't think I could be entirely comfortable here."

Rachael saw the lines of distress deepen in his face. It was definitely time to exorcise some ghosts.

"Don't be silly, Clay. I promise to do something that'll take your mind off everything except me."

She put her lips to his ear and whispered exactly what she planned to do. Clayton's face turned red and he grinned self-consciously. "That sounds wonderful, but shouldn't we close the drapes first?"

"On the fifth floor?" Rachael laughed. "Come on, Clay, loosen up."

Clayton hesitated. Then Rachael's fingers reached their goal and his reticence vanished completely.

Twenty Minutes before 10:57 AM

Jack St. James took the breakfast tray from the nurse and set it back down on the counter. "Never mind, Miss Woodard. I'll take her tray in this morning."

He didn't miss the nurse's frown as he filled a silver carafe with coffee and set it on the tray. The doctor had limited Betty's caffeine intake, but she loved coffee and it certainly couldn't do her much harm at this stage. She had so few pleasures left that it seemed cruel to deprive her of her morning coffee.

"Is that decaffeinated, Mr. St. James?"

"No." Jack straightened up to his full five and a half feet and neatly faced down Betty's nurse. This was quite a feat since Margaret Woodard was almost six feet tall and outweighed him by at least fifty pounds. A small man, slightly though powerfully built, Jack had learned the trick of intimidation early in life. All it took was an authoritative tone and an unwavering gaze.

"Since you're taking the tray, I'll come in to bathe her later."

He gave a smile of satisfaction as Margaret turned on her heel and headed back to her bedroom. It was nice to know he hadn't lost his touch, not that the skill of facing people down was needed very often at Deer Creek Condos. It had come in handy when the telephone installer had claimed it wasn't possible to run an extension of everyone's line to a console up at the spa. And it had worked admirably the few times that cars filled with teenagers from Vegas had turned into their driveway to drink beer and enjoy the private view.

Jack reached for the jar of honey butter and put it next to the croissants on the tray. Margaret claimed that Betty should watch her cholesterol, even though the doctor hadn't mentioned it. Since Margaret was on a low-fat diet, Jack suspected she just didn't want to cook two menus. Betty ate little enough as it was and Jack wanted her to enjoy her food. It was one of the reasons he came up to Betty's unit for breakfast every morning. It was no fun eating alone and he'd noticed that Betty's appetite increased when she had visitors. She seemed to enjoy the time he spent with her and Jack enjoyed it, too. Unlike the other women he knew, Betty didn't make any demands on him, and, even more important, he could tell her all about his job as security chief without worrying that his confidences would be repeated.

A couple of months ago, Jack had run a cable from the closed-circuit monitors in his security office to Betty's bedroom television set so he could keep his eye on the building while he was visiting her. He hadn't told anyone about the extra cable, and now he was glad he hadn't, since Betty often watched what the other tenants were doing even when he wasn't with her. Jack supposed it was an invasion of privacy, but he didn't see how it could possibly do any harm. He'd told Betty that the closed-circuit channels were secret; she shouldn't watch them when anyone else was there. And since Betty thought the glimpses she got into the other tenants' lives were movies, no one would be the wiser if she talked about them.

Jack smoothed his close-cropped sandy hair and pinned on the name tag he'd ordered a month ago. It was white plastic and it said "JACK" in large black letters. Betty knew him, but she had trouble remembering his name. Whenever that happened, she cried in frustration. His name tag solved the problem.

He carried the tray into Betty's room, shutting the door behind him. The big master bedroom had been especially designed to meet Betty's needs. There was a huge television set on the wall opposite the bed and a rack of DVDs was within Betty's reach. The DVD player/recorder sat on the bedside table so Betty could record or watch any movie she wished and a built-in bookcase next to the bed was filled with Betty's favorite things.

In bits and pieces over the past two years, Jack had acquired the stories behind Betty's mementos. There was a collection of shells she'd gathered in the Bahamas, several pieces of ebony sculpture she'd brought back from Africa, a hand-thrown clay pot she'd fallen in love with in Guatemala and a Royal Dalton tea service she'd shipped back from England. Clearly, Betty had come from a wealthy family, but Margaret had told him that she'd been hired by the law firm that paid her salary. She knew nothing personal about Betty; only the medical history in the doctor's report. No one in the building had any additional information, not even Marc, who'd purchased the land on Deer Creek Road from the lawyers who handled Betty's trust.

Ten years younger than Jack, Betty was thirty-four. That meant her parents would be in their fifties or sixties if they were living. Since Betty had no visitors in addition to the residents of the building and received no mail, Jack assumed she had no living relatives.

By nature curious, Jack had gone straight to the source. Betty's life was an unsolved puzzle and Jack hated loose ends. All she could tell him was that she had no family. Of course it didn't really matter, now that everyone in the building had adopted her as one of their own.

Betty was sitting up in bed, watching television. She was dressed in the green silk kimono that Clayton and Rachael had brought her from Japan and her light brown hair was tied back with a matching ribbon. She looked lovely and completely normal. There were no physical signs of the debilitating disease.

Jack set the tray on the table by the bed and leaned over to kiss her. Her cheek was a little too warm and he made a mental note to ask the nurse to check her temperature. "You look pretty this morning, Betty."

"Thank you." Glancing at his name tag, Betty flashed a big smile. "Happy to see you, Jack."

"I'm happy to see you, too. What are you watching?"

"Answers." Betty nodded. "I'm watching answers, Jack."

For a moment Jack was puzzled. Then he noticed that the television was turned to a quiz show. Questions and answers. Everything Betty said made sense if he thought about it from her point of view.

"Drink?" Betty looked hopeful as he poured two cups of coffee from the silver carafe. "Brown is better than green."

Jack grinned. "I know it is, Betty. And this is coffee. Real coffee, not that awful herbal tea."

Betty nodded and took a sip. Then she drained her cup and held it out for more. "Caffeine is contraindicated in cases of hypertension."

"What was that?" Jack stared at her in shock.

"I . . . I forget." Betty looked confused. "Shotgunning again, Jack."

Jack nodded. He knew exactly what Betty meant. Sometimes her words came out all in a rush, like the pellets in a shotgun shell. At those times she was amazingly fluent. On other occasions, when she reflected first, the words got short-circuited somehow.

"Go out today, Jack? Or is it ice?"

"It's cold today, Betty, but maybe tomorrow." Jack caught the disappointment on her face and quickly changed the subject. "Look at this. Croissants and honey butter. Shall I fix one for you?"

"No, please." Betty nodded and Jack began to butter the flaky pastry. At first he'd been thoroughly disconcerted when Betty said no and nodded yes. Then he'd realized that her body language was much more accurate than her words.

Betty took the croissant he offered and nibbled at it daintily. "Will the cowgirl come?"

Jack nodded. Jayne dropped by every morning. He'd have to call her and tell her to wear a name tag.

"She comes after breakfast, Jack?"

"That's right. Jayne'll be here after breakfast."

"Jayne." Betty repeated the name. "My in-between name is Jayne."

"Your middle name is Jayne? I didn't know that." Jack smiled at her. The doctor's report had listed her name as Betty Matteo with no middle name. Another piece of the puzzle.

"Call me B. J. The J for Jayne and the B for . . . what's my front name, Jack?"

"It's Betty." Jack turned away slightly to hide the moisture in his eyes. At times like this, he almost wished he wouldn't be around when Betty's illness took its unrelenting course and all the name tags in the world wouldn't help.

Fifteen Minutes before 10:57 AM

Marc Davies rolled out of bed, pulled on a red silk dressing gown with an elaborate *MD* embroidered over the pocket and hurried to open the blackout drapes that enabled him to sleep late after a night on the town. The wind was whipping up gusts of snow that rattled against the pane, creating the snare drum sound that had roused him after only three hours of sleep.

As he surveyed the scene, a smile replaced the frown on Marc's face. He ran his fingers through his curly dark hair and sighed in satisfaction. The sky was a mottled gunmetal gray and the wind was rising fast. Foul weather on the mountain was a great excuse to stay home most of the day.

Marc took time to pull on a pair of fur-lined slippers before punching out his office number on the bedroom phone. Waiting for his secretary to answer, he grabbed the aspirin bottle on the table by the bed and swallowed three.

"It's me, Tam. Cancel my noon meeting, will you? Tell Nicholson I'm sorry, but it can't be helped. There's a winter storm warning and I'm stuck up here on the mountain."

Marc grinned as Tammy asked the predictable question. "Hell, no. I'll be in later this afternoon. One other thing, call the electrician and ask if he finished those junction boxes at the Sandhill development. I need them in today."

Marc was halfway across the room before he remembered. He picked up the phone again and pressed the redial button. "Tam? If I don't get in before you leave, meet me at the Golden Steer at seven. I want you to soften up a prospective buyer for Johnny Day's unit. Name's Roy Perkins."

Just as soon as he'd hung up, Marc turned on his answer phone, started the coffee, and headed for the shower. He still felt a little groggy from lack of sleep, and last night had been a disaster. He'd entertained Sam Webber, the man who owned the land he needed for his next housing development, flying him in from Dallas first-class and picking him up at the airport in a limo. The little man in the ridiculous ten-gallon hat had seemed to enjoy himself during the dinner, but when Marc offered the services of a genuine showgirl for the rest of the evening, Sam had been less than interested. He told Marc he'd ordered a book on blackjack from a television ad, and he really wanted to try out its "sure-fire" system.

Marc had paid off the showgirl and sent her home in a cab. Whatever the pint-size Texan wanted was fine with him. So they'd started at one end of the strip and worked their way to the other, Marc watching while Sam swilled cheap booze, played impossible hunches, and hopped from table to table in casino after casino. The little Texan had been up five hundred dollars when they'd left for the airport at seven in the morning, despite the fact that he'd done everything wrong. As Sam had gone up the ramp to board, he'd thanked Marc effusively for the night on the town. He'd said that it was the best fun he'd had in years and he was real sorry, but he'd changed his mind about selling his land. He'd decided to hang on to it for a while, to see if it would go up in value.

Marc stepped into the giant shower stall and sighed as the hot water chased away the stiffness in his shoulders. Watching someone gamble was hard work. You sat or stood in one place for hours and the tension was just as bad as it would be in any high-powered business deal. And even though he'd managed to slip Sam enough chips to make him think he'd won, Marc had ended up with nothing but a giant headache.

He studied his image in the steamy mirror as he toweled dry. Pretty good for a guy approaching his fortieth birthday, lean and tall with what Tammy called devil eyes. They were a shade between dark green and blue, and his black eyebrows almost met in the center.

Marc tossed the towel in the hamper and dressed in a dark green velvet monogrammed sweatsuit. All his clothes were designer originals, carefully crafted to complement his dark complexion and accentuate his height. Several women had compared him to the tall, dark stranger who lived in their fantasies and he encouraged that image by living the life of a freewheeling bachelor. He enjoyed women, lots of them, as frequently as he could manage, but none had managed to lure him into one of Vegas's sixteen deluxe wedding chapels.

He went into the kitchen and poured himself a cup of coffee, black and strong. On his way out the door, he grabbed a couple of raspberry Danish from the bag on the counter and headed for his game room.

Marc flicked the wall switch and grinned as his pinball machines came to life. Moira had carpeted the room in midnight blue; the walls and ceiling as well. With recessed lighting, it resembled a dark cavern. Each pinball machine was set back in its own alcove. There were twelve in all, enough variety so he'd never be bored.

He hesitated in front of "Haunted House." It was a three-level wonder of mechanical precision, but it played a theme song. Paul Lindstrom had told him the piece was *Toccata and Fugue in D minor* by one of those composers that started with a *B,* Bach or Beethoven or Brahms, he could never remember which. It didn't really matter who'd written it. It wasn't the sort of music he wanted to hear first thing in the morning.

The second alcove contained a great little machine he'd played as a boy, and it was every bit as much fun now. "All-Star Baseball" took the player through a whole nine-inning game, with extra balls if you got over a five hundred average. It played "Take Me Out to the Ballgame," a melody that reminded him of hot dogs slathered with yellow mustard, and warm beer in waxed cups. Laureen swore that hot dogs prepared in a microwave tasted just like ballpark franks, but she was dead wrong. Nothing could compare with the real thing.

He hesitated for a moment and then moved on. All-Star Baseball brought back painful memories of his brief moment in the limelight. He could still hear the roar of the crowd when he'd nailed someone stealing second, feel the slaps on the back in the locker room when he'd pitched a no-hitter, relive his elation when he'd faced a power hitter with a full count and caught him looking. Even after almost twenty years, Marc still felt incomplete without a ball in one hand and a glove in the other. Most days he could handle it, but not after losing out on his land deal to a man like Sam Webber.

Marc pulled out a padded stool and sat down in front of "Front Line Invasion," a war game. There were three sets of flippers and two balls, one from either side, that were put in play simultaneously. It took six hits to knock out the big cannons at the rear and four hits to take out a sniper. Every time a ball missed its target and hit the surrounding bumper, the player lost points. The first time Tammy had played, she'd ended up with a minus score; her whole army was dead, and she'd lost the war. When the machine had played "Taps" and the rows of caskets had lit up, Tammy had gotten so bent out of shape that he'd ended up spending the rest of the evening coddling her. Of course he'd known that her father had been killed in 'Nam, but he'd never expected her to get so emotional about a game.

There was a pile of slugs in a bowl on top of the machine and Marc dropped one in the coin slot. Then he pulled back the twin plungers to release two balls in tandem. There was no way he'd ever understand how today's kids could be so fascinated by video games. With their synthesized voices and computerized graphics, they were about as boring as watching Saturday morning cartoons. Pinball machines were real. The player controlled the action completely and anything could happen. You could even cheat the odds a little by tilting the machine if you knew just how far to go. It was no wonder that kids today sat back and waited instead of getting out there and making their own luck.

Ten Minutes before 10:57 AM

Jayne Peters was doing her best to be cheerful, even though she'd been depressed ever since the divorce papers had been filed. Life just wasn't the same without Paul and how could she even begin to start a new life when she was surrounded by so many traces of the old?

Paul had designed every piece of furniture in their apartment. There was the built-in kitchen booth in the sunniest corner overlooking the ravine. And the bed with separate, cleverly shaded lamps built into the bookshelf headboard so they wouldn't keep each other awake with late-night reading. And the wall-mounted speakers in every room so she could listen to her favorite country-western music. And the rough pine paneling in her studio with cattle brands burned into the wood to give her the feel of a western ranch. And the huge wagon-wheel table he'd designed to hold her music. Perhaps she should have been the one to move out, but she hadn't wanted to give up the fabulous sound studio.

Balancing a piece of toast on top of a cup of coffee, Jayne opened the studio door with the other hand and headed for her piano. Years of coffee rings marred the finish already, along with other stains she couldn't begin to identify. Red wine perhaps, or the imported cocoa Paul had made for her when she had to work late to meet a deadline. Now that she was a successful songwriter, she ought to think about buying a nice new piano, but she liked the sound of the old, battered Kimball that had been in her family for forty-odd years. She'd written her first hit on that piano, a little piece of fluff called "Scattered Roses" that sold when she was still in high school.

The toast was cold and Jayne gave up on it after one bite. Always a compulsive eater, she'd lost her appetite right along with her husband, and now she existed predominantly on crackers and cheese. No time was required to fix crackers and cheese. She just got out the jar of Cheese Whiz and smeared it on a couple of saltines. It was true that she was a bit tired of eating the same thing, meal after meal, but she couldn't bear the thought of preparing a gourmet meal and eating it alone.

She frowned as she thought of Paul. He'd stopped trying to work things out and she couldn't blame him, since she'd been too stubborn to take his calls or even agree to see him. Now she was sorry she'd been so pigheaded, but it was too late to try to mend fences. Their divorce would be final in less than two months and her twelve years of being Mrs. Paul Lindstrom would be over.

Jayne blinked back tears as she picked out the melody of the song she was writing. It didn't sound as good as it had last night, but she'd promised to have it finished by the end of the week. Barbie Rawlins needed time to rehearse before she recorded it.

Her notebook lay open on the piano bench, and Jayne frowned as she faced the blank page. The melody was easy, but lyrics were much tougher going. It was lucky that most country-western songs fell into two categories: love found or love lost. Since Barbie's last song had been about losing a lover, this one should be about falling in love. It would be difficult to get into that mind-set since she was still grieving over losing her own lover.

Nothing was going right lately, including her work. The only good thing she'd written since Paul had left was a song about how much she missed him. Johnny Day had recorded it before leaving for Italy, but Paul would have no reason to tune in to a country-western station and no interest in a song by his soon-to-be ex. As hard as it would be, she had to face the fact that Paul was completely gone from her life.

Jayne got up to pace the floor. The words to the chorus were hovering somewhere just out of reach, something to do with a merry-go-round. "Buy me a ticket on the merry-go-round of love?" Jayne spoke the line aloud to check the meter. Too many syllables. What was another name for *merry-go-round*?

"*Carousel!* The carousel of love!" Jayne was so excited, she almost tripped in the headlong rush to get back to her notebook. "Carousel of Love" was a great song title. It would knock Barbie's socks off.

Jayne scribbled furiously for a moment. She had to get it all down before she forgot it. Then she picked out the melody from a standing position and started to sing.

> *It's the best ride in town and I wanna take it*
> *And this time I promise I'm not gonna fake it*
> *Mister, please buy me a ticket,*
> *A ticket to the carousel of love.*

She sang it once more to be absolutely sure, and then she started to work on the verses. The first three came easily, standard fare that she could write in her sleep, but the last one was tricky. Sometimes it helped to sing it all the way through, even though some words were missing.

> *It's the best ride in town and I wanna take it*
> *And this time I promise I'm not gonna fake it*
> *Mister, please buy me a ticket,*
> *A ticket to the carousel of love.*
> *I'll trade in all my lonely nights*
> *The tears I cried when I turned out the lights*
> *The smiles I smiled to try to hide*

If that'll buy me just one little ride.
Why am I standing down here on the ground
While the man I love rides around and around?
Mister, please buy me a ticket,
A ticket to the carousel of love.
I'll swap my plans to that singular dream
A lady alone with her get-rich scheme
'Cause all I need is a blankety-blank
And a ride on the carousel of love.

Paul had been a genius for coming up with the perfect rhyme, but Paul was gone and if she started thinking about him, she'd never finish. Jayne picked up the telephone and punched out Ellen's number. She wasn't socializing much either since she'd broken off with Johnny. As the only women in the building who went to bed alone, they really ought to stick together.

Five Minutes before 10:57 AM

Ellen ran for the phone as it rang, hoping it was Walker. She still hadn't located those mannequin arms. But it was Jayne.

"You got to help me, Ellen. I'm writing this song and I'm stuck between a rock and a hard place. What rhymes with *love*?"

Ellen grinned. Jayne was always asking for rhyming words. "How about *above,* or *turtledove,* or even *shove.*"

"Nope. This one's for Barbie Rawlins and she pronounces *love* like the museum in Paris."

Ellen frowned. "You mean the Louvre?"

"That's it. So what rhymes?"

"I'm not sure." Ellen thought for a moment. "How about *groove.*"

There was a slight pause while Jayne thought it over. "Close, but still not exactly right. Barbie's from North Carolina and there's no way I can match her accent. Maybe I should just ditch *love* and go with *affection.*"

Ellen chuckled. "That sounds like a good idea in more ways than one. A rhyme for *affection* would be easy. There's *direction,* or *protection,* or . . ."

"Erection?" Jayne let out a whoop of laughter. "Thanks, but I think I'd better hang on with *love.* You want to take a break and beat me in a game of tennis?"

"Not right now, Jayne. I'm stuck filling an emergency order and Walker's in town at the warehouse."

Jayne took on a serious tone. "Come on, Ellen, honey. We haven't played for a coon's age, and I need something physical to take my mind off Paul. Besides, it's not good for you to work all the time."

"I know, but I've got a rush order. And . . ."

"You've got all day to fill it," Jayne broke in before Ellen could think of another excuse. "I figured out that you're avoiding Vanessa, but you're going to have to face her sooner or later, living in the same building and all. You might as well take the bull by the horns."

"Well . . . all right. Is eleven-thirty good for you?"

"It's perfect. Keep thinking about what rhymes with *love,* will you?"

There was a thoughtful expression on Ellen's face as she hung up. It was true that she'd been avoiding Vanessa ever since catching her with Johnny, but she hadn't realized that anyone had noticed, especially since she'd been too embarrassed to tell anyone about that night. No one, not even Johnny himself, knew the real reason why she'd bought out his half of Vegas Dolls and hired Walker to

take his place. Falling for Johnny had been a terrible
mistake. He'd never promised her anything and she'd
been a fool to assume that he felt the same way she did.
At least she wouldn't make that mistake again.

The phone rang again and Ellen grabbed it, but it was
only a salesman peddling burial plots. Ellen told him she
didn't plan to die and slammed down the receiver. With
all these distractions, she'd never get anything done.
Ellen pulled out the drawer on her workbench to get a
list of her suppliers. It was ten fifty-seven and Walker
ought to be at the art supply store by now. She had just
begun to dial the number when the phone went dead.
Then she heard a noise like a freight train outside the
window and the whole building started to shake.

Ellen screamed as the banks of fluorescent lights flickered and went out. There was no time to run and no
place to go if there had been. Boxes of mannequin parts
flew from the shelves and broke open to reveal the arms
she'd been missing, but Ellen was too busy scrambling
for cover to notice. Then her huge oak workbench began
to tip and a crushing weight pushed her down.

FOUR

Jayne was the first one to reach the garage, the place they'd agreed to meet in the event of a building emergency. Since Jack had told them not to use the elevator in an emergency, she'd run down nine flights of stairs and she was breathing hard. They were to wait in an orderly fashion for the others to assemble, then, as a group, check on missing residents and assess the damage.

She paced, anxiously waiting for someone else to join her. She'd already broken one of Jack's rules by taking the time to stop off at Betty's floor, where Margaret Woodard had answered the door with a broom in her hand. A picture frame had fallen off the wall, shattering the glass, but that was the only casualty. According to the nurse, Betty had been watching television and hadn't even noticed the tremor. Jayne was glad they were both all right, even though she'd never liked Margaret Woodard. Perhaps it was her starched efficiency or the fact that she never smiled. Even though Jayne had stopped by to see Betty every day for the past two years, she still called the nurse Miss Woodard.

Just as Jayne was wondering what she should do, the

elevator doors opened and Alan Lewis stepped off. She was so surprised she said the first thing that popped into her head. "If Jack were here, you'd be in deep trouble."

"You mean because I used the elevator?" Alan grinned as Jayne nodded. "It's okay, Janie. I checked it out and the backup system's okay. Aren't you even going to ask me if I'm all right?"

"You look okay to me. How about Laureen?"

"She's fine. That big spice rack over the stove fell down and I left her cleaning up basil and oregano and God knows what else. How about you?"

"My coffee cup smashed and the studio's a mess, but nothing else broke."

The door to the stairwell opened and Marc came in, followed by Hal and Vanessa, who was clinging uncharacteristically to her husband's arm. It was obvious that Vanessa had been in the process of applying her morning makeup. She had blue eye shadow on her left eyelid with none on her right.

"Any damage?" Hal asked.

Jayne shook her head. "Nothing to write home about. Your place?"

"Vanessa's makeup mirror fell off the wall. That's major damage, according to her."

"How can you joke at a time like this?" Vanessa pulled away from him. "I could have been killed!"

Hal began to grin as he considered that possibility and Alan jumped in before he could reply. "How about your pinball machines, Marc?"

"They're okay. The one I was playing flashed a tilt, so the building must have taken a real jolt. Does everyone have power?"

Alan nodded. "We're running off the emergency generator. Did you go out to check the building?"

"That was the first thing I did. There's minor damage to one of the retaining walls, but that's easy to fix. Our phone lines are dead, though. And our cell phones won't work. I tried both of mine."

The door to the stairwell opened and Clayton and Rachael rushed in. Moira was right behind them, a smile on her face. "None of us have any damage, but wait till Grace hears! She says nothing exciting ever happens up here on the mountain. Did anyone see what happened?"

"Laureen did," reported Alan. "She was looking out the kitchen window and saw a solid wall of snow slide down the mountain."

Clayton nodded. "An avalanche, then. Or an earthquake that precipitated an avalanche. Rachael and I were . . . well, we weren't looking out the window, but we both heard a loud, rumbling sound."

"And then the earth moved, didn't it, Clay?"

Vanessa's eyebrows raised slightly, but then she decided to let Rachael's comment pass. Surely it couldn't mean what she thought it meant. "I bet they blew up a bomb at the Nevada test site."

Hal assumed his long-suffering look. "The Nevada test site shut down years ago."

"But they could still have a bunch of bombs down there. Maybe one went off by accident."

Hal snorted. "Try using that little brain of yours. If they'd set off any kind of thermonuclear device, we'd all be crispy critters."

Just then the elevator doors opened and Laureen stepped out. "Sorry I'm late. Who's missing?"

"Grace is," Moira answered, "but she left for work early this morning."

"How about Betty?"

"Betty and Margaret are fine," Jayne informed them. "I stopped off on my way down. Should I go up and check on Ellen?"

"Not until we find Jack. He's the one with the master plan."

Alan led the way to Jack's security office and pushed open the door. The sight that awaited them was total destruction. The bank of closed-circuit television monitors had toppled off the shelf and shards of glass were everywhere.

"Careful where you step," Alan cautioned. "Jack? You in here?"

There was silence for a moment and then they heard a moan. Jack lay behind his desk in a pool of blood. His lower leg was bent at a grotesque angle and his face was gray with pain.

"Oh, God!" Vanessa took one look and grabbed Alan, blocking the doorway.

Laureen pulled her away and shoved her into Hal's arms. "Shut up, Vanessa. And hang on to your own husband for a change."

"But Jack's dead! We're too late!"

Hal pushed his wife forward none too gently. "Dead people can't moan. Now get in there and make yourself useful. You told me you had some nursing training."

"Only two weeks." Vanessa looked panic-stricken. "And all we learned how to do was empty bedpans. I can't deal with this, Hal. The sight of blood makes me sick!"

Alan made his way past the group at the door and grabbed a chair cushion to protect his knees as he knelt down by Jack. After a moment, he motioned for Laureen. "Bring me all the blankets you can find, anything we can use to keep him warm. Rachael? Go up to Betty's and tell the nurse that Jack's got a compound fracture of the left fibula and send her down here on the double." Alan took one look at Vanessa's white face and added, "Take Vanessa with you before she faints."

Vanessa looked dazed as Rachael grabbed her arm and pulled her out of the room. The rest of them crowded around Jack as Alan covered him with blankets.

Clayton swallowed hard. He'd seen the jagged edge of bone that stuck out of Jack's shin and he felt a little faint, too. "Should we carry him to the bedroom?"

"Leave him right where he is. He'll go into shock if we move him."

"But won't he bleed to death?" Jayne's face turned almost as gray as Jack's as she stared down at the blood on the floor.

"There's still a little bleeding, but it's slowed. Go find a big pillow and some adhesive tape. We'll have to line up his leg. Lucky there's a nurse in the building."

"We're also lucky we've got you." Laureen squeezed her husband's arm and turned to the others to explain. "Alan was a medic in the army."

"Will Jack be all right?" Moira asked the question that was in everyone's mind.

"I think so. His ABC's check out." Since Moira was looking at him blankly, he explained. "ABCs. Airway, breathing, and cardiac function."

"I'm here." Margaret Woodard bustled into the room and everyone moved back a step as she knelt down next to Alan. It seemed to take forever to the anxious group, but at last she turned to look up at them. "Is there a shortwave radio? He's got to be hospitalized as soon as possible."

Hal nodded. "There's one in the next room. Jack showed it to me. I'll call for help."

Alan and the nurse slipped the pillow under Jack's leg. When they straightened it, Jack cried out sharply and sweat broke out on his forehead.

"Hold on, Jack." Alan's voice was gentle. "We'll work as fast as we can."

They had just finished securing Jack's leg in its pillow bandage when Hal rushed back into the room. "They'll be here in less than twenty minutes to airlift Jack out. I told them exactly what you said, Alan, a compound fracture of the left fibula. Let's go up and check on Ellen. If she's injured, they can fly her out, too."

"Go ahead." Margaret Woodard gestured for Alan to go. "I'll stay with this one."

Jayne frowned; Margaret Woodard's attitude irked her. Jack came to see Betty at least twice a day; yet she referred to Jack as "this one." The woman was a cold fish, no doubt about it.

There was an uneasy silence as they rode up to the eighth floor. After seeing Jack's condition, no one wanted to speculate. They all knew Ellen worked with power tools and might well have been using them when the avalanche hit.

Jayne was in the lead as they reached Ellen's unit and she waited anxiously for Alan to unlock the door with the master key he'd taken from Jack's office. They stepped in and Jayne called out, "Ellen? Are you here?" Jayne frowned as there was no answer. "Let's check the workroom first. She told me she had some things to finish before she met me for tennis."

There was something eerie about walking through someone else's home without being invited, and Jayne shivered as she pushed open the workroom door. They found even more damage than in Jack's security office. A heavy workbench had toppled and lifelike pieces of mannequin anatomy were strewn all over the room.

"Ellen? Where are you?" This time they heard a muffled answer.

"I'm under the workbench." Ellen's voice was faint. "I think I'm all right, but there's not much room under here."

Clayton took charge. "Come on. Everyone over here. Let's lift it so she can get out."

"Stop!" Jayne ran forward. "From that end, the weight'll shift. It's a classic cantilever and you have to lift along the axis."

Marc turned in surprise, then he nodded. "You're right, Jayne. Alan? Come over here. I'll show you where to lift. Clayton, you take it from the middle and I'll handle this end. Straight up now, on the count of three. You ladies get ready to help Ellen out."

In less than a minute, Ellen was freed. Bruised and shaken, she wasn't seriously hurt. "Is everyone else all right?"

"Except Jack." As usual, Jayne spoke without thinking and she winced at Ellen's anguished expression. "Don't worry, Ellen. Just a broken leg. They're coming with a helicopter."

"Thank God!" Ellen drew a sigh of relief, then looked around at the debris and started to giggle. "It looks like a morgue in here. Something about the sight of those heads over there is doing me in."

They followed Ellen's gaze and even Hal began to smile. It did look like a morgue. Several mannequin heads had rolled out of their boxes and one was sitting on the stomach of a torso.

"I'm glad you can laugh about it, Ellen." Jayne put

her arm around Ellen's shoulders. "I would have been scared straight out of my hide."

"I didn't have time to be scared when it was happening, but it was awful being trapped. I knew I couldn't get out by myself and I kept wondering what would happen if . . ." Ellen swallowed hard. "Well, it's over. No sense thinking about it now. I'm just glad you didn't panic, Jayne. How did you know about the cantilever business, anyway?"

Jayne shrugged. "I guess Paul must have talked about it. The whole thing looked a little like a bridge he designed."

"I'd better call Walker and tell him I'm all right. He's probably at the warehouse by now."

Alan stopped her as she reached for the phone. "The lines are down, Ellen. We had to use the shortwave to call for the chopper."

Just then, the sound of helicopter blades whirling became audible and Alan led Ellen toward the door. "Let's go out and tell them we're okay. They can call Walker for you."

Everyone was relieved as they rode down on the elevator, the aftermath of surviving a disaster relatively unscathed. The last one off, Ellen hung behind a little. She reminded herself that they were all alive and nothing was damaged that couldn't be fixed. She really ought to be thankful. But as she stepped out into the frigid air and watched her neighbors rush through the snow to the helicopter, she couldn't seem to shake a premonition of trouble ahead.

FIVE

Walker had noticed the sign on the shopping center as he'd driven past. It was ninety-eight degrees. Thanks goodness Ellen had air-conditioned the warehouse! He would have to go back out into the heat when he loaded Ellen's new van, a forest-green behemoth with VEGAS DOLLS printed on both sides in bright pink lettering, but at least he'd been treated to cool air inside.

As he stepped in, Walker saw the crate of mannequins was propped up against the wall with four of Ellen's creations inside. The packing slip from the department store in New York claimed that they had arrived in damaged condition. Walker closed the warehouse door and locked it, switching on the bank of overhead lights. Then he pried open the crate to find that all four of the hollow mannequin heads had been broken open. Running his finger around the inside of the skulls, Walker tasted the residue, and nodded.

Walker tossed the damaged mannequins in the trash bin and wheeled it out for the daily pickup. He had just finished loading the supplies that Ellen needed and was about to lock the door and go out to the van to head back up the mountain when the telephone rang.

"Mr. Browning?" The voice on the other end of the line sounded bored. "This is Officer Carillo from the North Las Vegas police department. The residents at Deer Creek Condos asked me to call to tell you that they have adequate supplies and power from their backup generator. No land lines or cell phones, but there's a shortwave for emergency use and the situation is under control."

Walker frowned. There was obviously something the officer had forgotten to tell him. "What situation?"

"You haven't heard?" Officer Carillo cleared his throat. "There was an avalanche up on Mount Charleston at ten fifty-seven. One resident was seriously injured, but the damage to the building is minor."

Walker felt the sweat break out on his forehead. "Who was hurt?"

"I'm sorry, Mr. Browning, but we can't release the name unless you're a family member."

"Come on, officer. I work for Ellen Wingate. Can't you at least tell me if she's all right?"

"Wait a moment, sir. I'll check on that."

There was a click and Walker was put on hold. It seemed to take the officer a long time to get back to him.

"Mr. Browning? I'm sorry, sir, but I don't have the authority to release any additional information."

Walker sighed. The bureaucracy always played by their own rules. "Okay, I'd better head right up there."

"That wouldn't be advisable, sir. The snow slid down to the base of the access road. Since it's not a high priority, the highway department says it'll take at least a week to clear, and there's no way you can get through in a conventional vehicle."

"How about a four-wheel drive?"

"Sorry, sir. The only way is by helicopter."

"Fine. How about hitching a ride on one of your choppers?"

"Just a moment, sir. I'll have to check."

Officer Carillo came back on the line almost immediately. "I'm afraid that's impossible, sir. It's against regulations."

Walker thanked the officer and hung up. Minutes later, he was speeding toward town. As Jayne Peters was fond of saying, there was more than one way to skin a cat and he had to get up to Deer Creek Condos on the double.

At six-ten in the evening, it was still over ninety degrees and Paul Lindstrom's shirt stuck to his back as he walked across the parking lot to the door of the Castle Casino. Some Vegas regulars took taxis from one casino to another, even if their destination was only a block away. Paul had always regarded this as a needless extravagance, but now, as a blast of refrigerated air transformed his shirt into a cold, clammy mess, he had to admit that stepping from one air-conditioned casino into an air-conditioned taxi that would take him to another air-conditioned casino made sense.

Walking past the blackjack tables, Paul stopped to watch an elderly lady with a blue rinse in her hair play a quarter slot machine against the far wall. Each time she put in a coin, she patted the machine four times before pulling the handle. When he'd first come to Vegas, Paul had noticed the superstitious mannerisms of slot machine players. Some talked to the machines using words that resembled incantations. Still others counted the seconds they held the handle down. There were as many rituals as there were players. When Paul had asked if these people really thought they could control an action that was specifically geared to be random, Jayne had explained what she called *slot behavior*. It was nothing but intermittent reinforcement, the type that was most difficult to extinguish. A laboratory rat who had received food pellets while pressing its nose against the corner of the cage would return to that position countless times in an attempt to acquire more pellets. Even when the reward was no longer forthcoming, the rat would continue to scurry for the corner every time the technician walked near. If Jayne's theory was correct, the blue-haired lady had once hit a jackpot after patting the machine four times.

After watching for a few more moments, Paul walked on. Jayne had once written a song called "Somethin' for Nothin'" and it was that very phenomenon which kept the casinos thriving. There were true accounts of gamblers who won enough money to retire in luxury and every player in Vegas had similar dreams.

In the lounge Paul took up a position near the doorway. It was quiet and dark inside, a welcome relief from the bright lights and noise on the floor of the casino. The lounge's only occupants were three men with red and white name tags, obviously from a convention, sitting at a table in the back of the room. A woman with flaming red hair was seated at the piano, playing old standards to the nearly empty room. Paul was early. Grace DuPaz had promised to meet him in the lounge at six-thirty, right after rehearsal.

The pianist noticed him and gave a little wave. "Hi, honey. Why don't you come over here and sit by me?"

"Thank you." Paul gave a little bow and reached out

to shake her hand before he took one of the seats by the piano. "I am early to meet a friend."

"Good. You can keep me company. This place is dead right now."

"Dead?" Paul looked puzzled for a moment, but then he smiled. "Ah, yes. There are not many people to listen."

"That's right, honey. Any requests?"

"There is one song I would like very much to hear." Paul nodded. "My Stubborn Heart."

The pianist broke into a smile. "I love it, but it's so new I haven't really worked it up yet. Want me to give it a whirl anyway?"

Paul smiled back. "I would be pleased. My wife wrote it."

The pianist did a double take and her professional smile grew much warmer. "Then you must be Paul! Glad to meet you. I'm Flame Richards and I'm a big fan of Jayne's."

As Flame sang, Paul reflected on the song about a husband who'd left and a woman's stubborn heart that wouldn't let her ask him to come back. Just as she struck the ending chords, Grace walked into the bar and Paul rose to his feet.

"Hi, Paul." Grace shook his hand and slid quickly onto a chair. After living in the same building for almost four years, she knew Paul wouldn't sit down until she did. "I've never seen you in jeans before. You look good. And that blue cowboy shirt just matches your eyes. Did you ditch it for good or did you just pack it away in mothballs?"

"Pardon?"

"I'm talking about the three-piece suit you used to always wear, even up at the spa when the rest of us were sitting around in sweats. I bet Jayne would faint dead away if she saw you like this. She used to buy you all those gorgeous cowboy shirts and you'd never even try them on."

"Yes, that is true." Paul frowned slightly. He'd been what Jayne called a stuffed shirt about wearing anything other than proper clothing, but now he only took out his suit for business meetings and sometimes not even then. Jayne had been right. Casual clothes were much more comfortable.

Grace turned to the piano player. "How's it going, Flame?"

"Just fine." The pianist gave her the high sign and segued into the music from Grace's last show. "How's the new show coming?"

"The costumes are awful, the music stinks, the lighting's horrid, and the girls all have two left feet. Other than that, everything's right on schedule."

"You always say that." Flame laughed.

A cocktail waitress, dressed in a low-cut gold lamé minidress, leaned over the piano. "Flame? That guy in the black shirt wants you to play 'Hey Jude.'"

"Again?" Flame raised her eyebrows. "I've played it three times already, but I guess I'd better keep those aging hippies happy and do my whole Beatles medley."

As Flame started up again, Grace leaned a little closer to Paul. "What's up? You sounded really upset on the phone."

"I have some distressing news, Grace. There was an avalanche on the mountain."

Grace looked alarmed. "An avalanche? When? Early this morning everything was fine, a little snow on the road, but I drove through it, no problem. Good heavens! You'd think someone would have called to tell me unless . . . Oh, my God!" Grace's face turned pale. "Is Moira hurt?"

"I am sorry, Grace. My friend from the police could not tell me as I am not of Moira's family. There was one serious injury which the police transported to hospital by helicopter, but that is all I know."

"Oh, Lord!" Grace jumped up and Paul also rose to his feet. "I'd better call right away."

Paul took Grace's arm and guided her back down to her chair. "It is not possible, Grace. The phone lines are no longer in service and the cell tower has toppled. That is why I asked to meet with you. I must go to Jayne immediately and I thought that you also would wish to go."

"Yes! Of course. Let's take my Jeep, Paul. It'll make it through anything."

Paul shook his head. "No, Grace. My friend has told me of a solid wall of snow. The authorities will not permit anyone to attempt the road."

"How about the police chopper?"

Paul shook his head. "Also not possible, Grace. The helicopter is reserved for emergency use only. I know we must go, but I am not sure how to accomplish this."

"How about a snowmobile?" Flame finished "Hey Jude" and began to play the chorus of "Strawberry Fields Forever."

Paul took a moment to think it over. "That is an excellent idea, Miss Richards. But where do we find a snowmobile in the desert?"

"You could try the Alpine Ski Shop in the mall." Flame finished the chorus of "Strawberry Fields" and switched to "Dear Prudence." "Use the bar phone."

Grace went off, but came back frowning. "They don't

carry snowmobiles. And they don't know anywhere we can get one."

"Just a sec." Flame struck the final chord. "Do either of you know any Beatles songs? If someone can spell me for a minute, I might be able to find you one."

"Sorry, Flame." Grace shook her head. "I never learned to play the piano. You know something about music, don't you, Paul?"

Paul nodded. "I play the violin, but I am not accomplished at the piano. Jayne attempted to teach me last winter, but I can play nothing of the Beatles except the chorus to 'Obladi Oblada.'"

"That'll do." Flame slid off the bench and motioned to Paul to take her place. "Just play it over and over until I get back. Those jokers will never know the difference, I guarantee it."

Paul was just winding up his twenty-fifth rendition when Flame came back, sliding over on the piano bench and replacing Paul at the piano. "I got you a great big Arctic Cat. Here's the address." She pushed a cocktail napkin across the bar. "It belongs to my boyfriend's landlady's cousin."

Grace pocketed the cocktail napkin and gave the pianist a grateful smile. Flame was just getting into the rocking rhythm of "Honey Pie" when the cocktail waitress rushed over with a note. "You're going to love this one, Flame. Those guys want to hear 'Obladi Oblada' again. They said you played it just the way they like it."

Grace and Paul were still chuckling as they headed to the parking lot. The sky was beginning to darken, but it was still over eighty degrees on the neon-studded Strip.

"It is summer down here." Paul opened the window to enjoy the warm night breeze as Grace pulled out of the parking lot and drove toward Henderson. Grace didn't reply, but she knew exactly what he was thinking. While it was summer in Vegas, it was winter on Deer Creek Road. And they were about to embark on a long cold trip up the mountain.

An hour had passed, and the residents of Deer Creek Condos were beginning to gather at the spa. No one wanted to spend the evening alone and Laureen had organized a potluck dinner.

Jayne had dressed for the occasion in a natural buckskin dress with fringes at the hem and matching moccasins. Paul had called her Pocahontas whenever she wore it. Her hair hung around her shoulders in a curly black cloud and she brushed it back with her hand as she surveyed the tables set up around the pool area. She'd set them with china and silver, even though Paul was no longer here to object to paper plates and plastic utensils. They'd fought over that issue bitterly throughout their marriage. Jayne had stubbornly maintained that picnic ware was perfectly adequate for everyday use while Paul had insisted that dining wasn't dining unless the food was properly presented. She'd never come out and admit it, but food really seemed to taste better his way.

"Okay, kids. It's vacation time!" Hal stepped out of the elevator with a pitcher of margaritas. He was wearing his favorite artist-at-home outfit, faded blue jeans and a long-sleeved black sweater. "As long as we're stuck here for a week, we might as well party."

"Here's the chili." Laureen set a huge pot on the buffet table. She wore slacks with an oversize shocking pink sweater. The sweater was intended to hide her extra weight, but the splash of bright color made her look even larger.

Hal rubbed his hands together. "Okay, we've got Laureen's incredible chili for starters. And Clay's brought . . ." Hal paused to grin. "Blue chips! That figures."

Clayton, dressed in chinos and the green and black rugby shirt Rachael had given him for Christmas, looked puzzled as he set down a bowl of blue corn chips. Hal figured he'd better explain. "Isn't that what you tell your clients to buy? Nothing but blue chips?"

"Oh." Clayton frowned. "I get it, Hal. Blue-chip stocks. But the connection is a bit tenuous."

"Here's the salsa." Rachael arrived with Vanessa and Moira. "The blue bowl is mild, for you, Clay. The one in the red bowl is dynamite."

All three women had a distinctive style. Rachael wore her yellow Tai Chi uniform with tire-tread sandals, Moira was impressive in an orange silk caftan which swirled around her ankles, and Vanessa was dressed for a cocktail party in a purple satin minidress that fit like a second skin and huge, dangling gold earrings.

"This is my special fat-free herbal dip." Vanessa's high-heeled gold sandals clicked against the tiles as she crossed the room to set a bag of potato chips on the table, along with a bowl of dip. "I know everybody's watching their weight. Or if they're not, they *should* be. You can have all you want because there's only eighty calories in the whole thing."

Laureen gave Vanessa a venomous glare. "Unless you count the chips!"

The door to the elevator opened again and Ellen stepped out, carrying the thirty-cup coffeepot. "Where do you want this? It's all ready to plug in."

"Over there." Alan pointed to the ledge by the Jacuzzi. "I rigged an extension cord."

Vanessa frowned as Ellen plugged in the coffee. "I wish Ellen would wear one of the dresses I helped her pick out. That big old shirt and those awful pants must have come straight from the men's department. No wonder Johnny dumped her. When I latch on to a really neat guy, I never let him get away."

"Of course you don't." Laureen gave her a withering look. "Parasites always cling to their hosts."

"I think Ellen did the right thing by cutting Johnny loose." Jayne jumped in before a full-scale fight could develop. "I like him, don't get me wrong, but he goes through women like Kleenex. I'm glad Ellen wised up before she got screwed."

"Maybe that was the problem." Vanessa giggled. "I don't think Ellen's ever been . . ."

Hal put his hand over his wife's mouth. "Cut it out, Vanessa."

The elevator doors opened again and Marc stepped out. He was wearing a maroon velour warm-up suit with his monogram, and he carried a large pink bakery box.

"Oh, God!" Laureen moaned. "A pink box. Those yummy pink boxes chase me in my dreams."

"Sorry, Laureen." Marc set the box on the table. "I was planning on taking these to my crew this morning, but now you'll have to help me eat them."

Laureen lifted the lid and groaned. "Raspberry Danish. There must be three dozen!"

"Thirty-four. I had a couple for breakfast."

"That means we have to eat three apiece." Jayne sighed. "I'd better put in my laps now or I'll sink like a stone. The pool's all right to use, isn't it, Marc?"

Marc nodded. They'd discovered a crack in the decorative tile of the pool, but since it was triple-lined, there was no leakage. "You might as well use it. Once we start the repairs, it'll be down for a while."

Jayne went off to the cabana to change and Ellen came over to take the empty chair next to Vanessa. Jayne was right; she couldn't avoid her forever.

"I'm glad you're all right, Ellen." Vanessa turned to her with a friendly smile. "I wanted to come up and help when you were stuck under that bench, but they made me go to Betty's. Everybody figured I'd faint or something."

Ellen nodded and tried to smile back. It wasn't fair to blame Vanessa. She'd been only one in the long line of Johnny's women, but Ellen had been too blind to realize it.

"Let's fix you up." Vanessa reached over to open the top three buttons on Ellen's shirt. "You need to show off your neck, Ellie. It's your best feature. And that awful denim shirt's way too big for you. No man's ever going to look at you twice if you dress like a bag lady."

Ellen's first instinct was to pull away, but she didn't want to cause a scene. Before she could think of a reply, Vanessa had unhooked the gold mesh belt she wore and cinched it around Ellen's waist.

"Not bad." Vanessa eyed her critically. "Of course, it'd help if you wore tighter pants, but sloppy's in this year. A little eye makeup and you'd look right in style."

"Thanks, Vanessa." Ellen couldn't help but smile. Vanessa didn't have a tactful bone in her body, but she was honestly trying to be nice.

"I need a list of your damage, Ellen." Clayton turned in his chair to face her. "We'll have to file a group claim."

Ellen nodded. "Will our homeowners' insurance cover it?"

"That depends entirely on the proximate cause of the damage. I reviewed our policy and I'm gratified to report that we elected the earthquake option. Even though an avalanche is subsumed under acts of God, we can claim vis-à-vis the exceptions provision." Clayton held up his hand as Ellen opened her mouth to ask a question. "On the other hand, if Vanessa's theory has any probative weight, we have an action for damages against the Nevada test site."

Ellen gave Rachael an expectant look. Since Rachael was also a lawyer, she was often called upon to assume the duties of translator.

"Clayton's trying to tell us that we're covered one way or the other. Oh, look!" Rachael pointed toward the springboard. "Jayne's going to do one of her dives."

Everyone watched as Jayne bounced on the springboard and executed a perfect one and a half gainer into the deep end of the pool. Alan whistled. "I wish I could dive like that!"

"And I wish I could look like that in a swimsuit." Laureen's voice was envious.

"Jayne's really a water-rat." Moira watched as Jayne came up for a breath of air and then disappeared beneath the water again. "She was swimming when she was nine months old. Her mother took her to Crystal Scarborough classes. You know, the woman who taught babies to . . . what's the matter, Jayne?"

Jayne's eyes were wide with fright as she came up in the shallow end of the pool and scrambled out of the water. Moira handed her a towel and helped her to a chair. "Are you all right?"

Jayne was shaking so hard, she couldn't speak. All she could do was point at the pool.

"I'll get her a hot cup of coffee." Ellen jumped to her feet and hurried to the coffeepot.

"Tell us what happened, Jayne." Laureen looked worried. "Was it a cramp?"

Jayne shook her head and gulped several times. "There's a . . . a hand down there!"

"A what?"

"A hand! It's down there behind that crack!"

"Try to calm down, Jayne." Laureen looked worried. Jayne wasn't an excitable person and she was clearly hysterical. "Alan'll go down and take a look."

Marc pushed back his chair. "I'll go, too. It's probably something that fell in during the avalanche."

Moira hurried to get one of the heavy terry-cloth robes they kept by the sauna and wrapped it around Jayne's shoulders. "It's all right, Jayne. They'll check it out. What made you think it was a hand?"

"I saw it!" Jayne insisted. "I dived down to look at the crack and there was something shiny behind it. So I grabbed it and . . . and it came loose."

"The hand came loose?" Clayton frowned as he tried to make some sense out of Jayne's words.

"No! The ring it was wearing came loose. I . . . I got so scared I dropped it."

Vanessa giggled. "You can't fool me, Jayne. I watch Vampira all the time and I saw the one where the skeleton comes up out of the pool."

Ellen came back with a steaming cup of coffee and set it down in front of Jayne. "Drink this, Jayne. You're still shaking."

Vanessa turned to Ellen and winked. "It's all an act. Jayne's trying to make us think that someone lost a hand in our pool. And Alan and Marc fell for it."

"It's no act!" Jayne shook her head. "There really *is*

a hand down there . . . or something that looks like a hand."

Vanessa examined Jayne's pale face for a moment and then nodded. "Okay. I believe you. You never could have pulled it off. After all, you're not an actress like me."

Laureen opened her mouth and then closed it again. They'd all seen the video of Vanessa's film debut. Supposedly terrified, her character had jumped from a sinking speedboat into a lake, wearing a white silk bikini that turned almost transparent when wet. Her acting had consisted of two piercing screams, which were later dubbed. Laureen figured that they'd cast the bikini and then looked around for someone to fill it, but this wasn't the time to critique Vanessa's acting ability.

Alan surfaced with a splash and climbed out of the pool. "There's something stuck in the plaster, but the crack's too narrow to see very much. Marc went back down for the ring."

"Got it!" Marc hauled himself out of the pool and brought the ring to the table.

"My grandfather had one of these." Laureen picked it up. "It's made from a horseshoe nail and he told me it was a good luck charm."

Alan gave a short laugh. "Well, it wasn't very lucky for the guy who lost his hand in the cement."

"Gunite, not cement," Marc corrected. "And we're not sure it's a hand."

Vanessa looked exasperated. "Of course it's a hand. What else wears a ring?"

"She's got a point," Hal conceded. "The question is, how did it get there? And who does it belong to?"

Jayne laughed shrilly. "It's a soap opera. All we have to do is tune in tomorrow to get the exciting answers to these and other questions."

"Easy, Jayne." Laureen patted her on the shoulder. "Maybe it's a fake hand, like the skeletons kids buy at Halloween. This could be some kind of dumb practical . . . Alan!"

"What did I do?" Alan flinched as Laureen glared at him.

"We all know who's the biggest practical joker in this group!"

"No way, Laureen. Whoopee cushions and dribble glasses are as far as I go."

Marc looked thoughtful. "It could have been somebody on my crew. Planting a fake skeleton in the liner is right up their alley. Maybe we ought to dig it out and . . ."

"That wouldn't be advisable," Clayton interrupted. "The police should handle something like this. After all, we don't want to disturb a possible crime scene."

Marc considered it for a moment. "You're right, Clay. I'll go call them on the shortwave."

"I think it's a real live hand." Vanessa's eyes were gleaming with excitement. "And I bet I know who it belongs to."

Hal turned to stare at his wife. "It's not live, Vanessa, not anymore. But I'll bite anyway. Who does it belong to?"

"Johnny Day!"

There was complete silence and Vanessa scowled. "Why are you all staring at me like that? It could be Johnny's. Maybe Johnny didn't go back to Italy at all. Maybe somebody killed him and stashed him in our pool. And all the time we've been diving off the board and playing in the water, we've been only inches from discovering poor Johnny's body!"

Hal was the first to recover. "And here we have another example of my charming bride's superlative logical abilities. Now listen carefully, Vanessa, and try to follow. The pool was built before anyone moved in. Is that right?"

Vanessa nodded.

"And that makes the pool over four years old. Do you agree?"

Vanessa nodded again.

"Now, here comes the tricky part. Since the hand was stuck in the liner, it had to get put there before the pool was finished. Got that?"

"Of course. I'm not stupid, Hal!"

"And that means the hand's been down there for over four years. Is that right?"

"Well . . . yes, but . . ."

"Now we know that Johnny left only five weeks ago and I think we can assume he took both his hands."

Vanessa pondered the whole thing for a moment and then she shrugged. "Okay, then. But I still think something funny could've happened to Johnny. He promised to keep in touch and he hasn't called once since he left."

"That's true," Jayne agreed. "He asked me to pack up his stuff, but he never called to tell me where to ship it. Has anybody heard from him?"

"I certainly haven't." Clayton scowled. "As his legal counsel, I naturally hold his full power-of-attorney, and speaking strictly in camera, I've been forced to assume the entire responsibility for his portfolio."

Everyone turned to Rachael and she laughed. "Clay's upset because he's had to wing it alone with all of Johnny's stocks and bonds."

"I know Marc hasn't heard from him either," Alan confided. "Johnny hasn't even called to find out if his condo sold and that's a million-plus property."

"But Johnny's got a lot on his mind right now." Laureen pointed out. "After all, his father just died and I'm sure he trusts us to take care of everything on this end while he sorts out things with his family."

The elevator doors opened and Marc got out carrying the shortwave radio in both hands. The case was smashed in on top and loose wires dangled down in back.

"My God! What happened?" Hal gasped at the broken radio.

"That jolt we took must have loosened the shelves in Jack's office. Either that, or we had some kind of aftershock. I found it under a pile of rubble."

"I think we're in big trouble."

There was a frown on Hal's face as he pried open the case and Vanessa stared up at him anxiously. "You can make it work again can't you, honey?"

Hal gave a bitter laugh. "I'd have a better chance of fixing a busted balloon."

SIX

"How much farther?" Grace leaned close to Paul and shouted into his ear. The roar of the big snowmobile's engine made communication difficult.

"Five or six miles."

Paul's words were whipped away by the wind and Grace huddled as close as she could. "What did you say?"

Paul turned his head and shouted. "Five or six miles! Do you wish to rest?"

"No! I'll turn into a solid block of ice if you stop." Grace huddled down a little in the seat. They'd both dressed in winter parkas and ski masks, but it was less than thirty degrees outside and the wind chill brought that down to below zero.

"Drink the brandy, Grace. It will warm you."

The snowmobile had come equipped with a plastic flask that fit in a holder on the dashboard. Grace reached for it and took a swallow. Flame's boyfriend's landlady's cousin had told them that the man who'd designed the holder and flask had made millions.

Paul swerved to avoid a pine tree. His fingers felt frozen even though he'd worn his choppers. The fur-lined leather mittens had been a gift from his relatives in Norway and he'd never had occasion to wear them before. Tonight he yearned for the whole outfit, including the fur-lined leather cap with the earflaps and the heavy woolen pants his ancestors had worn. Grace had given him a pair of warm-up leggings from her dance wardrobe, but they weren't designed for temperatures like this.

With great difficulty, Paul managed to pull up his sleeve to glance at his watch in the dim light from the dashboard. It was almost nine. They'd left Vegas at seven-thirty and it had only taken them twenty minutes to drive to the wall of snow in the road. Unloading the snowmobile had taken another five minutes, which meant they'd been out in this bitter cold for over an hour. They'd been forced to make several detours, and right now they were roughly paralleling the access road. Paul figured they should be able to see the lights of the building in a half hour or so. If they didn't run into more obstacles. If the snowmobile kept on running. And if he didn't smash into a snow-covered bump that was really a big rock.

They rode without speaking for what seemed like hours, with only the roar of the Arctic Cat's powerful engine to break the silence. Their headlight's narrow beam probed the frozen darkness and it reminded Paul of a bright yellow ribbon unwinding from an infinite spool. The moon was just rising over the tops of the trees and the snow seemed to glow with an icy blue light while the huge pines cast long purple shadows over its surface. If managing the snowmobile hadn't taken all his concentration, Paul might have enjoyed the sight.

"You all right?" Paul shouted back to Grace.

Grace leaned forward so her lips were close to his ear

and called back, "I'm as all right as I'm going to get. We're almost there, aren't we?"

"Yes, Grace. We are almost there." Paul tried to sound confident, even though he wasn't sure exactly where they were. The blanket of snow covered what landmarks the avalanche hadn't covered, but there was no sense in alarming Grace. They'd get there. He headed toward the peak of the mountain like a sailor taking his bearing from the polestar.

Grace tucked her head down and let Paul's body shield her from the full force of the wind. Even though the night was calm, the motion of the snowmobile created a blast of icy air past her face. She didn't want to look at the scenery. She just wanted to get to the building before she froze to death.

While Paul had inspected the snowmobile and received last-minute instructions from the owner, Grace had called every hospital in Vegas to find out if Moira or Jayne had been admitted. Neither name had been listed, but that hadn't changed their plans. They both had other reasons for making this long, cold trip.

Grace felt a little warmer as she thought of Vanessa. That damned woman made her blood boil. Perhaps it was a game to see how many men she could topple, but it was creating havoc in more than one household. Vanessa seemed to have one simple guideline: if a man was ambulatory and he belonged to someone else, she wanted to try him. And now she was snowbound without fresh victims. Would Vanessa turn to Moira when she ran out of men? Grace was betting on it.

As Grace sighed, her breath came out in a frozen cloud that was whisked away by the freezing wind. Moira was particularly vulnerable right now. She was forty-nine years old and gravity was taking its inevitable toll. She constantly complained about sagging and wrinkles and she couldn't help but feel flattered that such a gorgeous young girl was interested in her. Naturally Grace was jealous, but that wasn't the primary reason she was braving the elements to get up the mountain. She wanted to stop the woman she loved from making a fool of herself and getting badly hurt in the process.

Paul shouted something unintelligible and Grace leaned closer. "What was that?"

"The ridge!" Paul pointed off to the right. "We're almost there!"

They were climbing the steep ridge in switchbacks and Paul knew it was studded with boulders. But even though most of his concentration was required for negotiating the difficult terrain, he couldn't help but wonder what Jayne's reaction would be when they arrived. He hoped that the song he'd taken as an invitation wasn't just a song after all.

Walker had been skiing for over an hour before he reached the crest of Devil's Slope. He stopped for a moment to catch his breath and adjust the bindings on his cross-country skis. From his high vantage point, he could see the lights of the building glimmering in the darkness, but he knew it was still miles away. Distances in the mountains were always deceiving, as he'd discovered on his first backpacking trip in Colorado. He'd set out one morning to hike to a mountain ridge that looked no more than an hour away. When he'd stopped by a stream to rest after four hours, the ridge still appeared an hour away. It had taken him the whole day to reach it.

With a sigh, Walker dug his poles into the crusty snow and pushed off again. There were two more ravines to negotiate and it was better to go slowly than risk snapping his ankle on the uneven terrain. Since no one knew he was coming, any serious injury meant he'd lie out here for days without being discovered.

Even though Walker had been anxious to start, he'd taken the time to find out that Jack was the injured party, hospitalized with a compound fracture and in stable condition. He was sorry that Jack was injured. He liked Jack. But at least it wasn't Ellen.

Walker began to ski cautiously down the ravine. He knew his descent would be even more dangerous in the dark, but he couldn't afford to wait until morning. He imagined what Ellen would say when she saw him lugging a backpack filled with dye. She'd probably tell him he was crazy. She certainly hadn't needed supplies badly enough for him to hitch a ride on the KLV traffic helicopter and ski down from the ranger's landing pad on the far side of the mountain, but it was a convenient excuse. The image of the loyal employee who slogged through the ice and the snow to deliver the goods made Walker chuckle. He'd never expected all this when Jack had called him in.

The moon was bright overhead and Walker took a brief moment to enjoy the sight. There was no doubt in his mind that Ellen would be glad to see him. He'd finally gained her trust and it hadn't been easy. Ellen was very cautious around men, and he suspected it was because she believed she was ugly. True, she was taller than average and a little on the thin side, but she was unusually graceful. And when she smiled, she was lovely.

There was a sound in the brush and Walker crouched, the gun materializing in his hand almost like magic. It vanished almost as quickly when he saw it was only a deer crashing through a thicket. Combat training. Even though there was no enemy hiding in these Nevada mountains, his quick reflexes had saved him more than once.

A sound broke the stillness of the night, the high-pitched whine of a motor from a distant ravine somewhere below him. Walker listened, his body poised. A snowmobile. Three miles away, maybe four. The sound bounced off the sheer walls of rock and made it difficult to locate with any accuracy.

Walker dug his poles into the snow and set off again. There was no use hurrying. The snowmobile would arrive long before he did. He just hoped it was someone who belonged at Deer Creek Condos. He'd have enough trouble dealing with the regular residents without adding a couple of curious visitors to the mix.

At Clayton's insistence, they'd covered the pool with the solar blanket, but Marc drew the line at declaring the whole penthouse off-limits. "Come on, Clay. We don't even know if those bones are real or not."

"This is still a probable crime site and we have a civic responsibility to keep it intact for the police."

Moira looked exasperated. "Fu . . . fudge! Those bones are old and we've been tramping around up there for the past four years. Isn't it a little too late to keep it intact?"

"It's like locking the barn door after the horse has been stolen," Jayne jumped in. "Talk some sense into him, Rachael."

Rachael put her hand on Clayton's arm. "I think we've done our bit by covering the pool, dear. After all, that's where the alleged bones are."

"I don't agree. That cover is removable. If someone enters the water, the evidence could be dislodged."

"Yuck!" Vanessa made a face. "I'm not going near that pool until they clean it. I'll tell you what, Clay. If it'd make you feel any better, we can all take an oath to stay out of the pool, scout's honor. I used to be a Girl Scout."

Laureen couldn't resist. "And now she's a Boy Scout. She scouts out every boy she sees."

"Cut it out, you two and take a look out that window! Somebody's coming up the ridge!" Alan pointed at a bright light cutting through the trees.

Marc rushed over to look. "A snowmobile. It could be someone from the ranger station."

"That's not likely." Clayton joined them at the window. "We told the paramedics that we were all right and didn't need supplies."

Jayne came over to look. "It's got to be someone from town. The ranger would be coming down from the other side. I bet it's Grace."

Moira laughed. "Not a chance! You know how Grace hates the cold."

"Well, that thing's not driving itself." Vanessa came up to peer out the window. "Maybe it's my fitness instructor. I had a workout session scheduled for tonight."

Jayne's eyes widened. "Lordy, Vanessa! Your fitness instructor wouldn't drive all the way up here on a snowmobile, would he?"

"He might." Vanessa preened a bit. "He's dedicated to keeping my body in perfect shape. It's almost a religion to him. And he knows that there's no way I'd let myself get fat and dumpy like some of the women in this building."

Hal reached out to grab his wife's arm. "That's enough, Vanessa. If I were you, I'd shut up."

"You want *her* to shut up?" Laureen snorted. "The

only way to shut her up is to stuff something in her mouth. And I don't mean food!"

Jayne pulled Laureen over to the window. "Easy, Laureen. Don't let her push your buttons."

"I can't help it, Jayne. Every time that little bitch makes a crack about my weight, I want to kill her!"

"Don't say that, Laureen. You know darn well you'd never do anything like that."

"Maybe not, but I'm certainly tempted." Laureen sighed. "Vanessa's causing problems for all of us, and I don't understand why Hal doesn't divorce her. He knows what's going on."

"I don't understand it, either, but it's not our problem. Come on, Laureen, honey. Let's make sure we've got plenty of coffee. Whoever's on that thing's going to need some warming up."

Clayton headed toward the elevator. "I'm going down to see who's on that snowmobile, and I'm going to ask them to inform the police. We might be hindering an important investigation. Shall I invite them up here to thaw out?"

"Of course," Marc assured him. "But I wouldn't mention the bones, not to strangers."

"Why not?"

"I've got a perfect buyer all lined up for Johnny's unit and he's a nervous Nellie. Even if the bones turn out to be a fake, it might queer the deal."

Clayton looked thoughtful and then he nodded. "That does put an entirely different aspect on the situation. It's really no one's business except ours . . . and the police, of course."

Jayne turned back to the window and gave a wry smile as the elevator doors closed behind Clayton. His self-righteous tone had changed the moment he thought it would cost him money. She guessed she really couldn't blame him. Clayton had drawn up the corporation bylaws and knew they had only thirty days left to find an acceptable buyer for Johnny's unit. If they failed, they'd have to divide the cost and buy it themselves. Of course, they'd eventually sell it and get their money back, but that might take a while.

The snowmobile approached the windows, and Jayne peered out into the darkness. She could tell that there were two people on the machine and her heart beat a little faster as she noticed that both of them were wearing ski masks.

Jayne sighed and turned from the window, reminding herself that Paul wasn't interested in her any longer. It was probably a couple of hardy reporters, braving the wind and the snow to get a firsthand account of the avalanche. Or perhaps Vanessa was right and one of them *was* her fitness instructor. Jayne had met him once and while he had a perfect body, he seemed short enough on brains to head up here on that snowmobile.

SEVEN

Betty Matteo sat alone in her suite, watching the television monitor. Her secret friend hadn't come tonight. Perhaps it wasn't time. He'd told her he could never come when anyone else was awake.

The revolving shelf right next to her bed contained hundreds of her favorite movies. Betty could play a DVD any time she wanted, even though she sometimes had trouble remembering how to read the titles.

She knew there was something wrong with her mind. It was a disease, and at first, she'd been able to remember its name. Now that was gone, too. One of the symptoms of the disease was that people forgot its name. There was a word for that sort of thing and Betty concentrated on trying to remember it. It took a long time, but she finally remembered. The name of the disease she had was ironic.

The man called Jack had been very patient about explaining things to her. And he was so good about wearing his name sign every time. Betty knew that she loved him. There was a good, warm feeling when he came into her room. And he was much nicer than Nurse.

Sometimes Betty took great pleasure in the fact that she couldn't remember Nurse's real name. Nurse gave her shots that confused her, that reminded her of the piñata she'd brought back from Mexico City. The gaily painted papier-mâché sculpture shattered when a blind-folded child hit it with a stick, spilling the contents down like rain, and that was exactly what the inside of her head felt like after one of Nurse's needles.

Betty wished she could tell Jack to find someone new for Nurse, someone who was kind and cheerful, some-one who cared about her and wanted her to get better. But every time she tried to tell Jack about Nurse, she couldn't find the words. They were there in her mind and she thought she was pronouncing them correctly, but no one seemed to understand what she said. Names and words. They always eluded her. But she was proud that she still remembered how to use the remote control to switch through the forbidden channels.

It was growing dark outside and soon it would be time for her secret friend to come through the door. Betty was sure she'd known his name once upon a time, but she couldn't remember it now.

Betty turned her attention to the screen once again. The movie she was watching was very familiar and she put a blank disk in the machine to record it. She smiled as she saw the red light on the console start to glow. She could record a movie. That was almost as good as re-membering names and words, wasn't it?

This movie took place by the water. It was a big swim-ming place and she almost remembered where it was. They'd covered it after the cowgirl had found something that frightened her. Betty smiled as she watched. She loved scary movies as long as everything ended happily ever after. And this movie had her favorite actors.

There were footsteps in the hall and Betty quickly switched the channel to something safe. No one could know she was watching the forbidden channels, no one except the man called Jack. He had warned her about it so many times, it was almost like remembering.

"Do you need anything?" Nurse opened the door and stuck her head in. She was a black-haired woman who looked like the bird who said "Nevermore," with a sharp beak and beady eyes and black shiny feathers.

Betty tried to force out the word Nurse wanted to hear, but it was no use. She'd lost it.

"Water? A little snack?"

This time Betty remembered and she shook her head. That meant no.

"I'll let you watch television for another hour, but then you have to sleep." Nurse came into her room to draw the drapes. She even moved like the *Nevermore* bird, with quick little steps. Her head turned from side to side and her glittering eyes watched Betty as she pulled the drapes to shut out the night. Betty shivered as she remembered that the *Nevermore* bird ate dead things called carrion.

How could she remember a word like that and then forget her friends' names? This disease was very curious. Things she hadn't thought of in years would come back in startling detail. She would know them for a brief instant and then she'd forget them again. Alzheimer's, that was the name of her disease. And it was progressive. She couldn't quite remember what that meant, but suddenly sadness overcame her.

"Buzz if you need me." Nurse closed the door behind

her. Immediately, Betty felt better. She knew she'd done everything just right. Nurse was gone and she hadn't given her the needle. Now she could watch the forbidden channels again.

Betty smiled as she used the remote control to switch to another movie. This one was even better. Two people were getting off a machine on skis in a big garage. The man turned toward the camera and Betty clapped her hands. He was a very important foreign actor and she was glad he'd come back to star in her secret movies. The cowgirl who shared her in-between name was in love with him.

"Here comes the elevator." Vanessa watched the doors expectantly. "I bet it's my fitness instructor. Does anybody want to give me odds?"

Jayne shook her head. Even if she was a gambler, she wouldn't bet on anything concerning Vanessa.

Hal grinned. "What do you want to bet, Vanessa? Ten thousand? Twenty thousand? More?"

"You know something, Hal?" Vanessa looked suspicious. "You never bet money unless you're sure. Did you see who was on that snowmobile?"

Hal shook his head. "I didn't see a thing, Vanessa. But I know it's not your fitness instructor."

"How do you know that?"

"Because I called yesterday and told him you no longer required his services."

"What does *that* mean?"

"That means I fired him. I canceled your sessions, Vanessa. Since I'm paying the bills, I decided he was an unnecessary expense."

"How could you do that to me?" Vanessa looked at her husband in shock. "I need my workouts!"

"Then you'll just have to use the spa like the rest of us. Let's just say I didn't approve of all the exercises he had you doing, especially that last little session you had in your room."

Vanessa looked embarrassed for a brief moment. Then her expression changed to anger. "My workouts are private, Hal. You had no business spying on me! Besides, everything he does is part of my total body therapy."

"That particular part of your body doesn't need any more exercise."

"But, Hal . . ." Vanessa began to pout. "He's a trained expert. And I don't know how to do my workouts without him."

"You can always borrow my Jane Fonda tapes," Laureen said smugly. "She shows you how to do everything."

Vanessa glared at Laureen. "Jane Fonda's only good for women over forty."

The indicator light over the elevator blinked and Grace got out. Alone.

"Sh . . . shucks!" Moira gave a delighted laugh. "Grace! On a snowmobile?"

Grace nodded. "You never thought anything would drag me out in the cold. Right, Moira?"

"Right." Moira rushed to embrace her, then poured her a cup of coffee. "I'm *really* glad to see you. But whatever possessed you to drive all the way up here?" Grace just smiled and Moira's face turned slightly pink. "Well! It's just incredible, that's all. You're the last person I expected to see. But Jayne said there were two people on the snowmobile. Who's with you?"

"That's a surprise. Clayton took him out to check on the building. They'll be up here in a couple of minutes."

Jayne's heart began to pound in excitement. Who knew enough about the building to check on it? A structural engineer, of course. Or a builder. Or an architect. And he had to be someone they knew. If Grace had come up here with a stranger, she wouldn't have said it was a surprise.

The indicator light on the elevator blinked again and Clayton got out, followed by a man holding a red and yellow ski mask.

"Paul!" Jayne jumped from her chair and ran across the floor to meet him, barely managing to keep from throwing her arms around him. "My God! What happened to your suit?"

"It is in the mothballs. Are you well, Jayne?"

"Oh, I'm fine, but the avalanche almost killed us all and poor Jack's leg is broken something awful and just now I found a . . . a hand in our pool. And at first I thought it was yours!"

Paul looked down at her in total confusion. "You thought my hand was in the pool?"

"Yes, they have such a high suicide rate in Scandinavia. But that was only at first, before we found out that it was at least four years old. And I wrote you a song, but they'd never give it airtime on a classical station and I just couldn't call you on the phone. Something about talking into those little holes is so dang impersonal and I like to see a person's face when I . . . oh, I'm so glad you're here!"

"I think you had better sit down, Jayne." Paul led her over to a chair and sat down beside her. "You are beginning to sound like Grace."

Marc came over with a mug of coffee and set it down

in front of Paul. "Here, Paul. Drink this. I put some brandy in it."

"Thank you." Paul wrapped one hand around the mug, but he kept his other arm firmly around Jayne's shoulders. It was an uncharacteristic display of affection in public, but he didn't want to let her go. "Will you join us, Marc? And I would be very pleased if one of you will tell me about the hand from the pool."

It took five minutes with everyone talking at once, but finally Paul had the complete story. "So you can understand why we need to notify the police right away," Clayton continued, moving his chair closer. "As Marc pointed out, there's the possibility that the bones are artificial, but we need the authorities to confirm it and we can't contact them by phone or e-mail. We don't have any means of communication at all now that Jack's shortwave radio is broken."

Paul could see that Clayton was looking at him expectantly. "Is there something you wish me to do?"

"Yes. I know this is an imposition, but you obviously know how to operate the snowmobile. We think you should go back to get the police. As soon as you warm up, of course."

Jayne stared at Clayton in absolute shock. "No way, Clay! If you're all fired-up to report those old bones, get your tail in gear and do it yourself!"

"She's got a point, Clay." Marc laughed. "You're the only one here who thinks it's an emergency."

"Is that so? No one else thinks we should go to the police immediately?" Clayton waited, but no one spoke up. "All right, then. I've never shirked my civic duty. Come on, Rachael. Let's go!"

Rachael frowned. "How did I get in on this? I agree that we have to file a report, but there's no reason why it can't wait until someone digs us out. Driving down the mountain at night on the back of a snowmobile is *not* my conception of civic duty."

Clayton was about to make a sharp retort when he saw the tears that had gathered in Rachael's eyes. She was clearly terrified at the prospect of leaving and he reached out to pat her hand. "You're right, honey. The police can wait. I guess I just got rattled there for a minute."

"Cabin fever." Grace nodded. "I read a book about a family trapped in a blizzard, and how they were all going crazy knowing they couldn't get out, and the snow was rattling against the windows, and the wind was howling louder than a pack of wolves and they'd used up the last of their food three days ago, and . . . I know, Moira. I'm babbling again."

Moira grinned. "I hate like h . . . heck to say it, but I was already beginning to miss your babbling. What do Norwegians do when they get cabin fever, Paul?"

"My grandfather carved the furniture in winter while Grandmother needled."

"She what?"

"Perhaps the word is not right, but she used big balls of wool to make mittens and stockings."

"That's called knitting," Moira told him. "But they did something to take their mind off the weather, is that right?"

"Yes. The winter in Norway is many months."

"Well, I don't make furniture and I sure can't knit." Jayne began to smile. "Maybe we could do some work instead, like packing up Johnny's stuff. Will you guys help me?"

"I will help." Paul was the first to offer even though he was tired from his long trip. Jayne had obviously been glad to see him, but he didn't know if her warm welcome would be extended to sharing their bed. There was bound to be an awkward moment and it might be wise to delay it as long as he could.

One by one the others chimed in, all except Vanessa. "I'm not setting foot in Johnny's place. Those two guys might be hiding out in there."

"What two guys?" Hal turned to his wife with a frown.

"The mean-looking ones that were there the day he left. I went down to say good-bye, but I split right away. They were straight out of *The Godfather.*"

Alan pointed at the glowing indicator over the elevator door. "Somebody's coming."

"Probably those mean-looking thugs from *The Godfather,*" Laureen suggested with a chuckle. "Maybe they're afraid Vanessa can identify them so they've come back to get rid of her."

Vanessa jumped up. "I don't think that's very funny! You wouldn't either if you'd seen them."

"Just take it easy, Vanessa." Marc reached out to pull her back into her chair. "There's nobody hiding out in Johnny's unit. I personally guarantee it. I've shown it to buyers."

Vanessa nodded. "Okay, I believe you. But who's coming up on the elevator?"

"Probably Betty's nurse. I stopped down there to tell her we'd be up here if she needed us."

The elevator doors opened and Walker stepped out. While Marc rushed to get him some hot coffee, Jayne turned to catch the smile that was spreading across Ellen's face.

"Walker! How did you get here?"

"I took the KLV helicopter to the ranger station, and

then I skied down. Who was on that snowmobile I heard?"

"Paul and Grace," Moira spoke up. "What's in the backpack, Walker?"

Walker handed it to Ellen. "The dye Ellen wanted. And a couple other items for survival in the wild. So fill me in, Moira. What happened?"

While everyone talked at once, Ellen unzipped the backpack and peered inside. Along with the dye were two other packages. She opened the first and discovered a bottle of her favorite *Fumé Blanc,* perfectly chilled. The second package looked like a shoe box and she almost laughed out loud as she lifted the lid and found fluffy white slippers with the face of a bunny on the toes. Just yesterday she'd mentioned that she needed new slippers. Silly and whimsical, these were the sort of thing she adored but would never have considered buying for herself.

"What did he bring you?" As Vanessa tried to peer into the backpack, Ellen closed it quickly.

"Just some things I needed from town."

"Like what?" Vanessa wasn't the type to give up easily, but Ellen knew everyone would tease her mercilessly if she showed them her new slippers. She glanced at Walker and saw that he was grinning, waiting for her to think up some way out of this awkward situation.

Ellen cleared her throat. "I told you, Vanessa. There's the dye for my mannequins and some alcohol. And then, there's . . . uh . . . something personal I needed."

Vanessa zeroed in. "What is it, Ellen? You can tell us."

Ellen noticed that Walker was still grinning and she shot a daggerlike look. "It's nothing, Vanessa. I have a little problem with the hare on my feet."

"You have *hair* on your feet?" Vanessa glanced down,

but Ellen was wearing boots. "That's really gross, Ellen. I hope Walker brought you a good depilatory."

"Hold it!" Hal stood and held his arms up in a bid for silence. "My child-bride just used a five-syllable word. Cause for celebration."

"Cut it out, Hal. I know lots of five-syllable words. I even know one that's eleven. *Antidisestablishmentarianism.* So there!"

"I'm impressed, Vanessa. Now spell it."

While Vanessa sputtered, Ellen glanced at Walker, who was cracking up. "We're going down to pack Johnny's things. Want to come along?"

"Sure." Walker sobered instantly. He'd heard enough bits and pieces of gossip to put the whole story together, and packing her former lover's possessions was bound to be an ordeal for Ellen.

Jayne spoke up. "Maybe we can find an address or a telephone number. I have to know where to ship Johnny's stuff and I don't have a clue."

"I guess I'd better help you then," Vanessa offered. "I learned how to search for clues by watching *Columbo.*"

Marc snorted. "Do you have a rumpled raincoat?"

"What?"

"Never mind, Vanessa." Marc exchanged a sympathetic glance with Hal. "But if you come across a Sandy Koufax ball, I could sure use it. I know Johnny bought one at the auction last year."

Vanessa looked puzzled. "What kind of ball was that?"

"A baseball. Sandy Koufax was a pitcher and it's a ball from his perfect game."

"Okay, Marc." Vanessa nodded. "I'll look around for a used baseball. But wouldn't you rather have one that's brand-new?"

EIGHT

"This gives me the creeps." Vanessa shivered a little as they stepped into Johnny's unit.

"What do you think we're going to find?" Marc chuckled. "Johnny's corpse?"

Vanessa turned to him in alarm. "Don't say that! Nobody's heard from Johnny since I saw him with those scary guys."

"It's all right, Vanessa." Marc was still grinning. "I told you I showed this unit, and I would have noticed if Johnny's body was here."

"You didn't open every closet, did you?"

Hal laughed. "If Johnny's body was stuffed in a closet, we wouldn't be able to get within a hundred yards of this place. Relax, child-bride. I guarantee there's no body here."

"But how can you tell?"

Hal groaned. "Use your head, Vanessa. Have you ever smelled hamburger that's gone bad?"

"Yes, but . . ."

"Let's change the subject," Walker interrupted, noticing that Ellen was turning pale. "Is the electricity still on? We didn't bring flashlights."

"Hold on." Moira patted the wall until she found the switch and the hallway flooded with light. "Does anyone have a game plan?"

Jayne shook her head. "I thought we'd just start stuffing things in boxes."

Moira shook her head. "That's not the way to do it. I suggest we split up into groups. Do we have packing materials?"

"Johnny said he'd leave boxes and tape in the hall closet." Jayne opened it and looked inside. "Yup. Everything's here. Even a couple of wardrobe boxes and a dish pack."

Moira took charge. "There's a lot to do so let's get our uh . . . tails in gear. Jayne and Paul? Why don't you pack up the music rooms since you know about pianos and musical instruments. Ellen and Walker can help you. Grace and I'll take the living room. Marc? You start in on the master bedroom and Laureen and Alan can pack up the kitchen."

"Why do people always put me in the kitchen?" Laureen complained.

Alan put his arm around her shoulders. "Because you're the expert. You'll know what to pack and what to throw out."

"That's right," Moira confirmed. "No insult intended, Laureen, but I wouldn't know a truffle from a trifle and neither would anyone else in this group. Clayton and Rachael can take their pick of the rooms that are left over. And then they can wander around and poke their noses into everything, since they're the lawyers."

Rachael laughed. "That's your conception of lawyers? People who poke their noses into everything?"

"Well, I didn't mean it quite that way." Moira grinned. "Vanessa and Hal? You'd better take the den. There's a lot to pack in there. And if anyone finds a clue to Johnny's whereabouts, just holler."

Grace looked impressed. "You're really organized, aren't you, Moira?"

"Just used to directing my work crews. Is everyone set?"

Hal pulled Vanessa toward the den. "Come on, we'd better get started."

"But they never start with the den on *Columbo!*"

Hal propelled her through the door. "Johnny practically lived in that room. If he left an address or a telephone number, it might be in there."

"Oh." Vanessa looked slightly mollified, but she turned to deliver a parting shot. "At least we didn't get the kitchen. Laureen'll probably dig through the garbage to find out what Johnny had for his last meal."

Laureen started to sputter and Alan put his arm around her. "Easy, honey. Vanessa's just jealous, that's all."

"Of what?"

"Of you. You've got a husband who's crazy about you. That's more than she'll ever have. And she's too young and too stupid to understand why."

Laureen looked up at him suspiciously. "Do you really think she's jealous of me?"

"Of course. All she has going for her is her looks. You've got that plus a lot more."

Grace looked pleased as Laureen and Alan headed for the kitchen. "How sweet! They're actually holding hands. Think Laureen's finally forgiven him?"

"Maybe." Rachael shrugged. "And maybe not, but it's a good sign. Come on, Clay. I'm beginning to think

Vanessa's right. Something really could have happened to Johnny. Let's start with the bathrooms."

"The Harris case. Good thinking, honey."

"Hold it a second." Moira stopped them. "What's the Harris case?"

"It got a lot of press last fall in the scandal sheets," Clayton explained. "Harris was a doctor in Boston. His wife's friends got worried when she didn't show up for her bridge club a couple of weeks in a row and called the police. Dr. Harris told them that his wife had packed up all her clothes and left while he was at the hospital. He said he was so embarrassed that he hadn't told anyone. Since it was common knowledge that Mrs. Harris had been involved with several other men, the police were ready to file a missing person report and close their investigation."

Rachael picked up on the story. "Then some smart woman detective searched the house and found his wife's contacts in a bathroom drawer."

"That was the turning point." Clayton took over the story. "The optometrist confirmed that Mrs. Harris was too vain to wear glasses and she was legally blind without her contact lenses. It was so unlikely she would leave them behind that the police reopened their investigation."

"Did they eventually locate Mrs. Harris?" Paul asked.

"Oh, yes." Rachael nodded. "Dr. Harris had used some kind of acid to dissolve her flesh. Her skeleton was hanging in his lab at the hospital."

Jayne stuck close to Paul as they entered the huge music room. Even though she was sure they wouldn't find Johnny's skeleton, the Harris story had still unnerved her. Then Paul flicked on the lights and the sight of Johnny's collection took her mind off her concern. He had twenty museum-quality pieces in his studio, all set off with spotlights.

"Look at this!" Walker walked over to the huge upright mahogany cabinet in the center of the room. "It's awfully big. Did people actually have these in their homes?"

Jayne shook her head. "They were usually in restaurants or hotel lobbies. Do you want me to show you how it works?"

Walker nodded and Jayne flicked the switch. The two antique lamps on either side of the mahogany cabinet began to glow and the doors in the center slid open to expose a full-size piano keyboard. "This is an orchestrion. It mechanically replicates the sound of an entire orchestra. The music is recorded on a roll, just like a player piano, and those little levers behind the glass activate the whole thing. I think it plays a Strauss waltz, but I don't remember which one."

Ellen laughed in delight as the orchestrion began to play. "*Tales from the Vienna Woods.* I never could play that last part right."

"You played the piano?" Jayne turned to her in surprise.

"I *tried* to play the piano," Ellen corrected. "I was so awful that I finally convinced my mother that lessons were a waste of money."

"Were you awful on purpose?"

"Of course not!" Ellen stopped and looked slightly guilty. "Well . . . maybe I didn't exactly apply myself. It made me mad when I had to stay inside to practice. My mother was raised in the old school. She believed a girl should learn to embroider, play a musical instrument, and draw. I managed to learn how to draw, but that's only one out of three."

"That's not a bad average." Walker'd been around long enough to realize that Ellen had made a career out of selling herself short. "As Marc would say, they sure won't kick you out of the majors for batting three thirty-three."

"He's right, Ellen, honey." Jayne waited until the music had stopped, then flicked a switch and another set of lamps on the piece next to the orchestrion began to glow. It looked like an ordinary piano, but a glass case containing three violins was built in above the keyboard. "This one's called a Hupfeld Phonolizst-Violina. It's not quite as impressive as the orchestrion, but it's really very complicated. See those mechanical arms holding the violin bows? Now watch. And listen."

They were all silent as the mechanical arms began to draw the bows across the strings. Ellen sighed enviously. "Isn't that wonderful? It never makes a mistake. What is it playing?"

"*Sonata in C major*, by Mozart," Paul said. "It was the composer's first mature violin-piano sonata."

When the piece was over, Walker turned to Jayne and asked for one more. "These instruments are really something."

Jayne led them over to the lovely grand piano in the corner. "This is my favorite. The owners of the piano would hire a popular virtuoso to come to their home to give a little concert. The piano recorded it on a punch roll and the owners kept it to play whenever they wanted. I guess you could say that it's the great-grandpappy of the tape recorder."

Walker examined the piano carefully. "I see how it

works. Hey, Jayne! There's a shipping label on the side telling the movers to deliver it to your studio."

Jayne's mouth dropped open. "My studio? But why?"

"There's something written on the roll." Ellen peered down at it. "It says, *Listen to this, Jayne.*"

Jayne switched on the piano, which began to play a one-fingered melody. She looked at Paul and frowned. "What is it?"

Paul listened for a moment and then he shook his head. "I have never heard it before. Perhaps it is an original written by Johnny."

"It's not very good," Ellen pointed out, making a face. "If that's the best Johnny could do, I'm glad he hired you to write his songs."

Jayne switched off the piano and ran her fingers over its glossy surface, an amazed smile on her face. "I just can't believe a gift like this. It's incredible!"

Walker knelt to look under the piano. "It's on a dolly. I think we can move it by ourselves if we get a little help. What do you say, Jayne? Shall we wheel it up to your studio right now?"

"Let's wait until tomorrow. It'll be easier in the daylight. This is so exciting!"

Paul glanced at this watch. "We had better begin the packing. The others will be finished before we have started."

Jayne shrugged. Paul was right; she knew they had to get to work, but it was so damn typical of him to remind her. There were times when she liked to play hooky from her obligations. She knew she'd have to make up the time by working harder, but it was worth it. It was a basic difference in their personalities. Jayne sighed as she walked over to a standard player piano and looked through the box for a suitable roll. "Why don't you two start boxing the stuff in Johnny's practice room? And I'll put on the 'Maple Leaf Rag' to work by."

"Great." Walker nodded and headed for the alcove in time to Joplin's bouncy tune. "Come on, Ellen, let's go."

As soon as they were alone, Paul turned to Jayne. "I will now take the cow by her horn. You are angry because I reminded you of the work to be done?"

"Take the bull by the horns," Jayne corrected him. "And yes, I'm madder than a wet hen. We've got all week to do this packing and I was having such a good time showing off Johnny's collection. You've got a problem, Paul. You never did learn how to kick back and have fun!"

"Norwegians are by nature a humorless people." Paul looked very serious. "We eat lutefisk and enjoy it."

Jayne stared at him for a moment and then doubled over in laughter. "You made a joke, Paul! I never heard you make a joke before!"

"Does this mean that you have forgiven me for suggesting the work?"

"I guess so." Jayne blew the dust off an old metronome and put it in the box. "Why aren't you packing, Paul? I thought you were so hot to work."

Paul crossed the room and knelt down beside her. "Perhaps you have convinced me to boot back and have fun."

"Kick back." Jayne corrected him automatically. "And you don't know how to have fun."

Paul didn't bother to reply. He just lifted her to her feet and whirled her around the room until the "Maple Leaf Rag" had finished with a crashing finale.

"Was that not fun, Jayne?" Paul's voice was loud in the sudden silence.

Jayne laughed as she reached for another carton and opened it. "I take it all back. By the way, I need a rhyme for a song I'm writing. Can you help me out when we get home?"

"Of course." Paul glanced over at her, but she was busy filling the carton. *When we get home.* Was that Jayne's way of asking him to come back into her life? Or was it just a turn of phrase?

Ellen sighed as she took a stack of sheet music from the shelf and handed it to Walker. It was "Lonesome Hours," one of Johnny's early hits. Seeing Johnny's familiar smile on the cover made her feel like crying. She'd been so sure he loved her. And she'd been so wrong.

"Do you want me to do this, Ellen?" Walker's voice was gentle. "You could start on the stuff in the closet."

"No." Ellen picked up another stack of music and flipped it over so she didn't have to look at Johnny's picture. The closet would be even worse. Johnny kept his working clothes there, all the sequined shirts and satin tuxedos he'd worn for his performances. There would be the lingering scent of his expensive cologne and she'd have to fold them and pack them and try not to imagine how he'd looked when he'd sung her favorite songs.

Walker looked up at Ellen as he assembled the next carton. Perhaps she was trying to exorcise ghosts by helping to pack Johnny's things, but it wasn't working. "Why don't you take a break and see how Laureen's doing in the kitchen? I can finish up in here."

Ellen shook her head. She knew Walker was trying to spare her, but the kitchen would be even worse. They'd sipped coffee together at Johnny's kitchen table out of matching mugs. And shared take-out Chinese they'd picked up in town and reheated in his microwave. The silver chopsticks he'd given her for her birthday were still in the drawer by the stove, and the special rice bowl with her name on the side was in the cupboard. No, she didn't want to set foot in the kitchen.

Thank God Moira hadn't suggested they pack up the bedroom! One look at Johnny's bed and Ellen knew she would have been in tears. And the den would have been just as bad. They'd watched late-night movies together, cuddled up on the overstuffed leather couch, eating popcorn and drinking Johnny's favorite imported beer. The living room was out, too. She'd played hostess there at Johnny's parties, giving instructions to the caterers and florists, and meeting his friends. The picture she'd given him hung over the fireplace, an original drawing of Johnny onstage that had taken her months to complete. No room in Johnny's condo was safe from memories.

"Ellen? Are you all right?"

Realizing that Walker was staring at her, Ellen nodded shakily.

"I think that's enough work for tonight." Walker taped the box shut and pushed it against the wall. "Come on, Ellen. Let's go up and open that wine I brought."

"But there must be twenty boxes left to pack."

"They can wait." Walker took her arm and propelled her into the room where Jayne and Paul were working. "We're knocking off for tonight. Ellen needs some rest."

"She sure does." Jayne nodded. "Go to bed, Ellen, honey. You look like you've been rode hard and put up wet."

Less than ten minutes later, Ellen was sitting on her own couch in her own living room, wearing her new bunny slippers. It was a relief to be home again. Walker came in from the kitchen with the wine and stopped to smile at the slippers. "You look cute with hare on your feet."

"Thank you." It was an effort, but Ellen managed to return his smile. "These are the silliest things I've ever seen in my life."

"I knew you'd like them. How's the wine?"

Ellen took a sip and smiled again. "Perfect."

When Walker sat down in the big chair across the room, Ellen began to relax. He seemed to know that she didn't like close contact. She was lucky to have such an understanding friend.

They sat in silence until they'd finished their wine. Then Walker got to his feet. "Can I get you another glass of wine before I go?"

"Go where?" Ellen was puzzled.

"Marc said I could use Johnny's place since I'm stuck up here with the rest of you."

"But they've packed up all of Johnny's sheets and bedding. Why don't you stay here with me?"

The moment the words were out of Ellen's mouth, she wished she hadn't said them.

"Do you want to rethink that, Ellen? I know you're offering your extra bedroom, but some of your neighbors might talk."

He was reading her mind again! Ellen could feel the color rise to her cheeks. "Forget the neighbors. If you stay here, we can start cleaning up the workroom first thing in the morning."

"That's fine with me if you're sure it won't cause any problems." Walker got the wine bottle from the kitchen and refilled her glass. "Take this to bed with you, Ellen. I'm going to start on that cleanup before I turn in."

Ellen took his advice and finished the wine before she got ready for bed and turned off the lights. It was comforting, knowing that he was only a few steps away. Perhaps she wouldn't have another nightmare tonight. She'd been absolutely right to tell him she didn't care what the neighbors thought. It was time she started living her own life.

NINE

After two hours of packing, Clayton had called them all into Johnny's living room. "Any luck?"

Laureen shook her head. "Nothing in the kitchen. We even rubbed a pencil over the pad of paper by Johnny's kitchen phone."

"Why did you do a silly thing like that?" Vanessa giggled.

"It's not silly at all." Hal sighed as he explained. "When a person writes, it can leave an impression on the paper underneath. I thought you said you watched *Columbo*."

"I must have missed that one. So what did it say?"

"Where's Ellen?"

"That's what it said? *Where's Ellen?*"

"No." Alan looked as exasperated as Hal. "We just want to know where Ellen is."

Jayne spoke up. "Walker took her home. She was all dragged out."

"Good. We didn't want to say this in front of her, but one of Johnny's girlfriends left him a note. It said, *Roses are red, violets are blue. Thanks a lot for the screw.* And *violets* was misspelled."

"That figures." Marc snorted. "Johnny never picked his girlfriends for their brainpower."

Laureen noticed that Vanessa's cheeks were very red. "How *do* you spell *violets*, Vanessa?"

"*V . . . I . . .* oh, who cares." Vanessa glared at Laureen. "I'm sure you know how to spell it. Tell her what we found, Hal. That's much more important. It proves Johnny never left on that plane!"

Hal nodded. "We found Johnny's airplane tickets. One-way to Italy, still in the folder with his itinerary."

Laureen shrugged. "That doesn't prove a thing. Johnny might have forgotten them and asked for duplicates at the airport. Or maybe he decided he wouldn't bother with paper tickets and downloaded e-tickets. I've done that a couple of times."

"So has Gracie." Moira grinned at her roommate, who was starting to blush. "Except Gracie left the e-tickets at home, too. But we don't think Johnny left on that plane, either. Grace and I found his telephone bill and there's not one single overseas call."

"What does that have to do with the price of apples?" Marc frowned.

"It's just strange, that's all," Grace pointed out. "When my father died, I spent a lot of time on the phone making arrangements with my mother. Of course I tried to call after five when the rates were down, but there were so many things to take care of and the lawyers' offices were closed after three because there's a two-hour time difference between Vegas and Indiana and I don't think it was daylight savings time or there would have been three hours because they don't have it there, you know. So anyway, my total phone bill was simply . . ."

"I told you those tickets we found were important!" Vanessa interrupted. "Johnny wouldn't leave without calling Italy to tell his mother what time to meet the plane!"

Clayton held up his hand. "We may be jumping to erroneous conclusions. Johnny could have called from the casino."

"We thought of that," Grace continued, "but I was doing a show for Johnny then and I know he never got to the casino more than fifteen minutes before his show because his parking spot was right next to mine. They've got the nerve to call it executive parking, but it's really not because all the spots on the top level are uncovered and if it rains, your car gets wet and you have to walk all the way across . . . Okay, Moira. I know I'm babbling. Anyway, I used to see Johnny pull in at seven forty-five and my girls complained that he left right after the nine o'clock show without even signing autographs."

"So what does that mean?" Vanessa looked blank.

"It means he couldn't have called from the casino," Moira explained. "There's a six- or seven-hour time difference, and I don't think Johnny would call his relatives in the middle of the night."

Clayton looked impressed. "That's very astute!"

"But it still doesn't prove anything." Marc spoke up. "Johnny could have called from his cell phone, or a girlfriend's phone, or his relatives could have called him. I packed up the stuff in Johnny's bedroom and I'm positive he left. His suitcases are gone and he took his clothes."

"His toilet articles are gone, too," Rachael added. "Toothpaste, toothbrush, comb, razor, antiperspirant."

Marc looked pleased. "There you go! A man doesn't pack a suitcase unless he's planning on taking a trip."

"A point well taken." Clayton nodded. "On the other hand, if the two men Vanessa so graphically described engaged in any type of foul play, they may have confiscated the items in question."

"Huh?" Vanessa frowned.

Rachael assumed her role as interpreter again. "Clay's saying that if the thugs got to Johnny, they'd take the suitcases to make us think Johnny had left."

"That's what I said in the first place!" Vanessa was so excited, she almost shouted. "I told you those two guys looked mean enough to murder him!"

Hal grinned. "Sure, Vanessa. But what did they do with the body?"

"They dug a hole and they buried it. That's what you do with dead people."

"They didn't dig a hole up here. The ground's been frozen for over two months."

"Then they took him somewhere else to bury him. Or maybe . . ." Vanessa jumped to her feet. "I know! They chopped Johnny up in pieces and put him in the incinerator! I saw a movie where they did that. Do I win?"

"It's not a game, child-bride. Is that possible, Alan? Could someone cremate a body in our incinerator?"

Alan shook his head. "No way. Our incinerator doesn't reach temperatures that high. There'd still be big chunks of bone left behind."

Vanessa made a face. "Oh, yuck! I know it was my idea, but I'm not going down there to look for Johnny's bones."

There was a long silence before Jayne spoke up. "Nobody has to look, Vanessa. There's nothing in our incinerator except ashes."

"But how do you know?"

Jayne's face began to turn red. "Because I dropped something down there yesterday and I had to sift through the ashes to get it back."

"Grandmother Lindstrom's silver ice bucket?" Paul sighed as Jayne's face turned even redder.

"Well . . . yes. But it only got one little dent that you can hardly notice. And I polished it afterward. I'm sorry, Paul. I promise I'll never use it for a wastebasket again."

Paul nodded even though he knew Jayne would forget. She seemed to lack respect for the silver his family had given them as a wedding present. She'd been thrilled to receive it and she kept it beautifully polished, but a few months after their marriage he'd found the coffee server doubling as a vase for flowers and the cream pitcher sitting on top of her piano holding pencils and pens. The only piece that had retained its original purpose was the candelabra and Paul knew that was only because Jayne had yet to find something that would fit into the holes. When he had objected, Jayne had informed him that silver wasn't any fun if you kept it wrapped up in bags.

"Okay, let's call it a night." Clayton yawned and headed for the door. "We can finish up the packing tomorrow."

Hal took Vanessa's arm to pull her up, but she refused to budge. "Where's everyone going? I thought we were going to decide what happened to Johnny."

"We've got all week." Hal got a better grip on her arm and hauled her to her feet. "I'm tired and I want to go to bed."

"Oh, sure. You want to go to bed, but you sure don't want to . . ." Hal squeezed her arm and Vanessa let out a little yelp as he pushed her through the doorway.

"We're leaving, too." Moira stood up. "Poor Grace is beginning to droop."

"True enough," Grace sighed, "but I wish you wouldn't point it out in public. You're no spring chicken either, you know."

Moira let out a whoop of laughter. "I guess I deserved that one. Come on, Gracie."

"Me, too." Marc headed for the door. "I have to check my answer phone. I'm expecting an important call."

"I'll bet you ten bucks you didn't get it." Rachael looked smug.

"You're on. This guy promised he'd call right after dinner and he must have called the land line, because I didn't get any calls on my cell . . . oh, hell!" Marc started to laugh. "I forgot. The phone lines are down and none of our cell phones work."

Clayton waited until they were all out the door. "Hold the elevator while I lock up."

"Why bother?" Alan asked him.

"Because someone could walk right into the building and steal Johnny's possessions. Our security system's down."

"But we've got a natural backup system."

"We have? Jack never mentioned it."

"That's because Jack didn't know. It's called the avalanche system and nobody's getting in or out until they move that wall of snow."

I'll swap my plans to that singular dream
A lady alone with her get-rich scheme
'Cause all I need is a blankety-blank
And a ride on the carousel of love.

Jayne swiveled on the piano bench to look at Paul. "So what do you think? Do I need a teensy shove? A black satin glove? Or the stars above?"

"I do not care for any of the three." Paul frowned slightly. "They do not meet your usual standard, Jayne."

"I know that. Come on, Paul. I've got to come up with

a finale, but I can't think of anything else that rhymes with love."

"Perhaps you should attempt to rhyme with *A* and *B* and permit your strongest line to stand alone."

"Can I do that?" Jayne looked dubious.

"Certainly." Paul nodded. "Many excellent poets have written in this manner."

"Okay, if you say so. But I'm still stuck for a rhyme."

Paul hummed the melody twice. Then he smiled. "If you'll give me one chance to grab the brass ring when I ride on the carousel of love."

Jayne scribbled on her pad of paper and sang the stanza again.

> *I'll swap my plans to that singular dream*
> *A lady alone with her get-rich scheme*
> *If you'll give me one chance to grab the brass ring*
> *When I ride on the carousel of love.*

"I like it, Paul. I like it a lot. But ring doesn't exactly rhyme with dream and scheme."

"It will when Miss Rawlins sings it."

Jayne turned to him in surprise. "You've been listening to Barbie's records?"

"This is true. I have attempted to identify her most unusual accent."

Jayne began to smile. "Sure you have. And the Pope just turned Lutheran. You were listening to country-western because you missed it."

"No, Jayne. I did not miss the music. I missed you."

Jayne felt suddenly shy. The moment she'd been avoiding was close and she wasn't sure how to react. She'd missed Paul, too, but should she come right out and say it? Instead, she changed the subject. "You must have missed dinner. Do you want something to eat?"

Paul nodded. "Do you have the Cheese Whiz, Jayne?"

"Cheese Whiz?" Jayne's voice was incredulous. "You always said that you hated processed cheese. Wild horses couldn't drag you to try it."

"I have changed my mind, Jayne. I recently purchased a jar and I have developed the taste."

Jayne was thoughtful as she went into the kitchen and fixed a plate of crackers. She set the jar of Cheese Whiz in the center and prepared to carry it into the studio. Paul had definitely missed her if he'd listened to Barbie Rawlins songs and tried Cheese Whiz, but that didn't mean that he could just waltz up here and pick up the threads of their marriage. They'd both learned how to compromise in the months they had been apart, but basic issues persisted.

They sat on opposite ends of the piano bench and munched crackers in silence, passing the jar of cheese back and forth. Jayne blushed as she realized that Paul was staring at her. Damn that cool Scandinavian exterior! She never had been able to read his expressions. Did he want her as much as she wanted him? Or should she observe the proprieties and insist he sleep on the couch? It was all so confusing that she was ready to jump out of her skin, especially since she couldn't seem to stop imagining how good it would be if they were in bed together.

"What is wrong, Jayne? Are you unhappy that I am here?"

"Of course not." Paul was looking at her with concern and Jayne decided to confront him straight on. "I'm just trying to decide whether I should follow my instincts and drag you to bed."

"That would be very wonderful." Paul began to smile.

"Yes, but we haven't settled anything yet. Remember that awful argument we had?"

"I remember. And I must offer to you my apology."

Jayne sighed deeply. "You can't apologize if you didn't start it and you didn't, I did. I flew off the handle and I knew I was wrong, but I was too damn ornery to admit it."

"That is not true, Jayne. I am the one who left and I am also the one at fault."

Jayne shook her head. "No, Paul. I pushed you too hard and I should have known better. You had to leave. I didn't give you any other choice."

"No, Jayne. You had worked all night and you were very tired. I failed to appreciate your exhaustion."

"That's ridiculous!" Jayne's voice was rising. "You're just making excuses for me. You always make excuses for me. I'm adult enough to admit that I was wrong!"

"You were not wrong! The blame belongs to me!"

Paul realized that he was glaring at Jayne and she looked just as upset. Unable to resist, he started to chuckle.

"What's so funny?"

Jayne glared at him, arms crossed, and Paul laughed out loud. Clearly reconciliation had its pitfalls, too.

"Answer me, Paul! What's so funny?"

Jayne's eyes were flashing and Paul could tell she was growing furious, but he couldn't seem to stop laughing. The whole argument was utterly absurd.

"If all you can do is stand there and laugh like a hyena, you can turn right around and go back down that damned . . ." Paul pulled her into his arms and silenced her with a kiss. At first she sputtered, but then her arms tightened around him and she kissed him back.

"What was that for?" Jayne looked confused when he let her go at last.

"If we had continued to argue about our previous argument, it would have been another six months before I saw you again."

"But it really was my fault. You've got to see . . ."

Paul grabbed her and kissed her again. Why hadn't he thought of this before? When he let her go, Jayne was giggling.

"I get it. Every time we start to fight, you kiss me. Is that right?"

"That is correct. It is impossible to disagree if we cannot talk." Paul stood up and extended his hand. "Come, Jayne. Let us go to bed before we begin another quarrel. It is also impossible to argue in bed."

Jayne took his arm and let him take her to the bedroom. She sighed in pure enjoyment as Paul undressed her and she felt his warm hands on her skin. Oh, how she'd missed his hands and his lips and his strong, warm body that made her cry out in delight! Her last rational thought, before passion turned her body into a trembling cluster of needs and desires, was that Paul was right. They had never argued in bed. If they just stayed between the sheets forever, they wouldn't have any problems at all.

TEN

An hour passed while he paced the floor in the garage security office until he was sure that everyone had gone to bed. Then he retrieved the pricey, compact, shortwave radio from his vehicle and carried it up to the penthouse spa.

He glanced at his watch as he switched it on. Almost midnight. The Old Man would be in bed. The device crackled as he attempted to connect and he moved to a better spot next to one of the glass windows where the static was minimal. His contact was almost out of range, but the altitude worked in his favor, a straight shot down the mountain with no obstacles.

"Yes?" A female voice with a slight foreign accent answered immediately. Since the Old Man's wife had died in childbirth over thirty years ago, he'd surrounded himself with a succession of beautiful women. This one was Colette, a young French showgirl, his personal companion for the past six months.

"I'm calling from Deer Creek and I need to talk to him."

"May I please say who needs to speak with him?"

"I'm the Caretaker." He frowned, hating his code name. Every time he used it, he felt like an actor in a cheap movie. Unfortunately, precautions were a necessary evil.

"Just a moment. I'll get him."

The voice he heard next was sharp with concern. "Is she all right?"

"She's fine." The Old Man always asked about her. He didn't give a damn about anyone else and he never had. "I need some advice."

"You woke me. This had better be good."

"It is. The people who took care of your problem last month left the tickets behind. They were discovered tonight."

There was a long silence with nothing but static while The Old Man considered the problem. Moments before he'd switched on the device, he'd decided that there was no sense in mentioning the bones in the pool. He'd already removed them and substituted a couple of steak bones from the garbage. It could all be chalked up to post-avalanche panic.

The old geezer who'd seen too much when he'd cleaned up the construction debris had been completely expendable. The soldiers had dumped him behind the liner and no one except the mission do-gooders had missed him. They'd figured that he'd wandered off to try his luck in another city. It was one less mouth to feed and the bums down there dropped in and left whenever they wanted. The horseshoe ring was no problem, either. It had no identifying marks and for all anyone knew, it could have belonged to a worker on the construction crew. There was no sense in bothering the Old Man with details. The problem had been solved and that was what counted.

"Hello?" he asked, wondering if he'd lost his connection. This was taking too much long. There was no answer and he was about to disconnect and try again when the Old Man spoke.

"You can talk now. I hooked up a scrambler. How about those suitcases?"

"Your soldiers put them in the gardening shed. They barely had room for the body in the truck."

"Get rid of them."

"I will, as soon as I can get down the mountain. They're safe. I put on a new padlock and I have the only key."

"There's nothing else to tie us to that rat?"

"Nothing concrete, but one of the women spotted your soldiers. She said they looked mean and scary."

"They are." The Old Man chuckled. "Contact me if there's any problem. You got that?"

"I got it." He was still scowling as he switched off. He'd been well rewarded for being the Old Man's errand boy, set up in a business that netted all the money he'd ever need and served as a laundry besides, but he'd never been trusted to act on his own. He knew he was much more capable than others who held positions of honor. All he had to do was prove it.

Rachael sat in one of Clayton's big leather armchairs and watched him pace. He was restless tonight and even though she was tired, she didn't want to go to bed without him.

"So what do we have for damage, Rachael?" Clayton stopped by the couch to pick up one of the legal pads on the coffee table.

"Nothing of any consequence. A couple of broken glasses from the bar and . . ."

"The crystal?" Clayton looked worried as he interrupted her.

"No, the tumblers I bought for parties. They weren't expensive. And my Mexican piggy bank's cracked, but I can always get another. Five dollars at the flea market."

Clayton made a note on the pad. "Anything else?"

"Only the big clay pot for the rose tree. It's been looking sick anyway. I'll have someone take care of it just as soon as the road's clear."

"The rose tree with the yellow flowers?" Clayton frowned as Rachael nodded. "Those are Darby's Marshall Golds. She worked for years on that strain. Will it live until we can call in a gardener?"

Rachael hesitated. "I think so, but you know how lousy I am with plants. Do you want to take a look?"

"I guess I'd better."

Rachael watched as Clayton opened the sliding glass door to the rose garden and stepped out. She knew he hated to go into the rose garden, which had been virtually neglected since Darby had died. It was too beautiful to go to waste, but Rachael's gardening skills were minimal and now that their regular gardener had quit, she had to find someone else to take over his duties.

Clayton came in, frowning. "It's root-bound. That's probably why the pot broke. And it doesn't look like it'll last for long. Do you think you could help me move it to another pot? There's a whole stack of them in the gazebo."

"Of course I can." Rachael jumped to her feet. Working together in the rose garden would be wonderful therapy for Clayton, almost as effective as making love in Darby's sitting room.

It took twenty minutes of backbreaking effort with Clayton lifting and Rachael steadying the tree while he poured in the potting soil, but they'd finally managed to transplant it into a big earthenware pot. Rachael stepped back and brushed off her hands. "Done! Now let's hope it thrives."

"Not without more potting soil." Clayton bent down to point at the base. "See that line around the trunk? It's called a crown and the soil has to come up far enough to cover it. I'd better put in another couple of bags."

"You can't. I brought out the last one. Shall we dig some dirt from the garden and fill in with that?"

"Not advisable." Clayton shook his head. "This is a special mixture for plants in pots, and garden soil has a different composition. I guess we should have left it and hoped for the best."

Clayton looked so disappointed that Rachael knew she had to do something. "Maybe there's some soil in the gardener's shed. Let's go down and take a look."

"I don't know who has the key."

"Never let a little technicality stand in your way. That's the first thing I learned after I passed the bar. This junior lawyer's been picking locks since she was six years old."

Clayton looked shocked and Rachael explained as they rode down on the elevator. "I was a latchkey kid. When I was little, I used to forget my key at school so I learned how to pick the lock on the front door. That came in so handy, I started to practice on other locks, too. I got into my foster mother's desk and my foster father's liquor cabinet and I even learned how to pick the padlock on my foster brother's ten-speed so I could take it for a spin when he was away at summer camp. Even more important, I was the only girl on campus who didn't have to wake up the housemother when she came in late."

"It's amazing you didn't turn to a life of crime." Clayton grinned down at her. Rachael never ceased to surprise him.

"Well, I wasn't quite that good," Rachael admitted with a giggle. "But I know I can pick the flimsy padlock on that gardening shed."

The gardening shed ran the width of the garage and Clayton watched while Rachael examined the lock. "It's the same kind of padlock my foster brother had on his bike. If I remember correctly, I just twisted to the left while I poked a hairpin halfway in and . . . I did it, Clay!"

Rachael stepped to the side while Clayton opened the door and switched on the lights. There was a whole shelf of potting soil and they each grabbed two bags. "Anything else we need before I lock it back up again?"

"I don't think so." Clayton headed for the door. "Don't trip on those suitcases, Rachael."

Rachael looked puzzled. "What are suitcases doing in here? We've got individual storage bins for things like that."

"Good question. Do you suppose they belonged to our gardener?"

Rachael put down the potting soil. "There's only one way to tell."

"I'm not sure we should . . ." Clayton stopped in midsentence as Rachael unzipped the little carry-on bag. It was too late to protest and he was just as curious as she was.

"Passports!" Rachael held up the distinctive folders and began to flip through them. "Look at this, Clay. They're issued in different names, but they all have

Johnny Day's picture on them! Why would Johnny have fake passports?"

"Got me . . . but we'd better take them with us. And I'm definitely calling the authorities as soon as our phones start working again!"

Rachael stuffed the passports in her pocket, grabbed the bags of potting soil, and followed Clayton to the elevator. She didn't bother to relock the door since they'd be coming back down in the morning to show the others.

When they got back to their own apartment, Clayton went out to pour the potting soil around the rose tree while she sat down on the couch to examine their find. Four different passports with Johnny's picture, issued to Joe Perrino, Ramone Bertoni, Frederic Sorrento, and Johnny Day.

"I think we saved the Marshall Golds." Clayton was smiling when he came in, but he quickly sobered when he saw her face. "What is it?"

"This passport's got Johnny's real name on it." Rachael held it out to him. "He couldn't have left the country without it, could he?"

"Of course he could. He probably used another fake one. Still, it's definitely another piece of the puzzle. We'll discuss it with the others in the morning. How about a nightcap before we turn in?"

"That would be nice." Rachael smiled at him. Clayton always suggested a nightcap when he wanted to make love to her. It had become one of their private rituals, a small glass of sherry preceding an enjoyable interlude in bed.

When they'd finished their sherry, Rachael rinsed out the glasses while Clayton showered, and then she hurried to her dressing room to put on Clayton's favorite negligee, a floor-length wisp of rosy pink lace. She creamed her face, brushed her hair, and sighed as she took her toothbrush out of the holder. She didn't feel like going through the whole routine tonight with the plaque rinse and the brushing and the flossing, but she had an appointment with her dentist next week and he'd go through the roof if he knew she hadn't followed his instructions.

While Rachael rushed through her prescribed dental hygiene program, she thought about the passports again. Now she wished she'd taken the time to open the other suitcases. Were there more passports inside? Or did they contain something even more interesting, like smuggled jewels or contraband drugs? If Clayton was still in the shower when she got through, she'd slip on a robe and run down to the gardener's shed to check.

Clayton was waiting for her when she emerged from her bathroom. He was wearing nothing but a towel and it was obvious that he'd been thinking about her. When he switched out the lights and put his arms around her, Rachael decided that the suitcases could definitely wait.

Betty smiled at her secret friend and took another piece of candy. She was getting very sleepy, but that was all right. Her friend had told her to go to sleep anytime she wanted and he'd even covered her with her favorite blanket. She felt warm and happy, just knowing that he was taking care of her. He was much nicer than Nurse.

They were watching a movie on forbidden channel five, but it wasn't very interesting. The actor and the actress were in bed and the man had just switched on the light. He was reaching for a glass of water when Betty's secret friend began to smile. Perhaps this was a comedy and she'd missed something. She thought she'd nodded off a few minutes ago, but she wasn't sure. Her head felt as light as the pink fluff from the carnival. What was it called? *Cotton candy*, those were the words.

Betty was proud of herself. She'd remembered something. She wished she could tell the man called Jack, but he had gone to the hospital. She'd try to remember to tell him when he came back all about the comedy that wasn't very funny and the candy cotton and how her secret friend had smiled.

Clayton woke up to reach for the water glass and poured in the packet of bromo he kept by his side of the bed. Despite Rachael's warning, he'd eaten some of her hot salsa. His stomach was still on fire and the corn chips had made him terribly thirsty.

He glanced over at Rachael's side of the bed and noticed that her water glass was empty. She must have been thirsty, too.

"Rachael? Do you want me to get you more water?" Clayton waited for a moment, but Rachael was sound asleep. He knew that filling her glass would be the gentlemanly thing to do, but he was so tired, he couldn't face the thought of walking all the way to the bathroom and back. If Rachael wanted more water in the middle of the night, she'd just have to get it herself. Wasn't that what women's lib had been all about?

He frowned as he settled back against the pillow. The water had a bitter aftertaste. Perhaps the avalanche had loosened some rust in the pipes.

There was a burning sensation in Clayton's chest and he wished the bromo would work faster. He was utterly exhausted, and it had nothing to do with the packing they'd done for Johnny or repotting Darby's Marshall Golds. He was a middle-aged man, in good shape of course, but he'd acted like a randy teenager today. He'd made love to Rachael twice, once before the avalanche and again tonight.

A smile spread across Clayton's face as he remembered what they'd done. He considered rolling over, waking Rachael, and doing it again, but he didn't have the energy. He was so tired that he had no feeling at all in his legs and when he tried to reach out to adjust his covers, he could barely manage to wiggle his finger. His entire body felt numb and there was a horrible taste in his mouth. His last waking thought before the deep night closed in was that they really ought to order bottled water. Just as soon as their phone was working again, he'd call to find out how much it cost.

Betty was awake again and the television was still on. The movie on the forbidden channel five was still running. She glanced at the chair, but her secret friend was gone. The clock by the side of the bed had the big hand on the six and the little hand halfway between the two and the three. She wasn't sure what that meant, but she knew it was nighttime outside. Her friend had left before the movie was over. Betty reached out to slip a blank disk in the machine. She would record the ending and if he wanted to watch it, she could play it for him. She'd try to remember to tell him the next time he came.

At last the movie was getting exciting. Another man had appeared in the bedroom. The actor and actress were dead. Betty could tell by the way he wrapped them in blankets that covered their faces. He wasn't a doctor because he didn't have a black bag. And if he wasn't a doctor, he must be playing an undertaker. She remembered that word. The man who took you under was the undertaker. There was another word now, a new modern one. She couldn't remember it, but that was all right. One word for one man was perfectly adequate.

Betty watched the screen intently, but she couldn't quite make out the undertaker's face in the dim light. He lifted one bundle and carried it out the door. She wasn't sure how she knew, since there was nothing on the screen to tell her, but she was sure the door led to a garden. Red and yellow and pink roses. Betty remembered them so vividly, she could almost smell their lovely perfume. Someone had grown roses in this garden. Had she seen this movie before?

There was a way to switch cameras and Betty pushed the proper button. The scene shifted to the garden, where the undertaker was digging a hole. This must be a funeral, but there were no mourners. That was the name for the people who came to watch someone buried. There were no flowers, either, at least not many. The rosebushes looked sad and neglected. Perhaps the woman who'd taken care of them had been in another movie on a different channel.

The undertaker was very strong. Betty watched him dig until the hole was deep, then roll one blanket-wrapped bundle into the grave and go back inside for the other. Betty winced as he rolled the second body right in on top of the first. There was no casket. That must be why this scene was taking place in the middle of the might. The family was ashamed that they couldn't afford a proper funeral.

As soon as he'd finished with the dead people, the undertaker went to the garden building and came back with a package to throw in the hole. It had a flag on the front, something to do with the men who sailed ships and wore gold hoops in their ears. Then he went inside to bring out three suitcases and the type of bag that was designed to fit under seats in an airplane. Betty laughed as she recognized the bag. The blue folders were inside and they were from the movie she'd watched with her secret friend on forbidden channel zero. This movie must be a sequel, like *Rocky II*.

The undertaker threw the suitcases into the hole and went back inside to get two parkas and two pairs of boots. These were very strange things to bury. But when the undertaker added two water glasses to the pile in the grave, Betty began to understand. The dead people were playing ancient Egyptians. The pharaohs had buried things for the afterlife in their tombs.

It took a long time for the undertaker to fill in the grave and level the earth next to the sad rosebushes. At last he was finished and he disappeared from the screen. Betty watched for a long time, but nothing else happened. This movie must be over. Since she was wide-awake now, she switched through the forbidden channels to see what else was playing.

Channel nine was showing a movie with two people in bed. All the movies this time of night seemed to star people in bed. Betty smiled as she recognized the cowgirl who shared her in-between name. The foreign actor was sleeping next to her and they were nestled together like two spoons in a drawer. Something about the scene made Betty feel happy and she watched for a long time before she tried another channel.

On eight the doll-lady sat in a living room chair, huddled in a blanket. There were two fuzzy white rabbits wrapped around her feet and she looked as if she'd been crying. She was silent and the rabbits didn't move a whisker, so Betty turned on the camera in the dollhouse.

Betty gasped as the camera scanned the room. Pieces from the dolls were scattered all over the floor and it was a terrible mess. They must have shot a disaster movie and she'd missed it. Betty loved disaster movies, and she was very disappointed. She'd have to remember to check this channel again in case they reran it.

The forbidden channels weren't very interesting tonight. Betty had to switch all the way down to three before she found another movie to watch. This one was a detective show. The young actress was searching through a drawer in a desk. She was looking for something, and she was very careful not to make any noise. Betty watched for several minutes, but the actress never found what she was looking for.

Forbidden two was Betty's favorite channel. She liked the animals and she knew some of their names. One was *giraffe* and another was *bear*. There was also a big animal with horns and she frowned as she tried to think of what it was called. *Moose,* that was it. *Alces Americanus,* and this one had its head stuck right through the wall. She watched it for a long time, but it never moved at all and since she couldn't seem to figure out how they'd trained it to do that, she switched to channel one. It was more of the same old thing. Two people sleeping. They didn't make movies the way they used to. Betty couldn't find any action at all until she pressed the button for forbidden channel zero.

As soon as she saw the picture on the screen, her face lit up in a smile. She'd finally found something interesting! The actor who'd played the undertaker was pushing the machine on skis across the snow. Betty followed him with the outside camera as he moved it up the steep hill and hid it behind a big pine tree. He stood on top of the hill with a kind of black box for a long time and then he walked back to the garage and came inside.

Betty felt her eyelids droop. There were no interesting movies this time of night. Perhaps there would be better television tomorrow, she thought, as she clicked off the monitor and went back to sleep.

The Caretaker was frowning as he hid the compact shortwave radio under the bed in Jack's apartment. He'd tried to call the Old Man twice, once from the spa right after they'd found the suitcases and again from the top of the hill where he'd hidden the snowmobile. There must have been some sort of atmospheric disturbance because he'd failed to make contact either time.

Naturally, the Old Man would hit the roof, but this had been an emergency situation. There was no way his soldiers could get through to do the dirty work and they hadn't done such a great job with Johnny, anyway. Too many loose ends.

The Caretaker's mouth tightened into a straight line as he thought about Johnny. No loyalty, that was the problem. The Old Man had taken him out of a two-bit lounge in North Vegas and made him into a star as a favor to his father, a pal from the old country. And when Johnny had blown all his money and begged for another chance, the Old Man had set him up in the candy business. Johnny had known that holding out on the Old Man was a capital offense, but he'd tried it anyway and the Caretaker had caught him red-handed.

That was the one and only time the Caretaker had wanted to take care of a contract himself. Looking back on it, he knew he could have done a better job. It was definitely time for the Old Man to recruit some new soldiers. Perhaps they ought to contact the guys they'd hired down in New Orleans two years ago. The Marshalls had been a neat piece of work, especially since the police had written it off as a mugging with no suspects. It was unfortunate that they'd been forced to hit Charlotte Marshall, but she'd come a little too close researching her genealogy of the building and the Old Man hadn't wanted the chain of ownership to be scrutinized. The land where Deer Creek Condos now stood had been in the Old Man's hands for years. They'd used the old mine tunnels for storage of booze during the prohibition years and then arms and dope and the bodies of the rats who'd crossed the Old Man. Of course, everything had been cleared out when the condos were built, but the Old Man didn't want anyone sniffing around.

Lyle Marshall had been the hard luck story of a guy who'd been in the wrong place at the wrong time. They'd tried several times to get Charlotte alone, but she'd stuck to her husband like a second skin and there had been no choice but to hit him, too.

Tonight there hadn't been time to make any arrangements from the outside, or even to ask the Old Man's advice. He couldn't stand by twiddling his thumbs and waiting for orders while Clayton and Rachael told the others about the suitcases. Like it or not, he was on his own up here and he'd been forced to make the decision. The Old Man ought to be grateful that he'd handled the problem so competently. Perhaps it would get him that long-overdue promotion.

The Caretaker was smiling as he checked the gardening shed to make sure everything was in order, then re-locked it. It was a lucky break for him that Darby hadn't believed in natural gardening and even luckier that she'd stocked up on insecticides before her death. The skull and crossbones on the package of rose dust had given him the method, and the execution had gone off by the numbers. Poison was a quiet, hands-off solution, a way of accomplishing his task with a minimum of personal involvement. Unlike the Old Man's soldiers, he had never been a violent man and the obvious enjoyment they took from their work had always struck him as the sign of an aberrant personality.

ELEVEN

Ellen glanced at the clock on the living room wall. It was past three in the morning and Walker was gone. But where was he? She was beginning to worry.

The wine had relaxed her, just as Walker had promised, and she'd fallen asleep the minute her head had touched the pillow. Then, almost an hour ago, a nightmare had jolted her from her sleep. Ellen remembered the dream vividly, even though she tried not to dwell on it.

She was all alone, walking down a path through a graveyard late at night. The moonlight cast dark black shadows on the path. She was wearing her favorite pajamas, the pink flannel ones with white elephants that her mother had given her when she was a child, but the sandals she'd bought last summer were on her feet.

Her footsteps were loud in the quiet night, a crunching of gravel beneath her feet. Frightened, she glanced behind her to make sure no one was following. She wasn't certain why she was in this graveyard, but she knew that she had to follow the path, and that it was leading her deeper and deeper among the towering headstones.

The night breeze was cold and she wrapped her arms around her chest, unsure whether she was shivering from the chill wind or from fear. Then, as she passed a carved marble headstone with angels surrounding a name she couldn't quite read, the earth below her feet trembled and split apart. A bony hand reached up from the yawning black abyss to fasten around her ankle. As it began to drag her down, Ellen woke up with a scream.

Of course, she'd known it was a dream, a perfectly natural reaction to everything that had happened today. The avalanche. Being trapped under the workbench. Finding that hand in the pool. She'd switched on the light and gone to the guest room, hoping to find Walker still awake, but he was gone.

Ellen shivered. The terror of the dream was still with her. Even though she'd turned on every light in the living room, vestiges of terror were difficult to dispel at this time of the night. Familiar objects like the mirror over the fireplace and her denim doll in the corner took on an eerie quality when the darkness closed in and there was nothing but the yellow glare of incandescent bulbs to vanquish it.

Ellen despised the night. It was the loneliest time and she'd always been lonely, even as a child, set apart at birth, the misfit in a long line of beautiful people. Her mother had wanted a golden-haired doll to dress up and show off to her friends. Instead, she'd ended up with a baby ostrich, too shy to curtsy and sing a song for the grown-ups, too clumsy to dance in patent leather shoes and a frilly dress, and too tall to cuddle on a lap and chuck under the chin. Ellen had been a misfit all her life and she was a misfit here, too. If there had been any doubt in her mind, Johnny had proven it.

Even though she tried not to think about it, Ellen's

mind turned back to the night, six months ago, when all her dreams had been shattered. And as she remembered everything in detail, it was exactly as if it were happening all over again.

Johnny arrived at eight with a bottle of champagne to celebrate Vegas Dolls' new contract with Knock-offs, an upscale clothing chain with over two thousand shops. While Johnny opened the wine, Ellen went to get the lovely champagne glasses that had belonged to Aunt Charlotte. They were Waterford crystal and Ellen held her breath every time she washed them.

Johnny filled both glasses and lifted his in a toast. "You look different tonight, Babe. New dress?"

"Yes. Vanessa helped me pick it out." Spots of color appeared in Ellen's cheeks as Johnny looked at her appraisingly. She knew the dress was perfect, a pale blue designer silk that draped softly over her shoulders and transformed her sharp angles into an oriental mystery of curves. The saleswoman had sighed when she'd taken Ellen's measurements. Her waist curved in as a woman's should, but her hips were slim and boyish, and her bust-line wasn't really there at all. The designer had relied on quite a bit of padding.

"We're a great team, Ellen." Johnny touched the rim of his glass to hers and took a sip of champagne. "Getting excited about designing those new punk mannequins?"

Ellen nodded. Ecstatic was more like it. And just being with Johnny made her feel like the most beautiful woman in the world. Perhaps she could compete with all those gorgeous showgirls after all, as long as she always dressed like this.

Johnny led her over to the couch, and draped his arm

around her shoulders. Ellen shivered in anticipation and
tried not to look impossibly eager. He'd been a perfect
gentleman, escorting her to dinner or a show at least
once a week and then bringing her back home after a
friendly good night kiss. Ellen had heard enough rumors
around town to know that the time would come when
Johnny would want more than a kiss. Would it happen
tonight?

"Your hair looks different, too." Johnny reached out
to touch it. "I like it this way. I never noticed those gold
highlights before."

As Ellen opened her mouth, she remembered
Vanessa's advice. "Thank you, Johnny," she said. She was
doing her best to learn what everyone called feminine
wiles. There was no need for Johnny to know that she'd
treated herself to gold highlights at the most expensive
salon in town.

There was an expression in Johnny's eyes she couldn't
quite read as he pulled her into his arms and kissed her.
The kissing was wonderful, but she hoped he wouldn't
wrinkle her new dress. Of course, that was the reason
she'd bought it, wasn't it?

Johnny was breathing heavier now and his body
pressed against hers. Ellen didn't pull away. At last he was
treating her like a woman. "So what do you think, Babe?
Want to cement our permanent partnership in bed?"

Ellen took a deep breath, then met his eyes boldly.
"I thought you'd never ask."

Johnny threw back his head and laughed. Then he
picked her up in his arms and carried her to the bedroom.

Her clothes didn't fall to the floor like rain. They had
to be awkwardly unbuttoned and unclasped. And while
the sight of his naked body thrilled her, she couldn't
help but notice that he wasn't fully aroused. She told

herself that this must be normal, that after all, he was over forty and he worked long hours. Only teenagers were in a state of perpetual readiness and she really ought to do something to help him, but she wasn't sure exactly what it should be.

"Hold on a sec, Babe. And keep it nice and hot for me."

They weren't the romantic words she'd longed to hear, but Ellen smiled up at him anyway as he picked up his pants and carried them into the bathroom, shutting the door behind him.

It seemed to take a very long time to do whatever he was doing in there. Ellen shut her eyes and prayed that everything would be all right. What if he'd guessed that she was a virgin and decided it wasn't worth it? Or what if he was sitting in there, trying to think of a nice way to tell her that she didn't turn him on?

By the time he came out, at least five minutes later, Ellen was a bundle of nerves. And then, without a single word or even a kiss, he was probing between her legs and pushing himself inside of her.

She must have fallen asleep, after, because when she woke up, Johnny was gone. She switched on the light and found the note.

You're terrific, Babe. Wish we could do it again, but I'll be a nice guy and let you sleep. J.

Ellen slipped the note into a drawer and sighed deeply. It hadn't been at all what she'd expected, but she remembered her college roommate telling her the first time was a disappointment and after that, it was heavenly. She must have done something right because Johnny had written that she was terrific. She could kick herself for falling asleep, but there would be plenty of other opportunities now that they were lovers at last.

Her new dress was in a crumpled heap by the side of the bed and she hung it carefully in her closet. She'd go right out tomorrow and order another, maybe two, in different colors.

The nap she'd taken had refreshed her and she felt sexy and elegant as she ran a hot bubble bath and relaxed in the steaming water. When she climbed out of the tub, she put on the lovely silk robe Johnny had given her for Christmas and glanced in the mirror. Her hair was perfect, it hadn't lost its body at all, and she knew she'd never looked better. She wandered into the living room and poured herself a glass of champagne, feeling like a woman of the world as she sipped it. Even though it was almost midnight, she was wide-awake. There was work to do on her new mannequin design, but what she really wanted to do was make love with Johnny again.

Ellen began to smile as a wonderfully bold idea occurred to her. Johnny's note had said he wanted to make love again. Why should she make him wait? He'd given her a key to his apartment just last week in case she needed to get something from the files. A second glass of champagne helped Ellen make up her mind. She needed to feel Johnny's arms around her again, his body pressing against hers.

Ellen shivered slightly. The tile floor in the elevator was cold beneath her bare feet, but she didn't bother to go back after her slippers. She was sneaking out in the middle of the night to meet her lover. It reminded her of countless romance novels.

The ride seemed to take forever, but at last the elevator came to a stop on the fourth floor. Ellen fairly ran down the hallway and opened Johnny's door. There was a light in the living room, but he wasn't there. Then she heard water running in the shower. She'd climb into his bed and be waiting when he came out.

Johnny had a heated water bed and Ellen giggled as she got under the covers. This was definitely a night for firsts and she could hardly wait to make love on a water bed. She had just settled down when she heard Johnny laughing over the sound of the shower. That was odd. Lots of people sang in the shower, but she'd never heard of anyone who laughed.

Ellen got out of bed and padded over to listen at the bathroom door. She had almost decided to open the door and ask him what was so funny, when she heard another voice. A woman's voice.

"I missed you, Johnny. What took you so long?"

Ellen gripped the edge of the door so hard, her knuckles turned white. It was Vanessa! She'd taught Ellen how to dress, given her advice on how to attract a man, and even helped her with her makeup. Ellen had poured her heart out to Vanessa, thinking she'd found a friend, and here she was in the shower with Johnny!

"Couldn't be helped, Babe. I told you I had to go up to Ellen's place."

"You spend more time with her than you do with me." Vanessa sounded slightly miffed. "And you know my time is limited. Hal keeps me under lock and chain whenever he's home."

"But you still manage to slip away, don't you?" Johnny chuckled. "And if I'm not home, you knock on Marc's door. He told me you were up there twice last week."

"What else can I do? You know I'm not getting any at home, and a girl like me gets lonely. But you made me wait for over two hours and I was bored out of my skin."

"I told you I'd be gone for a while. And I made up for it when I got back, didn't I?"

"You sure did." Vanessa gave a contented sigh. "So what's going on, Johnny? I know Ellen's crazy about you because she told me. What are you going to do when she gets romantic?"

Johnny groaned. "That's what happened tonight. You should have seen her, all dressed up and acting sexy, trying to drag me to bed."

"So what did you do?"

"I put her off. We spent some time talking about the business and then I hightailed it back down here to you."

"And that's all you did with Ellen? Just talk?"

"I sure didn't jump in the sack with her if that's what you mean! Relax, Babe. No reason to be jealous. There's no way in hell I could get it up for Ellen."

"Really?"

"Well, maybe one way," Johnny answered. "It might work if I put a bag over her head and pretended she was you."

Ellen stifled a gasp. Not only was Johnny lying, now she knew why he'd turned off the lights on his way back to bed. That two-timing bastard hadn't made love to her at all. He'd pretended she was Vanessa!

"You should be ashamed of yourself, Johnny Day!" Vanessa sounded angry. "Ellen's a nice person and she can't help the way she looks. I think it's time for you to be honest with her."

"I should tell her she doesn't turn me on?"

"No, that'd only hurt her feelings. You should say something like . . . uh . . ." Vanessa began to giggle. "That you really want to, but you've got a terrible disease and you don't want her to get it."

"Oh, sure. Or maybe I could tell her I got it shot off in the war."

"Don't be silly. Anyone who looks at you can tell that . . . never mind. Just think of a real good excuse that won't hurt poor Ellen's feelings."

"Like what?"

"You could say that you respect her too much to treat her like a casual romp in the hay. Ellen's innocent enough to go for that, and it'll make her feel good besides."

"You're really a good friend to her, aren't you?" Johnny sounded surprised.

"Of course I am and I'll scratch your eyes out if you ever touch her. There's no way I want you to get all hot and bothered thinking about me and then waste it all on Ellen!"

Ellen came back to the present with a sigh, brushed away a tear that was rolling down her cheek, and straightened a little in her chair. When Johnny had come to see her the next morning, she'd gone into her speech before he could open his mouth. She'd told him that she knew he respected her too much to treat her like a casual romp in the hay. And wouldn't it be wiser to keep their relationship on a platonic level? Johnny had blinked twice and exclaimed that she'd taken the words right out of his mouth. Vanessa's words, but he didn't know that she knew. She wasn't about to admit that she'd hidden in his bedroom like an eager, blushing bride only to overhear his conversation in the shower with Vanessa. Then, after he'd left, she'd thrown every one of his CDs down the incinerator chute. It was a childish gesture and it hadn't made her feel any better, but at least it was appropriately symbolic.

During the next few months, she'd been friendly and businesslike despite her breaking heart, and when she couldn't stand the strain for one moment longer, she'd consulted Rachael and dissolved their partnership.

Even though she was no longer involved with Johnny in any way, his betrayal still hurt. Ellen knew it was partially her fault. She'd tried to be something she wasn't. An expensive hairdo, makeup applied by an expert, and a designer gown could camouflage the package, but nothing could change the contents. And as she became accustomed to being alone, she admitted that it was a considerable relief not to have to worry about how she looked and what she said. Now she was just plain Ellen, and if people didn't like her, that was too bad.

Of course she'd missed the hours she'd spent with Johnny, so to compensate, she had poured all her energy into running her mannequin business. Ellen knew her products were good, but orders were slow and her expenses were much higher than she'd figured on. She knew it took time for a small business to show a profit, but she was barely at the break-even point and she was running herself ragged, trying to handle everything on her own.

One morning she'd run into Jack St. James and when he'd casually asked how her business was doing, she'd burst into tears. It was just too much for one person to handle alone, she was losing money every time she turned around, and she wished she'd stayed in Minnesota and never tried to go into business for herself. After a couple of astute questions, Jack had told her she needed a business manager and recommended his friend, Walker Browning. Walker had spent the first two weeks examining the books and he'd discovered that Johnny had contracted with several firms who were bleeding off Ellen's profits. Their shipping charges were ridiculously high and the company they used was only minimally responsible for damages. Walker had found another carrier who guaranteed all losses at a much lower tariff, and Ellen had agreed to switch the moment their contract ran out. They were also changing warehouses as soon as their lease was up. Vegas Dolls had been paying through the nose for a prime location they didn't need.

When Walker had handed her his set of recommendations, Ellen had been astounded. She knew nothing about business, and obviously, Johnny hadn't either. If she followed Walker's plan, her running expenses would be cut by more than a third!

Next, Walker had concentrated on generating new business. He'd persuaded Ellen to ship out a free sample mannequin to several chains of clothing stores and every one of them had placed an order for more.

There was the sound of a key in the lock. Walker looked startled to see her sitting there.

"Ellen! I never expected you to wake up. You all right?"

Ellen nodded. "I'm fine. I just couldn't sleep, that's all. Where were you?"

"Up in the spa, enjoying the view."

Walker smiled his contagious smile. He seemed honestly glad to see her awake and Ellen couldn't help but smile back. She couldn't thank Jack enough for sending her Walker. He didn't mind working long hours and seemed just as excited as she was when they came up with a good model, even suggesting some new features of his own. He never pried into her personal life and he'd caught on to her moods so quickly it amazed her. If she didn't want to talk, he did his share of the work in silence. If she was in the mood for conversation, he treated her to stories of growing up in Chicago that had her in stitches. She knew he liked her and she didn't have to be on her guard.

"Tell me about it, Walker." Ellen tucked her knees up and the blanket slipped down a little. She saw her image in the mirror over the fireplace and smiled again. Here she was in her blue flannel granny gown, the bunny slippers on her feet, alone in her living room with a man and not even the slightest bit embarrassed. Perhaps if Johnny had truly been her friend, things might have worked out better between them.

Walker sat down on the couch. "It was spectacular, Ellen. You know those little crystal balls you find in the stores at Christmas, the ones with the winter scenes and the snowflakes?"

Ellen nodded.

"Up at the spa with the dome overhead and the snow falling outside, I felt like I was trapped inside one of those crystal balls. It was a strange feeling. I was all alone, but I wasn't alone because some big hand up there was shaking the ball to make the snow swirl. That sounds pretty crazy, doesn't it?"

"Nope." Ellen shook her head. "I wish I'd been there."

"It's not too late. Why don't you go put on your suit and we'll sit in the Jacuzzi with the lights out. Then I can show you what I mean."

Ellen began to smile. Her former coworkers at Garfield Elementary would have had a collective fit if they thought she was even considering such a thing. She was glad she didn't have to worry about proper behavior for a teacher anymore.

"Come on, Ellen. I really want you to see it. It's the chance of a lifetime."

Ellen smiled and got up. She turned at the doorway with a smile. "It's really strange, Walker. Somehow, you've plugged into my fantasy. When I was a little girl, I always dreamed of hiding inside the little crystal ball my mother had on the mantel. Now here I am, over thirty years old, and I'm finally going to do it."

TWELVE

Jayne woke up to feel her husband's arms around her. God, how she'd missed him! She burrowed a little deeper under the covers and thought about how good it was to have him home again. Last night had been like a second honeymoon. If only they could stay like this and ignore their problems. Perhaps they needed blackout drapes like Marc, so they could sleep and make love all night and all day.

The sun streaming in through the shuttered window cast a bright pattern of gold stripes against the knotty pine-paneled walls. Moira had burned cattle brands into the wood at strategic intervals and the bedroom had the look of an elegant bunkhouse. Jayne squinted and tried to read the time on the Lone Ranger alarm clock Paul had found for her in an antique shop. Seven-fifteen. At seven-twenty, the clock would whinny like Silver and play the first eight bars of the *1812 Overture*. She reached out and pulled the plug so it wouldn't go off. The button had broken off while Paul was gone and she hadn't gotten around to fixing it.

The bedroom was filled with promotional objects that

had been sold in the forties by the enterprising cowboys and cowgals of the silver screen. It had all started when Jayne had casually mentioned that she'd always wanted the Tonto Trick Lasso she'd seen as a child, advertised in the back of a Lone Ranger comic book, and Paul had turned it into a holy quest. Now she had the lasso, along with a Gene Autry hat rack, a Roy Rogers Happy Trails phonograph that played only seventy-eight RPM records, a Gabby Hays Sidekick trunk that sat in the corner next to her dressing table, and a Dale Evans Little Cowgirl mirror framed with rope. Paul had even managed to find a Cisco Kid poncho, obviously a product of some tongue-in-cheek promoter. He'd spent hours searching for cowboy movie memorabilia until she'd begged him to stop. That was another of their basic differences. She'd always enjoyed trying new activities, but Paul threw himself into them with such zeal that they ended up as work instead of fun.

Jayne grimaced as she remembered suggesting they camp out at the Grand Tetons for a week last summer. She'd always wanted to see Jackson Hole. Paul had agreed that it might be fun and the next thing she knew, their living room had been loaded with camping equipment. She could see the need for backpacks and sleeping bags and she hadn't objected to the three tents: One for sleeping, one for cooking, and one for storing their supplies. Paul said he wanted to be prepared for any contingency and he'd pored over countless volumes on life in the wild, taking notes on the proper procedures for setting up their base camp and making detailed lists of the supplies they'd need. Jayne had thought all this preparation was silly. They were just going for a week and if they ran out of something, they could get in the car and drive to the store. And if the tent blew down, or the air mattresses went flat, or it was too cold at night, they could always dash up to the lodge to get a nice comfy room there. Absolutely not, Paul had been firm. Jayne had wanted to camp out and that was exactly what they were going to do.

Paul had been so thoroughly prepared that absolutely nothing had gone wrong. But what Jayne had thought would be a carefree week of romping through the park and sleeping out under the stars had turned into a test of their survival skills.

The same thing had happened when they'd taken up tennis. She'd watched Laureen and Alan play and it looked like fun, so she'd asked Paul if he'd pick up a couple of racquets and a can of balls while she took care of the rest of the things she had to do in town. She should have known better. Paul had purchased every conceivable item of tennis equipment, all the proper clothing the salesman insisted they'd need, and a stack of instructional videos. He'd even arranged for them to take lessons from a pro three times a week. Naturally, the fun had gone out of it.

Jayne sighed. Paul researched a subject to death while she tended to go off half-cocked. There simply had to be a happy medium.

"What is wrong, Jayne?"

Jayne opened her eyes to find Paul staring at her. "I was just thinking about tennis, that's all. And how it's no fun anymore."

"I know. I have thought similarly. Perhaps it would be more enjoyable if we failed to keep score."

"You'd go for that?" Jayne was clearly surprised. "I thought you were keeping a log of how many matches we won."

"I deep-fived it."

"You mean deep-sixed. Then you're willing to play just for fun?"

Paul nodded and glanced at his watch. "We can go to the court before brunch. Unless you would rather argue first."

"But I don't want to . . . oh, you mean *that* kind of argue." Jayne began to smile. "I'd love to, but I can't think of anything to argue about."

"Speak the words *grumble-mumble*. And then *walla, walla, artichoke*."

"What?" Jayne pulled back a little to stare at him.

"It is a crowd noise. A month ago, I became the additional in a movie of the television."

"You were an extra? How did it happen? Tell me!"

"I was walking to the office of Marc, and the director invited me to join them."

"And you did? Just like that?" Jayne was clearly surprised. It was totally out of character for Paul to do anything spontaneous.

Paul grinned. "I knew you would say to have fun and I did. They first divided the group into two sections. One was to speak the *grumble-mumble,* and the other the *walla, walla, artichoke*. The director told us it would simulate the sound of many persons arguing. Which words do you choose to speak, Jayne?"

Jayne frowned slightly. "I think we'd better postpone this, Paul. We're supposed to meet the gang for brunch in less than an hour."

"It does not matter to me if we are late."

"It doesn't?"

"No. You are of more importance than the clock which tells the time."

Jayne wrapped her arms around his neck and kissed him. Paul had definitely mellowed.

* * *

Hal popped the last of a strawberry muffin in his mouth and waved Jayne away as she passed the plate. "I had three already and I couldn't eat another bite. We'd better save a couple for Clayton and Rachael."

"What's keeping them?" Vanessa looked thoughtful. "I knocked at their door on the way up here, but they didn't answer. I know Clayton's not exactly the passionate type, but maybe . . ."

"That's enough, Vanessa!" Hal cut her off before she could finish. "They probably just overslept like Jayne and Paul. Yesterday was quite a day, right, Jayne?"

"Right." Jayne felt the blush rise to her cheeks and hoped she didn't turn the color of the red cowgirl shirt she was wearing. She wasn't sure whether Hal was referring to Paul's return, or to everything else that had happened. "Anyone want another piece of Laureen's quiche?"

Alan rubbed his stomach. "Just one more. My wife makes the best quiche I ever tasted."

"That's sweet, Alan." Marc winked at him. "And pretty sly, too. Did you marry Laureen to get a controlling interest in her quiche?"

"No, he didn't," Laureen laughed. "I was a terrible cook when we got married."

Vanessa looked puzzled. "I don't get it. If you were a terrible cook, I don't see why in the world he'd ever . . ."

"Vanessa!" Hal clamped a hand over her mouth. "I don't believe you were ever a bad cook, Laureen."

"I was, though. The first time I made breakfast for Alan, I burned the toast and the eggs were as hard as rocks."

"And I didn't even notice." Alan smiled at her. "I was

thinking about how pretty you looked across the table. I could have been eating cardboard."

Grace laughed. "Now that's true love. Moira won't even let me try to cook. She says I break too many dishes. Five years ago, right before that last big party we had for all Moira's clients on Thanksgiving, or maybe it was Halloween, I really can't remember which, I had all the china sitting out on the counter, two dozen salad bowls and two dozen plates and two dozen cups and saucers in that wonderful old-fashioned gold leaf design and I reached for the silver coffeepot and . . ." Grace cut herself off in midsentence and turned to look at Moira in alarm. "Why aren't you stopping me, Moira? I know I'm babbling."

"I was waiting to see how long you'd go on." Moira reached for Grace's hand under the table and squeezed it, and then she turned to the rest of the group. "Gracie's impossible in the kitchen. I don't see how she can be so graceful on the stage and such a total fu . . . klutz in the kitchen."

Jayne glanced at the clock on the wall and frowned. "Do you think I should go down to check on Clayton and Rachael? They're over an hour late."

"I will go also, Jayne." Paul stood up and bowed. "Excuse me. And please to hold down the rampart until we return."

"It's hold down the fort," Jayne corrected automatically. "Better make some more coffee, Ellen. I think I drank that whole pot all by myself."

Jayne frowned as they got into the elevator. "Better stop at our place, honey, just in case. Rachael gave me a key when they delivered the new dishwasher and I think I still have it."

"They purchased a new dishwasher?" Paul looked surprised. "The one they had was under warranty."

"I know, but Rachael bought a whole bunch of new glasses that wouldn't fit in the rack so they traded it in for a different model. Hold the elevator. I'll be right back."

When they got down to the fifth floor, Paul rang the doorbell repeatedly with no result. "I am not sure that we should use the key, Jayne. It is an invasion of their privacy."

"Oh fiddlesticks! They won't mind. Come on, Paul. Let's roust them out of bed."

The apartment was silent as Jayne and Paul walked from room to room. The bed looked as if it had been slept in, but Rachael and Clayton were nowhere in sight.

Paul was clearly unsettled by the sight of the deserted rooms. "This is very curious. Where could they be?"

"Uh, oh." Jayne rushed to the hall closet and looked inside. "Their coats are gone and so are their boots. Remember how Clayton was so hot to take the snowmobile last night? I think we'd better check to see if it's still here."

Several minutes later, they had their answer as they stared at the empty spot where Paul had parked the Arctic Cat. There was nothing to do but go back to the spa.

Everyone was stunned, most of all Grace. "I can't believe that Rachael would let him start out on the thing in the dead of night."

"Well, that's exactly what they did." Jayne gave a rueful laugh. "I swear, Clay doesn't have the brains that God gave a barrel cactus!"

"Maybe they waited until morning," Marc suggested. "It wouldn't be as dangerous in the sunlight."

Laureen shook her head. "I know for a fact they left

before daybreak. I got up at six-thirty to start the quiche and I would have heard them."

There was a long, tense silence while everyone imagined the worst. Then Ellen spoke up. "There was plenty of light last night. It was a full moon. I saw it from the Jacuzzi."

"What were you doing in the Jacuzzi in the middle of the night?" Vanessa wanted to know.

"I couldn't sleep. Too much excitement, I guess. So Walker and I went up there to enjoy the view."

Vanessa looked shocked. "Really, Ellen! You went up to the Jacuzzi in the middle of the night with a . . ."

Hal clamped his hand over Vanessa's mouth. "Sorry about that. So what shall we do about Clayton and Rachael?"

"I don't know that we can do anything." Marc shrugged. "They took off with our only means of transportation. I guess we just have to hope that they got through all right."

It was seven in the evening when they finished packing the things in Johnny's kitchen. Laureen glanced down and groaned. "That's enough work for today. Just look at my hands! They're black from all the newsprint."

"Not as black as . . ."

Hal clamped his hand over Vanessa's mouth, a gesture that had become pure reflex. "I think I'll stay and finish a couple more boxes. It's too early to go to bed."

"How about a game of charades?" Grace rose to her feet from a cross-legged position and stretched.

"We could play at our place," Moira chimed in. She loved charades. "Are you up for a game, Ellen?"

Ellen nodded. "I'm terrible at charades, but I'll play anyway. Walker?"

"Sure. How about you, Jayne?"

Jayne hesitated. There was something bothersome about Clayton and Rachael's disappearance, but she couldn't put her finger on what it was.

"Come, Jayne." Paul squeezed her shoulder. "You have always enjoyed the charades."

Reluctantly, Jayne nodded. There would be time to think about Clayton and Rachael later. "All right. I'll play if Hal's on my team. He always guesses the ones I have to act out."

"You want me?" Hal looked surprised. "The last time we played, you said I didn't have the brains that God gave little green apples."

"That was only a figure of speech, so don't get your underwear in a bunch. Are you playing, Vanessa?"

"I haven't decided yet. Is Laureen bringing brownies?"

Laureen began to smile. Vanessa loved her brownies and it was a perfect way of getting back at her. "Nope. I've only got one batch left in the freezer and I'm saving those for Alan."

"In that case, I'll pass." Vanessa got up and yawned. "All this packing has given me a headache. I'm going to sit in the Jacuzzi for a while and then I'm going to bed."

Hal couldn't resist a parting shot. "What's the matter, Vanessa? Afraid we'll all find out what a lousy actress you are?"

Vanessa turned to give him a withering glance. "I told you, Hal, I have a headache. And don't wake me when you come in. Not that you'd have any *reason* to."

Everyone was silent until Vanessa had left. Then Grace broke the awkward moment.

"Hal? I know I'm butting my nose in, but why don't you two just split up? You fight all the time."

Hal nodded. "It's complicated, Grace, but the bottom line is we can't."

"You can't get a divorce?" Moira raised her eyebrows. "Come on, Hal. You certainly have enough grounds."

Hal gave a bitter laugh. "Don't I know! But I did a really stupid thing when we got married."

"Don't tell me." Grace sighed. "You forgot to have her sign a prenuptial agreement?"

"No, I'm not quite *that* stupid. She signed one. I drew it up myself."

"Uh, oh." Marc groaned. "What did it say, Hal?"

"It said that if she filed for divorce, she'd end up with nothing but a small monthly allowance."

"What's wrong with that?"

"Absolutely nothing. But I neglected to put in what happens if *I'm* the one to file for divorce. And since I didn't stipulate otherwise, the Nevada divorce laws apply."

"I get it." Marc nodded. "If you're the one to file for divorce, Vanessa gets half of everything you earned during your marriage."

Hal nodded. "And you all know I've made a lot of money since then. Naturally, Vanessa won't file for divorce. And I can't file either. So here we are, stuck together like glue, and there's not a damn thing either one of us can do about it."

Laureen gave a deep sigh. She finally understood why Hal hadn't done anything drastic when she'd told him about Vanessa's affair with Alan. "Well, don't let it get to you, Hal. If she keeps on being so obnoxious, maybe somebody'll help you get rid of her permanently."

Alan looked shocked. "Laureen!"

Laureen got to her feet. "Come on, everybody. Let's stop by our place so I can pick up my reading glasses."

"Good idea, honey." Alan grinned at her. "I remember when you got *The Joy of Sex* and you acted out *The Joy of Cooking*."

"And I spent the entire five minutes trying to figure out what sex had to do with Laureen stirring something and licking her fingers." Moira stopped and her face began to turn red. "Oh, sh . . . shucks! I don't believe I said that!"

Marc laughed. "I don't either. I've got a jug of wine I can bring, if you don't mind stopping at my floor. And while I'm there, I'll just check my . . ."

"Answer phone?"

They all spoke in unison and Marc laughed. "I keep forgetting. Well, I just hope you all can read my mind like that when it's my turn to do a charade."

There was a determined expression on Vanessa's face as she pulled on a black turtleneck sweater and a pair of black slacks. The game of charades would keep everyone busy for at least two hours, which gave her plenty of time.

She reached up to take off her earrings and reconsidered as she caught her reflection in the mirror. The sparkling diamonds lent a touch of elegance to her all-black outfit. The heart-shaped earrings had been a present from Hal for their first anniversary, the last present he'd given her, but she was about to cash in for a whole lot more.

The call had come the morning the avalanche had hit. Since Hal was working, Vanessa had taken the message and she'd been immediately suspicious. When she'd asked, Hal had told her that a Swiss bank was handling some property he owned over there, but of course she'd heard all about those numbered Swiss bank accounts, and she was positive that Hal was hiding his money from her.

She'd spent all last night searching for some sort of evidence. She knew that if she found the number to Hal's Swiss bank account, she could fly over there and clean it out. She'd seen a movie just like that. But she hadn't found the number, even though she'd gone through everything in the apartment. And then, just this morning, while they were in Clayton's unit, she'd realized that Hal might have given the number to Clayton to keep for him. Vanessa gave one last glance in the mirror and turned to go out the door. Clayton had given her a key before Rachael had moved in and he'd forgotten to ask for it back.

Her hands were trembling slightly as she reached for the elevator button. Then she remembered that the elevator shaft was right outside Moira and Grace's living room. If Hal heard the elevator running, he'd realize that she was awake, and he might come up and find her.

Vanessa turned on her heel and headed for the stairwell. Clayton's unit was only two floors up. She felt proud of herself for thinking it through. Maybe her luck was changing and she'd find what she needed to get away from Hal for good.

THIRTEEN

Jayne was watching the oven timer impatiently when Paul came up behind her to wrap his arms around her waist.

"Do not look at it, Jayne. A watched clock never ticks."

"It's a watched pot that never boils, but you've got the right idea." Jayne turned and kissed him. "The smell's killing me and my stomach's growling worse than a grizzly in heat."

They both turned to look through the oven window. It had all started when Marc said he was dying for pizza and wished a delivery truck could get through. Laureen had remembered the refrigerated pizza dough she was testing for her cooking show, and offered each of them a batch for individual pizzas with toppings of their choice. If anyone was interested, they could have a contest to see who could come up with the best pizza. Laureen would be the judge, along with Alan. There were no hard-and-fast rules. If you didn't have what you needed, you could borrow from someone else. And everyone would have plenty to eat.

"Your pizza is giving a delicious aroma." Paul studied

Jayne's entry, which was browning nicely. "I think you will surely win the contest."

Jayne shrugged. "I doubt it, not with plain old sausage and cheese. But I figured somebody in this family had to make a pizza that's edible."

"Is this a personal criticism, Jayne?"

Jayne giggled. "I don't know. I've never had a sardine and cream cheese pizza before."

"But you say you like lox and bagels. My pizza is almost similar, except for the difference in fish."

"Some difference!" Jayne giggled again. "And lox and bagels aren't served hot."

"I fail to see why they could not be. And this will not squeeze from the sides when it is bitten. Is it baked enough, Jayne?"

"Two minutes to go. Why don't you get out that big basket in the cupboard?"

Paul had just finished lining the basket with towels when the stove timer rang. Jayne lifted out the pizzas and set them inside. "All set and rarin' to go. Let's hustle over before they get cold."

As they walked down the hallway, Paul was smiling. "What type of pizza will Ellen and Walker bake?"

"Ellen'll bring pineapple and Canadian bacon. She told me that was her favorite. I don't know about Walker, though."

"Watermelon pizza?"

"Paul!" Jayne was shocked. "You shouldn't say things like that!"

"I do not understand why. Walker does not seem to be sensitive about his race. I am sure he would smash up if I told him that joke."

"Crack up, not smash up, and no, he wouldn't. That's

how racial problems get perpetuated. Everyone starts believing those awful stereotypes."

The elevator stopped at the eighth floor, and Walker and Ellen got on, bearing two pizzas wrapped in a towel.

Jayne inhaled as the elevator started to descend again. "Whatever that is, it really smells good. What did you bring, Ellen?"

"Canadian bacon and pineapple. Walker made his own creation with his favorite things on top."

Jayne gave Paul a warning glance. "Like what?"

"Oh, the usual." Walker grinned at her. "Chitlins and collard greens. I was going for the watermelon when Ellen stopped me."

Paul laughed and turned to Jayne. "You see? I was correct."

Both Walker and Ellen looked puzzled and Jayne sighed. "It's a little complicated. Paul was going to tease Walker about watermelon pizza, but I assured him that it was in bad taste."

Walker nodded solemnly. "It certainly would have been. I tried watermelon pizza once and it was awful."

At the sound of a key in the lock, the Caretaker flicked off the light and pressed himself against the kitchen wall. The footsteps headed down the hallway toward Clayton's office and he followed silently in the semidarkness. The hallway had floor-to-ceiling windows and the lights from Betty's suite above reflected harshly against the freshly fallen snow.

The figure darted into Clayton's office and when he reached the door, he saw the glimmer of a penlight traveling across the floor, stopping at Clayton's file cabinet. The drawer opened almost noiselessly and the intruder propped the light on the handle of the drawer above to shine down on the files below.

Delicate hands, small-boned. It was a woman, but which one? And what did she want?

They'd all gone to their own kitchens to bake the pizzas, and any one of them could have come here on the pretext of borrowing something from Clayton's refrigerator. Then he noticed a wedding ring, which eliminated Ellen. And Grace and Moira. Jayne had long, strong fingers from years of practicing the piano. And Laureen's hands were larger, he recalled from close-ups on her cooking show. It certainly wasn't Betty, which left the nurse and Vanessa.

He watched as she located a file and flipped through the contents, pulling out a single piece of paper. As she sat down in Clayton's chair to study it, he could almost make out her face. Something glittered by her left ear, reflecting the tiny glow from the penlight. It was a diamond earring shaped like a heart. Vanessa had heart-shaped diamond earrings. But why was she so interested in Clayton's files? He took one step closer, and then another. When he got close enough to make out the label on the file, he smiled. Vanessa was going through Hal's papers. That was nothing to worry about, but he'd keep an eye on her until she left.

Vanessa almost laughed out loud. Hal had moved over four million dollars into his numbered Swiss account. He was a real bastard, and a dumb one at that. His birth date was the access code. Jack had once told her how common that was, when she'd asked him about the security business.

She put the file back in the drawer and closed it. Now she'd act perfectly normal until the access road was cleared, then take off for Switzerland on the very first flight.

Vanessa smiled. Switzerland. She'd always wanted to go there and she might just do that once she'd gone to the bank and cleaned out Hal's account. They had wonderful skiing, and she'd always wanted to shop in the boutiques at St. Moritz. Best of all, there wasn't a thing Hal could do. There was nothing illegal about a wife making a withdrawal from her husband's Swiss bank account. That's exactly what had happened in the movie she'd seen.

She shined the penlight all around the office, checking to make sure she hadn't left anything out of place and then she headed for the door. If Hal decided to check up on her, she wanted to be in bed, sleeping like a baby.

Vanessa was nearing the end of the hallway when the lights in the rose garden came on. She whirled and bolted for the door before remembering that Clayton had them on a timer. There was no need to be so jumpy. She stopped and took a calming breath as she looked out at the garden. It had been beautiful the first time she'd seen it, with tiny sparkling lights and a white latticework gazebo. Two round wrought-iron tables, painted dazzling white, were surrounded by eight matching chairs. Darby had been fond of having her morning coffee in the garden, surrounded by the sweet scent of her beautiful roses.

Things were a lot different now that Darby was dead. The paint was peeling off the wrought-iron tables and the roses looked as if they were growing wild. Nevertheless, one perfect pink rose bloomed on a bush in the back. It would look lovely in the silver vase she had in her bedroom. Hal hadn't given her roses in at least a year and they were her favorite.

Opening the French doors, Vanessa stepped into the garden. It was lovely out here in the climate-controlled dome. There was something magical about flowers blooming in the dead of winter. Roses in the snow. A great title for a movie and now that she was about to become a wealthy woman, she might just decide to finance it.

She grabbed the clippers from the nail in the gazebo and headed for the perfect rose. It would only take a moment. As she took a detour around two bushes that had grown together in a tangle of branches, her sandal sank into a patch of soft ground. Someone had been digging out here and the soil was loose. Had Clayton hired a new gardener? Vanessa bent over for a closer look.

Lines of concentration creased Betty's forehead as she tried to make sense out of the talk show. The host had a towel wrapped around his head and the audience laughed every time he spoke. Betty didn't think he was very funny, but the people did. Perhaps you couldn't appreciate him when you had a disease like hers.

She was watching the regular channels now because Nurse would be back in a minute to give her the needle and put her to bed. It had been a pretty good night for television, and she'd enjoyed the charades on forbidden channel two. The cowgirl had been very good and so had that nice colored man. Betty seemed to remember that *colored* was an obsolete term. Now they wanted to be called black, or maybe Afro-American, she wasn't sure which. When the colored man came to visit her, she'd just say hello and avoid calling him anything. That was the smart thing to do.

When the charades had stopped, Betty had switched through the other forbidden channels. There had been a lot of cooking shows on tonight and she didn't feel like watching those, but she'd found something very interesting on channel five.

That pretty young actress was back, searching for something. She seemed to be typecast in the role of searcher. When she left the room where the papers were kept, Betty had assumed the movie was over. She had been about to switch the channel when she'd seen the actress open the doors to the garden, the same one she'd seen in the funeral movie. Would the undertaker appear? Betty hoped so.

There he was! Betty had clapped her hands together in delight. He was her very favorite actor, unless you counted Jack, who was in the hospital. They didn't run many hospital movies now.

Betty reached for a blank disk and put it into the machine, pushing the button to record. She'd start a collection to show Jack when he came back home. While the undertaker series wasn't as funny as the movies that Jack had recorded for her, it was still very exciting. She gasped as the sharp metal thing crashed down. You'd never guess they made those things out of Styrofoam so they couldn't hurt anybody. Then the actress had crumpled to the ground very gracefully, and since she was pretending to be dead, she hadn't moved at all.

Would the undertaker bury her in another funeral? Betty had leaned forward to peer at the screen intently. No, he just put the Styrofoam shovel back in the gazebo, wrapped the pretty actress in a big plastic tarp, and carried her down the hall to the stairwell. Once they'd gone through the door, Betty had known that the forbidden channel five movie-of-the-night was over, but she might be able to catch the rest of the film on another channel.

She had been looking for the ending of the movie when she'd heard Nurse coming with the warm milk and cookies she always had before bedtime. She'd barely had time to switch to a talk show before Nurse had come into her room with the tray. It had been a close call. Very close. She had to remember to be more careful in the future now that Jack wasn't here to remind her.

The man who loved Budweiser beer was rolling his eyes at something Johnny had said and the audience was laughing again. Betty frowned. She liked the forbidden channels much better. Should she take a chance and scan them to see if she could find the end of the movie?

There was water running in the bathroom. That meant Nurse was fixing her face. Nurse took a long time every night in the bathroom. She'd explained it all to Betty. When people got older, their skin dried out. That meant they had to use moisturizers. Nurse put a pink cream on her face every night that had to stay there for five minutes. Then she washed it off and put on a moisturizer. Betty hadn't said what she'd been thinking out loud, that nothing could help Nurse from looking like one of those big black birds.

Betty took a chance and reached for the remote control. She had to find out where the undertaker would bury the actress. It was a very important part of the movie.

There he was again on forbidden channel one, carrying the searcher into a room of ice. There was a word for a place like that, but Betty couldn't think of it. She winced as he rolled her out of the tarp, then chuckled at her own foolishness. Of course they'd stopped the cameras to put in a mannequin just like the doll-lady made, so the actress could go back to her dressing room to rehearse her next scene. It looked so real, it had almost fooled her. Movie magic was wonderful!

When the water stopped running, Betty put on the talk show again. She was laughing at the towel around the host's head, it took a certain amount of courage to appear on television in a silly-looking thing like that, when Nurse came in with the bedtime needle.

They all sat on pillows covered with Royal Stewart plaid, the tartan Moira claimed she was entitled to use since her grandfather's name had been Stewart. The pizzas were arranged on the living room table, a huge, round knee-high slab of black marble and the only furniture in the room. The walls were still white, the windows bare, but Moira had lit a cheerful blaze in the black marble fireplace and the cavernous room was a perfect place for games. When Paul had inquired, Moira had called the effect her Terminally Lazy Look and sworn she'd finish with her decorating just as soon as the roads were clear.

Laureen and Alan sat at one end of the table, passing slivers of pizza back and forth. There were the standard varieties: Jayne's sausage and cheese, Ellen's Canadian bacon and pineapple, Moira's was Italian meatballs and fresh tomato, and Walker's was pepperoni and onion. There were also some very unusual creations like Paul's sardine and cream cheese, Hal and Grace's feta cheese and Greek olive, which they'd made together in Grace and Moira's kitchen because Hal hadn't wanted to wake Vanessa, and a strange concoction which Marc refused to name. When they'd tasted them all, Laureen looked at Alan with a question in her eyes. He took another bite and nodded.

"And the winner is . . ." Laureen paused for dramatic effect. "Marc's braunschweiger and Swiss cheese with pesto sauce. It's the most unusual thing we've ever tasted."

"Pesto sauce?" Marc looked surprised. "I thought it was green onions, all ground up."

Laureen laughed. "Why did you use it if you didn't know what it was?"

"I don't know. I didn't have any tomato sauce and I had to use something. It looked kind of interesting when I opened the jar, so I just spread it on the top."

"Then it was a lucky accident." Laureen nodded. "Tomato sauce would have been horrible. And Paul gets an honorable mention. I don't know anyone who ever tried to put sardines on a pizza before. Moira? Bring out the prize."

Moira got up to present Marc with a long, narrow package wrapped in newspaper.

"Uh, oh." Marc accepted it gingerly. "Is this one of your father's things, Grace?"

"Open it and see," Grace ordered with a grin.

Ellen studied Marc carefully as he started to unwrap the package. Why on earth would he buy pesto sauce if he didn't know what it was? Of course, she'd bought tofu ice cream once, and she hadn't been sure what that was. She guessed it wasn't so strange, after all.

Everyone leaned forward as the wrapping fell away from a large stuffed rattlesnake.

"Just what I needed!" Marc lifted it up, taking his unusual prize in stride. "I'll put it on my desk when the roofer comes in with his bid. That way he'll feel outnumbered."

"Let's eat." Moira passed out plates and napkins. "Will you open more wine, Gracie?"

"I'd be glad to, but we're out and I was going to pick up some on the way home, but then there was the avalanche and I forgot all about it and we couldn't have brought it up on the snowmobile anyway because there was barely room for the two of us in all those bulky . . ."

"Never mind, Gracie," Hal interrupted her. "I've got a jug, if no one minds drinking jug wine. Vanessa bought it and she doesn't know much about wines."

Grace nodded. Vanessa didn't know much about anything, but it would be uncharitable to point it out. "If you don't mind getting it, that would be nice. And if Vanessa's still awake, why don't you ask her to join us? There's plenty of pizza."

After Hal had left, Laureen turned to Grace. "Why did you have to be so polite? Nobody wants Vanessa down here."

"That's precisely why. She's got feelings after all, plus we have to live in the same building with her so we might as well make the effort because we all like Hal and . . ."

"Okay, Gracie." Moira patted her arm. "We understand."

Hal was back in a couple of moments, carrying the jug of wine. "Is Vanessa here?"

"We haven't seen her. Did you stop at the spa?" Hal nodded and Grace frowned slightly. "Don't worry, Hal. Maybe she went out for a tramp in the snow."

"A tramp in the snow!" Laureen burst into laughter. "Sorry, Hal. Do you want us to help you find her?"

Hal looked concerned. "It's just that she always wears those ridiculous high-heeled boots, and she could have slipped or something."

"If you will all excuse me, I will get my parka." Paul stood up and bowed. "A brisk walk will stimulate the appetite."

As the other men got to their feet, Hal looked doubly concerned. "But the pizzas will get cold."

"Don't be an as . . . idiot!" Moira patted his shoulder. "Laureen knows how to reheat pizza."

Laureen nodded. "Of course I do. You guys go look for Vanessa and we'll take the pizzas to my place. They'll be even tastier if I heat them on bricks. It's the only way to get the crusts properly crisp."

It didn't take long to cart the pizzas to Laureen's kitchen, where she stuck them in her huge, restaurant-size oven. Ellen had brought down her thirty-cup coffeepot and the five women sat around Laureen's butcher-block work island on bar stools. A full array of copper pans and kitchen utensils hung above their heads, suspended by hooks on a revolving frame, and Ellen pointed up at a big slotted spoon with prongs around the circumference of the bowl. "What's that?"

"A spaghetti separator," Laureen informed her. "I have two. One here and one in the bedroom."

Jayne giggled. "Some days you step in it, other days you don't, but I have to ask anyway. Why do you have a spaghetti separator in the bedroom?"

"Because Alan uses it for a back scratcher. He says it's a lot better than those little plastic ones you buy in the store."

"I wonder if they found Vanessa yet." Grace looked worried.

"Oh, who cares?" Laureen sighed deeply. "Remember how much nicer it was before Hal married her? Personally, I wish she'd take a hike for good. We'd all be a lot better off."

"True enough." Grace admitted, pouring herself a cup of coffee before it was quite through perking. "But not tonight. I saw a pack of wolves right next to the building and I know they don't attack humans unless they're starving, but the avalanche may have cut off their food supply and my dad told me stories of how hungry wolves band together and if they see any kind of prey they . . . okay, Moira, I won't go into details."

Laureen said snidely, "Wolves wouldn't bother Vanessa. She'd just invite them up to her bedroom for a drink."

"Come on, Laureen, honey." Jayne reached out to take her arm. "You'd be a lot better off if you could just put that whole mess behind you."

Laureen gave a bitter laugh. "I still wish she'd rot in hell! And I don't think you'd be quite so charitable if she'd taken off after Paul."

"Well . . . maybe that's true." Jayne smiled slightly. "That's the only good thing about our fight. It took Paul out of the lineup."

"So how may scalps did she actually get?" Moira wanted to know.

Laureen counted them off on her fingers. "Marc, and Clayton, and Alan, for sure. I'm not sure about Johnny or Jack."

Ellen winced at the mention of Johnny's name, but this wasn't the time for confidences. "I know that Jack managed to keep his distance."

"How about Walker?" Jayne changed the subject before anyone could notice that Ellen hadn't mentioned Johnny.

"Oh, she counted Walker out from the beginning."

"She did?" Moira was amazed. "But Walker's a handsome man, and single."

"Vanessa's a Southern girl. She might not have many scruples, but black is one of them."

"Well, she's got a fu . . . screwed-up sense of priorities,

that's all I have to say. I can't believe she left Walker alone and tried to pick up on me."

"She tried to seduce *you?*" Jayne was clearly shocked.

"You don't have to look so surprised, Jayne. For an aging broad, I'm not so bad."

"I didn't mean it that way." Jayne's face turned red. "I just didn't realize that Vanessa swung both ways."

"I doubt she did. She just ran out of men, and it was desperation time. If she'd had any brains at all, she'd have known that I'd never look at anyone except Grace."

Grace reached out to squeeze Moira's hand under the table, feeling pleasurably foolish and insanely relieved. Moira had known exactly what was going on.

"Well, I'm going to make another pizza." Laureen reached for the last can of pizza dough. "If I recommend this stuff, I have to test it myself, and nobody made a pizza with anchovies."

Jayne laughed. "That's because nobody but you goes to the gourmet shelf in the grocery store. How about anchovies and Cheese Whiz? I've got a couple of jars you can borrow."

"No, thanks." Laureen laughed. "That sounds almost as bad as your husband's sardines and cream cheese. And I don't buy my anchovies in cans at the grocery store. I get them flash-frozen direct from the distributor."

"I just love anchovies, but Moira hates them so we always have to make our pizzas half-and-half, and if one little piece of my anchovy gets over on Moira's side, she threatens me with . . . okay, I'll stop." Grace grinned at Moira. "Tell me where you keep your anchovies, Laureen."

"In the walk-in freezer, right side, second shelf. I can get them, Grace."

"Stay there and make the pizza. I have to get more coffee, anyway."

Jayne whistled as Laureen threw the dough in the air to shape it. "Lordy! Look at that!"

"All it takes is a flick of the wrist, hours of practice, and someone to clean up the kitchen if you miss." Laureen laughed. "I spent the whole day at Papa Luigi's before I did my gourmet pizza show."

"Well, you won't catch me trying it. I went to flip a flapjack once and it ended up sticking to the ceiling. Poor Paul had to climb up on a ladder and . . . what's the matter, Grace?"

Grace stood motionless before the open door to Laureen's huge freezer. When she turned to face them, no words came out, only a terrible scream.

They all rushed over to see. Vanessa was crumpled on the floor of the freezer, her eyes staring up at the ceiling. For a moment they just stood there in shock, but then Ellen moved Grace aside. "Let me through."

Ellen knelt down next to Vanessa and took her wrist. After a moment she looked up and shook her head. "She's dead. I think she must have hit her head on something."

"Go for the men, Grace." Moira took Grace's shoulders and turned her around. "The fresh air'll do you good."

When Grace had left, Moira pointed to the metal table in the center of the freezer. "I didn't want to say anything in front of Grace, she's always been squeamish, but there's a lot of blood down there. Vanessa must have hit her head on that table. But what was she doing in Laureen's freezer? And why was the door closed?"

It took Laureen a moment, but then she caught the unspoken accusation. "You don't think I shut her up in there, do you? Just because I said I wished she'd rot in hell . . ."

"Hush up, Moira," Jayne scolded, putting her arm around Laureen. "You're going to make this poor girl feel like a treed 'possum. We all know Laureen didn't mean it, isn't that right, Laureen, honey?"

"No, I meant every word," Laureen admitted with difficulty. "But I didn't trap her in my freezer. And I certainly didn't shove her against that table. Think about it for a minute. I hated Vanessa enough to kill her, but do you actually think I'd let her bleed all over those wonderful lobster tails I just got in from Maine?"

FOURTEEN

An hour later, they were gathered in Grace and Moira's living room again. They'd decided to hold the body in Laureen's freezer until the police could be notified. Naturally, Laureen had put up some resistance. She'd waited years for her walk-in freezer and there was no way she wanted it turned into a morgue! It had taken some persuading, but she'd finally yielded.

Walker and Marc had volunteered for the unpleasant task of wrapping Vanessa in a sheet and laying her out on the floor of the freezer, while Alan and Paul kept Hal company. When Walker and Marc rejoined the rest of the group in Moira and Grace's living room, they were grim faced and solemn.

"Brandy?" Moira passed the bottle that Alan had brought. "I think we could all use a drink."

Hal held out his glass for a refill.

"Careful, Hal." Moira poured just a bit more in his glass. "That stuff is pretty potent."

"It's just what I need. I still can't believe that Vanessa's dead. And even worse, I don't know whether I should drown my sorrows or celebrate. Vanessa was a real piece of work, but at least she was interesting. I think I'm going to miss her."

Laureen clamped her mouth shut and avoided Hal's eyes. It was apparent that she wanted to say something, but she managed to remain silent.

"I am sorry, Hal." Paul patted Hal's shoulder. "I wish to offer condolence, but I do not know which words to say."

Hal nodded and took another sip of his brandy. "Well, I do. I say there's something rotten in Denmark, and don't take that personally, Paul."

"I am Norwegian. You may say what you wish about Danes."

"Right." Hal gave a lopsided grin and turned to Marc. "You said her skull was smashed?"

"Hal, please," Moira soothed, reaching for his hand. "Don't dwell on it."

"I'm not dwelling. I'm just trying to make some sense out of it." He turned to Marc again. "You think she hit her head on that metal table in Laureen's freezer?"

Marc nodded. "That's what it looked like, Hal. Of course I'm no expert, but . . . ."

"What was she doing in there in the first place?" Hal interrupted. "The first time she saw Laureen's freezer she said she thought it was scary. She told me that it reminded her of a television show where a guy was impaled on a meat hook. I just can't picture her going in there for no reason."

"We think she went after the brownies. There was an open package on the floor and everyone heard Laureen say she had a batch in the freezer."

"Well . . . maybe." Hal looked dubious. "Vanessa was crazy about those brownies. But that doesn't explain how she got into your unit."

Alan responded immediately to Laureen's questioning look. "I know what you're thinking, but you're wrong! I never gave her a key, and I have no idea how she got in. Are you sure you locked the door when you ran down to get the pizza dough?"

Laureen frowned. "I think I did. But I could've left it open. I do that sometimes, when I'm just going somewhere in the building."

"That explains it, then." Hal nodded. "But why did Vanessa hit her head on that table? There wasn't anything on the floor to trip over, was there, Laureen?"

"Only a case of lobster tails, but that was in plain sight. I'm sure she would have seen it."

"Not if the light went off." Alan hurried to explain. "The freezer has two switches for the lights. The first one goes on and off with the door, the same as a refrigerator. But there's a wall switch that overrides it. That's on a ten-minute timer."

"That's too complicated for me right now."

Alan patted Hal on the shoulder. "That's all right. You're entitled to get a little smashed. You see, there are times when you want to spend more than a couple of minutes in the freezer, rearranging the shelves or whatever, and you don't want to leave the door open that long. That's when you use the wall switch, and if you forget to turn it off when you leave, it shuts off automatically after ten minutes."

"So Vanessa used the wall switch and closed the door. Is that what you're saying?"

"That's right. Now picture this. Vanessa's in the freezer looking for the brownies. She finally finds them and she's opening the package when the lights click off. Naturally, she panics and runs for the door, but it's pitch-black, and she trips over that case of lobster tails and crashes into the corner of the table."

Hal reflected for a moment. "That tracks, Alan. Even better than *Columbo*. Vanessa used to love reruns of *Columbo*."

"Buck up, old bean." Jayne patted Hal's shoulder. "I think you'd better stay in our guest room tonight so we can keep an eye on you."

Hal struggled to his feet. "No, I'm okay. I'll just take the rest of this brandy with me, if Alan'll let me."

"Go ahead, Hal." Alan got up to offer a steadying arm. "Laureen and I'll walk you home. And if you need another bottle just bang on our door."

They all said good-bye to Moira and Grace and went out.

"Shall we hold the elevator?" Paul offered at the third floor. Laureen shook her head. "We'll take the stairs down to our place. It's good exercise."

Ellen stared glumly at the indicator light as they passed Johnny's unit on the fourth floor. He was a two-timing rat and she was glad he was gone, but she hoped he was safe in Italy. Those plane tickets bothered her. She'd driven him to the airport a couple of times, and before leaving he'd always checked to make sure he had his tickets.

Number five flashed next and Ellen shivered a bit. Had Clayton and Rachael made it down the mountain on the snowmobile? Or were they at the bottom of a ravine somewhere, under a pile of twisted wreckage? The sixth floor was Betty's and thinking about her didn't make Ellen feel any better. At least number seven was Marc's floor.

"See you tomorrow." Marc gave a wave and Ellen sighed with relief. Eight was hers and nine was Jayne and

Paul's. But ten was the spa and that's where they'd found the hand in the pool. Ellen blinked hard. Suddenly this whole building seemed like a tomb to her, or a death trap for those still living.

"Ellen?" Walker tapped her on the shoulder and she almost jumped out of her skin. "We're home."

"Oh, sorry. I must have been daydreaming." Ellen turned and managed a smile for Jayne and Paul as she stepped off the elevator.

"Night, Ellen, honey." Jayne gave a little wave. "See you tomorrow, Walker."

As Walker unlocked her door, Ellen turned to watch the indicator light on the elevator. The up-arrow glowed, then flickered off at the ninth floor, where it would stay until morning unless somebody called for it in the middle of the night.

"Ellen? Coming?" Standing by the open door, Walker looked concerned. Ellen forced a smile. As she stepped inside and closed the door behind her, the indicator light began to glow again as Betty's secret friend rode to the sixth floor for another long night of surveillance.

Moira released her tight chignon and ran her fingers through her hair. This upswept hairstyle hurt like hell, but it was worth it if Grace didn't notice her wrinkles. She scowled at her reflection in the mirror of the white French vanity Grace had bought her for her birthday. It was rumored to have once belonged to Marilyn Monroe, and Moira hadn't had the heart to tell Grace that claiming reproductions had once belonged to the rich and famous was a thriving business. Once, when a client had specifically requested a Napoleon Bonaparte bed, Moira had spent months looking. She'd found six, each with papers testifying that the little dictator had slept in them. And every one had been a fake.

The workmen had delivered the vanity while she was at work and when Moira had come home, she'd found it sitting in the bedroom with a note from Grace stuck in the corner of the mirror. Moira had left it there. It said, *This once belonged to MM. You're not blond, but you're still my bombshell.*

Moira pulled open the drawer to take out her hairbrush. The rollers on the drawer were made of a plastic that hadn't existed when Marilyn was alive, but she'd never tell Grace. She was brushing her hair, preparing to pull it back up into its uncomfortable twist, when Grace came in. "Leave it down, Moira," she suggested gently. "You're not going to have any hair left if you keep pulling it up so tight, and I like it better down, anyway. Think we ought to go up and check on Hal?"

"Hal's a big boy, Gracie. He can take care of himself."

"I suppose so," Grace sighed, "but he had a lot of that brandy."

"Don't worry. He'll come down if he needs anything, and if we hear any loud crashes, we'll run upstairs."

"Moira? Could I ask you a question?"

Moira studied Grace's anxious expression. "What is it, Grace?"

"Did you mean what you said at Laureen's?"

"I said a lot of things at Laureen's. Did I mean what?"

"That you knew what Vanessa was doing all the time. And that you'd never look at anyone but me."

Moira turned to face her lover, who looked very beautiful in lavender baby-doll pajamas, an effect thoroughly sabotaged by the old blue and red flannel shirt draped over her shoulders. "I meant it then. Right now, I'm not so sure."

"What do you mean?" There was a quaver in Grace's voice.

"Oh, you know how it is, Grace. You live with someone for years and they start taking you for granted. When bedtime rolls around, they wear ugly flannel shirts over absolutely scrumptious baby-doll pajamas."

Grace let out a relieved sigh and began to grin. Moira loved to tease her about her flannel shirts.

"I know what you mean. I was in love with a woman who went to bed in an old college sweatshirt. Can you imagine that?"

Moira smiled. She was wearing her college sweatshirt, so old that the red was now a washed-out pink and the mascot was totally unrecognizable. "Must have been grim, Grace. Did you love this woman a lot?"

Grace sighed. "Oh, yes, much more than she deserved. One night when I couldn't stand seeing her like that any longer, I ripped that sweatshirt right off her body and covered her all over with kisses."

"You did?" Moira flicked off the lights in the dressing room and took Grace's hand. "Come on, Gracie, tell me more."

Betty glanced at her secret friend and smiled. At last she knew who he was, and she felt proud that such an important actor had come to visit her. She wished she could find the words to ask him why he only made scary movies, but perhaps he'd take that as an insult. Sir Laurence Olivier had refused certain movies when he hadn't approved of the scripts, but her secret friend might not have that kind of bargaining power.

There was something she'd meant to tell him, something about his appearance in the undertaker movies.

Betty frowned and searched her mind, but her head felt light and empty, almost as if she were dreaming. Even the forbidden channels showed people sleeping, except for channel three where the funny animal man did nothing but sit on the floor and look through big piles of papers. Letting random images pop into her mind was much more interesting.

Her secret friend had brought the candy again. Someone must have told him what she liked. As she reached for her second piece, an image popped into Betty's mind and she smiled. A boy was handing her a box of this very same candy, wrapped in silver paper. There was a little green and red bow on top so it must have been Christmas. The card had a reindeer with a very red nose and the boy's name was Rudolph. No, that was the reindeer's name. The boy's name was Charles, Charles G., and he'd drawn her name from the basket at school. No present over four dollars. No exchanging names if you got someone you didn't like. Miss Parker was very strict about that. She could see Miss Parker now, playing the old upright piano in their classroom. They were all sitting at their desks, five rows across, seven in each row, hers second from the front in the middle row. Amy C. sat in front of her and Doug S. behind.

She heard Miss Parker playing the Christmas songs as everyone sang.

We three Kings of Orient are. Smoking on a big fat cigar. It was loaded, and exploded. Blam!

But only Charles had sung it that way. And never when Miss Parker could hear him.

Then they were opening their presents and Charles was watching her out of the corner of his eye, every freckle on his face standing out because he was blushing. Chocolate-covered cherries. She'd never liked them that much before, but she thanked Charles and told him they were her favorites. And every Christmas after that, even after Charles was grown up and had an important job with the government, he had given her a big box of chocolate-covered cherries.

Betty frowned in concentration. There was a word for what Charles had done, a bad word. It started with a *T* and ended with an *R* and it had been in one of the crossword puzzles she'd loved before she'd gotten so sick. The clue was "one who informs or betrays." And the word was . . . *traitor!* Betty shivered a little, even though the room was nice and warm. Charles, the traitor, was dead and he hadn't loved her after all. He'd just used her to try to hurt Daddy. Still . . . sometimes she missed him, and she missed Daddy, too. She was almost sure that Daddy hadn't come to see her since she'd moved into this lovely mountain chateau. Was Daddy dead like Charles?

"What's the matter, Betty?" The image vanished as her secret friend reached over to wipe a tear from her cheek. He was so kind, she couldn't help but smile.

"That's better. I like to see you happy. Have another piece." He was holding out the box, so she took one, just to please him, even though the candy didn't taste like it used to. She put it into her mouth before she remembered that she had to tell him about her undertaker collection, but it wasn't polite to speak with your mouth full. She chewed, and swallowed, and, as her eyelids closed, her message for him turned into a shimmering butterfly with gossamer wings and drifted away.

* * *

Hal sat on the floor of his office, surrounded by stacks of his discarded work. He figured he must really be drunk, or he'd never have dragged out all his old portfolios. These drawings were his slush pile, the stuff he hadn't used for one reason or another.

He picked up an early drawing and examined it critically. This was a stripped-down version of Chiquita Chicken without her lace mantilla and red high-heeled shoes. Probably no one would recognize her.

Hal frowned as he noticed the date on the bottom. This drawing had won the local cartoon contest. He had been seventeen that year, a senior at Jefferson High and wildly in love with a stunning blond cheerleader named Marcie Wilson, who didn't seem to know that he existed even though her locker was right across the hall from his. Hal still remembered the morning that his winning cartoon had appeared in the paper, and Marcie Wilson, the lovely subject of every one of his adolescent fantasies, had actually stopped him in the hall to congratulate him. "That was a great chicken you drew, Hal. Are you going to the dance tonight after the game?"

Hal had shifted from foot to foot. He hadn't even planned on going to the game. "I don't know. I might drop in for a couple of minutes."

"Oh, I hope so!" Marcie had reached out to squeeze his arm. "Shall I save you the last dance? And then maybe you could drive me home."

Hal had walked away in a daze, right past the room where his European history class was meeting. He'd turned around and run back, sliding into his seat just as the final bell rang. Mr. Harmon had given a rousing lecture on the battle of Waterloo, but Hal hadn't heard a word.

* * *

Just as soon as they'd parked up on the overlook, Marcie shrugged out of her blouse and turned that dazzling smile on him. "Everyone says you're going to be famous, Hal. Isn't that just wonderful?"

"Yeah." Hal wasn't thinking about fame and fortune. He was too busy staring at Marcie's lovely white breasts in the moonlight. "They're wonderful, all right!"

Marcie giggled. "Oh, Hal, you're so funny. Touch them if you want to."

Hal reached out to run tentative fingers over her smooth warm flesh. His fingertips tingled, but Marcie's little groaning sounds made him draw back quickly. "I'm sorry, Marcie. I didn't mean to hurt you."

Marcie giggled again. "You didn't, silly. It felt wonderful." She reached out to pull him closer. Hal's head swam with the sensation of being this close to her deliciously soft skin.

Marcie groaned again and held his head tighter. Hal thought he'd died and gone to heaven and then a headline popped into his mind. *Promising young cartoonist found smothered by Marcie Wilson's breast.* What a way to die!

It could have gone on for hours, Hal didn't know. He was vaguely aware of the cars whizzing past on the causeway below, but maybe that was the sound of the blood coursing through his veins. Marcie's fingers played in his hair, combing and twisting playfully. He'd never known that individual strands of hair could tingle with delight.

"Will you do a drawing of your darling chicken for me, Hal? I'd just love to have one to hang in my bedroom."

"Sure. I'll do that, Marcie." Hal didn't even recognize

his own voice. It was low and muffled, and he felt himself gasping for breath. He wondered if he was too young to have a cardiac arrest.

"I want you to sign it, too." Marcie was very serious as she wiggled away. "An original Hal Knight to hang where I can look at it every time I get ready for bed. Will you promise to do that, Hal?"

"I promise, Marcie." Hal would have promised anything just as long as Marcie didn't put on her blouse again.

"You're so nice, Hal. And I've got something for you, too. Just look."

Hal looked down just in time to see Marcie pull up her skirt. He gasped out loud as he saw she was wearing only a baby blue garter belt.

"God!" It was a combination sigh and prayer. He'd seen pictures of women with no clothes on before, but he'd never expected to see Marcie Wilson like this.

Marcie giggled and caught his hand. "I just don't know if I should let you or not. Maybe if I had that drawing, I might. You have some art paper with you, don't you, Hal?"

"Art paper?"

It took a minute for Hal to understand what she wanted. Then he straightened up in the seat and grinned as he reached for the drawing pad he always carried with him. He'd dash off a drawing of Chiquita Chicken for her and Marcie would let him do what he'd been dreaming about for months. What a deal!

His hands were trembling and he had to take a couple of deep breaths to make them steady enough to draw. He'd spent a lot of time perfecting Chiquita Chicken and it should have been no problem to draw her now. But Marcie had slipped down in the seat and she hadn't put any of her clothes back on, even though he'd flicked on the dome light. He ruined three sheets of drawing paper before he finally got a rendition of Chiquita good enough to give her.

"That's wonderful." Marcie smiled as he showed her his drawing. "Sign it, Hal. And then turn off the dome light. You've been so nice to me that I'm going to be just as nice to you."

Hal's head reeled as he scrawled his name on the bottom of the drawing. What a night this would be!

Hal poured himself another drink and didn't bother to sip it. Marcie Wilson was probably an overweight matron by now, but the thought of that night still made him sick. The most beautiful girl in the senior class and he hadn't been able to do it. Naturally, she'd told her girlfriends, and they'd spread it all through the school. Hal had spent the remainder of his senior year in an agony of embarrassment.

He stuffed the drawing back in its portfolio and reached for another. Marcie's drawing was worth real money now, and he was sure she'd kept it. That's what she'd been after in the first place.

Far away on the West Coast, the chances of running into anyone who knew Marcie Wilson had diminished considerably. But it had still taken Hal a full year before he'd tried to make love to another woman. He'd picked an expensive call girl knowing that high-priced hookers with big mouths didn't last long in a city like Vegas. But even then he hadn't been able to go through with it, not then and not in several attempts after that.

So he'd gone to a shrink who'd suggested a therapy that had made Hal laugh out loud. He'd told Hal to find a girl who looked just like the Marcie he remembered and attempt to reenact that night. It hadn't crossed his mind in the years since . . . until he'd met Vanessa.

Vanessa was a ringer for Marcie, right down to the cute little mole on the side of her neck. And she'd had no idea that he was rich. The dinner she'd made for him in her run-down apartment had been the nicest thing anyone had done for him in years. That's when he'd made up his mind to marry her, if she'd have him. He hadn't been able to resist the girl of his adolescent dreams.

Hal sighed as he opened another portfolio and drew out a whole series of drawings he'd shelved to preserve his marriage. In a moment of weakness, when he'd still thought it might work between them, he'd offered to name one of his cartoon characters after her. Naturally, Vanessa had been delighted.

Unfortunately, all Hal's previous characters were alliterative. He'd used it as a gimmick at the beginning of his career and now names like Skampy Skunk, Benny Bunny, and Chiquita Chicken had become the Hal Knight trademark. If he used Vanessa's name, her character would have to start with the letter *V* and he couldn't think of any *V* animals. Vanessa had been insistent. So late one night, Hal had sat down in front of his drawing board, determined to come up with a character that would please his wife.

It had taken hours, but he'd finally come up with a series of drawings for Vanessa Varmint, a cute little red weasel that flew in from Paris to tug on the heartstrings of everyone's favorite character, Skampy Skunk. And he'd introduced her in his Sunday strip.

Hal still remembered Vanessa's shocked expression when she'd picked up the paper and caught the first glimpse of her personal cartoon character. A weasel? She didn't care how cute it was!

That Sunday strip had been Vanessa Varmint's debut and her swan song, all rolled into one. She'd never seen the light of day again. And here Hal was, stuck with a whole portfolio of drawings he'd never used.

Hal sighed. They really were pretty good. He guessed he could reintroduce Vanessa Varmint now that her namesake was no longer around to object, but Skampy Skunk was better off as a freewheeling bachelor. Right now he was in the midst of a tenuous romance with Penelope Possum, the unwed mother of six. There was a problem with the babysitter and Skampy Skunk couldn't seem to get his ladylove alone. Since Penelope's sister, Patricia, was now working for the postal service and using her pouch to carry the mail, Penelope and Skampy had to take the kids along on all their dates.

Hal picked up the portfolio with the Vanessa Varmint drawings and started to toss it into the trash, until it dawned on him that someday someone would pay top dollar for an unpublished series by Hal Knight. As he stuffed the portfolio back in the file drawer, Hal wondered whether the real Vanessa would have changed her attitude toward varmints if she'd known just how valuable that little red weasel might turn out to be.

It was past midnight and Hal yawned as he got to his feet and headed for bed. At least he wouldn't miss Vanessa there. They'd had separate bedrooms for over a year.

A key fell out of his pocket as he slipped out of his shirt. Bending over to pick it up, Hal saw it was on a little gold ring with a tag that said, *Smiling Bill Korman in Henderson. I've Got a Deal for You!* Hal was thoroughly puzzled; he'd never bought a car from Smiling Bill in his life.

Then he remembered that Walker had given it to him when he'd come back to Grace and Moira's apartment, explaining that he'd found it on the floor next to Vanessa's body. Hal had slipped it into his pocket without even looking at it, assuming that it was Vanessa's door key.

Turning the key over in his hand, he reached for his own door keys. The notches didn't match up, and he was willing to bet it wouldn't fit Alan and Laureen's door, either.

His mind was reeling, and despite the effects of the brandy, he slipped back into his shirt. He couldn't sleep now. He staggered to the bathroom and splashed cold water on his face, which helped a bit, and took three aspirin. If he kept on taking aspirin, maybe the hangover wouldn't have time to hit between doses.

Three cups of instant coffee later, Hal felt almost human, still a little woozy but clearheaded. It was all beginning to add up. Vanessa hadn't gone into Laureen's freezer under her own steam. Someone had carried her there after she was already dead.

"This key's the key." Hal spoke aloud and chuckled at his own wit. If he could manage to sober up enough, he'd try it on every door in the building.

FIFTEEN

The Caretaker was scowling as he switched off the shortwave. The Old Man had no idea what hell was breaking loose up here, and again, he'd failed to get through. It was a good thing he'd been able to handle it without any help.

When Vanessa had discovered the loose patch of earth, he'd had no choice. At least he'd covered his tracks brilliantly in the process, even setting the stage with the box of brownies. It was something the Old Man's soldiers seemed incapable of doing.

He sighed as he shut the door to Jack's apartment and headed for the elevator. How many gruesome accidents and disappearances would these people swallow before someone got suspicious? Even though he'd always wanted this kind of responsibility, keeping his eye on everyone was exhausting. The only thing that made it possible was the monitor in Betty's unit. Jack would probably have a heart attack if he knew that he'd done the Old Man a real favor.

* * *

There was the sound of irregular breathing in the darkness. "Alan? Are you sleeping?" The voice quavered slightly.

Alan opened his eyes to find Laureen sitting on the edge of the bed, staring out at the big pine tree, her shoulders slumped and her arms folded across her chest as if she were hugging herself for comfort. After twenty-two years of marriage, he knew that she was close to tears.

"What's the . . . what's the matter, honey?"

Laureen's voice was still quavering. "It's the freezer, Alan, it's haunting me. Every time I close my eyes, I see what's in there."

Alan rubbed the sleep from his eyes. Problems he'd encountered during the day seldom kept Alan awake, but he wasn't as sensitive as Laureen. He hated it when she cried. Laureen didn't cry often, but when she did, it took hours to soothe her.

"I've got an idea." He went over and put his arms around her. "Since we're both awake, let's go up to the spa and enjoy the Jacuzzi. No one else will be up there and it'll be nice and relaxing. And then we'll take a nap on the lounge chairs. The freezer won't bother you as much if you're nine floors away from it."

"That might help," Laureen agreed hopefully. "But you were sleeping just fine before, and you always get a backache when you fall asleep on those lounge chairs. Are you sure?"

"I'm sure. My back won't bother me if I take along a pillow. I'll get a bottle of wine and we'll sit in the Jacuzzi and look at the stars."

"It's snowing, Alan. We won't be able to see the stars."

"Then we'll look at the snow. Come on, honey. It'll be fun."

"Well . . . all right. I'll just pack up a couple of things

and get into my suit." Laureen began to feel a little better as she packed up their pillows and blankets. She took her new blue swimming suit out of the drawer and struggled into it. It had a special tummy-slimming panel, but nothing short of a miracle could hide all the extra pounds. She'd been a perfect size eight when they were married, but now, as she caught her reflection in the mirror over the dresser, she sighed. This shade was perfect for her coloring, but she looked like a big blue beach ball.

Alan went into the kitchen and put together two huge sandwiches, roast beef and cheddar on whole wheat bread with a generous dollop of horseradish sauce, and packed them into a picnic hamper. He stuck in a bottle of wine and two glasses and two napkins. Maybe a full stomach and a couple glasses of wine would make Laureen sleepy. Then he went to get some brownies for dessert. He loved Laureen's brownies.

Alan stopped with his hand on the freezer door, recoiling at the thought of Vanessa in her plastic shroud. Forget the brownies. There was no way he wanted to go in there.

As he walked away, he turned to look back at the freezer door, its brushed steel gleaming in the fluorescent glare of the kitchen lights. Even at wholesale, it had been an expensive addition to their gourmet kitchen, but Laureen found it indispensable for storing those hard-to-find ingredients sometimes required for her show. The industrial appliance was twelve feet long and six feet wide, holding thousands of cubic feet. Its motor was powerful, guaranteed for ten years, and its hum was barely discernible. Although the appliance appeared perfectly benign unless you knew what was inside, Alan certainly couldn't fault Laureen for being jumpy around it. He was a little jumpy, too. They'd never had a dead neighbor stored in their freezer before.

"Laureen? Ready?"

She appeared almost immediately, carrying a tote bag with their towels, two pillows, two thermal blankets, and a change of clothing for each of them.

Alan's breath caught in his throat as he stared at his wife. Her eyes were puffy from lack of sleep, but she still looked pretty. And the swimsuit reminded him of one from a long time ago.

Laureen caught his expression and flashed a shy smile. "I just got this suit last week. Do you like it?"

"It looks great. It reminds me of the one you wore on our honeymoon."

"I didn't think you'd remember!" Laureen stared at him in pleased amazement. "That's the reason I bought it. It's exactly the same shade. Not the same size, of course."

"So who can wear the same size?" Alan glanced down at his expanded waistline. "People change, Laureen. Besides, you were much too thin when we got married."

"I was?"

Alan nodded. "We were both pretty skinny back then, and those hipbones of yours almost killed me. Remember?"

"I do." Laureens's smile grew wider. "You said you'd have bruises in the morning—and you did. Did you know that I ate nothing but cottage cheese and fruit for three solid months before our wedding?"

Alan looked puzzled. "Why on earth did you do that?"

"I wanted to fit into my mother's wedding gown and that meant losing thirty-five pounds. It looked nice on me, didn't it, Alan?"

"You looked ravishing. Where's our wedding album, anyway? I haven't looked at those pictures in years."

"Right here." Laureen opened the drawer to the table by the couch and handed him a heavy leather book embossed with gold. They'd hired the best photographer in town, and it'd been worth it.

While Laureen looked over his shoulder, Alan opened the book. It was like stepping back in time. "Look at that, Laureen." Alan pointed to the picture of them at the altar. "We certainly were a handsome couple. And I was right, you did look ravishing."

Laureen smiled as she examined the photograph, remembering her tears right before the wedding when she thought her hair hadn't curled right. It looked just fine. Chalk it up to bridal jitters.

Alan flipped the page, "Here's the one where you're tossing the bouquet. Who caught it, anyway?"

"Your sister, Shirley. And I had to toss it again because she was already married."

"Oh, yeah." Alan nodded. "Pure reflex. In high school Shirl was a star shortstop, so she just reached up and fielded that bouquet."

Laureen giggled. "I wish the photographer had gotten a picture of her. She was so embarrassed."

Alan flipped through several photographs of the reception and Laureen smiled as she noticed that the photographer had caught her mother, Millie, nervously rearranging the flowers on the tables. Millie had been in an absolute tizzy for months before the wedding. She'd bought a book with a checklist of everything that had to be done and she'd quizzed Laureen constantly. Had she gone down to pick out the bridesmaids' flowers? Arranged the ceremony with the minister? Chosen the music? Put down a deposit on the Elks Hall for the reception? And was she absolutely certain the invitations had gone out to all of Alan's relatives?

A month before the wedding, Laureen's father had pulled them into the kitchen for a private talk. He'd heard Millie say it might be nice if white doves were released from a net as the bridal couple left the church, but he didn't think Reverend Thurgood would go for bird shit all over the steps of the church. Millie's idea of a perfect wedding was not only costing him a fortune, it was turning poor Millie into a nervous wreck. Rather than go through all this nonsense for another four weeks, he'd be glad to write them a check for the whole amount the wedding would cost, provided they eloped right now.

Laureen had turned to Alan for the final decision. They could use the money for a new car or even a down payment on their first house. But just as they were about to agree, Millie had stormed into the kitchen. She'd heard the whole thing and she was furious. He was depriving his only daughter of the precious memories she'd treasure for the rest of her life! And besides, what would everyone think if they called off the wedding now? Only brides who were "that way" ran off to elope . . . unless there was something that Laureen wasn't telling her?

So the wedding had gone off as scheduled, minus the doves. Laureen's father had been firm about that. And Millie had talked about Laureen's wonderful wedding until the day she died.

"Laureen?" Alan reached out for her hand. He looked very solemn. "Will you promise to be honest if I ask you a question?"

"I promise, Alan."

"After all that's happened in our life together, would you marry me again? Knowing what you know now?"

Laureen nodded. "I'd marry you, Alan, anytime you asked me. And you?"

"Absolutely." Alan smiled at her. "You're the only one I've ever loved."

Laureen blinked away happy tears. It was true. She knew that. And she'd forgiven him for his affair with Vanessa.

Alan turned back to the album. "Look at this one, honey. You're raising your skirt to show off your garter and my brother Harry's leering at your legs. He certainly looks different with all his hair."

Laureen nodded in agreement, distracted by a terrible twinge of conscience. For one brief moment, she'd almost confessed an affair, too, a long time ago. But it would only hurt Alan if he knew, and she'd vowed to carry her guilty secret to her grave.

Alan turned the page and pointed at them cutting the cake. "They always take this shot, don't they?"

"It's a standard." Laureen pasted on a smile and banished her guilty thoughts. "This is my favorite photo, the one of us feeding each other."

"I remember that moment." Alan chuckled and squeezed her hand. "You were so nervous you missed my mouth with the cake."

"And you gave me such a big piece that I nearly choked."

They were quiet for a moment, reliving the memories. Laureen was the first to speak. "We were so young and naive back then. Think we've learned anything important over the past twenty-two years?"

"That money and success don't matter nearly as much as we thought they would. We were just as happy in our first efficiency apartment as we are in this big expensive place. And we've learned that love can survive all sorts of obstacles."

"That's true."

Alan started to grin. "Of course, I didn't mention the most important thing we've learned since this picture was taken."

"What's that, Alan?"

"We're *much* better at feeding ourselves."

Staggering slightly as he got off the elevator, Hal steadied himself with one hand and tried to fit the key into the hole. It was the right kind of lock, but Alan had been telling the truth. He hadn't given Vanessa a key because this one didn't fit Alan and Laureen's door.

"One down, eight to go." Hal mumbled. He was almost positive Vanessa's key wouldn't open Grace and Moira's door, but he had to try. Still too drunk to make any sort of assumptions, he was having trouble enough just remembering which floor he was on. When he reached the second floor, he was very quiet. Moira might come out and bean him with a hammer or something if she thought he was a burglar. But the key didn't fit in Moira and Grace's door, and he dropped it into his pocket again. Two floors down, seven floors to go.

He was out of the elevator before he realized that the third floor was his floor, and that he'd already compared Vanessa's key to his key. Hal got back into the elevator and resumed what he thought of as his quest. Heroes of ancient times had searched for the Holy Grail, and Excalibur, and the Golden Fleece. His quest for the Unlockable Door wasn't quite that romantic, but he didn't have to encounter fire-breathing dragons and armor-plated knights, either.

Hal leaned against the wall for a long time after trying Johnny Day's lock, wishing he could stretch out on Johnny's thick green carpeting and close his eyes. It took great resolve to press the button for the fifth floor. The coffee had worn off and that last snifter of brandy was catching up with him.

By the time Hal stepped off, he was seeing double. He weaved his way down the hallway and braced himself against Clayton's door. Concentration. Hal blinked hard and the two doors he was seeing merged into one. It took several tries, but he finally managed to get the key in the lock and turn it. What happened next almost made him fall on his face. Clayton's door swung open on its well-oiled hinges.

"Aha!" Hal let out a whoop of pleasure. Now he could go home to bed. If he could get there.

Hal's legs refused to carry him any longer, and he sat down on the rug with a thump, staring at the darkness inside. What had Vanessa been doing in Clayton's apartment?

He ran his hand through the thick pile carpeting and frowned, trying to think of a connection. He shut his eyes to concentrate, but before he could draw any conclusion, he passed out cold.

Betty frowned as she stared at the screen. The moment she'd realized that her secret friend was in this movie, she'd pressed the button to record. And then she'd seen that it was another scary movie, the kind she didn't like. Why had they typecast him in roles like this? He was handsome enough to play a romantic lead, and he might be able to do comedy, too, if they'd only give him a chance.

Even though she knew it was only make-believe, Betty still felt very afraid. The man who drew the funny animals was dead, and her secret friend had killed him. She wasn't so sure she wanted him to visit her again, not even if he brought her candy.

She remembered a trick that Charles had taught her when they were young and saw the movie about the vampire. She'd wanted to leave. Charles had told her to cover her eyes with her hand and peek out through her fingers and she'd remember it was only a movie.

Betty put her hand over her eyes and peeked through. It worked. This was only a movie on her television set, all pretend. She watched as her secret friend dragged the body into the elevator and the doors closed behind them. Now she had to take her fingers down so she could use the remote control to find the rest of the movie.

It wasn't on forbidden channel four. They were running a late-night commercial for a company that sold pianos. These were old pianos and she'd seen this commercial many times before. It must be a very effective sales device because the cowgirl had bought one and moved it up to forbidden channel nine.

Betty smiled as she switched to channel three. She'd found it! It was just like reading a story in the newspaper. When they ran out of space on one page, they continued it on another. Television was like that now. Betty was forever having to switch channels to watch the ends of movies.

Her secret friend had thrown a rope over a beam on the ceiling. Now he was tying a loop in one end and hooking it around the funny animal man's neck. Betty got her eyes covered just in time. She watched through the space between her fingers as he pulled on the rope and hoisted the funny animal man up in the air to dangle. Then he tipped over a chair and put it underneath and the movie was over at last.

Betty knew that there was something very frightening about all the movies she'd seen lately. It had to do with the forbidden channels and the actors who appeared on the screen. She thought she remembered Jack telling her that they weren't really actors. Of course they could be part of a neighborhood theater group. Sometimes public access television ran amateur programming and that would explain why the movies weren't very professional. Once upon a time, Jack had sat right here in this very room and told her all about it, but she'd forgotten most of what he'd said.

Her frown changed to a smile as she pressed the button for forbidden channel eight. The doll-lady was sitting on a couch, paging through a magazine. There were bunnies around her feet again and Betty wished she had some, too. But why didn't they hop away? She was trying to figure it out, when the doll-lady raised her foot and a word popped right into Betty's head like magic.

"Slippers!" Betty was so delighted she said the word out loud. The doll-lady was very generous. She'd given Betty the big patchwork doll, so she could have company now that Jack wasn't here. Maybe, if she could remember the words, the doll-lady would let her wear the fuzzy bunny slippers.

Betty reached for the notepad by the side of her bed and wrote down a *B* for bunny. That wasn't enough. *B* was for bunny, but it was also for ball. She sang the rhyme out loud. A *is for apple and* B *is for ball.* C *is for cat and* D *is for doll.* She needed more letters for the bunny slippers, but that was as far as she could remember. Perhaps she could draw a picture.

She worked very hard at the drawing and when she'd finished, she had a good picture, almost as good as a photograph. She circled the things, she'd forgotten their names already, and put in the mark that meant question. Now all she had to do was show it to the doll-lady.

She stared at the picture for a moment and then frowned, vaguely recalling that young children wore things like these. Was she too old to have them? She glanced down at her hands. She'd heard Nurse say that her job was like taking care of a big baby, but hers were adult hands. How did people judge age if they couldn't remember birthdays?

Betty searched her mind for the answer. If she had been a horse, she could have gone to the mirror and looked at her teeth. Horse traders could tell an animal's age by checking its teeth. *Never look a gift horse in the mouth.* It was clever if you knew what it meant.

Then a funny thought popped into her head and Betty laughed out loud. If she'd been a tree, somebody could have counted her rings. She had two on her left hand and one on her right. That told her absolutely nothing, but the rings were certainly pretty. She held up her right hand and the big Tiffany-cut stone glittered in the light. It was a diamond and diamonds were forever. Charles had said that when she'd opened the box. It was too bad that Charles hadn't been as forever as the diamond.

At a sound outside her door, Betty switched off the television set. Then she pulled up the blankets and closed her eyes so the Nurse-bird would think she was sleeping when she came in to do the bed check.

SIXTEEN

Walker moved close enough to recognize Alan and Laureen stretched out on the lounge chairs. Alan was sleeping on his stomach, snoring softly, and he looked very uncomfortable. Laureen was on her back with the blanket pulled up to her chin, as if she were taking the air on the deck of a cruise ship.

He studied their sleeping faces for a moment. Walker couldn't blame them for fleeing their own apartment. Dead bodies made him uncomfortable, too. He'd never grown used to seeing the slack features and wide-open eyes staring up at nothing. Sometimes there was a surprised look, a perplexed expression, or a grimace that didn't quite fade as death froze the features into a mask.

Walker'd had several close encounters and he had the scars to prove it, a six-inch knife cut that had nearly spilled his guts out on the ground, and a shoulder wound that still twinged whenever it was about to rain. Usually it didn't bother him, but there were times like tonight when he wanted out. They'd offered to let him retire after this job, but now that his family was gone, there was really no reason to take them up on it.

Some people accepted death as inevitable. Others sought all sorts of ways to ensure immortality, like spending a fortune to be preserved at subzero temperatures and thawed when modern medicine had found the cure for their fatal disease. Walker had decided that he'd be better off ignoring death and living each day as it came, which seemed to work just fine until something happened to remind him that his luck couldn't last forever.

Many might argue that his luck was relative. Walker had lost his wife and his six-year-old daughter in an auto accident. At least that was what he'd told people, omitting that the accident involved a bomb under the hood of his car. If you had good protection, they moved on to your family.

As Walker reached out to press the elevator button, his hand was trembling. His still got the shakes every time he thought about that morning, five years ago. The phone had rung at eight o'clock, just as Jenny had been sitting down to her favorite cereal, a gruesome concoction that turned pink and soggy when she poured milk on it.

"I'll get it, hon." Cheryl had sprinted across the floor to grab it before he'd even pushed back his chair. She'd been a long-distance runner before they were married and had almost made the Olympic track team. She probably could have made it four years later, but she'd married him and had Jenny by that time.

"He did? Right next to his eye? That sounds nasty, Mavis." Cheryl had held the phone with one hand and refilled his coffee cup with the other. "It's not really serious, is it?"

Walker had studied the furrow that appeared on his wife's forehead and sighed. Definitely a problem.

"Of course." Cheryl's voice had been very sympathetic. "We'll just switch weeks, all right? And tell Danny he'll look like a pirate."

Cheryl had hung up the phone and poured herself a cup of coffee. Then she'd flopped down in a chair and sighed. "Danny had an allergic reaction to a spider bite. His eye's swollen shut and Mavis has to keep him home from school. Do you mind driving the bug today, Walker? I have to do the car pool."

"Sure, no problem." Walker had agreed immediately, even though he hated to drive Cheryl's bug. When rust spots had appeared on her lime-green car, she'd covered them up with flower decals. From a distance, it looked polka-dotted, which was bad enough, but when people got a close look at the pink and purple and yellow daisies, they smirked.

Cheryl had laughed and Walker had known she was reading his mind. "Sorry, hon. I know how you feel, but I can't cram six first graders into the bug, and there's no time to run over to get Mom's station wagon."

"I told you, no problem. It's probably good for me to drive around in a flowered car. Builds character. What was that business about the pirate?"

"Oh, that." Cheryl had smiled. "The doctor gave Mavis a patch to put over Danny's eye. Naturally, he hates it. I just thought he might leave it on if she tells him he looks like a pirate."

Jenny had nodded solemnly. "Danny wants to be a pirate when he grows up. He loves airpranes." Walker and Cheryl had exchanged amused glances over the rims of their coffee cups. "Want to explain?" Walker had done his best to maintain a straight face. Jenny had developed a slight lisp and she was very sensitive about it.

"On the drive to school." Cheryl had pushed back her chair and stood up. "Any gas in the van?"

"Not much. I was planning on filling it this morning."

"Never do today what you can put off until tomorrow. Isn't that our motto, hon?" She'd given Walker a quick kiss on the forehead. "There's not much in the bug, either. Come on, Jenny. Give Daddy a kiss and get your coat. We have to leave right now or we won't make it to school on time."

He'd still been sitting at the table, drinking the last of his coffee, when he'd heard the explosion. By the time he'd run out the door, his van had been an inferno. The doctor had said they'd died instantly, but that had been small comfort.

For the first few weeks, Walker had been in a state of shock. And when that had worn off, his guts had churned with white-hot anger at the men who'd killed his family. He knew that a man hell-bent on revenge took foolish chances, so he'd waited, and two years later the opportunity had come. His retaliation hadn't brought Cheryl and Jenny back, but it had been sweet. And then he'd closed the book on his dream for a normal life. A man in his profession had to be a loner.

Walker thought about Ellen as he got off the elevator and walked down the hall. It was a real pity they'd raised questions about Johnny Day, and he was glad that Ellen hadn't joined in their speculation. He hated to think of what would certainly happen if she started adding up the facts. If there was some way to warn her off, he'd be tempted, but the orders he'd been given were very specific.

In spite of his orders and training, Walker had still gotten personally involved. He'd liked Ellen the first time he'd met her. She was bright and witty, and because she was so totally defensive around men, he'd spent a lot of time trying to bring her around. The turning point had come just a week ago, when he'd found her on a ladder, arranging supplies on her storage shelves. She'd asked him to please give her a hand, so he had. Right out of the box of spare parts.

Ellen had stared at him for a moment and then cracked up. She'd laughed so hard, he'd had to help her down from the ladder and she hadn't stopped laughing for at least five minutes.

Now she even teased him back occasionally. And she was an absolute master of the pun, Walker's favorite form of humor. That crack she'd made to Vanessa after he'd given her the bunny slippers had almost finished him off. And as her ability to laugh had grown, so had her trust in him. That had been his real objective. Ellen had to trust him enough to believe the lies he was required to tell her.

Walker smiled. He'd actually talked her into going up to the Jacuzzi with him last night, a step in the right direction. Of course she'd worn a discreet one-piece suit, and over that, a terry-cloth robe. She'd taken it off to jump into the Jacuzzi, but only after asking him to turn off the lights. Even though she had the perfect body for a bikini, Walker knew it would reveal too much of what she thought she had to hide. He'd never met a woman so paranoid around men before, which made his job even more difficult. There were times when Walker felt like marching Ellen over to the mirror, stripping off every stitch of her clothing, and forcing her to look at herself objectively.

Reaching for his key, Walker paused at the door for a moment. Part of him wished that Ellen would be awake again tonight, waiting up for him. No one had cared about what time he came home since Cheryl and Jenny had died. On the other side of the coin, she might get suspicious if she realized that he'd been out two nights in a row. Then she'd start asking questions and that could be very dangerous for her.

Ellen glanced at the clock. It was three-thirty in the morning and Walker was gone again. She sighed and turned back to the eight-month-old issue of *Newsweek* she'd bought for the article about Justin Holmes, an artist who made life-size dolls in New York. She hadn't bothered to read the rest of the magazine and now the news was too stale to hold much interest.

Even though she tried not to think about it, Ellen's mind turned to Vanessa. The thought of anyone trapped in a cold, dark place, bleeding to death all alone, was horrible. Ellen put the magazine back on the table and got up to pace across the floor. She'd give Walker another ten minutes before going up to the spa to look for him. She needed some company tonight to take her mind off the nightmare that had shaken her screaming from her bed, a recurrence of the graveyard dream she'd had last night. The only difference was that tonight's version had gone on longer.

Again, the hand from the grave had reached up to pull her down, and although she'd dug her fingers into the grass until her hands bled with the effort, it had dragged her down to lie in the damp, cold earth. Then something had embraced her there in the frigid ground, something cold and repulsive and evil. She'd been powerless to resist while it probed and fondled the most intimate recesses of her unwilling body, leaching the warmth from her flesh until she'd been waxen and paralyzed. Then, satisfied, it had given a maniacal shriek. And she had opened her eyes to see two people standing at the edge of the grave, watching her violation. She'd screamed so loud it had jolted her from the awful nightmare, but not before she'd recognized Vanessa and Johnny, laughing down at her.

Now that the dream had run its course, its message was obvious. Her experience with Johnny had been even more traumatic than she'd realized. And even though she'd vowed not to trust any man again, the nightmare still roused its ugly head whenever she'd had a troubling day.

After she'd hired Walker, it had stopped for a while, but now it was back with a vengeance. Was it because she was beginning to rely on Walker? If that was the case, she'd have to be very careful to see it went no further.

Ellen walked across the room and confronted her image, the same old Ellen in the mirror, skinny as a stick and about as alluring as a wet dishrag. At the sound of a key in the lock, she raced back to the couch, picked up the magazine again, and flipped it open. She didn't want Walker to think she'd been waiting up just for him.

Walker looked startled to see her sitting up, two nights in a row. "Don't tell me you couldn't sleep again?"

Ellen shrugged off his question. "I got up to make a sandwich. Then I didn't feel like going back to bed."

"Want to go up to the Jacuzzi? It's beautiful again tonight." Walker gave her a smile that made her heart beat faster and Ellen smiled back. So that's where he'd been all this time!

"No, thanks, Walker. My bathing suit's still damp from last night."

"Probably for the best. We'd have to be too quiet, anyway. Alan and Laureen are up there, camping out on the lounge chairs. The freezer must have gotten to them."

"I can understand that! I certainly wouldn't want to sleep right next to . . ." Ellen stopped and shivered.

"Me neither. How about a walk? It's not that cold, and the snow's stopped falling."

"Great." Ellen got to her feet. "We've been cooped up inside since the avalanche hit. Just let me get my parka."

Walker glanced down at her feet and his grin got wider. "Better put on your boots, too. I don't care if you go out in your nightgown and robe, but I don't think those bunny slippers are snowproof."

"Wake up, Paul. I need you!"

Paul opened his eyes to find Jayne leaning over him. He pulled her down and tried to kiss her, but she shook her head.

"Not that. At least not right now. Are you awake?"

Paul sat up and yawned. "I am awake. What is it, Jayne?"

"I know what was wrong at Clayton and Rachael's. I finally figured it out."

"Tell me." Paul reached out for her hand. It was ice cold.

"Rachael didn't take her fur hat, the one she always wore to keep her ears warm. She told me she got terrible earaches if she didn't wear it."

"Rachael may have had two hats. I would take the precaution of buying an additional, if I were that sensitive to the cold. I think you are mortgaging trouble, Jayne."

"Borrowing trouble." Jayne flipped over on her stomach so her voice was muffled by the pillow. "I guess you're right. It just bothered me, that's all. Will you rub my back, honey? I missed your back rubs more than a greenhorn misses targets."

Paul straddled her body and began to massage her back, trying not to think of the other enjoyable things they could be doing in this very same position. He wasn't successful, but Jayne relaxed at last and he continued to rub until her breathing was deep and regular and he was sure she was asleep. Then he covered her with the blankets and slid over to sit on the edge of the bed. Now he was wide-awake, wishing he'd given in to his impulse. Jayne would have welcomed him, he was sure, but he didn't have the heart to wake her. Had Rachael owned two fur hats? The only person who could tell them was Rachael, herself.

Paul got up and walked to the window, where he had an unobstructed view of the pine grove below. The moon, a bright silver sphere in the dark velvet sky, sparkled like gemstones on the smooth sheet of unbroken snow. He smiled as he recognized Ellen and Walker out for a midnight stroll.

As he watched, Walker took Ellen's arm to help her over an icy patch of ground, and Paul was pleased that Ellen didn't pull away. He thought back to the first time he'd met Ellen, right after she'd moved into Charlotte and Lyle's apartment. Painfully shy, she'd been friendly enough when she met her neighbors in the hall, but Johnny had been the only one she'd really talked to.

Jayne had made the effort, inviting her to their brunches and parties, and by the end of the first year, they'd been playing tennis every morning, Jayne and Paul against Ellen and Johnny. Ellen had turned out to be a natural on the tennis court. Tall and built for speed, she was amazingly agile and her backhand was dynamite.

Then the tennis had tapered off as the mannequin business had gone into production. Jayne had come home one day, awed by her first glimpse of Ellen's mannequin, so Paul had gone to see the prototype for himself, and had barely been able to believe his eyes.

The skin tone was wonderful, but he'd been much

more impressed with Ellen's design. How had she come up with those wonderfully neutral yet expressive features? And the pliable body that could be arranged in any of a thousand incredibly natural positions?

They'd sat there sipping the champagne they'd brought and Ellen had shrugged off his praises. It had been pure luck, a pigment she'd mixed by accident while she was in college. Paul had sighed as he'd congratulated her, exasperated that Ellen didn't recognize her own talent.

One night, a few months later when they'd driven down to Vegas for a night on the town, they'd seen Ellen and Johnny in a restaurant. Jayne and Paul had been seated in another room, but a lattice room divider gave them a clear view of Ellen and Johnny's table. There had been only one word for the expression on Ellen's face and that meant trouble. Jayne and he both knew Johnny's reputation.

Jayne had tried to prepare Ellen for the inevitable, but there had been only so far she could go, and then the whole thing had blown up. Ellen had gone back to wearing her shapeless clothes and burying herself in her workroom. She'd turned down their invitations, claiming she was simply too busy to socialize. It wasn't until Ellen had hired Walker as her general manager that things had begun to look up.

Jayne whimpered in her sleep, reaching out for him, and Paul hurried back to the bed. He cuddled up to his sleeping wife, shaping his body around hers, and then he went back to sleep, home once again with the woman he loved.

SEVENTEEN

Ellen's mouth dropped open in surprise. "You want me to do *what?*"

"Come on, Ellen, just try it. It's really a lot of fun."

"Forget it, Walker. That snow's cold. And flat on my back? No, thanks!"

Walker looked down at her with amusement and Ellen felt herself blushing. If anyone overheard them, it would be all over the building in no time flat. "Have a little common sense, Walker. What if someone saw us? I'd never be able to face them in the morning."

"That's just an excuse." Walker looked very serious. "You know no one's up this time of night. And even if they see us, so what? They'd probably say, *Isn't that nice? Walker and Ellen are having fun in the snow.* You're just paranoid, Ellen. My wife showed me how when we first started dating, and we must have done it in every vacant lot in Chicago."

Ellen couldn't help it. She almost fell over, she laughed so hard. Walker stared at her in confusion for a second, and then he started to laugh with her. "Okay,

okay. I know how it sounds. But I still don't see why you won't try it. It'll only take a couple of minutes."

"Only a couple of minutes?" Ellen doubled over with an attack of the giggles. "Okay, I'll do it just to shut you up, but you'll have to teach me. I've never done it with anyone else before."

That sent them off into new gales of laughter. Finally Walker calmed down enough to give her instructions.

"Ready?" Walker pulled her over to a spot where the snow was an unbroken sheet of sparkling white. "Now remember, Ellen. You're falling uphill and the snow is deep, so it'll be just like landing on a feather bed. After you're down, don't move a muscle until I tell you what to do next."

Ellen gave a little cry as they fell backward. Her first instinct was to scramble to her feet, but she certainly didn't want to do this twice.

"Ellen? Are your arms tight against your hips?"

"Yup." She giggled.

"Good." Walker sounded very serious. "Did you ever do an exercise called the jumping jack in school?"

"Of course I did. I used to teach first grade and Mary Christine Fanger lost her hair ribbon the first time we did it in gym."

"Good, you've got plenty of experience. We're going to do a jumping jack with our arms. Leave them level with the snow and drag them up over your head. Then back down to your side again. That'll make the wings."

"Got it." Ellen raised her arms and brought them back down again. Walker was right. The snow was like a feather bed, a very cold feather bed, and she looked up into the deep black night to see thousands of stars sparkling overhead. They looked so close, she felt she could almost reach up and touch them. She shivered as she was suddenly struck by the vastness of space. She was only a miniscule speck of warm life in the icy void, so small and insignificant that she could disappear without anyone noticing or caring.

"Now the legs." Walker's disembodied voice pulled her back and she had an almost overpowering urge to reach out to touch him, just to make sure he was real.

"It's almost the same as the arms. Spread them out as far as you can, then bring them back together again. And then don't move. Ready?"

"Yes." Ellen pushed her legs out to the side and brought them back. Then, rather than risk feeling that terrible loneliness again, she shut her eyes and told herself that she wasn't alone, that Walker was only a few feet away.

"And now I bet you're wondering how we get up without ruining it, right?"

"I guess so." Ellen smiled to herself. That problem hadn't even occurred to her until right now. She turned her head just a fraction of an inch and watched Walker roll forward in one fluid motion until he was up on his feet. And then he was standing in front of her, smiling.

"Hold out your hands and keep your body as stiff as a board."

Ellen hung on as Walker pulled her forward. A second later they were both standing at the foot of their creations.

"They *do* look like angels!" Ellen studied them with an appraising eye. "That was fun in a crazy sort of way."

"Told you. And these are superior angels. If it doesn't snow anymore tonight, they'll still be there in the morning."

Ellen stomped her feet and brushed the powdery snow off her clothes. The night was friendly now that she could see Walker, and the air was crisp and clean with the scent of pine. "Come on, let's walk through the pine grove. I've always wanted to go out there at night, but it's frightening by yourself."

"Most things are." Walker took her hand to help her down the steep incline, but they both slipped several times anyway. Ellen's face was flushed and she was out of breath as they ended up running the last several feet to keep from falling.

When they reached level ground, Walker still didn't release her hand and Ellen found she was glad. It felt good to walk across the huge glittering sheet of snow, swinging arms.

It was much darker when they entered the pine grove, where giant branches filtered the blue-white moonlight into lacy patterns against the snow. Ellen sighed in pure contentment; it was just as beautiful as she'd imagined. Pinecones hung from the branches like Christmas tree ornaments and icicles glistened in the blue-white light.

"Come here for a minute, Ellen." Walker reached out with one mittened hand and pulled her under the branches of a huge pine tree. "I used to love to play under these things when I was a kid."

Ellen ducked under a low branch. The top of her head brushed against it, sending down a shower of snow. Walker pulled her next to the trunk of the tree and dusted her off.

"Look around. What do you think?"

"It's enchanting." Ellen looked up at the dark cavern of branches above them, drooping down to touch the ground. "It's like a little house under here, and it smells so good."

Walker nodded. "When I was a little kid, I told my

mother I wanted to live under the pine tree in our backyard."

"I can see why." Ellen looked down at the ground. There was no snow, only a cushion of aromatic pine needles. "Did she point out that it would get chilly in February?"

"That's exactly what she said. But I kept on dreaming of that little room under the pine tree, and when summer rolled around, I asked her again."

Ellen smiled. "And she said no?"

"Nope. She said it'd be fine with her as long as I came in to wash up once in a while. So I fixed up a room under there with a sleeping bag and my comic books and a stash of cookies."

"She actually let you move out there?" Ellen turned to him in surprise. "If I'd tried to do something like that, my parents would have told me to grow up and quit acting so foolish."

Walker grinned. "My mother was a very smart woman. That night, she went upstairs to bed and I went out to my pine tree."

"What happened?"

"Exactly what she figured. Bugs crawled on me, mosquitoes bit me, and it rained. One night was all it took." Something about the wistful tone in Walker's voice made Ellen feel sad. Perhaps a dream should be an end in itself. It was too easy to be disappointed when fantasies came true and weren't like you'd imagined at all.

"Why so sad?" Walker slipped his arm around her shoulder and gave her a little hug.

Ellen swallowed hard before she could answer, and her voice was shaking. "You lost your dream forever. Don't you think that's sad?"

"I didn't lose my dream," Walker protested gently. "I just tempered it with a little reality. I decided I'd rather live under a tree that had walls and a Plexiglas roof."

Ellen smiled, but before she could stop, the bitter tears of longing, the tears she had held back for so long, were rolling down her cheeks. Walker tightened his arms around her and Ellen felt herself falling into an abyss, a sheer drop of thousands of feet that was cushioned every inch of the way by his sheltering body. He held her for a long time. And then he parted the branches and led her back to the building.

Marc was passing the window when he happened to look out and see them heading for the entrance of the building, holding hands. Ellen and her faithful slave. He had absolutely nothing against blacks personally, hired them all the time for his construction crews, but this guy had a bad habit of poking his nose into places where it didn't belong. Of course, he was a pretty good business manager for Ellen, digging out all those contracts that Johnny had arranged for Vegas Dolls. Marc had suspected that Johnny was up to something, but he hadn't known the details until Walker had asked his advice on the shipping contract.

He gave a wry smile, wondering whether they were sleeping together. The concept of a black guy getting to Ellen bothered him, although he supposed it shouldn't. It was Ellen's business and he had no stake in it. He'd never tried to pick up on her and he never would. She wasn't his type. And if you looked at the whole thing objectively, Walker was a lot better bet than Johnny Day.

Marc watched as they went into the building, then went to the liquor cabinet to pour himself a splash of vodka. He knew he ought to get some sleep, but his nerves were shot. Vanessa's death bothered him a lot more than he'd figured and helping Walker lay her out in the freezer had been a total bummer. Perhaps it was because he'd slept with her just a couple of nights before, and the memories were still fresh. Vanessa had known how to please him and she'd been up for anything. Whenever she'd knocked on his door, he'd known he was in for a wild night. He hadn't loved her, far from it, but they'd been two of a kind. On their last night together she'd told him they were animals in bed but nothing more than neighbors with their clothes on, a pretty deep thought for Vanessa. Knowing that he'd never get the chance to enjoy her gorgeous body and her warm, moist lips again was a real downer.

He finished his drink and set the glass on the bar next to the one he'd used last night. It was over a week since Ramona had cleaned, and the mess was beginning to get to him. There was a film of dust so thick he could write in it on top of his smoked-glass and chrome coffee table, the white carpet in the living room had a red stain where he'd dropped a raspberry Danish, and his pinball machines needed a shot of Windex. He would have cleaned the place himself, but Ramona brought in her own cleaning supplies and he'd never bothered to stock them. Here he was, living in the most expensive condo he'd ever built, and it was turning into a dive.

He pushed the dirty glasses to the back of the bar and scowled as his elbow twinged. He'd bumped it on that damn case of lobster when he'd helped Walker lay Vanessa out in the freezer and it had been bothering him ever since. Maybe he should have gone in for the operation his doctor had recommended last year. With the new techniques in orthoscopic surgery, his arm could be repaired completely. If they'd had the technology ten years ago, he would have jumped at the chance, but it had seemed pointless at this stage of the game. It was too late for him. No major league ball club would consider hiring a forty-year-old rookie.

There was no sense getting riled up about it. Marc filled his glass to the brim, took another gulp, and then headed for the game room. It was only natural to be jumpy after everything that had happened in the past few days. He needed some distraction or he'd go crazy, stuck up here in the condo with nothing but his anxiety for company.

Marc took off his shirt and flexed. Women still came on to him all the time and it wasn't because of his money. His newest lady couldn't seem to get enough of him. Myra wasn't much in the brains department, but he didn't go out with a woman to talk to her.

She was one crazy lady with an incredible body. He'd learned to spot silicone from a mile away and Myra was all natural. She was also a serious cokehead, but that didn't bother him. Then there was Myra's daughter. When he'd gone to pick Myra up last week, the little nymphet had waltzed out of her bedroom stark naked. At sixteen, she'd already developed a figure to rival her mother's, and all that rosy young skin had nearly driven him crazy. Naturally, she'd acted all surprised, but Marc knew she'd heard him come in. If he'd guessed that damned avalanche was going to hit, he would have invited them both up here for lunch.

Ellen could still feel the imprint of his lips on hers when she pulled away. They were standing in the middle of the living room, still in their parkas and boots. "Look, Walker. I like you a lot, but this is impossible."

"A kiss is impossible?" Walker raised his eyebrows as he shrugged out of his parka. "Could've fooled me. I thought we just did it. Take off your coat, Ellen, you're going to get overheated."

"I just mean that we shouldn't get involved. It really won't work." Ellen unzipped her jacket and threw it on the couch.

"Because I'm black and you're white?"

"That has nothing to do with it and you know it!" Ellen sat down to pull off her boots.

"Didn't think so." Walker flashed her a smile. "Then you're not attracted to me?"

Ellen took a deep breath and threw her boots in the corner. "I just don't want to get involved with any man."

"But, Ellen, I'm not just *any* man."

The color rose in Ellen's face. She was beginning to get exasperated. "You're being deliberately obtuse! What do I have to do, spell it out for you?"

Walker placed his boots next to Ellen's, taking time to straighten both pairs, then came to sit next to her on the couch. "Spell it out for me, Ellen, the whole thing. I want to know exactly why you won't let me love you."

"Oh." Ellen's voice was very small. She hadn't expected this. "All right, then. I had a bad experience. With a man."

"But it wasn't with me, was it, Ellen?"

"Look, Walker, it doesn't really matter what happened. The point is, I'm bright enough to realize my limitations and stay away from the obvious pitfalls."

Walker pulled her into his arms and kissed her again. Ellen felt herself falling again, swimming in a pool of pure sensation. She knew she couldn't take much more of this. It was far too dangerous.

"You're crazy, Ellen." Walker released her at last. "And you're so damned defensive you make me want to cry. But I'm crazy about you anyway."

He was giving her that smile again, the smile she had to return. And then he was pushing her down on the couch. And kissing her again and again, the way she'd dreamed someone would kiss her. And this time their clothes *did* fall away like rain, perhaps because her head was whirling so hard she could barely think. And then he was carrying her into the bedroom, carrying *her*, Ellen Wingate, with her too-tall awkward body that seemed amazingly petite in his arms. And the light was on in the bedroom, and she wished he'd turn it off, but he seemed to want to look at her and touch her, running his hands over her skin with a feathery sweeping motion that made her breath catch in her throat. And then she was on top of her quilt, her face pressed against the smooth muscles of his chest and oh God! She knew she'd die if he didn't kiss her again!

And he did, his lips painting a pattern of crimson pleasure that blossomed and rippled and ran through her in such a rushing torrent of desire that she wrapped her arms around his neck and cried out for him to love her. There was no hesitation, no painful shyness, no shame as she lifted her hips to meet him. And then she was whirling away in a glorious rainbow of pleasure that made her gasp. And sob. And laugh with delight at the incredible beauty of it all as he carried her with him to ecstasy.

EIGHTEEN

There was a little foil packet on her tray and Betty picked it up to examine it. Letters were on the top. *S . . . T . . . R . . .* and the rest were so smudged she couldn't read them. She pulled off the top and stared at the contents. Red berries inside, to spread on the whole wheat toast Nurse had brought her for an afternoon snack. Now she missed Jack more than ever. He'd always brought her cookies with strawberry ice cream.

Strawberries! Betty held the packet to her nose and sniffed. There were strawberries inside the packet, but they didn't smell as wonderful as the strawberries in Aunt Sophia's garden. She remembered helping to pick them while Aunt Sophia held the basket. *One for Betty, and one for the basket,* over and over until she couldn't eat any more. And then, in the middle of that warm, sticky summer, Aunt Sophia had given her a beautiful white ruffled dress and said to get ready, she was a birthday girl and they were having a party. The whole family was coming, even cousins from across the sea, and there would be music and games and clowns and balloons, everything to make the birthday girl happy, even her very favorite strawberry ice cream.

Car after car had pulled into the compound, people laughing and everyone hugging and kissing her. The big table in the dining room had been heaped with presents wrapped in gold and silver and pink and blue, all gifts for the birthday girl. She'd met all her cousins and tried not to get dirty as they'd played hide-and-seek in the yard. And then she'd sat in a folding chair next to Aunt Sophia and Daddy and her brother, Mario, to watch the clowns do their tricks.

One clown had a funny bicycle with only one wheel, and he'd ridden it around and around, swerving and swooping down the garden paths as all her cousins had laughed. Another clown had brought a little white dog who could prance on his back legs and jump through hoops. The clowns had been very funny in their polka-dot suits with too-big shoes and bright red hair. They had chased each other and turned cartwheels on the grass until there was a loud bang and Daddy had pushed her down so hard she'd cried.

Then the birthday party wasn't fun anymore because Mario had a strawberry stain on his shirt and everyone was screaming. Aunt Sophia had taken her into the house when they came with the loud sirens and flashing red lights, and she'd heard them say that Daddy had been damn lucky he'd moved just then. But Mario was gone and he'd never come back, and opening her presents hadn't been as much fun.

There were drops of wet on her dressing gown and Betty frowned. It was silk and the wet would leave a stain. Dishes rattled in the kitchen and Betty reached for a tissue to wipe her eyes. Soon Nurse would pick up her tray and she'd go for the needle if she suspected that Betty had been crying.

Betty sat up a little straighter and concentrated on the game show. A man in a yellow and green flowered shirt was trying to answer a question worth twenty thousand dollars. The host read the question out loud. *What term do scientists use to describe the large boulders left by glaciers during the Ice Age?*

The name popped into Betty's mind like magic. The boulders were called erratics. She'd learned that a long time ago when they'd studied glaciers and she'd helped Charles make a mountain out of flour and salt and water. But the man in the yellow and green shirt didn't know and he'd lost the game.

There was a happy smile on Betty's face as Nurse opened the door. If she had been the contestant on that game show, she would have won twenty thousand dollars.

"Not very hungry?" Nurse took the tray. "You've got company, so we'll have our bath later."

Betty was careful not to laugh out loud. Since Nurse had never bathed with her, why did she use the plural? Perhaps Nurse was using the "royal we," pretending she was Queen of England. And then Nurse was gone and the cowgirl was there, along with her foreign actor. Betty smiled, always glad to see faces besides Nurse's.

The quiz program was over and a movie was on, something with stirring music. It was about a runner in an important race and the cowgirl watched for a minute. "That looks like *Chariots of Fire*. Have you seen it before, Betty?"

Betty shook her head, even though she really wasn't sure. With this horrid disease, she sometimes forgot the movies as soon as she watched them. If everyone in the country had her disease, the television station could save a lot of money by running the same movie over and over.

The cowgirl spoke again. "You look tired. Did you stay up late watching television?"

Betty nodded. Yes, she had, she remembered, and she recalled the movie, too, because it had frightened her.

"Which program did you watch, Betty?" The foreign actor asked the question and Betty turned to look at him. He really wanted to know. She wished she could tell him about it, but the words were very difficult to catch.

"Movie." She heard herself speak and she was very surprised. It must have been right because he nodded.

"That sounds like fun." The cowgirl smiled. "Do you remember what it was about?"

Betty frowned. Of course she remembered, but now she'd forgotten the word for it. She opened her mouth and nothing came out.

"Was it a romance?"

Betty shook her head. It hadn't been a romance. She knew that. Suddenly she had an idea, and she put her hands up to her eyes to peek through her fingers.

"It was a horror movie!" The cowgirl looked very excited. "Did someone get killed?"

Betty smiled. That was exactly right, someone had died.

"Were they shot? Or maybe stabbed?" The cowgirl turned to the foreign actor. "Help me, Paul. I can't think of any other ways."

"Perhaps there was a drowning? An explosion? Poison?"

Betty shook her head each time he spoke. If only she could find that word! Then, before she really thought about it, her hands moved up to her neck.

"Choking!" They both spoke at once and Betty gave them a smile. That was almost right so she did it again.

"Strangling?" the cowgirl guessed. "Or maybe someone got hung?"

"Hanged," Betty corrected. "Clothes get hung, people get hanged."

The cowgirl looked very shocked and then she reached out to hug Betty. "That's right! Hanged. I never could remember which was which."

Betty laughed out loud, glad there was something someone else had trouble remembering. And the cowgirl didn't even have the disease.

"So the subject was hanging." The foreign actor smiled at her. "That is very frightening. Are there no comedies for you to watch?"

Betty shook her head. No comedies, just awful movies where people got killed.

"I bet it was a western!" The cowgirl looked excited again. Betty knew she must like westerns because she always dressed in the costumes. "Channel eleven runs all those old cowboy movies. Were you watching channel eleven?"

Betty held up three fingers. She had been watching forbidden channel three.

"But we don't even get channel three. Are you sure, Betty?"

Betty tried to concentrate on the question. What had the cowgirl asked? Suddenly her mind was blank. This was an interesting game to play, but her eyes kept falling shut.

"Come, Jayne." The foreign actor stood up. "Would you wish us to come back later, Betty, after you have rested?"

Betty nodded. He was so nice. It was lucky the cowgirl with her in-between name had found him again.

* * *

It was almost one in the afternoon when Moira and Grace knocked on Hal's door bearing a pitcher of orange juice and a large bottle of aspirin, just in case Hal didn't have any. Moira knocked again, then used the key Hal had given them so they could keep an eye on things when he was out of town.

Silence greeted them, and the bed didn't look as if it had been slept in. "He must be in his studio," Moira said, leading the way. "He probably holed up in there."

Grace blushed. "Yes, but what if he's . . . I mean . . . what if he doesn't have any clothes on?"

"That shouldn't bother you, especially if he's passed out cold. Come on. You'll probably have to help me carry him back to bed."

Grace found she was holding her breath as Moira opened Hal's studio door.

"Hell!" Moira spun Grace around and pushed her through the doorway. "Go get a couple of the guys."

"But I can help you," Grace started to protest. "What's wrong?"

"Move it, Grace! Get the hell out of here!"

Grace hurried to the elevator and frantically stabbed at the button. When it didn't come right away, she ran up the stairs. Moira had said *hell* twice without even trying to think of a substitute, and that meant that something was terribly wrong.

They'd all gathered at Grace and Moira's again, and it had been almost eleven at night before they'd split up to go home. Jayne had claimed they were like spooked cattle herding together, and she wasn't far wrong. No one had wanted to be alone. Hal's suicide on the heels of Vanessa's awful accident had been just too much to handle.

Laureen frowned as Alan opened the door to their apartment and they stepped inside. "I can't do it, Alan. I simply can't survive another night in those lounge chairs."

"I know what you mean." Alan winced a little and rubbed his neck. "I guess we should have taken Jayne and Paul up on their offer after all."

"No, you were right. They need their time alone right now. I thought about asking Ellen if we could sleep there, but I know Walker's using her guest room. Maybe we should have stayed at Grace and Moira's."

"We can still do that," Alan pointed out. "Moira told us to knock on the door if we couldn't sleep."

"But Grace could hardly keep her eyes open, Alan."

"Then how about Marc's place? He's always up late, playing his pinball machines. He'd put us up in his guest room."

Laureen shook her head. "Remember the last time you slept on a water bed?"

Alan grinned. They'd gone to one of those adult motels once, and the water bed had thrown his back out for a week. "It seemed to me it was worth it."

Laureen giggled and her face turned slightly red. It had definitely been worth it.

Alan started to grin. "I know what we can do. We'll go up and sleep at Hal's. After all, we're putting him up in our freezer."

"Oh, Alan!" Laureen looked shocked. "How can you joke about a thing like that?"

"If I don't, I get scared. I can handle it if I joke about

it. Betty's place is out. The nurse is using her guest room, but how about Johnny's? His place is vacant."

"Not Johnny's. I know it's ridiculous, but I can't seem to shake the idea that we'll open a closet and find his body."

"Then the only place left is Clayton and Rachael's. Would that bother you?"

Laureen took a moment to think, then she shook her head. "Rachael's such a good housekeeper, she's probably got the guest room all made up. You don't think they'd mind, do you, Alan?"

"If they were here, they'd be the first to invite us. Come on, honey. Let's get our things together and go."

The Caretaker frowned as he watched them step inside. Alan was carrying a bag and Laureen had two pillows. Clayton's apartment was a lousy choice, but perhaps it would be all right as long as they didn't start snooping around.

Betty was still sleeping soundly, but her lips were moving. Perhaps she was trying to speak. He leaned over to listen and smiled as he made out the word. Friend. Poor Betty, with her confused mind and her love for everyone. For the first time, he almost felt sorry for her. What would she think if she knew that he was the one who'd supervised the hit on her boyfriend and come up with the plan that had turned her into a vegetable?

Naturally, the Old Man had objected, but he'd finally seen that there was no other way, not if he wanted to keep his darling daughter alive. The Caretaker had hired Margaret Woodard himself. No one knew that he'd recruited her more than ten years ago, the daughter of one of the Old Man's soldiers who'd been killed in the line of duty. It had been a brilliant move, training her in a profession that might prove valuable.

Margaret was smart enough to know what would happen if she didn't repay her debt. She hadn't been happy about her assignment, but she'd done an excellent job so far. The only problem he could see was her sympathy for Betty, an occupational hazard in the nursing profession. Of course, it didn't really matter. If she made any wrong moves, she was expendable.

He smiled as Alan turned down the covers, a typical domestic scene. There was no need to turn up the audio as long as they went straight to bed. Other people might enjoy being voyeurs, but not him, and Laureen and Alan's sex life was bound to be dull.

Now Laureen was yawning. That was good. Once they were asleep, he could catch a snooze himself. He'd confiscated Johnny's stash. By rights it was theirs anyway, since the rat was cutting into family territory, but he hated to use it on such a regular basis. There was no substitute for sleep. And now Alan and Laureen were sitting down on the bed and . . .

The Caretaker groaned as he saw Alan reach for his robe. Now both of them were up again and he used Jack's fancy system to track them into the kitchen. A late-night snack. He might have known. Laureen took out one of Clayton's frying pans while Alan assembled the ingredients. It was almost like watching one of her cooking shows. In less than ten minutes, Brie and prosciutto omelets with a dollop of sour cream were ready.

Garnished with chives and ripe olive slices, they looked delicious.

Laureen handed the plates to Alan and picked up the napkins and silverware. No problem. But he swore softly under his breath as they bypassed the dining room and headed out to the rose garden.

"It's nice out here, isn't it, honey?" Laureen smiled at her husband. They'd finished their omelets and were enjoying a glass of Chablis from Clayton's refrigerator.

Alan nodded. "Yes, but you can tell Clayton's no gardener. The rosebushes need pruning."

"And the gazebo needs a new coat of paint." Laureen frowned. "I'm surprised at Rachael. She keeps the rest of the apartment in such good shape."

Alan fumbled in the breast pocket of his robe for a cigarette, wishful thinking since they were still safely hidden in his father's desk. He really wanted a smoke, but he never smoked a pipe right before bed. It took about forty-five minutes to smoke a bowl and there was no way he'd risk ruining a good pipe by knocking it out before it was finished. The moisture and oils from the tobacco would sour the pipe. He settled for a walk around the garden instead, examining the rosebushes.

"Look at this, Laureen," he called out, pointing to a patch of ground. "Maybe Clayton's hired a gardener."

Laureen walked over to join him. "I know I'm probably being ridiculous, but doesn't this look a lot like a . . ." she swallowed hard, ". . . a grave?"

Alan laughed. "More like a flower bed to me. Remember that bed of zinnias you put in by our old house? I think it was about this size."

Laureen gave a sigh of relief. "I guess my imagination

is running away with me, honey. It's just that so many people have died."

"Yeah. And they're all in our freezer. Pretty soon there won't be enough room for your brownies."

"Alan! You're terrible!" Laureen was shocked, but she couldn't help laughing.

Alan grinned and hugged her. Then, catching a glitter in the dirt, he stooped down to pick up a heart-shaped diamond earring. "Look at this, honey."

Laureen stared down at the earring for a moment and then she gave a little cry. "That looks just like the earrings Hal gave Vanessa."

"Might as well keep it." Alan stuck it in his pocket. "I've got the other one. I found it on the floor of the freezer. She must have been wearing them the night she died."

"But what was she doing out here?" Laureen shivered. "This doesn't make any sense, Alan."

"Maybe we'd better wake the others. Come on, honey."

Laureen could feel her knees shaking as she walked through Clayton's apartment and out the door. The lights on either side of Clayton's door were out. She hadn't noticed that earlier.

"It's really dark, Alan."

"I must have turned off the hall lights by mistake." Alan led her calmly down the hall.

Laureen leaned against the wall as Alan pressed the elevator button. At least the arrow lit up, its faint glow reassuring her.

The elevator doors slid open, but the inside light was off. Laureen shuddered and stepped back. "I'm not getting in there in the dark."

Alan put his arm around her shoulders. "The bulb's just burned out. The elevator's still working just fine."

"But what if the power's going out? We could get stuck!"

Alan sighed. There were times when his wife was terribly obstinate. "The doors opened and they're electrical, and the button lit up. Come on, Laureen, we don't have time to argue about this."

"Let's take the stairs. Please?"

"Be reasonable, honey. You told me your legs were stiff from sleeping on the lounge chair. Do you really want to walk down all those stairs? We'll get there much faster in the elevator."

Laureen took a deep breath and squared her shoulders, as Alan took her arm to lead her forward. Then she let out a cry and pulled him back. "It's not there! Oh, my God, Alan! The elevator's not there!"

Alan took a step back, away from the brink of the yawning shaft, and reached out to wrap both arms around her. "Jesus, Laureen! You saved our lives!"

"Thank God I noticed! If we . . ." Laureen's voice broke and she found she couldn't go on. Thinking about what could have happened was just too horrible. As they stood there hugging each other, glorying in the fact that they were still alive and safe, something connected solidly with the small of Laureen's back, hurtling them forward into the empty shaft. They had a brief moment to clutch at the empty air as they fell five floors to the garage. Alan had been right. The elevator was much faster than the stairs. They didn't even have time to scream.

NINETEEN

Betty let out a little cry. Her secret friend had gone down to forbidden channel zero to open the big box that ran the elevator and then he'd come back to channel five to push them. Now they were falling to the bottom of the elevator shaft to play dead. She didn't want to watch the end of this movie. It was so scary that holding her hand in front of her eyes wouldn't help.

Outside snow was falling again. Betty knew it was late at night because the other channels were playing their sleeping movies. Her secret friend had been here again and he'd given her more of her favorite candy. This time she had taken three pieces, but she'd saved them for later. Of course, she hadn't let him see her. He was so nice to bring the candy and she didn't want to hurt his feelings.

The thought of the candy made her mouth water, and Betty reached under her pillow. It was still there, wrapped in a tissue, but it didn't look much like candy anymore. She tossed the gooey mass in the wastebasket by her bed and reached for a cracker instead. At least crackers didn't melt, they only crumbled. She was just about to put on one of the Doris and Rock movies that Jack had given her, when she found something interesting on forbidden channel two.

"Did you hear something?" Moira sat up in bed. "Grace? Are you awake?"

Grace sat up and swung her feet out of bed. "I am now. What was it?"

"It sounded like something crashed into the living room wall. I think I'd better take a look."

"I'll go with you."

Grace got into her robe and slippers and followed Moira into the living room. They switched on the lights, but there didn't seem to be anything out of place.

"Maybe one of the animals fell over," Moira guessed. "We'd better check."

Grace lagged behind a bit as she followed Moira to the storage room. When her father had died, she'd wanted to sell off the whole collection, but Moira had been delighted with the variety of species her father had preserved. Grace never liked going to the storage room, but it was even worse at night. Paul had designed a huge temperature-controlled room to house and preserve her father's legacy. It had a rustic look, almost like the inside of a log cabin, and Moira had arranged the specimens in a manner that was much too realistic. It frightened Grace every time she saw the big upright Kodiak bear, huge paws extended to rake her into his deadly embrace.

The black panther was another animal Grace avoided. His yellow glass eyes glittered savagely in the light and his lips were pulled back in a vicious snarl, exposing his long, sharp incisors. He looked ready to pounce on her and rip her flesh into shreds.

"Everything seems to be all right." As Moira walked down the rows of animals, she reached out to pat the lion's head. "Check on Penny, will you, Grace? If she fell over, she'd make an awful racket."

Penny was Moira's nickname for the giraffe, and Grace dutifully headed to the back of the room, giving the bear and the panther a wide berth. At least the giraffe didn't scare her. She'd never heard of anyone being attacked by a giraffe.

"Penny didn't tip over." Grace's voice quavered slightly and she was ashamed of her timidity. She'd never mentioned her fears to Moira, but she was very glad when they closed the door on her father's menagerie and went back into the living room again.

"Your picture's crooked." Moira pointed to the publicity photo of Grace in her first role as a featured dancer. "Something must have bashed against the other side of this wall. That's the elevator shaft, isn't it?"

Grace nodded. "Maybe it got stuck and someone pounded on the wall to get our attention."

They hurried out into the hall and pressed the elevator button. In a moment, the doors slid open. Moira was about to step in even though the inside of the cage was dark, when Grace pulled her back.

"Oh, my God!" Moira's mouth dropped open as she peered into the empty shaft. "Thanks, Grace."

Both women looked at each other for a moment and then Moira took charge. "Get the flashlight, Grace."

Light in hand, Moira got down on her stomach and leaned over the shaft. When she spoke, her voice echoed hollowly. "There's something down there."

"Does it look like a . . . a person?" Grace wasn't sure

she wanted to know, but perhaps knowing was better than imagining.

Moira got to her feet. "More like a bundle of clothes. Come on, Grace. We've got to warn everyone so they won't use the elevator."

They ran down the stairs as quickly as they could and rang Alan and Laureen's doorbell. When no one answered, Grace turned to Moira with fear in her eyes. "You don't suppose . . ."

"Don't be silly," Moira interrupted. "I heard Jayne invite them to stay in her guest room."

The third floor was Hal and Vanessa's, the fourth floor Johnny Day's. By the time they got to the fifth floor landing, Moira's legs were trembling with fatigue.

"There's no use stopping here." Grace grabbed Moira's arm. "We know Clayton and Rachael aren't home. Come on, Moira. You can make it."

"Oh, sure. That's easy for you to say. You're the dancer in the family. My legs will never be the same."

"Only one floor to go." Grace pulled her up the stairs. "Jack hooked up a battery intercom in Betty's unit. We can call everyone from there."

Sabotaging the elevator had worked perfectly. Naturally, some of them had been hysterical, but they'd pulled themselves together enough to carry the bodies to the freezer which was fortunately, only one floor up. He hadn't found the earring, it must have fallen out of Alan's pocket when he fell, but that didn't really matter as long as it was out of the rose garden. And now they were all back in their own apartments, trying to sleep after the latest tragedy.

The Caretaker clicked through the closed-circuit

channels, checking on everyone, watching Betty out of the corner of his eye. She was wide-awake, staring at the television screen, even though she'd eaten three pieces of tranquilizer-laden candy.

"Sleepy, Betty?" He reached out to take her hand, but she pulled away, almost as if she knew what he'd done. It was such an unexpected reaction that he turned to look at her closely. Of course that was impossible. He must be even more tired than he'd thought. The Caretaker sighed as he took the little gold vial out of his pocket and laid out a couple of lines. This whole thing was growing much too complicated.

What would the police do when the road was cleared and they were faced with a suicide and five accidental deaths? Not even the Old Man and his big-name friends had enough juice to stop an investigation. They'd go through this place with a fine-tooth comb and some eager-beaver young cop would discover something. Given the odds, it was inevitable. Perhaps it would be better to clean out the building floor by floor since they were all sitting ducks. Then he could arrange a convenient explosion.

He forced himself to think carefully. He didn't want to make a mistake. A gas line weakened by the avalanche was a natural, and by the time they'd finished sifting through the debris, he'd be someone else. Their plastic surgeon had plenty of practice. The whole setup was even more thorough than the federal witness program. A couple of days from now he'd be recuperating at the resort, eating lobster, and reading about the terrible accident that had killed him.

But what about Betty? He looked over to find her watching him. Unfortunate, but it couldn't be helped. Since the Caretaker had come up with the scheme to keep Betty alive, the Old Man would never suspect he'd killed her.

He stood up to look out the window. The winds had died down and he should be able to get through tonight. He'd call the Old Man to tell him that his beloved daughter had died peacefully in her sleep, heart failure or some such thing. And how he'd busted his ass to protect the family after the soldiers had botched the job with Johnny. There was no need to fill him in on the details, he'd just say it was impossible to cover any longer, that they were too close to the truth. The Old Man would have to agree that blowing up the building was the only way out.

There were tears in Margaret Woodard's eyes as she punctured the top of the vial and filled the syringe. She'd done her best not to get personally involved, but she hadn't been able to harden her heart against Betty completely.

As she punctured the top of a second vial and drew back the plunger, she considered the man waiting in Betty's room. Once she'd administered Betty's lethal shot, he wouldn't need her services any longer.

The Caretaker wasn't sure what had warned him, perhaps the expression in her eyes or the way her fingers tightened around the syringe. He whirled just in time; one well-placed blow was all it took to guarantee that she would never move again.

Turning back to Betty, he found her staring at him in horror. He smiled to reassure her and patted her hand. "It's all right, Betty, just a bad dream. Now close your eyes and I'll make it all go away."

Betty closed her eyes obediently as he walked over to pick up the syringe that had fallen out of the nurse's hand. Used to her bedtime shots, she hardly seemed to feel it as he slipped the needle into her vein and depressed the plunger. "Good night, Betty. And good-bye."

He pulled the nurse's body into the bathroom and shut the door. Betty might open her eyes again and there was no need to upset her. When he went back into her room, her breathing was slow and even. Mission accomplished. The double dose would push Betty into unconsciousness, and soon it would be over. There was a satisfied expression on the Caretaker's face as he went down to Jack's apartment to retrieve his shortwave radio.

Moira reached out to flick on the light, then shook Grace's shoulder. "Wake up, Grace. I finally figured it out."

"Figured what out?" Grace opened her eyes and groaned.

"The bodies, Grace, think about Alan and Laureen's bodies."

"Do I have to?" Grace mumbled, blinking groggily. Moira sounded very excited.

"Did they look as if they'd fallen only one floor?"

Grace winced. "I'm not sure. I tried *not* to look."

"Well, I think they fell a lot farther than that. Besides, we live above them. How could they bang into our wall if they fell from their own floor?"

"You're absolutely right." Grace perked up. "I never thought of that before. What shall we do?"

Moira sighed. "I hate to even think of it, but we'd better go up to Jayne and Paul's to see if Alan and Laureen were staying with them."

"Wouldn't they have mentioned it?"

"Not necessarily. We were all so stunned. And it never occurred to me to ask. Come on, Grace. Let's go."

"Do you really want to walk up seven flights of stairs?"

Moira shook her head wearily. "No, Grace, I don't. But I'll never be able to get to sleep if I don't find out. You can stay here if you're too tired, but I'm going."

"Then I'll go with you." Grace got out of bed and grabbed her clothes. There was no arguing with Moira once she'd made up her mind.

Betty was shaking as she reached for the remote control. Her arm still hurt where he had poked it with the needle, but she'd seen most of the medicine squirt out of the syringe when he'd knocked it out of the Nurse-bird's hand and she hadn't made a sound. The drawing she'd made of the doll-lady's slippers had reminded her and she'd remembered what rabbits did when they were cornered. They froze and hoped for the best. Now he was gone and she had to see if the other actors and actresses were all right.

Something was happening on forbidden channel two. The nice actresses were coming out the door. Betty hoped they wouldn't use the elevator and she held her breath until she saw they were going through the door to the stairs. She couldn't see them as they climbed from channel to channel, but she could catch them on the landings. She switched to forbidden channel three and waited. Yes, there they were. And now they were climbing up to channel four.

Suddenly Betty knew she should go out to the landing for channel six and stop the actresses as they passed by. It would be difficult because she wasn't very good at walking, in fact, she'd heard Nurse tell her secret friend that she was almost as weak as a baby. Remembering that gave Betty a wonderful idea. She knelt down on the rug.

Babies crawled and she could, too. At least she hadn't forgotten how to do that.

It seemed to take a long time to get from the bed to the door. But even though she was weak, her head seemed much clearer now, clearer than it had been in a long time.

It was strange being down here on the rug, and Betty smiled as she crawled through the bedroom doorway and out into the living room. Here the rug was brown, a beautiful rich chocolate brown.

Betty giggled. Everything was very different from this vantage point. No wonder babies were always smiling! She crawled past the coffee table and past her swivel rocking chair. She'd never realized that the living room was so large before, and it seemed to take a long time to crawl the length of the room to the front door.

The front doorknob was too high. What should she do? Stand up, of course. She needed something to hold. Using a table by the door, Betty pulled herself up. Her hands seemed to recall the motions and she slipped off the chain, turned the knob, and opened the door to the empty hallway stretching out before her.

Betty took one step forward, then dropped back down to her knees. It would be faster, and she wouldn't hurt herself if she fell. The stairwell seemed a very long way away.

TWENTY

Getting out of bed, Ellen pulled on an old pair of jeans and a sweatshirt, looked back at Walker, sleeping peacefully, and sighed. At least someone was getting some rest. Every time she closed her eyes, she saw Laureen and Alan, crushed almost beyond recognition at the bottom of the elevator shaft.

She went into the kitchen to make herself a cup of hot chocolate and carried it into the workroom. She was so on edge, she doubted that anything could relax her except work and there was plenty of that. Walker had found the missing box of mannequin parts and there were still a half dozen to assemble.

As she walked past the big metal bin in the corner, she caught sight of the damaged mannequin inside. It had been returned from a store in Los Angeles and she'd saved it to use for spare parts since only the head was smashed. She shuddered as she stared down at it. Just like Alan and Laureen.

Chiding herself for being so morbid, Ellen lifted the mannequin up to her workbench. She'd take it apart, put all the pieces in the appropriate boxes, and throw the rest away.

She was removing the head when she noticed a thin film of white powder coating the inside surface. She used no powder in her molding process, only liquid plastics. Touching the top of her finger to her tongue, she noticed a bitter taste followed by a strange sensation.

Ellen gasped out loud as she realized that the powder could mean someone was using her mannequins to transport drugs. But no one touched those mannequins except her. And Walker . . . but it was disloyal to even think it. Still, there were all those new contracts he'd arranged, a whole distribution network that stretched across the country.

With a sinking heart, she went to the spare bedroom where he had stored his things. The backpack was there and she looked inside. Pajamas, toothbrush, a disposable razor, and . . . a gun. She forced herself to stand there and think calmly. Many people carried guns. It *could* be perfectly legal. But why had he brought it up here unless he intended to use it? Something else caught her eye, something glittering at the bottom of the backpack. She reached down to retrieve it, her hands starting to tremble as she recognized Vanessa's diamond earring.

Calm. She had to stay calm. Walker had been with her the night Vanessa died, except when she sent him up to borrow a can of tomato sauce from Jayne. Had he been gone long enough to kill Vanessa and drag her down to the freezer?

She didn't like the path her thoughts were taking her, but she couldn't seem to stop them. He'd been up at the spa all alone the night that Clayton and Rachael had left. And he'd been gone again the night that Hal had died. What if all these awful accidents weren't accidents at all?

Tonight, while she'd soaked in a nice, relaxing bath, he would have had plenty of time to sabotage the elevator.

With her heart pounding so hard she was almost afraid it would wake him, Ellen tiptoed to her bedroom and peeked in. Still asleep. Then she turned and went out, blinking back tears of grief and fright. The man she'd been learning to love was a killer. She had to warn the others about him.

By the time they reached the sixth floor landing, Moira's legs were trembling so hard she could barely stand. "I'm too old for this, Grace. I've got to rest a minute." She stopped and leaned against the railing, struggling to catch her breath. Then her left leg suddenly folded beneath her and she dropped heavily to the floor. "Da . . . drat! I knew this was going to happen!"

"What's wrong?"

"Charley horse, in my left leg. I don't think I can stand on it."

Grace climbed up the last step and joined Moira on the landing. "Give me your leg, Moira. I'll rub it for you."

As she kneaded the trembling muscle in Moira's leg, Grace gave a defeated sigh. There was no way Moira's rebelling muscles would make it any farther.

"I think it's a little better, Grace." The pain in Moira's eyes belied her words. "Maybe I can lean on the railing and pull myself up."

Grace shook her head. "You've got to rest or you'll injure the muscle."

Moira frowned and pulled herself to her feet in spite of Grace's protests. She hobbled one step and turned to Grace with a stubborn expression. "There's no time to rest. Come on, Grace. I think I can . . ." Moira stopped in midsentence as the door to the hallway began to open. "Oh, my God! It's Betty!"

* * *

"Okay." Jayne turned to a blank page in her music notebook. "Turn it on, Paul. I'm ready."

Paul flicked the switch on the piano Johnny had given her, and the strange atonal music began to play. The melody had been bothering him ever since he'd heard it, and tonight he'd remembered the game his violin teacher had taught him, creating a melody from the letters in a name.

Jayne frowned as she transcribed the melody into musical notation. "The lower octave is normal and the upper ones follow the rest of the alphabet. Is that right, Paul?"

Paul nodded. "*A* through *G* are obvious. The letter *H* is high *A*, and the letter *I* is high *B* and so on."

"This'll take a minute." Jayne turned back to her notebook. "I hope you're right, Paul. Johnny's song has been driving me crazy, too."

Just then there was a knock on the door. Paul went to answer it and came back with Ellen.

"Ellie, honey. You look worse than a whipped puppy." Jayne dropped her notebook and hurried to help Ellen into a chair. "What's wrong?"

"I . . . I looked in the backpack and I found this!" Ellen drew the gun out of her pocket.

Jayne grabbed for the barrel and lowered it. "Careful with that thing! It might be loaded!"

"Of course it's loaded." Ellen started to laugh, but it came out as a sob. "He couldn't kill us without the bullets, could he?"

"Whoa!" Jayne took the gun and handed it to Paul, then patted Ellen the way she'd calm a nervous filly. "Easy there, honey. Who couldn't kill us?"

"Walker. He was using my mannequins to ship drugs. And then I found his gun and I . . . I took it."

Paul frowned. It was difficult to believe that Walker had been dealing in drugs, but Ellen was clearly terrified. "You are safe now, Ellen. Where is Walker?"

"Still sleeping. But when he wakes up . . ."

The intercom buzzed, startling all three of them. Jayne hurried to answer it and when she came back, she looked dazed. "We've got to get down to Betty's right away. Grace and Moira just found her crawling out in the hall."

"You're all right now, Betty." Jayne held her hand. "Do you know where your nurse is?"

Betty frowned and tried to force out the word, but she was too exhausted to talk. She just knew she didn't want to go back to sleep, not when the awful movies might start to play again. She had to find some way to tell them. But what was the word for what had happened to Nurse?

"Cold!" Betty frowned. That wasn't right.

"Of course you are." Moira reached for a blanket and covered Betty's shoulders. "Your nurse is here, isn't she?"

"Hot!" Betty nodded. That wasn't the right word either, but it would have to do. Nurse was here. Right there in the bathroom with the door shut. And her secret friend had killed her.

"Jayne?" Paul came into the bedroom looking puzzled. "The nurse is not here in Betty's apartment."

"It's three in the morning, for Pete's sakes! Where could she be?"

"Hot!" Betty managed to get the word out again.

"Would you like a drink of water, Betty?" Grace did her best to understand.

Betty could feel her face light up in a smile as the dancer took a glass and opened the bathroom door. She flicked on the light and then she screamed, a much better scream than the ones Betty usually heard in the movies.

Jayne rushed to the bathroom to look and then she pulled Grace out by the arm. "Betty's nurse is dead and that's why she was out in the hall. She was trying to tell someone!"

"Do you know what happened to the nurse, Betty?" Paul leaned over to ask.

Betty nodded. She knew. But how could she tell them?

"Did your nurse have an accident?"

Betty shook her head. No, it wasn't an accident, but she'd forgotten the word. She had to make them understand about the scary movies. It was terribly important, although she couldn't remember why. Suddenly she had an idea and she reached for the remote control. If she couldn't tell them, she could show them. She turned on the set and pressed the button for forbidden channel nine.

"That's our living room." Jayne blinked as she stared at the screen.

Paul nodded. "It a closed-circuit surveillance system. The monitors in the security office broke in the avalanche, but it still works here. Jack must have run a second cable up here and hooked it to Betty's television set so he could keep an eye on things when he was visiting her."

Betty switched to forbidden channel zero and used the outside camera that was focused on the hill. Would they recognize what it was?

"I see it, Betty." Moira peered at the screen. "There's

something hidden behind that tree on the ridge. What is it?"

Betty frowned. She'd forgotten the word, but she knew the sound it made. *"Brmmmmm!"*

"The snowmobile!" Ellen gasped. "You've got to tell us, Betty! Do you know what happened to Clayton and Rachael?"

Betty nodded. She switched to forbidden channel five and pressed the control for the camera in the rose garden.

"That's Darby's rose garden." Jayne identified the image on the screen. "And somebody's been digging out there. See that loose dirt in the back?"

Grace began to shiver as she stared at the screen. "It looks like a . . . a grave."

Betty frowned in concentration. They almost had the connection. And then she remembered the word that would explain everything.

"Murder!" she said, as she zoomed in on the grave.

Jayne helped to push the snowmobile up to the top of the ridge. There were tears on her cheeks and the bitter wind turned them into streaks of icy cold.

Paul gave her arm a squeeze. "Just a little farther, Jayne. We can make it."

"I still don't think we should have left them." Jayne wiped her cheeks with her mitten and bent down to push again. The nurse's boots were a size too small, but they hadn't dared run upstairs for their own. Paul was wearing the nurse's parka, which had a hood. And she had Betty's mink coat and a woolen scarf.

"They told us to go," Paul reassured her. "I have knowledge of this snowmobile."

"But what if Walker finds them? They'll be trapped up there!"

"We will be back with the police in less than an hour." Paul swore in Norwegian as the snowmobile hung up on the drift. "Push, Jayne."

Jayne dug her heels in and they heaved at the heavy snowmobile until it had cleared the drift. It was tough going, and they had to reach the crest of the ravine to muffle the noise of starting it.

"We should have left the gun with them," Jayne gasped, leaning against the back of the snowmobile.

"Grace went down to get her father's gun and Moira is watching Walker on the surveillance camera. They will be fine provided we do our part. Push, Jayne; we are almost at the top."

Jayne bent over to push again, but she knew Paul was just trying to make her feel better. They'd tried to look in Marc's unit to make sure he was all right, but the rooms had all been deserted. And the blackout drapes at his bedroom windows were so effective, they hadn't been able to see if he was in bed or not. Paul had risked running up one flight to ring his doorbell. They had to alert him and send him down to safety with the others, but no one had answered.

"Do you think Marc's all right?"

"I do not know, honey." Paul stopped to catch his breath. "There is no time to worry now. Are you ready to push once more?"

"I'm ready." Jayne shivered, but it wasn't from the cold. Then she bent down again, trying to muster more muscle.

Paul smiled at her and Jayne did her best to smile back. Sneaking down the stairs had been harrowing,

searching every shadow to make sure they weren't being
followed.

"This is enough." Paul laid his hand on her arm. "Get
on, honey."

Jayne climbed on the snowmobile and held her
breath as the engine roared into life. Thank God! She
didn't begin to breathe again until they were over the
next ridge. Then she huddled close to Paul's back and
prayed they'd reach the police in time.

Grace held her breath as she unlocked the door, listening for the buzzing of the intercom. All was silent and
she breathed a sigh of relief. They'd worked out a signal,
Moira and Ellen would buzz her on the intercom if
Walker moved.

Even though she'd always hated the sport in the past,
Grace was finding herself grateful for her father's hobby.
He'd been quite a sportsman, going on safari in Africa,
moose hunting in Canada, and fox hunting on a private
estate in England. When she packed up his taxidermy
shop, she'd sold most of the guns, but several were on
the wall. Moira had insisted they lent a touch of authenticity to the room.

As she approached the door to the storage room,
Grace couldn't stifle an involuntary shudder. Moira had
wanted to come down with her, but her leg was still sore
and she might need her strength later. Grace held her
breath as she pushed open the door. Moira had warned
her not to turn on any lights that might cast a reflection
on the snow outside the window. She clicked on her
flashlight and forced herself to step inside, training the
beam of light on the huge Kodiak bear. She knew she

was being foolish, but she still wanted to make sure it didn't move as she walked past it.

There was a gun on the wall next to the bear, but Grace knew it was an antique muzzle-loader. Her father had shown her a picture of a man measuring out black powder from a horn to load it.

Grace stopped and shined the beam around the room. The eyes of the black panther glittered and she stepped back a pace, nearly impaling herself on the horns of a gazelle. She had to stop being so childish and find a gun they could use.

A rifle hanging on the wall caught her eye, a hefty weapon dating back to the Civil War called a Springfield Trapdoor. Grace grabbed it, then hurried to the cabinet where her father had kept his supplies. It was a mammoth piece of furniture, made of solid mahogany, and Moira had insisted she keep it. Since her father had been an organized man, the hundreds of drawers were labeled neatly in his Spencerian script. Grace started at the top row and worked her way down. Screws. Nuts. Bolts. Wads. Grace pulled out that drawer. She thought she remembered her father saying something about wadcutters once.

The moment she pulled out the drawer, she knew these wads weren't for a gun. She wasn't sure what her father had used them for, but they looked disgusting. Her father's handwriting was difficult to read and Grace decided it would be quicker to pull the drawers out one by one. She found a lot of interesting things that way, but none of them looked helpful. There was even a drawer of glass eyes that she promptly slammed shut again, but she finally found some shells in a drawer labeled "snap caps." As she stuffed them into her tote bag, she noticed a long, narrow drawer under the others. There was something that looked like a giant ice pick inside with a funny piece of metal sticking out where the handle should be. She picked it up, wrapped it in a piece of fur so it wouldn't stick her, and put it into her bag. She wasn't sure what it was, but it certainly looked nasty.

Grace flicked off the flashlight and headed for the door. Done! She was about to turn the knob when she heard footsteps outside.

The Caretaker had decided to start with Grace and Moira and work his way up to the top floor while everyone was sleeping. If someone got wise, he'd be able to trap them on the stairwell. Naturally, he'd fixed the elevator. It had been a simple matter to replace the cable he'd loosened and there was no way he wanted to tire himself out by climbing up and down all those stairs.

When morning came, he'd blow up the building. That part would be simple. The plate glass windows on the north and east sides of the building were doublesealed, designed to make the huge furnace in the garage run more efficiently and to reduce drafts. The only windows that could be opened were the bedroom and bathroom windows on the west side and the patio doors on the south, and it wouldn't take long to secure them. Then he'd turn up the gas and wait. Once the highly combustible mixture had built up to a concentrated level, he'd fire a shot from the outside to create a spark. Even though the Old Man had been grief-stricken about his daughter's death, he'd pulled himself together enough to agree that it was a solid plan.

He walked silently through Grace and Moira's living room and opened their bedroom door. Grace was smaller and it would be easier to snuff out her life without waking Moira. Then he'd finish off Moira.

The bed had been slept in, but it was empty now. He should have gone up to Betty's first and used the camera to track everyone. He was making mistakes already, and he hadn't even started. He'd check out the rest of the rooms, and if he couldn't find them, he'd run up to Betty's and let the closed-circuit system do his hunting for him.

Grace flicked off her flashlight. Why hadn't they called on the intercom? Had he found them and killed them all? She was paralyzed with fear as she realized her worst nightmare was coming true. She was trapped in her father's stuffed menagerie with no escape!

Suddenly Grace remembered the pile of animal skins behind the Kodiak bear and forced herself to move. The room was pitch-black and she had to orient herself by touch. Grace shuddered as her fingertips grazed the black panther's smooth fangs. It seemed to take hours, but at last her hand touched the bear's huge claws and she felt her way around the back. She'd just pulled a large water buffalo skin over herself, its musty animal scent still strong, when the door opened.

There was a small opening where the skin was slightly torn and Grace could see his feet as he flicked on the bright overhead lights. He was wearing green and white designer tennis shoes she'd seen before. If Moira were here, she'd quip that it was probably what well-dressed killers wore when they stalked terrified middle-aged women in rooms full of stuffed animals.

Grace bit her lip to silence the terrified scream that threatened to tear from her throat as he stopped right next to her. She held her breath and shut her eyes. Moira had shown him around the menagerie when he'd first come to work for Ellen, and she prayed he wouldn't notice there was anything out of place. Then the lights went out and the door shut her in with the darkness and the Kodiak bear that suddenly seemed like a very dear friend. She stayed there, hardly daring to breathe, until she heard the front door close. Then she hoisted herself up on trembling knees and grabbed the rifle and her tote bag.

She rushed to the front door and peeked through the fisheye peephole to observe the newly repaired elevator. The green arrow flickered six times. He was going up to Betty's floor and that meant they were still alive!

Grace's fingers were trembling as she fumbled in the tote bag and slipped a round into the chamber. Then she ran to the stairwell and took the stairs as fast as she could, blessing her dancer's legs. There was no way she could get there first, but they were barricaded in Betty's bedroom. And she was coming with the gun that would save them.

"Oh, God! I was right!" Ellen's voice was shaking. Since she was good at puzzles, Jayne had given her the notebook and she was frantically working to divide the letters from Johnny's message into words.

"What does it say?"

Moira didn't take her eyes from the screen as she changed cameras and locations, desperately trying to locate Walker. They'd buzzed Grace on the intercom to tell her that he was up and moving, but there had been no answer.

"The words are, *Jayne If You Get This I Am Dead Cocaine In Dolls Watch Out Marc.* And then it stops. Johnny must have discovered that Walker was putting cocaine in my mannequins and he was killed before he could tell anyone. And the last part is a warning for Marc. Oh, I hope he's all right!"

"There he is!" Moira pointed to the screen where Marc had appeared.

"He's coming down the hallway. Thank God!"

Ellen jumped to her feet. "I'll get him. You keep on trying to find Walker."

TWENTY-ONE

Marc was approaching the door when Ellen opened it, pulled him inside, and threw her arms around him. "Thank God it's you! We thought Walker had killed you!"

"What?"

"Come on." Ellen tugged him toward Betty's room. "We're all holed up in here."

Marc still looked dazed and Ellen realized that she hadn't explained the situation. "Sorry, I forgot that you don't know what happened. Johnny left a warning for you on Jayne's piano and Betty's all right now, but Walker killed her nurse. Grace went down to get one of her father's guns and we think she's okay, but we lost Walker when we tried to track him on Betty's television and now we don't know where he is."

"There's Grace and she's got the gun." Moira pointed at the screen where Grace was just reaching their landing. "Go let her in, Ellen. I'll keep trying to find Walker."

Grace came in and rushed over to hug Marc, who was sitting in a chair by the door. "You're alive! We thought . . . it doesn't matter now, but Walker came down to the menagerie while I was there and I had to hide behind the Kodiak bear and thank God he didn't spot me! I rushed right up here as soon as he'd left, and I managed to load this thing, but I hope to God you know how to shoot it!"

"Uh . . . sure, I do. No problem."

Marc's voice sounded strange. Ellen hoped he'd recover enough to do them some good. She patted him on the shoulder and handed him the notebook with Johnny's message. "Here, read this. Johnny left a coded message warning you that Walker was using my mannequins to transport drugs, but he . . . he was murdered before he could write the rest."

"We think Walker's still in the building," Moira explained, turning back to the screen. "He hasn't come out of the entrance and I've been switching back there every couple of seconds."

"Don't worry, I'll find him." Marc stood up. "You ladies stay right here. It's safer that way. And don't open the door for anyone but me."

"But . . . will you have to kill him?" Ellen's voice was shaking. "He doesn't have a gun."

"Then there's no problem. Give me the rifle, Grace." Marc smiled as Grace handed him the rifle and the extra shells. "Perfect. You loaded the rifle with these?"

"Yes. Did I do something wrong?"

"Not a thing. I don't want to leave you unarmed, so you keep this one. I'll run up and get my hunting rifle."

After Marc had left, Moira clicked the button for his floor and they all watched anxiously for him to appear. Ellen let out a relieved sigh as they saw him crossing the living room floor. "He made it!"

"Thank God!" Grace reached out to grip Moira's hand tightly. "I don't know whether he's brave or foolish, but I'm sure glad I don't have to go out there again."

* * *

Paul kept the snowmobile on a path across the ridge that roughly paralleled the access road. There were clouds over the moon and the wind whipped up the loose snow to drive it against his face in what felt like needles of ice. He could feel Jayne shivering on the seat behind him and he wished he'd been able to run upstairs to get her parka. Betty's fur coat was stylish, but no match for warmth.

"Are you all right, honey?" The wind whipped his words away in a blast of freezing air, but Jayne leaned close to him and shouted that she was fine, although she suspected the tip of her nose was already well on its way to turning into an icicle.

The engine of the snowmobile coughed once and started to sputter as it came slowly to a stop. Paul swore in Norwegian again, and got out of the driver's seat.

"What's the matter?" Jayne felt her heart beat faster. She hoped nothing was wrong.

"We are out of petrol."

"Out of gas?" Jayne gave a cry of alarm. "Oh, no."

Paul patted her shoulder. "It is just that I now must switch to the second tank."

Jayne gave a sigh of relief as Paul went around to the side of the machine and flipped a switch, then got back on and tried the motor. She could hear it turn over, but it didn't catch. Not on the second time, or the third, or fourth.

Paul frowned. "I think it is submerged."

"Flooded," Jayne corrected him. "What can we do?"

"We must wait until the extra petrol drains out and then it will start."

Jayne sat for a moment, realizing that all the time

they'd saved by cutting over the ridge was being lost now. Then the clouds rolled past the moon and it was bright once more. Jayne was just beginning to feel some hope, it would be easier to travel now that they could see clearly, when she spotted a dark furry shape barreling out of the trees ahead, charging straight at the snowmobile.

"Black bear!" Jayne pulled the gun out of her pocket and steadied it with both hands. "Get behind me, Paul."

Jayne lined up the sights and fired. Thank God Jack had talked her into taking that firearms safety course after Paul had left! She hadn't gotten around to buying a gun, but she'd learned how to use six different types of weapons, a forty-five automatic among them.

The bear gave a roar that nearly deafened them and kept right on coming. Jayne was sure she'd hit it, but the bullet must have bounced off its thick skull. She seemed to remember hearing that someone had pumped twenty rounds into a black bear before it had dropped. She had to make every shot count.

Jayne could see the bear's teeth now, viciously sharp and gleaming in the moonlight. She squeezed off another shot, aiming right into its open mouth, and then another and another. This wasn't the same as shooting at paper targets. This was real!

She tried to stay calm as she aimed carefully and emptied the magazine. The bear was almost on top of them when it staggered and dropped to the snow.

Paul's voice was shaking. "I thought we had bought the ranch, honey."

Jayne was too rattled to correct him. "Just try the engine again. And hurry!"

While Paul tried the engine, Jayne stared at the bear. It was a big one, five hundred pounds at least, with claws twice as long as her fingers and jaws powerful enough to rip a man's leg right off his body. Black bears were known to be vicious when awakened in the winter, and one half this size could kill with a swipe of its claws. Jayne didn't know what she'd do if it got up again. The gun was empty. She kept on staring at it, as if she could keep it motionless by the sheer effort of her will.

On the third try, the engine started, and as they sped away Jayne turned to look over her shoulder at the lifeless bundle on the snow, the dark stain of blood spreading beneath it. Then she started to shake. She'd just shot the most dangerous animal in the woods. It could have slaughtered them both, but it was a pussycat compared to the man who was stalking the halls of Deer Creek Condos.

Walker stared out the window, searching for movement in the shadows outside the building. Where the hell was Ellen? He'd rushed up here, hoping to find her before she could do any damage, but the spa was deserted.

He glanced out at the thermometer. Thirty degrees outside and the way the wind was howling past the windows, he was sure she hadn't gone out for a walk. That meant she was still in the building, but where? She'd taken his forty-five when she'd left and that meant she'd put the pieces together. He had to stop her before she alerted the others or all hell would break loose.

He turned and headed for the stairwell. Even though he had a master key, it would be a waste of time to check out every apartment in the building. Ellen was holed up somewhere, and she'd kill him with his own forty-five rather than turn it over to him. She had courage, a trait he admired, but right now he wished she were a shrinking violet. He loved her, no doubt about that, but he'd been a fool to let down his guard. And while he wasn't the first to be taken in by a woman, he sure as hell wasn't going to roll over without a good fight.

Walker was frowning as he pushed open the door to the sixth floor. There was only one way to locate Ellen. He'd find her with Jack's closed-circuit system and pin her down. There would be time for explanations later, but first he had to get his weapon back one way or the other.

Ellen put her arms around Betty as they watched Marc on the monitor. He'd taken his rifle from the case, an ugly-looking object that reminded Ellen of the ones she'd seen on movie posters, and now he was filling his pockets with clips of ammunition. She didn't blame Betty for being frightened. She was frightened, too. Why did he have to take so much ammunition if he was just going to find Walker and tie him up?

"It's all right, Betty." Ellen tried to calm the poor dear, who was trembling so hard, her teeth were chattering.

"No!" Betty started to cry. "Nice man!"

Ellen patted her shoulder. "Of course he is. Marc is going to help us."

"He's got his parka and gloves." Moira kept them posted. "He must think Walker's outside. He'd better change his shoes, though. Those sure won't make it in the snow."

Grace swiveled around to look at the screen. "Oh, my God! I saw the killer's feet, down in the menagerie and . . ."

There was a sound of a key in the lock and Moira switched cameras. "It's Walker! And he's got a key!"

Ellen's hands were trembling as she picked up the antique rifle Grace had brought. There was no other choice.

"No!" Grace shouted, whirling toward Ellen, but Betty was faster. Her arm shot out, knocking the gun from Ellen's hands.

"Killer Marc!" Betty insisted. "Walker is nice."

"That's what I was trying to tell you." Grace hurried to unlock the dead bolt. "I saw the killer's shoes and . . . and Marc's wearing them!"

"Oh, Walker!" Ellen hurled herself in his arms. "I thought you were the killer and I almost . . ." She stopped and swallowed hard, unable to speak the words aloud.

"I figured you'd try to kill me." Walker grinned down at her. "But I also figured you'd miss. Where did you get that antique? And where's my forty-five?"

They all spoke at once, trying to explain, but Walker caught enough to understand. Although Johnny's musical message had been accurate, they'd misinterpreted its meaning. *Watch out Marc* had been a warning for them, not him.

"Ellen? See if you can find coats and boots, everything we need for the outside. Stuff it all in one bag. Grace, you help Betty get dressed into something warm. Keep Marc on that monitor, Moira. Don't take your eyes off him and holler for me when he makes a move for the door."

"You'd better take this." Grace handed the Springfield to Walker proudly. "I went all the way down to the menagerie to get it and here's the box of bullets. Marc really blew it by leaving it here."

As Walker looked over the munitions Grace had

risked her life for, a quizzical expression came over his face. "Isn't it any good?" Grace asked.

"It's a good rifle, but those are dummy rounds. It makes a great club, though." Walker hefted the Springfield. "Don't feel bad, Grace. It's more than we had before."

"I've got this, too." Grace handed him the fur-wrapped bundle. "It's just a big ice pick without a handle, but it looked plenty dangerous. Can you use it?"

Walker grinned as he unwrapped it. "Watch this, Grace." He butted the ice pick up against the end of the rifle and twisted. There was a click as it locked into place. "It's a bayonet, a real pig-sticker. It's the perfect thing for hand-to-hand combat."

Grace beamed. She'd gotten something useful, after all. But even without it, the trip hadn't been wasted: she'd never be afraid of the panther or the Kodiak bear again. She turned to find Betty smiling up at her. "Sweatsuit in closet. Help me, Grace?"

"Of course I will!" Grace could hardly believe her ears. It was the first time Betty had remembered her name. As she hurried off to get the sweatsuit, she thanked God this was one of Betty's good periods. They were going to need all the help they could get.

Ellen was stuffing the last coat in a duffel bag when Walker joined her. "Anything for me?"

She nodded and handed him a bright pink jacket. "I think it was the nurse's, but it's the only thing that's close to your size."

"Not my best color, but I'll take it." Walker slung the jacket over his shoulder and picked up the duffel bag. "Think carefully, Ellen. Did you tell Marc that Jayne and Paul left on the snowmobile?"

Ellen frowned as she tried to remember, then shook her head. "No, I'm almost positive I didn't."

"Good. He doesn't realize the clock is ticking, and that's a big break for us."

Ellen put her hand on his arm. "Walker? Who are you?"

"Later, Ellen. I work for the good guys. Will that do for now?"

Ellen nodded. "Do you really know Jack, or was that just a part of your cover?"

"Jack's a friend. He called me in when he tumbled onto Johnny's cocaine pipeline. That's all I can tell you, Ellen, except that I'm retiring right after this one. Is the job as your business manager still open?"

"Oh, yes." Ellen smiled up at him. "I wouldn't want anyone but you."

Just then, before either of them could say another word, Moira called out. Marc was heading for the door.

"Jayne, honey. We're here!"

Jayne opened her eyes and nodded. Her teeth were chattering so loudly, she hadn't even realized the sound of the motor had stopped. She half-fell from the seat and steadied herself on legs that felt like frozen poles of ice.

"Hurry, get inside. I will start the heater."

Paul helped her up into Grace's truck and started the motor. Its shelter seemed warm, and soon heat would be coming from the vents.

It took her at least five minutes before she could stop trembling enough to speak. "How long did it take us?"

"Less than an hour. We made good speed."

Jayne nodded. They'd made excellent time, despite switching the gas tank and killing the black bear. It would take another fifteen minutes to reach the police station. Then, if everything went like clockwork, it might be no more than forty-five minutes before the police chopper reached Deer Creek Condos. Jayne shut her eyes in a fervent prayer.

"What's he doing?" Moira whispered as she watched Marc walk down the hall toward the elevator. They hadn't answered when he'd pounded on the door.

"Keep him on camera. He's bound to make a mistake." Walker's optimism wasn't totally wishful. Marc wasn't a trained killer. Walker could tell because he'd made too many stupid errors, and he was making another big one right now. Walker would have blown the lock off the door. Four women with dummy bullets was no threat to a man with an assault weapon. And then he would have used the closed-circuit system to track anyone left in the building.

"He's ringing for the elevator!" Ellen watched him with disbelief. "Why?"

Grace sighed. "I forgot to tell you, it works now. Count the times the arrow flickers and we'll know where he went."

"I've got him." Moira switched cameras. "He's down in the garage."

Sitting up in bed, fully dressed except for her shoes, Betty looked much more alert. She'd played the part of the cornered rabbit again, hardly daring to breathe while her secret friend was here, but now he was gone and she knew she had to help the nice man with the dark skin. "Eyes and ears."

"Right." Walker turned to Betty in surprise. "He'll cut off the monitor. Better find a flashlight."

Betty reached into the drawer by the bed and handed

Walker a flashlight. Then she swung her feet out of the bed and pushed them into her fur-lined slippers. "Ready."

"Good." Walker nodded. "Grab hands and stand at the door. Grace first with this flashlight. Unlock it and get ready to go. Moira? Right behind her. Then Ellen. Think you can take this rifle?

Walker smiled at her as Ellen grabbed the rifle and took her place in line. Then he lifted Betty in his arms. "We're going straight up to the spa, and we're going now, while we've still got light. If the power goes out, don't turn on the flashlight. Just slide your hands along the railing and keep on going."

"Movies!" Betty reached out and pulled five tapes from the shelf. "For evidence."

"You recorded the killings?" Betty nodded and Walker began to grin. "Okay, Grace, let's move it!"

They were all the way up to the ninth-floor landing before the lights went out.

"Quietly now," Walker whispered. "Hold onto the railing and keep climbing."

They climbed in silence until they reached the door to the spa. Grace pushed it open and blinked in the bright glow of the moonlight shining down through the dome.

"What now?" Ellen helped Betty to a chair while Walker secured the door to the stairwell.

"Now we wait." Walker sighed. "He doesn't expect us to come up here, so we've bought ourselves some time. Spread out at the windows and watch for anything moving outside. I think he'll try to get us out of the building somehow. It's the only way he can pick us off."

They waited at the windows for what seemed like an eternity. Then Ellen gave a low cry. "There he is!"

Walker rushed to her side and looked over to see

Marc moving toward the big pine tree on the south side of the building.

"I see him." Grace peered out into the darkness. "He's still got that gun."

"It's an assault rifle, Grace, probably with a night scope."

"But aren't they illegal?"

"I don't think he cares about that. The balconies are all on that side of the building, aren't they?"

"That's right," Moira confirmed. "Paul wanted a southern exposure."

"Smoke!" Betty exulted as the word came easily to her lips. She pointed toward the air-conditioner vent and said it again. "Smell the smoke. Building on fire?"

"Nope." Walker shook his head. "I kept an eye on the monitor while you were lining up at the door and I saw Marc doing something to the furnace. He must have backed it up to smoke us out. Probably plans on picking us off when we stick our heads out for air."

Grace began to smile. "At least he can't come into the building again, not until the smoke clears."

"That's true," Ellen agreed. "But there's no way for us to get any fresh air, either. The whole dome's sealed off."

"Washer." They turned to look at Betty. "We can open the window-washer."

"You're right!" Moira exclaimed, leaning over to give her a big hug. "There's a panel that lifts out for the window-washing equipment. Over on the other side of the swimming pool."

"Okay, everyone over here." Walker motioned for them to join him. "Now, don't make a sound. We'll lift out the panel and then I'll go down the side of the building on the scaffolding."

Moira frowned. "But how? The equipment's electrical."

"See that handle?" Walker pointed to a hand crank mounted on the wall beneath the panel. "It's a safety device and there's another crank mounted on the side of the scaffolding. I'll crank myself down as fast as I can and the moment I'm on the ground, crank the scaffolding back up again. Got it?"

Ellen grabbed his arm. "Don't do it, Walker. He'll shoot you before you get close enough to use that bayonet."

"You're forgetting that he's positioned himself to concentrate on the balconies and the front door. He'll never expect anyone to come down this side and circle around."

"But we've got fresh air now. Why can't we just wait until Jayne and Paul bring the police?"

Walker pulled her over to the side where no one else could hear them. "Look, Ellen, we can't count on them to bail us out in time. I didn't want to say anything in front of the others, but after Marc finished with the furnace, he went over to inspect the gas lines. If smoking us out doesn't work, I figure he'll blow up the building with us in it."

Ellen shuddered and Walker pulled her into his arms. He kissed her and reached out to cradle her cheek. "I know what I'm doing, Ellen. It's our best shot. Watch from the windows and if I can't take him out, get everyone down on the scaffolding and head for the woods."

"But if we go down on the scaffolding, we can't crank it back up."

"It won't matter then. He'll already know that I used it to get down and he'll figure the rest of you are still up there. We have to do it this way, Ellen. We don't have any other options."

Tears came to Ellen's eyes. Walker was right. But as she watched Walker crank himself down and she brought the empty scaffolding back up, she was working on her own backup plan.

Sergeant Dennis Rawley sighed. She'd been crying for the past ten minutes and nothing made him feel more helpless than a woman's tears. A veteran officer only a year from retirement, he'd been shot five times, once nearly fatally, and had lost three partners. Two of them had been killed in the line of duty and one had eaten the barrel of his own gun. He'd seen every kind of abuse that humans could dish out and had been on the receiving end more than once, but the sight of a woman with silent tears rolling down her cheeks still turned his insides into jelly.

"It's all right, Ma'am. They're loading up right now and they'll be there in less than twenty minutes. That's guaranteed." Tears were still streaming down her cheeks and he reached out to pat her hand. "How about coming up to the roof and watching them take off? It's against regulations, but I can swing it."

"Oh, yes. Thank you!" She gave him a blinding smile and Dennis felt ten feet tall as he led her up the stairs and showed her where it was safe to stand. Her husband was going in with the SWAT team, to give them the layout. Dennis watched the men pile in, carrying rifles and equipment. They looked like an invasion team and that's really what they were. He didn't envy them the dangerous assignment.

In the harsh glare from the lights he could see she was still half-frozen from the exposure. Dennis had called in the Doc. A patch of white skin on her left cheek looked like frostbite, a rare sight under the blazing Vegas sun.

"Hurry! Please hurry!"

"They will, Ma'am."

Jayne didn't realize that she'd spoken aloud until he answered. She could see a blinking neon sign in the distance, four-thirty AM, eighty-five degrees. Another warm Vegas night, but she was still shivering in Betty's fur coat.

The rotor started and the deafening noise filled Jayne with hope as she watched the huge helicopter lift off. She watched until it was nothing but a speck in the night sky and then turned to the officer beside her. "Twenty minutes?"

Dennis nodded. "That's right, Ma'am. How about a cup of coffee?"

Jayne let him lead her back into the building. Her knees shaking as they walked back down the stairs. As she watched the steaming liquid pour into the cardboard cup, Jayne couldn't help but think of the four friends they'd left behind, Moira, Grace, and Ellen, barricaded in poor Betty's room. How long could they hold out against a trained killer?

TWENTY-TWO

The west side of the building was landscaped with a hedge of juniper and Walker crouched behind it for cover. He worked his way around the building, wincing at the open field of snow ahead, still showing the blurry indentation of their snow angels. That happy time seemed far in the past, though it had actually been less than thirty hours ago.

Feeling the adrenaline rushing through his veins, he forced himself to slow down. Time was not of the essence, but caution was, and his breathing was already ragged. The Springfield weighed approximately eleven pounds, the bayonet probably bringing the total up to twelve. He'd trekked through the muck of Vietnam carrying at least fifty pounds, but he'd been much younger then.

As soon as his breathing had slowed, Walker assessed his chances. The wind had died down and now it was as quiet as a tomb. To make matters worse, the temperature had dropped, causing the snow to crunch underfoot.

Just then a crash sounded back in the trees on the far side of the building, as a fairly large animal moved through the brush. A coyote, perhaps, or a deer. It was an unexpected break. The moment he heard it, Walker was up and moving, streaking across the bare field of snow, using the sound for cover.

A shot shattered the stillness of the night. Marc had spotted him, but only after he'd reached the safety of the pine grove. Here only light snow dusted the ground, and less than five minutes later he was in the center of the grove, about a hundred yards directly behind Marc's position. There was still an exposed patch of snow to cross, but he had to wait for his chance.

Walker settled down and forced his tense body to relax. The bright pink jacket had only a thin lining of flannel inside. It had been designed for warmer temperatures, but it was better than nothing. Luckily, he'd been wearing his boots. Ellen had found a perfectly adequate pair of leather gloves, but Walker knew he couldn't last indefinitely out here in the cold. He had to hope his chance would come soon, while he could still move rapidly and efficiently.

His opportunity could come in several ways. If the wind picked up from the north behind him, it would be difficult for Marc to use his rifle sight in the blowing snow. There was also the possibility of diversion from another animal. All he had to do was be patient, and waiting was the most difficult task of all.

The Caretaker checked his ammunition and smiled. He'd brought enough to take care of everyone and then some. Although it seemed impossible, Betty was still alive. The nurse must have sabotaged that injection somehow. He should have thought to check it. Another mistake that he shouldn't have made.

He figured Walker was the one who had run for cover. The rest of them would still be huddled in Betty's room, trying to decide what to do. They might have hooked up with Paul and Jayne by now, but that wouldn't help them much. Not a man of action, it took Paul days to make a decision, and he'd never dash across the snow in a foolish attempt to outrun a man with a rifle. It had to be Walker. Of course the shot had given away his position. It was a bad break for him, but nothing he couldn't handle. Walker still had a clear patch of snow to cross, and that would be suicide, especially since the absence of return fire meant that he was unarmed. Either Walker was stupid or he had real balls; it didn't really matter which.

They'd plugged the air-conditioner vent with wet towels and were gathered at the windows. The open panel provided adequate ventilation. Grace peered out the window and frowned. "Marc's got Walker pinned down in the grove. Think he's hit?"

"Marc's shot went wild." Ellen let out her breath in a shuddering sigh. She'd seen the snow kick up at least ten feet in back of Walker.

"But now Marc knows that Walker's out there." Grace's voice was shaking. "We've got to help. If we had a gun, we could draw Marc's fire."

Betty spoke up. "Race gun! Ready, set, go?"

Moira stared down at Betty in shock. "The starter pistol. Je . . . Jeepers, Betty! Alzheimer's or not, you're smarter than all of us put together."

Paul's knuckles were white by the time they passed the outskirts of town. He didn't like planes, and helicopters were even worse. He stared down at the darkness below and hoped that the pilot had plenty of experience.

"Ten floors and there's only one entrance to the building, is that right?" An officer wearing camouflage fatigues and carrying a clipboard sat down next to him.

"Unless you count the balconies, nine on the south side of the building. Someone could reach the first-floor balcony, but the sliding glass door to the unit will be locked from the inside with a metal post which slides into a hole on the frame. It is the type of burglar-proof lock the police recommend."

"No problem." The officer made a note. "And there's no way for us to land on the roof?"

"No, the roof is a dome made of Plexiglas. However, there is a field one hundred and eighteen yards from the building on the east side. That is where the other helicopter made its landing."

"Garage?"

"It covers three-quarters of the ground floor. The main entrance is there, served by an elevator which is not functioning. My wife and I used the stairs. The remainder of the space is subdivided into a one-bedroom apartment and security office."

"And how many civilians are inside?"

It took Paul a moment to realize that anyone who wasn't a police officer must be a civilian. "Four, perhaps five. I do not know if Marc Davies is still alive."

"Four confirmed with a possible five," the officer noted, handing Paul the clipboard.

"Make a rough layout of the building, including the elevator shaft and the stairwells. Use red marks to indicate where you last saw the civilians. Our ETA is ten minutes."

Paul bent over the clipboard and began to sketch. The bright splashes of color against the white paper, one each for Moira, Grace, Betty, and Ellen, with a question mark on the seventh floor for Marc, made him shiver. Perhaps it was because red was the color of blood.

"This is a real treat." The doctor closed his bag and smiled at her. "No bullets, no knife wounds, not even a broken bone. You ought to see the ones they usually call me in for."

Jayne laughed. He was a wonderful doctor, old enough to be trusted and young enough to be up-to-date.

"Are you currently taking any medication, Mrs. Lindstrom?"

"No. Oh, I almost forgot!" Jayne reached into her pocket and took out the vial of Betty's medication that Paul had grabbed from the nurse's bag. "My neighbor has to have a shot of this every six hours. We were afraid they'd forget to bring it along when they rescued her, especially now that her nurse is . . . is dead." Jayne's voice broke and she began to sob. She wasn't sure why, since she hadn't cared for Margaret Woodard much when she'd been alive, but her death put a different perspective on things.

"That's all right, Mrs. Lindstrom. You've been through a real strain." The doctor patted her shoulder as he reached out to take the vial. Puzzled, he read the label. "What's wrong with your neighbor?"

"She has Alzheimer's."

"Does she have a history of violent behavior?"

Her tears were gone now, as quickly as they'd come, and Jayne wondered if she was turning into a basket case. "I don't think so. At least Dr. Glaser never mentioned it. He drives up to examine her every month and he brings a supply of her drugs for the . . . the nurse."

"Dr. Glaser?"

"Dr. Harvey Glaser. I ran into him in the elevator a couple of months ago, and I'd rather take my chances with a ten-foot rattler than let him . . ." Jayne stopped and winced, realizing that she was bad-mouthing the doctor in front of a colleague. "Well, let's just say I didn't much care for his manner. But I'm sure he's very competent."

"He was, before his death four years ago."

"But I don't understand! He told me he was Dr. Harvey Glaser."

"He lied. Do you know what this is, Mrs. Lindstrom?" The doctor pointed to the vial and Jayne shook her head. "It's Melahydroflorizine, a sledgehammer of a drug used to calm violent psychotics. The side effects are short-term memory loss, slurred speech, and the inability to form sentences. If I wanted to give someone the symptoms of Alzheimer's, I'd use this drug on a regular basis."

Jayne's mind was spinning. It was beginning to add up. "Then Betty doesn't have Alzheimer's?"

"I'd be willing to bet she doesn't. But someone sure as hell wanted you to think she did!"

Ellen stepped onto the scaffolding and held the rope with both hands. She'd found a utility belt in the office and cinched it around her waist. The starting pistol was in a pouch on the right, along with a coil of rope. She'd slipped her tennis racket into a loop on the left, not much of a weapon, but at least she knew how to swing it. On the ground, she'd take up a position on the south side of the building where the juniper was thick, then fire the pistol. And while she was drawing Marc's fire, Moira, Betty, and Grace would come down on the scaffolding and head for the woods.

She shut her eyes as Moira began to lower her with the crank. She'd always been afraid of heights and what awaited her on the ground wasn't exactly reassuring. The only thing that kept her going was the thought of Walker out there alone, pinned down by Marc's assault rifle.

The scaffolding swayed and Ellen bit back a moan of fear. She couldn't make a sound. It was vital that Marc not see the scaffolding. It was their only means of escape.

Walker rubbed his hands together to warm them. It was bitter cold despise the windbreak under the pines. He knew he had to move soon, before the sky began to lighten. The darkness was his only advantage.

Gunfire sounded on the south side of the building. Walker didn't take time to analyze who was firing what and why. He was up and running on legs painfully stiff from the cold. In the darkness, Walker saw Marc's rifle blast at the bushes beneath the first-floor balcony. Another shot and a return shot and then Walker hurled himself forward with the bayonet.

Marc heard the steps behind him and whirled, deflecting Walker's blow. The point of the bayonet buried itself in the sleeve of his jacket and the Springfield went flying to the snow. And then they were struggling, Walker clawing for the rifle barrel. An earsplitting shot missed Walker's head by inches and he managed to knock Marc's hand off the trigger, but his chilled arms had lost their strength. The two men grappled for long moments in the darkness of the night, but Marc was bigger and dressed for the weather. Walker felt his stamina ebbing in the biting wind.

Then something whizzed toward Marc's head, connecting solidly enough to throw him off balance. He dropped to one knee and another blow sent the assault rifle flying. Marc was down, and Walker was on him before he could move, pulling his hands roughly behind his back. When he looked up, he saw Ellen standing over him with her tennis racket tucked under her arm, handing him a piece of rope. He secured Marc's arms with hands that felt like blocks of ice. And then there was the welcome sound of a chopper in the distance, coming closer. Paul and Jayne had made it.

The next few moments were a blur of motion. Two officers rushed to take charge, handcuffing Marc and leading him away into the belly of the helicopter. Moira and Grace came around the side of the building supporting Betty between them, and two burly members of the SWAT team raced over the snow to help. Paul led four men into the building to inspect and secure it and Ellen and Walker found themselves momentarily alone, staring down at the trampled area in the snow where it had all happened.

Walker reached out to take Ellen's arm. He wanted to tell her that she was the most beautiful, courageous woman in the world. At the same time, he wanted to yell at her for being so incredibly foolish and crazy. It took a real idiot to come out here armed with nothing but a starting pistol and a tennis racket. And then he wanted to pull her close and kiss her. And tell her he'd do anything for her, that he was ready to settle down with her for the rest of his life if she'd have him. But there wasn't time for all that. Instead, he turned to her and said the first thing that popped into his mind. "Nice backhand, Ellen."

EPILOGUE

It was noon in Vegas and the temperature had hit the hundred-degree mark. The desert sun was merciless, glaring against the sides of the mirrored tower building and causing several passing tourists to fumble in their purses and pockets for sunglasses. Inside, it was cool and dark with the drapes drawn tightly and the air-conditioner turned up as high as it would go. The twentieth floor was an oasis of soothing relief from the blazing heat, but the four men at the table took no pleasure in their comfortable surroundings.

The tanned blond man frowned as he addressed the senior member of the group. "I got the word that they're moving him tomorrow. I made the arrangements, just like you said."

"Good!" The older man smiled in satisfaction. "He betrayed my trust. A rat like that does not deserve to live."

The short, thin man sighed deeply. "We respect your grief at your daughter's death. He will not die peacefully."

"I have no daughter!" The older man thumped his fist on the table. "It was an old man's foolishness to agree to his plan. I see that now. If she had lived, I would have killed her myself. I swear it!"

The heavyset man nodded. "I called this meeting to discuss a new plan for distribution, since the mannequins are no longer possible. We own a mail-order company. Computers and printers. It would be a simple matter to switch over the whole operation."

The older man frowned. "It is a risk to move my supplies."

"It's more of a risk to leave them where they are." The blond man pushed back his chair and stood up. "We've located a new storage place and our truck is ready. You'll go with me to supervise the move?"

"Do I have any choice in the matter?"

The blond man shook his head and there was silence until they had left. Then the heavyset man wiped his perspiring face with a handkerchief and sighed. "Your man knows what to do?"

"We went over the details this morning. It's unfortunate, but he's getting too old. He's already made several mistakes."

"I know that. Do you really think he would have killed his own daughter?"

The short, thin man shrugged. "Does it matter?"

Jack glanced at his watch for the third time in as many minutes and pressed the buzzer to summon the nurse. After a moment a tall woman with a mass of curly red hair bustled into the room. She was wearing a name tag that identified her as Miss Cooper.

"You buzzed, Mr. St. James?"

"Right. I've got ten to three. They said they'd be here at three, didn't they?"

"That's right." The nurse reached out to adjust his pillows. "Just relax, Mr. St. James. I'm sure they'll be here on time."

Jack frowned as he looked up at the crank and pulley that kept his leg stiffly elevated. "What are the odds of getting out of this thing, just while they're here? Jayne's going to say that I'm trussed up like a Christmas turkey."

"The odds are better at rigged roulette. The doctor says your leg has to be in traction for another two months."

"Come on, Miss Cooper. Can't you do something? I heal fast."

"Not that fast." The nurse laughed. "And I'm sure Jayne Peters won't say word one about a Christmas turkey."

"Want to bet a fiver?"

"Sure." The nurse nodded. "I'd better get some more chairs in here. Seven visitors, is that right?"

Jack shook his head. "Six. Jayne and Paul, Moira and Grace, and Ellen and Walker."

"I thought they said seven. I'll bring in an extra chair, just in case they're bringing a friend."

Jack sighed as he watched the nurse move in the extra chairs. Here he was, stuck in a hospital bed for at least two months, when he really wanted to be back up at Deer Creek Condos taking care of Betty.

"Here they come." Miss Cooper glanced out the door and hurried to fuss with his pillows one more time. "Just remember that bet you made."

"Jack, honey!" Jayne raced into the room and planted a kiss on his cheek. "Look at you, all trussed up like a Christmas goose!"

"A Christmas *goose?*" Jack groaned and handed Miss Cooper a five-dollar bill. "I thought for sure you'd say Christmas turkey!"

"No way. Turkeys are for Thanksgiving and geese are

for Christmas. I even wrote a song about it. 'Don't be a Turkey at Christmas.' You never heard it?"

"No, but Miss Cooper did." Jack glared at the nurse, who laughed and made a hasty exit. Then he turned to Paul. "Hi, Paul. Sorry I can't stand up to shake your hand. I tried, but they wouldn't let me out of this rig."

"It is no big contract."

"No big deal." Jayne corrected him automatically. "Come on, Jack. Shake his hand so he'll sit down."

Paul bowed slightly and extended his hand. "It is good to see you, Jack. Grace and Moira will be here shortly. They are arranging permission for the refreshments."

There was a knock at the door and Grace came in, followed by Moira with a picnic basket. While Moira opened the basket and set out glasses on Jack's bedside table, Grace came over to kiss Jack.

"The doctor said it's all right, that you're allowed to have the cake and ice cream we brought and a glass or two of champagne as long as we don't get you so drunk that you break out of that traction thing you're hooked up to and start swinging from the light fixtures or something equally destructive and, oh, I'm so glad to see you, Jack!"

"Say good night, Gracie." Jack grinned at her. "Hey, Moira . . . don't I get a kiss?"

"Dam . . . I mean, darn right you do!" Moira rushed over to the bed, her red and purple caftan flapping, and bussed Jack on the cheek. "Ellen and Walker are on their way up. They had to stop at the kitchen because Grace forgot to pack the silverware."

There was another knock at the door and Walker and Ellen came in. He was carrying a bucket of ice and she had a handful of spoons.

"Sorry about this, Jack." Ellen plunked the spoons

down on the table and kissed him. "They couldn't spare any knives and forks."

"They don't give us sharp implements. I guess they're afraid we'll stab one of the doctors and make a break for freedom. Hey, Walker. I hear you picked up a couple of biggies this afternoon."

Walker came over to shake Jack's hand. "Still got your sources, huh?"

"You bet."

"What are you guys talking about?" Moira looked puzzled. "We know that Marc is in jail, but who else got busted?"

Jack smiled. "Three kingpins in the drug-smuggling business. That's the reason Walker couldn't blow the whistle any sooner. I tumbled onto the fact that Johnny was running drugs in Ellen's mannequins months ago, but the agency wanted to hold off until they could nail his source."

"Then you're a narc?" Jayne turned to Walker with surprise. "You sure don't look like a narc."

Paul shook his head. "No, Jayne. Walker was kind enough to explain it to me. He is not a narc. He is actually a spook."

Jayne looked horrified. "Really, Paul! They might say that in Norway, but we certainly don't say it here!"

"But it's true." Walker chuckled. "I'm a member of the Spook Squad. We're the agents who go undercover on the big cases."

Ellen reached out to take Walker's hand. "You mean you *were* a member of the Spook Squad."

"You're finally retiring?" Jack began to smile as Walker nodded. "About time you let the young guys take over and started to lead a normal life. And you're settling down to make mannequins, right?"

"That's right."

Jack raised himself on his elbows until he was sitting up slightly. "You need my testimony to tie up any loose ends? All you guys have to do is subpoena me, and the doctors'll have to let me out of this thing."

Walker shook his head. "Nice try, Jack. But if you're not out in time, they can always do a deposition from your hospital bed."

"Okay, okay. If I can't get out of traction, how about opening that champagne? At least it'll take my mind off my troubles."

Ellen stood up. "Good idea. We've got two bottles and a surprise waiting out in the hall. I'll go tell her to come in."

Jack felt his heartbeat quicken. Her? But it couldn't be Betty. She wasn't well enough to wait alone in the hall. He was happy his friends were here and he was glad to see them, but it made him miss Betty even more than ever.

"Hi, Jack."

Jack's mouth dropped open as Betty walked in, unassisted. She looked so healthy and so beautiful that he could hardly believe his eyes. He swallowed hard, but his voice still came out in a strangled croak. "Betty?"

"It's me, Jack."

Betty handed the champagne to Moira to open and came over to the bed to kiss him. She smelled wonderful from some kind of expensive perfume, her hair was done in a soft, flattering style, and her dress was the most beautiful thing he'd ever seen. Jack blinked and fought down the urge to pull her down for another kiss, the kind of a kiss that might just embarrass them both.

"I told them it might be too much of a shock to spring

on you this way, but they just couldn't resist. Should I sit on the edge of the bed? Or will that hurt your leg?"

"Oh, no. Please sit." Jack's voice was still hoarse. "What happened to you? You look . . . uh . . ."

"Normal?" Betty laughed. "I'm getting there, now that the drugs are almost out of my system."

"Drugs?" Jack swallowed again, but it didn't seem to help his voice.

"Her father had her drugged to keep her from talking," Walker explained. "Betty's responsible for the arrests we made this morning. And she made tapes of the murders on that close-circuit system you hooked up in her unit. She's our star witness."

Jack gazed at Betty in shock. "Then you don't have Alzheimer's?"

"No. The whole thing was Marc's idea, and my father gave his approval. Walker says they've been trying to get the goods on our family for years."

"But that means you're in danger!"

"True, but it's minimal." Walker spoke up. "Marc told Betty's father that she was dead and we haven't said anything to the contrary. When the story breaks in the papers tomorrow, they'll list Betty Matteo as one of the victims."

"Come on, Walker." Jack shook his head. "That might work for a while, but you know they'll get wise sooner or later. Somebody's got to protect Betty and I'm stuck in this damn hospital bed."

Walker grinned at him. "Hospital beds can be moved. They can even be loaded onto a plane and taken to a nice safe tropical hideaway where you can recover with the aid of your private nurse."

"My nurse?"

"Meet Margaret Woodard, RN. I'm assuming her

identity." Betty handed him a glass of champagne. "Drink up, Jack. We're leaving in an hour."

"An hour?" Jack's head was spinning and he hadn't even tasted his champagne.

"It's all set. You took care of me for over four years and now it's my turn. You won't mind if I play nurse, will you?"

Jack began to smile. If playing nurse was anything like playing doctor, it was the best proposition he'd ever had. "I won't mind. And you certainly look prettier than the last time I saw you, Miss Woodard."

WHERE INNOCENCE DIES . . .
Expectant parents Karen and Mike Houston are
excited about restoring their old rambling Victorian
mansion to its former glory. With its endless maze of
rooms, hallways, and hiding places, it's a wonderful
place for their nine-year-old daughter Leslie to play
and explore. Unfortunately, they didn't listen to
the stories about the house's dark history.
They didn't believe the rumors about
the evil that lived there.

. . . THE NIGHTMARE BEGINS.
It begins with a whisper. A child's voice beckoning
from the rose garden. Crying out in the night.
It lures little Leslie to a crumbling storm door.
Down a flight of broken stairs. It calls to their
unborn child. It wants something from each of
them. Something in their very hearts and souls.
Tonight, the house will reveal its secret.
Tonight, the other child will come out to play . . .

**Please turn the page for an exciting sneak peek of
Joanne Fluke's
THE OTHER CHILD
coming in August 2014!**

PROLOGUE

The train was rolling across the Arizona desert when it started, a pain so intense it made her double over in the dusty red velvet seat. Dorthea gasped aloud as the spasm tore through her and several passengers leaned close.

"Just a touch of indigestion." She smiled apologetically. "Really, I'm fine now."

Drawing a deep steadying breath, she folded her hands protectively over her rounded stomach and turned to stare out at the unbroken miles of sand and cactus. The pain would disappear if she just sat quietly and thought pleasant thoughts. She had been on the train for days now and the constant swaying motion was making her ill.

Thank goodness she was almost to California. Dorthea sighed gratefully. The moment she arrived she would get her old job back, and then she would send for Christopher. They could find a home together, she and Christopher and the new baby.

She never should have gone back. Dorthea pressed her forehead against the cool glass of the window and blinked back bitter tears. The people in Cold Brook were hateful. They had called Christopher a bastard. They had ridiculed her when Mother's will was made public. They knew that her mother had never forgiven her and they were glad. The righteous, upstanding citizens of her old hometown were the same cruel gossips they'd been ten years ago.

If only she had gotten there before Mother died! Dorthea was certain that those horrid people in Cold Brook had poisoned her mother's mind against her and she hated them for it. Her dream of being welcomed home to her beautiful house was shattered. Now she was completely alone in the world. Poor Christopher was abandoned back there until she could afford to send him the money for a train ticket.

Dorthea moaned as the pain tore through her again. She braced her body against the lurching of the train and clumsily made her way up the aisle, carefully avoiding the stares of the other passengers. There it started and she slumped to the floor. A pool of blood was gathering beneath her and she pressed her hand tightly against the pain.

Numbness crept up her legs and she was cold, as cold as she'd been in the winter in Cold Brook. Her eyelids fluttered and her lips moved in silent protest. Christopher! He was alone in Cold Brook, in a town full of spiteful, meddling strangers. Dear God, what would they do to Christopher?

"No! She's not dead!" He stood facing them, one small boy against the circle of adults. "It's a lie! You're telling lies about her, just like you did before!"

His voice broke in a sob and he whirled to run out the door of the parsonage. His mother wasn't dead. She couldn't be dead! She had promised to come back for him just as soon as she made some money.

"Lies. Dirty lies." The wind whipped away his words as he raced through the vacant lot and around the corner. The neighbors had told lies before about his mother, lies his grandmother had believed. They were all liars in Cold Brook, just as his mother had said.

There it was in front of him now, huge and solid against the gray sky. Christopher stopped at the gate, panting heavily. Appleton Mansion, the home that should have been his. Their lies had cost him his family, his inheritance, and he'd get even with all of them somehow.

They were shouting his name now, calling for him to come back. Christopher slipped between the posts of the wrought-iron fence and ran into the overgrown yard. They wanted to tell him more lies, to confuse him the way they had confused Grandmother Appleton, but he wouldn't listen. He'd hide until it was dark and then he'd run away to California where his mother was waiting for him.

The small boy gave a sob of relief when he saw an open doorway. It was perfect. He'd hide in his grandmother's root cellar and they'd never find him. Then, when it was dark, he'd run away.

Without a backward glance Christopher hurtled through the opening, seeking the safety of the darkness below. He gave a shrill cry as his foot missed the steeply slanted step and then he was falling, arms flailing helplessly at the air as he pitched forward into the deep, damp blackness.

Wade Comstock stood still, letting the leaves skitter and pile in colored mounds around his feet, smiling as he looked up at the shuttered house. His wife, Verna, had been right; the Appleton Mansion had gone dirt cheap. He still couldn't understand how modern people at the turn of the century could take stock in silly ghost stories. He certainly didn't believe for one minute that Amelia Appleton was back from the dead, haunting the Appleton house. But then again, he had been the only one ever to venture a bid on the old place. Amelia's daughter Dorthea had left town right after her mother's will was read, cut off without a dime—and it served her right. Now the estate was his, the first acquisition of the Comstock Realty Company.

His thin lips tightened into a straight line as he thought of Dorthea. The good people of Cold Brook hadn't been fooled one bit by her tears at her mother's funeral. She was after the property, pure and simple. Bringing her bastard son here was bad enough, but you'd think a woman in her condition would have sense enough to stay away. And then she had run off, leaving the boy behind. He could make a bet that Dorthea was never planning to send for Christopher. Women like her didn't want kids in the way.

Wade kicked out at the piles of leaves and walked around his new property. As he turned the corner of the house, the open root cellar caught his eye and he reached in his pocket for the padlock and key he'd found hanging in the tool shed. That old cellar should be locked up before somebody got hurt down there. He'd tell the gardener to leave the bushes in that area and it would be overgrown in no time at all.

For a moment Wade stood and stared at the opening. He supposed he should go down there, but it was already too dark to be able to see his way around. Something about the place made him uneasy. There was no real reason to be afraid, but his heart beat faster and an icy sweat broke out on his forehead as he thought about climbing down into that small dark hole.

The day was turning to night as he hurriedly hefted the weather-beaten door and slammed it shut. The door was warped but it still fit. The hasp was in workable order and with a little effort he lined up the two pieces and secured them with the padlock. Then he jammed the key into his pocket and took a shortcut through the rose garden to the front yard.

Wade didn't notice the key was missing from his pocket until he was out on the sidewalk. He looked back at the overcast sky. There was no point in going back to try to find it in the dark. Actually he could do without the key. No one needed a root cellar anymore. It could stay locked up until kingdom come.

As he stood watching, shadows played over the windows of the stately house and crept up the crushed granite driveway. The air was still now, so humid it almost choked him. He could hear thunder rumbling in the distance. Then there was another noise—a thin hollow cry that set the hair on the back of his arms prickling. He listened intently, bent forward slightly, and balanced on the balls of his feet, but there was only the thunder. It was going to rain again and Wade felt a strange uneasiness. Once more he looked back, drawn to the house . . . as though something had been left unfinished. He had a vague sense of foreboding. The house looked almost menacing.

"Poppycock!" he muttered, and turned away, pulling out his watch. He'd have to hurry to get home in time for supper. Verna liked her meals punctual.

He started to walk, turning back every now and then to glance at the shadow of the house looming between the tall trees. Even though he knew those stories were a whole lot of foolishness, he felt a little spooked himself. The brick mansion did look eerie against the blackening sky.

"Mama!" He awoke with a scream on his lips, a half-choked cry of pure terror. It was dark and cold and inky black. Where was he? The air was damp, like a grave. He squeezed his eyes shut tightly and screamed again.

"Mama!" He would hear her footsteps coming any minute to wake him from this awful nightmare. She'd turn on the light and hug him and tell him not to be afraid. If he just waited, she'd come. She always came when he had nightmares.

No footsteps, no light, no sound except his own hoarse breathing. Christopher reached out cautiously and felt damp earth around him. This was no dream. Where was he?

There was a big lump on his head and it hurt. He must have fallen . . . yes, that was it.

He let his breath out in a shuddering sigh as he remembered. He was in his Grandmother Appleton's root cellar. He'd fallen down the steps trying to hide from the people who told him lies about his mama. And tonight he was going to run away and find her in California. She'd be so proud of him when he told her he hadn't believed their lies. She'd hug him and kiss him and promise she'd never have to go away again.

Perhaps it was night now. Christopher forced himself to open his eyes. He opened them wide but he couldn't see anything, not even the white shirt he was wearing. It must be night and that meant it was time for him to go.

Christopher sat up with a groan. It was so dark he

couldn't see the staircase. He knew he'd have to crawl around and feel for the steps, but it took a real effort to reach out into the blackness. He wasn't usually afraid of the dark. At least he wasn't afraid of the dark when there was a lamppost or a moon or something. This kind of darkness was different. It made his mouth dry and he held his breath as he forced himself to reach out into the inky depths.

There. He gave a grateful sigh as he crawled up the first step of the stairs. He didn't want to lose his balance and fall back down again.

Four . . . five . . . six . . . he was partway up when he heard a stealthy rustling noise from below. Fear pushed him forward in a rush, his knees scraping against the old slivery wood in a scramble to get to the top.

He let out a terrified yell as his head hit something hard. The cover—somebody had closed up the root cellar!

He couldn't think; he was too scared. Blind panic made him scream and pound, beating his fists against the wooden door until his knuckles were swollen and raw. Somehow he had to lift the door.

With a mighty effort Christopher heaved his body upward, straining against the solid piece of wood. The door gave a slight, sickening lurch, creaking and lifting just enough for him to hear the sound of metal grating against metal.

At first the sound lay at the back of his mind like a giant pendulum of horror, surging slowly forward until it reached the active part of his brain. The Cold Spring people had locked him in.

The thought was so terrifying he lost his breath and slumped into a huddled ball on the step. In the darkness he could see flashes of red and bright gold beneath his eyelids. He had to get out somehow! *He had to!*

"Help!" the sound tore through his lips and bounced off the earthen walls, giving a hollow, muted echo. He screamed until his voice was a weak whisper but no one came. Then his voice was gone and he could hear it again, the ominous rustling from the depths of the cellar, growing louder with each passing heartbeat.

God, no! This nightmare was really happening! He recognized the scuffling noise now and shivered with terror. Rats. They were sniffing at the air, searching for him, and there was nowhere to hide. They'd find him even here at the top of the stairs and they would come in a rush, darting hurtling balls of fur and needle teeth . . . the pain of flesh being torn from his body . . . the agony of being eaten alive!

He opened his throat in a tortured scream, a shrill hoarse cry that circled the earthen room then faded to a deadly silence. There was a roaring in his ears and terror rose to choke him, squeezing and strangling him with clutching fingers.

"Mama! Please, Mama!" he cried again, and then suddenly he was pitching forward, rolling and bumping to the black pit below. He gasped as an old shovel bit deeply into his neck and a warm stickiness gushed out to cover his face. There was a moment of vivid consciousness before death claimed him and in that final moment, one emotion blazed its way through his whole being. Hatred. He hated all of them. They had driven his mother away. They had stolen his inheritance. They had locked him in here and left him to die. He would punish them . . . make them suffer as his mother had suffered . . . as he was suffering.

ONE

The interior of the truck was dusty and Mike opened the wing window all the way, shifting on the slick plastic-covered seat. Karen had wanted to take an afternoon drive through the country and here they were over fifty miles from Minneapolis, on a bumpy country road. It wasn't Mike's idea of a great way to spend a Sunday. He'd rather be home watching the Expos and the Phillies from the couch in their air-conditioned Lake Street apartment.

Mike glanced uneasily at Karen as he thought about today's game. He had a bundle riding on this one and it was a damn good thing Karen didn't know about it. She'd been curious about his interest in baseball lately but he'd told her he got a kick out of watching the teams knock themselves out for the pennant. The explanation seemed to satisfy her.

Karen was death on two of his pet vices, drinking and gambling, and he'd agreed to reform three years ago when they were married. Way back then he'd made all the required promises. Lay off the booze. No more Saturday-night poker games. No betting on the horses.

No quick trips to Vegas. No office pools, even. The idea of a sportsbook hadn't occurred to her yet and he was hoping it wouldn't now. Naturally Mike didn't make a habit of keeping secrets from his wife but in this case he'd chosen the lesser of two evils. He knew Karen would hit the roof if he told her he hadn't gotten that hundred-dollar-a-month bonus after all, that the extra money came from his gambling winnings on the games. It was just lucky that he took care of all the finances. What Karen didn't know wouldn't hurt her.

"Cold Brook, one mile." Leslie was reading the road signs again in her clear high voice. "Oh, look Mike! A church with a white steeple and all those trees. Can't we just drive past before we go home?"

Mike had been up most of the night developing prints for his spread in *Homes* magazine and he wasn't in the mood for extensive sightseeing. He was going to refuse, but then he caught sight of his stepdaughter's pleading face in the rearview mirror. Another little side trip wouldn't kill him. He'd been too busy lately to spend much time at home and these Sunday drives were a family tradition.

"Oh, let's, Mike." Karen's voice was wistful. Mike could tell by her tone that she'd been feeling a little neglected lately, too. Maybe it had been a mistake insisting she quit her job at the interior decorating firm. Mike was old-fashioned sometimes, and he maintained that a mother's place was at home with her children. When he had discovered that Karen was pregnant he'd put his foot down insisting she stay home. Karen had agreed, but still she missed her job. He told himself that she'd be busy enough when the baby was born, but that didn't solve the problem right now.

Mike slowed the truck, looking for the turnoff. A little

sightseeing might be fun. Karen and Leslie would certainly enjoy it and his being home to watch the game wouldn't change the outcome any.

"All right, you two win." Mike smiled at his wife and turned left at the arrowed sign. "Just a quick run through town and then we have to get back. I still have to finish the penthouse prints and start work on that feature."

Leslie gave Mike a quick kiss and settled down again in the backseat of their Land Rover. When she was sitting down on the seat, Mike could barely see the top of her blond head over the stacks of film boxes and camera cases. She was a small child for nine, fair-haired and delicate like the little porcelain shepherdesses his mother used to collect. She was an exquisite child, a classic Scandinavian beauty. Mike was accustomed to being approached by people who wanted to use Leslie as a model. Karen claimed she didn't want Leslie to become self-conscious, but Mike noticed how she enjoyed dressing Leslie in the height of fashion. Much of Karen's salary had gone into designer jeans, Gucci loafers, and Pierre Cardin sweaters for her daughter. Leslie always had the best in clothes and she wore them beautifully, taking meticulous care of her wardrobe. Even in play clothes she always looked every inch a lady.

Karen possessed a different kind of beauty. Hers was the active, tennis-pro look. She had long, dark hair and a lithe, athletic body. People had trouble believing that she and Leslie were mother and daughter. They looked and acted completely different. Leslie preferred to curl up in a fluffy blanket and read, while Karen was relentlessly active. She was a fresh-air-and-exercise fanatic. For the last six years Karen had jogged around Lake Harriet every morning, dragging Leslie with her. That was how they'd met, the three of them.

Mike had been coming home from an all-night party, camera slung over his shoulder, when he spotted them. He was always on the lookout for a photogenic subject and he'd stopped to take a few pictures of the lovely black-haired runner and her towheaded child. It had seemed only natural to ask for Karen's address and a day later he was knocking at her door with some sample prints in one hand and a stuffed toy for Leslie in the other. The three of them had formed an instant bond.

Leslie had been fascinated by the man in her mother's life. She was five then, and fatherless. Karen always said Leslie was the image of her father—a handsome Swedish exchange student with whom Karen had enjoyed a brief affair before he'd gone back to his native country.

They made an unlikely trio, and Mike grinned a little at the thought. He had shaggy brown hair and a lined face. He needed a shave at least twice a day. Karen claimed he could walk out of Saks Fifth Avenue, dressed in the best from the skin out, and still look like an unemployed rock musician. The three of them made a striking contrast in their red Land Rover with MIKE HOUSTON, PHOTOGRAPHER painted on both doors.

Mike was so busy thinking about the picture they made that he almost missed the house. Karen's voice, breathless in his ear, jogged him back to reality.

"Oh, Mike! Stop, please! Just look at that beautiful old house!"

The house was classic; built before the turn of the century. It sprawled over half of the large, tree-shaded lot, yellow brick gleaming in the late afternoon sun. There was a veranda that ran the length of the front and around both sides, three stories high with a balcony on the second story. A cupola graced the slanted roof like the decoration on a fancy cake. It struck Mike right away: here was the perfect subject for a special old-fashioned feature in *Homes* magazine.

"That's it, isn't it, Mike?" Leslie's voice was hushed and expectant, as if she sensed the creative magic of this moment. "You're going to use this house for a special feature, aren't you?"

It was more a statement than a question and Mike nodded. Leslie had a real eye for a good photograph. "You bet I am!" he responded enthusiastically. "Hand me the Luna-Pro, honey, and push the big black case with the Linhof to the back door. Grab your Leica if you want and let's go. The sun's just right if we hurry."

Karen grinned as her husband and daughter made a hasty exit from the truck, cameras in tow. She'd voiced her objections when Mike gave Leslie the Leica for her ninth birthday. "Such an expensive camera for a nine-year-old?" she'd asked. "She'll probably lose it, Mike. And it's much too complicated for a child her age to operate."

But Mike had been right this time around. Leslie loved her Leica. She slept with it close by the side of her bed, along with her fuzzy stuffed bear and her ballet slippers. And she'd learned how to use it, too, listening attentively when Mike gave her instructions, asking questions that even Karen admitted were advanced for her age. Leslie seemed destined to follow in her stepfather's footsteps. She showed real talent in framing scenes and instinctively knew what made up a good photograph.

Her long hair was heavy and hot on the back of her neck and Karen pulled it up and secured it with a rubber band. She felt a bit queasy but she knew that was natural. It had been a long drive and she remembered getting carsick during the time she'd been carrying Leslie. Just a few more months and she would begin to show. Then she'd have to drag out all her old maternity clothes and see what could be salvaged.

Karen sighed, remembering. Ten years ago she was completely on her own, pregnant and unmarried, struggling to finish school. But once Leslie was born it was better. While it had been exhausting—attending decorating classes in the morning, working all afternoon at the firm, then coming home to care for the baby—it was well worth any trouble. Looking back, she could honestly say that she was happy she hadn't listened to all the well-meaning advice from other women about adoption or abortion. They were a family now, she and Mike and Leslie. She hadn't planned on getting pregnant again so soon, but it would all work out. This time it was going to be different. She wasn't alone. This time she had Mike to help her.

Karen's eyes widened as she slid out of the truck and gazed up at the huge house. It was a decorator's paradise, exactly the sort of house she'd dreamed of tackling when she was a naive, first-year art student.

She found Leslie around the side of the house, snapping a picture of the exterior. As soon as Leslie spotted her mother she pointed excitedly toward the old greenhouse.

"Oh, Mom! Look at this! You could grow your own flowers in here! Isn't it super?"

"It certainly is!" Karen gave her daughter a quick hug. Leslie's excitement was contagious and Karen's smile widened as she let her eyes wander to take it all in. There was plenty of space for a children's wing on the second floor and somewhere in that vast expanse of rooms was the perfect place for Mike's studio and darkroom. The sign outside said FOR SALE. The thought of owning this house kindled Karen's artistic imagination. They *had* mentioned looking for a house only last week and here it was. Of course it would take real backbreaking effort to fix it up, but she felt sure it could be done. It would be the project she'd been looking for, to keep her occupied the next six months. With a little time, patience, and help from Mike with the heavy stuff, she could turn the mansion into a showplace.

They were peeking in through the glass windows of the greenhouse when they heard voices. Mike was talking to someone in the front yard. They heard his laugh and another, deeper voice. Karen grabbed Leslie's hand and they hurried around the side of the house in time to see Mike talking to a gray-haired man in a sport jacket. There was a white Lincoln parked in the driveway with a magnetic sign reading COMSTOCK REALTY.

Rob Comstock had been driving by on his way home from the office when he saw the Land Rover parked outside the old Appleton Mansion. He noticed the painted signs on the vehicle's door and began to scheme. Out-of-towners, by the look of it. Making a sharp turn at the corner he drove around to pull up behind the truck, shutting off the motor of his new Continental. He'd just sit here and let them get a nice, long look.

This might be it, he thought to himself as he drew a Camel from the crumpled pack in his shirt pocket. He'd wanted to be rid of this white elephant for years. It had been on the books since his grandfather bought it eighty years ago. Rob leased it out whenever he could but that wasn't often enough to make a profit. Tenants never stayed for more than a couple of months. It was too large, they said, or it was too far from the Cities. Even though the rent was reasonable, they still made their excuses and left. He'd been trying to sell it for the past ten years with no success. Houses like this one had gone out of style in his grandfather's day. It was huge and inconvenient, and keeping it up was a financial disaster. It seemed nobody wanted to be stuck with an eight-bedroom house . . . especially a house with a reputation like this one.

Rob finished his cigarette and opened the car door. Maybe, just maybe, today would be his lucky day. He put on his sincerest, most helpful smile and cut across the lawn to greet the owner of the Land Rover. He was ready for a real challenge.

Leslie and Karen came around the corner of the house in time to catch the tail end of the sales pitch. Mike was nodding as the older man spoke.

"It's been vacant for five years now, but we check it every week to make sure there's no damage. It's a real buy, Mr. Houston. They don't build them like this anymore. Of course it would take a real professional to fix it up and decorate it but the price is right. Only forty-five even, for the right buyer. It's going on the block next week and that'll drive the price up higher, sure as you're standing here. These old estate auctions bring people in from all over; you'd be smart to put in a bid right now. Get it before someone buys the land and decides to tear it down and put in a trailer court."

"That'd be a real shame." Mike was shaking his head and Karen instantly recognized the thoughtful expression on his face. She'd seen it enough times when he was in the market for a new camera. He really was interested.

Of course she was, too, she thought, giving the house another look. They'd already decided to get out of the Twin Cities and Mike could work anywhere as long as he had a studio and darkroom. The price was fantastically low and there was the new baby on the way. They couldn't stay in their two-bedroom apartment much longer. Out here she could raise flowers and enjoy working on the house. They might even be able to swing a tennis court in a couple of years and Leslie would have lots of room to play.

"I'd really have to think about it for a while," Mike said, shrugging his shoulders. "And I'd have to see the inside, of course. If it needs a lot of work, the price would have to come down."

"No problem, Mr. Houston." The real estate agent turned to smile at Karen and Leslie. "Glad to meet you, ladies. I'm Rob Comstock from Comstock Realty and I've got the keys with me, if you folks would like to take a look. We've got at least an hour of daylight left."

Karen had a sense of inevitability as she followed Leslie and Mike inside. She'd been dying to see the interior and here she was. One look at the huge high-ceilinged living room made her gasp. This room alone was bigger than their whole apartment! Stained-glass panes graced the upper sections of the floor-length windows and the hardwood floors were virtually unblemished.

"Oh . . . lovely," Karen murmured softly. Her voice was hushed as if she were in a museum. She began to smile as she followed Rob Comstock up the circular staircase and viewed the second floor. Huge, airy bedrooms with polished oak moldings, a separate dressing room in the master suite with an ancient claw-footed dresser dominating the space—the interior was just as she had imagined. If only they could afford it.

"The furniture on the third floor is included." He was speaking to her now and Karen smiled. Rob Comstock could see she was interested. There was no denying Karen's excitement as she stepped up on the third-floor landing and saw what must have been the original ballroom, filled with old furniture covered by dropcloths. What she wouldn't give to poke under the shrouded shapes and see the intriguing pieces that were stored and forgotten in this enormous shadowed space.

A small staircase with a door at the top led to the cupola and Leslie was scrambling up before Karen could caution her to be careful. The steps were safe enough. The whole house seemed untouched by time, waiting for some new owners to love and nourish it, to bring it back to life again. Karen could imagine it was almost the same as it had been when the original occupants left, with only a bit of dust and cobwebs covering its intrinsic beauty.

"Plenty of real antiques up here, I'll bet!" Rob Comstock was speaking to her, but Karen only half heard him. She anticipated squeals of delight from Leslie over the view that stretched in all directions from the windowed cupola. Strange that there was only silence overhead.

Karen excused herself reluctantly. "I'd better go up and check on Leslie." A prickle of anxiety invaded her mind as she started up the narrow staircase into the dusty silence.

Karen was convinced there was something wrong when she reached the landing and pushed open the door to the cupola. Leslie was standing at one of the twelve narrow windows, staring out blankly. She looked preoccupied and started as Karen spoke her name.

"Kitten? What's the matter?" The still, stiff way Leslie was standing made Karen terribly nervous. She rushed to put her arms around her daughter.

"Huh? Oh . . . nothing, Mom." Leslie gave her a funny, lopsided smile. She looked miserable. "I'm afraid Mike won't buy it!" There was a quaver in her voice. "This house is perfect for us, Mom. We just have to live here!"

"Now, don't be silly, darling." Karen gave her a quick squeeze. "This is the first house we've seen and it really is awfully large for us. We'll probably see other houses you like just as much."

"No! We have to live here in this house!" Leslie's voice was stronger now and pleading. "You know it's the right house, Mom. We can't live anywhere else. This house was built just for us!"

"I think you should have Mr. Comstock's job," Karen said, smiling down indulgently. "You're an even better salesman than he is. But really, kitten, we have to be sensible. I know you love this old house and I do, too, but the final decision is Mike's."

Karen was firm as she turned Leslie around and guided her toward the stairs. "Come on now, honey. We have to get back downstairs before it gets dark. The power's not turned on, you know."

"But you'll help me convince Mike to buy it, won't you, Mom?" Leslie asked insistently, stopping at the top step. "You know it would be perfect for us."

"Yes, I'll help you, silly," Karen promised, brushing a wisp of silvery-blond hair out of Leslie's eyes. She breathed a sigh of relief as her daughter smiled fully and hurried down the stairs in front of her. Leslie would be persistent and she might just manage to convince Mike. Leslie was right. It was almost as if the house had been waiting all this time just for them.